MY BIG GOBLIN SPACE PROGRAM

ALSO BY SCOTT WARREN

War Horses Series

Chevalier

Ymir

Serpent Valley

Dog Soldier

Grand Melee

The Sunstone Imperative

Union Earth Privateers Series

Vick's Vultures

To Fall Among Vultures

Where Vultures Dare

Standalone Fantasy Novels

Oathbreakers Anonymous

The Dragon's Banker

Ought to be Dead

MY BIG GOBLIN SPACE PROGRAM

SCOTT WARREN

Podium

Cover design by Mary Cruz

ISBN: 979-8-89539-402-1

Published in 2025 by Podium Publishing
www.podiumentertainment.com

Podium

MY BIG GOBLIN SPACE PROGRAM

"She is not hatched."
"She is grown too large."
"We will die as she slumbers."
"Our magic cannot reach her. Our prayers go unheard."
"But our magic can reach worlds unknown."
"We have tried that before."
"We must find one who can reach her for us."
"Call them here."
"Will it succeed this time?"
"We must try."

CHAPTER 1

PUBLICITY STUNT

"*Ignition—go flight. Navigation—go flight. Operations—go flight.*"

I'd waited my whole life for this moment. Six years of college, two master's degrees in aviation and engineering, and everything almost derailed by a truck accident in university. I glanced down at the twin prosthetics attached below the knees of my space suit. After the accident, I thought I would only ever *build* rockets. Now, thanks to the CEO of Project NuEarth drunkenly exposing himself to twenty million followers on social media, I was a much-needed PR win in the making. I was three days away from being the first person without legs to walk on the moon.

Thank God for publicity stunts. I'll take it.

"*Primary ignition on. Transferring primary control to atmospheric NAV computer. All systems go flight, people. Luna 2 is TACAMO.*"

The rocket started to rumble to life underneath me as the primary motor kicked on. I looked to my left and right as the roar mounted. My mission commander, Major Dave Sanders, and the backup pilot, Sandra Davis (I know, trust me, they've heard all the jokes), gripped their restraints. Dave looked over and met my gaze.

"Let's hope this bucket you designed doesn't spring a leak halfway to LP1, eh Chris?" called Dave over the rolling thunder of twenty-two independent rocket motors. He grinned. I'd known him even before I worked to design the self-sustained command module for NuEarth's second manned moon mission. Hell, he'd recruited me from grad school and fought for me to receive astronaut training even after the accident.

I laughed. "The SC-Mod is golden, sir. As long as the first and second stages separate without a hitch, ain't nothin' keeping me off that moon dust by Friday."

"Keep your legs on," shouted Sandra. Her voice came through tinny over the internal radio. She reached out and gripped my space suit. I looked over, and she smiled. "You made it, Chris."

I felt a push against my chair as the motors opened up and the monolithic rocket began to move.

"*Liftoff!*"

"We're not there yet," I shouted. "But we're on our way!" My knuckles tightened on my own restraints. Laughing was a struggle as the G-forces mounted. I'd trained for this in the centrifuge. Ironically, I had even better G-force tolerances than most of the other astronauts at NuEarth, since my blood could no longer go past my knees. But the pressure still squeezes the air out of your lungs like a whoopee cushion.

The tone of the motors started to change.

"Approaching first-stage separation," gasped Dave.

"Acknowledged, first-stage separation," said Sandra.

A vibration started to mount. I narrowed my eyes, trying to think what a vibration at this stage entailed.

The radio crackled in my ear. "*Luna 2, nothing to worry about, but you might start feeling some shakes. We're picking up a slight variance in the first-stage separators. Nothing to worry about, well within toler—*"

I lay on my back, staring up at the sky—or rather, staring up at a box superimposed on the sun. Too blurry and bright to read, I reached up and pawed at it before suddenly freezing. My vision might have been blurry, but I'm pretty sure my hand only had four fingers, was about half the length as usual, and was covered in *blue fur.*

I lurched to a sitting position, groaning and putting both hands to my head. I squeezed my eyes shut. My head felt *huge,* and every cubic centimeter of it throbbed. What had happened? I had been on my way to the moon. My dream had come true, *finally,* after years and years of hard work (and maybe a few nights of drunken debauchery). Then there was a slight variance, and then . . . what?

It had exploded, I realized. That's what. I should have been dead. Instead I was . . . well, I wasn't myself. I forced my eyes open long enough to adjust to the light. I wiped gunk out of them with my claws (claws?!?) and tried to focus on the words in the box that had stayed front and center in my field of view.

<Your previous life has ended. You have been granted a new life! Your assigned race has changed from Human to Goblin. Your job has changed from Systems Engineer to Goblin King.>

"What the hell? A new life? Hold up, what was wrong with my last one?"

The window changed.

<Would you like to review your final moments?>

Huh. Voice-activated menus. Was I getting some sort of an afterlife tutorial? It's not like the UI wasn't intuitive, I just wasn't supposed to have one. People just don't *see* little boxes floating in front of their faces. I waved my hand through the box, and it wavered like a heat mirage before reforming. I looked at the prompt again. My final moments.

"Yes. Definitely."

The window expanded, this time, showing a bird's eye view of a rocket leaving the pad on a trail of exhaust, cruising into the upper atmosphere, and then exploding in a giant fireball.

"Oh . . ." I said.

Yep. We'd *Challenger*ed ourselves. Didn't even make it to the thermosphere. Friggen' first-stage booster goons blowing the transition. Vibrations well within tolerance my new little blue butt. Which reminded me:

"Are Sanders and Davis here, too?"

The System was slow to open the next window in response to my query.

<Request for information is denied.>

Well, that wasn't a *no.* But it wasn't a *yes*, either. It was only a few moments ago that I'd looked over at them as the rocket carried us up toward space. But my circumstances were so strange it still felt so . . . surreal. Like their absence hadn't fully set in. Maybe I was in shock? It certainly didn't feel like it.

I looked at my hands, and then the window again. Goblin king, huh?

<Would you like to view details on your new job?>

I shook my head. This was impossible. Except, it was happening, so it must not be. I've never had much use for religion, being raised vaguely Lutheran. And I didn't see any pearly gates or a bearded guy waiting to check my ID, so Heaven was out. Was this some sort of simulation? That was a theory gaining traction in scientific circles. Or worse, a *game*? The rational part of my brain warred with the little engineer side of me that just wanted to explore these new, impossible parameters apparently defining my current existence. Or maybe my life before was the fiction? I didn't know enough about philosophy to start unpacking *that* just yet. But I could take things one step at a time, troubleshoot, and work the problem in front of me.

"Yeah, lay it on me. Tell me about being a goblin king, now."

This window was populated enough that the text extended beyond the lower limit of the message box. I reached out a claw and swiped the page up as if it were a tablet, scrolling through the list of class features that were at least as strange as a world with information windows. Whoever had designed these interfaces had done a good job making them intuitive.

<Goblin King
Tribe size: 1
Primary Skills:
Head of the Snake: You cannot die unless you are the last living member of your tribe. Lethal damage will automatically transfer to a random member of your tribe.
Undying Loyalty: All goblins will exhibit absolute devotion upon meeting you. Defeating a rival goblin king will transfer his subjects to your tribe.
Without Number: Expanding your tribe will unlock additional benefits.
Tribal Knowledge: Practical skills and technology unlocked will transfer to all members of your tribe.
Natural Leader: Increasing your tribe size will unlock additional benefits.
Goblin Ingenuity: You have been granted access to the Goblin Technology Tree advancement path.
Reduced Mobility: You are ambulatorily challenged. Kings don't walk anyway.>

Ambulatorily challenged? My eyes went wide at that last one. I looked down at my legs—which ended in two stubby knobs just below the knees.

"Oh, come on!" I shouted across the plain. Granted a new life in a new world (simulation?), in an entirely new body, and I was *still friggen' legless!*

It hadn't even been congenital in my last life. I'd lost my legs in a motorcycle accident when a truck driver blew a red light. This seemed really, *really* unfair. I sighed. Well, it wasn't like I was any worse off. Also, I was alive. And since I didn't *see* Davis or Sandra anywhere, I had to assume I was the only one of the three who had been plucked from Earth and put . . . wherever this was. The wide grass prairie stretched out as far as I could see. But about forty degrees above the horizon . . .

"Woah . . . close the window for a second."

<Goodbye.>

The box faded out, and I got a look at the biggest moon *ever* glowing above me. It took up at least a tenth of the sky, at minimum. It was pale blue, veined with pink minerals, and *gigantic.* I was pretty sure I could see forests on it! And even a sea of cerulean waves. It was so incredible that, for a moment, it made me not want to think about the possibility of losing what little connection I still had to everyone I'd ever known on Earth.

I looked up at it, mouth agape, stunned as it shimmered in the morning sky. I don't know how long I watched it. But then I looked down at my legs. *If I did it once.*

"Tell me about the Goblin Technology Tree."

The window returned.

<The Goblin Technology Tree is a form of alternate advancement to achieve practical results through impractical means, materials, and methods, often more rapidly and less safely than traditional advancement.>

I looked around, seeing a couple of stones. Shale, I thought. Though since I'd always been more interested in space, terrestrial geology was never really my thing. But engineering . . . ? I picked one up and banged it against another until I'd chipped away enough to have a workable edge, hissing as I cut myself on a shard. Red blood trickled off my thumb.

<Your tribe has advanced! Goblin Technology Unlocked: Stone Stabbies>

A stone knife—or *stabby,* as the System dubbed it. Basically, the most primitive tool ever manufactured. I looked at the crude, dirty edge that would probably take five minutes to saw through a piece of 550 cord. Then I looked up at the sky. I pointed my hand like a rocket and made a whooshing noise as I lifted it above the horizon and centered it over the blue-and-pink moon. This world's moon looked a lot closer than the 250,000 miles thereabouts of the moon of Earth. Gears started to turn in my head. Was it possible? Could I really speed run through six thousand years of human development based on nothing but engineering know-how, half-remembered survival shows, and a dubious, goblinized technical library waiting to be discovered?

Hell yeah, I could. Death be damned. I was still going to the moon.

CHAPTER 2

A LEG TO STAND ON

It's not as simple as that, of course. You have to bang a whole lot of rocks together in the right order. And it's not a one-person job. It had taken hundreds of employees at NuEarth to get my rocket off the ground (at least, for a little bit). People I would never see again. After losing my folks, first my mom when I was young and then my dad before I graduated school, I didn't really have anyone except for a grandmother who didn't realize we'd stopped sending astronauts to the moon in the seventies, or that most televisions came in color now and weren't adjusted using dials. The team at NuEarth had become something of a found family. Now, it seemed like I was on my own again. But I did have one advantage this time around.

If the System was to be believed, I couldn't die unless I was the last living member of my tribe. Unfortunately, I was currently the *only* member of my tribe. I hadn't played many fantasy games, but I knew goblins were generally bottom of the barrel in terms of individual power level. Looking at my scrawny arms and absent legs, I saw no reason why that trend might deviate here.

My objective might be to get to the moon, but step one and *ongoing* was: Don't die. I wasn't going to take the chance of getting a third go-around. I needed to put that survival training from the Space Program to use. And ideally, I had to get out of this hot, dry prairie and find some goblins to pump those tribal numbers up before some wildcat made a meal of me. The head of a snake isn't very useful without a body behind it. To do *any* of that, I had to be mobile. Unfortunately, I was also *ambulatorily deficient*. Which was a fancy way of saying *Lieutenant Dan, you ain't got no legs.*

In one direction across the fields, I could see a tree line. But that was miles away, and the idea of dragging myself across that much open ground sounded like suicide. That was a problem, but it was a problem I could work. One step at a time—metaphorically *and* literally. I needed new prosthetics.

There were a few scraggly trees closer to my location. I started crawling my way over the grass and rocks, stone stabby kept close. I doubted it would do me much good if I were attacked, but it was better than my stubby, dull claws.

There was a surprising amount of strength in my new goblin limbs, despite their apparent scrawniness. I'd had a lot of upper body strength as a human from being on the rowing team in college, both before the accident and after rehab, and from rolling a wheelchair through NuEarth. But crawling to the roots of the gnarled, spindly deadwood tree with these stick-thin goblin arms would have exhausted even the best para-athlete. Once I made it to the tree, I tried and tried to haul myself up the trunk to some of the live branches and couldn't manage it without feet to grip with. Every attempt ended with me sliding back down to the roots.

My prosthetics before had been top-of-the-line, 3D-printed carbon fiber blades that I was going to use to bounce around the surface of the moon. Well, if goblins were a thing in this world, I doubted anyone here had heard of *carbon fiber*, let alone *additive manufacturing.*

The dead branches along the grass were twisted, gnarled, sap-covered things half-ready to snap. More tinder than wood, at this point. But they were the only thing within reach. I dragged myself around, tossing all I could find to a central location.

<Goblin Technology Unlocked: Sticky-Spinny Smacker>

By the time I made a circuit around the tree, I had about a dozen sticks. None of which were suitable. I dragged myself back to the pile and sighed, considering. High-grade medical devices, these weren't. But I wasn't making high-grade medical devices. I was using the Goblin Technology Tree. Rapid iterations, impractical means, and lowered safety. Pretty much every engineer's dream, when you think about it.

I took my stone knife and used it to peel down some of the bark from the old tree.

<Goblin Technology Unlocked: Sticky-Stringy Thingies>

It came off in long, thin strips that were tough enough that I couldn't break them by pulling them. Though I also just wasn't very strong. I selected the two straightest sticks I had. One was reasonably straight but twisted like a corkscrew. The other had a bumpy knob at the bottom that looked a bit like a shoe, which I hoped would offer some stability. I pulled them close and tugged up the simple hide wrap that protected my goblin modesty. With the bark, I lashed each of the sticks to my legs. The bark still had a little sap on the inside, and it helped act as an adhesive that bound the whole thing together far better than I felt it should have. *Achieve practical results through impractical means, methods, and materials.*

I selected the third-sturdiest stick to use as a cane. I'd had to use one to learn to walk again after the accident, and luckily this new body seemed to have kept my muscle memory from the old, freshly exploded body and human brain. By pushing off one of the larger roots and steadying myself, I was able to take a few tentative steps with the cane.

"Hot Christmas!" I said. "It's working!"

I took two more steps before my left leg snapped and my face planted itself in the dirt.

<*Often faster and less safely*>, the System reminded me.

"Owww . . ." I muttered with a face full of dirt.

<*Goblin Technology Unlocked: Sticky-Stilts*>

Progress!

I rolled over and looked at the damage. My left prosthetic had snapped cleanly in two. There'd be no fixing it. I set to the task of peeling back the bark so I could swap it for a new one, but stopped when I heard a howl in the distance. And then I started peeling faster.

The bark came away, and I bound two of the smaller sticks together to form a brace for the broken section. Again, it seemed to hold better than I thought it should, so again, with a bit more urgency, I strapped the bundle to my thigh and climbed to my, erm, *sticky-stilts*. This time, I spread the weight across two canes, rather than one single cane. I made a quick circuit around the tree to make sure there'd be no more breakage and then set off toward the tree line.

It wasn't long before I heard the howl again, closer this time. I hesitated to put on too much speed, lest I break these primitive prosthetics and leave myself a sitting duck. But I could feel the wind blowing past me, carrying my scent deep into the prairie.

Goblins aren't large creatures—or, at least, *this* goblin wasn't. Even with the stilts, I was maybe a meter tall. The grass rising on either side of the narrow trail was like the walls of a canyon, except that anything might lurk within and burst out at any moment.

I thought back to media containing goblins. They were always shown as devious, dangerous creatures to be dispatched by the main characters early on in their journey to prepare them for tougher foes. They attacked in swarms, ate rotten meat, served dark lords, and all that jazz. But at that moment, a lone goblin seemed quite the vulnerable creature. If goblins were real here, what other fanciful creatures existed? Trolls? Ogres? Chupacabras?

All of the above, knowing my luck. I limped faster, flinching every time one of my improvised legs creaked underneath me. I didn't know much about goblins, but I got the distinct impression that I was a forest creature. The trees shouted *safety* to the goblin part of my brain. I just wish they'd shout it from a little closer. I felt like a tiny puppet scurrying around. As I huffed and puffed with exertion, the tree line started to grow ahead.

Something startled a flock of birds in the grass behind me, and the howling came again, even closer this time. I froze, looking back, and raising one of the improvised canes. Sweat ran down my little goblin body. Nothing appeared, and I willed my shaking stumps to move. I had to get to the woods.

As I reached the scrubby brush before the tree line, I heard a growling behind me, and turned to see some sort of large canine with red fur, four eyes, and fangs the size of my index finger emerge from the tall grass. I stared at it. It stared at me, drool dripping down its chops. Thick claws dug at the turf beneath its paws. It lowered its head, ready to charge.

One cane would have to do. I pulled back with my right hand and sent the stick spinning toward the monster. It must not have ever encountered a goblin using a, what was it the System had named it? A *spinning smacky*. It watched the lazy arc of the oncoming projectile with confusion right up until the knobby end of the stick thumped into its forehead, right between the eyes.

It yelped in pain, falling over and scrabbling against the ground. I turned and hobbled my way away as fast as I could. The yelps behind me turned to growls of fury, but I had reached the tree line.

I heard snuffling and scrabbling behind me.

"Stay away!" I ordered. "Bad dog!"

My voice was high, tinny like an old-fashioned radio broadcaster. I felt like I should be advertising soap flakes. Not exactly intimidating. Clifford, the big red (snarling hungry) dog, didn't think so either. He lunged at me, just as my right leg gave out with a *snap.*

I fell to the ground, losing my other cane as it was snatched out of my hand by a red, furry comet streaking overhead. Rolling onto my back, I pushed myself up and watched the wild dog snap the branch between its teeth. It padded toward me. I reached about for something, *anything* that I could use in my defense. The only thing quick-to-hand was a rotten fruit on the ground. I picked up the bulbous, foul-smelling thing and recoiled. Maybe a direct hit would overwhelm its senses and frighten it off. I pulled it back for a throw right as the dog lunged. A small window appeared at the corner of my vision.

<Careful with that.>

The fruit sailed out of my hand. This time, the dog knew what was coming. He opened his jaws and clamped down on the fruit before it could hit him. Then, there was a bright flash, a wave of pressure, and I found myself airborne with ringing ears.

<Goblin Technology Unlocked: Simple Boom-Fruit Poppers>

CHAPTER 3

BLASTOFF

I felt like I was back aboard the rocket. I flew through the foliage and got a bird's-eye view of the woods as they blurred past. My ears rang, and I had just enough time to consider that if the explosion hadn't killed me, the fall certainly would, before I reached the top of my parabolic arc and curved downward toward the forest. I shouted, windmilling my arms, and fell straight on my head, which *squished*, and recoiled, bouncing me another five meters in the air where I got stuck in a tree.

I groaned, putting my hands on a tender spot at the top of my head. "How am I not dead?"

The box returned.

<Would you like to view your racial information?>

"Yes, please."

<Race: Forest Goblin
Innate Traits:
Meek: Goblins are among the weakest creatures. Goblins start at level 1. Goblins cannot level up.
True Omnivore: Goblins can derive nutrients from any meat, fruit, or vegetable, even those toxic to most other species.
Rapid Reproduction: Goblins are naturally occurring. Where there are goblins present, more goblins will regularly appear. No funny business required.
Inert: Goblins are incapable of using magic.
Soft-headed: Goblins are resistant to blast damage and immune to fall damage. Happy landings.>

Resistant to blast and fall damage, huh? I guess that was lucky.

<Goblins would probably be extinct otherwise.>

Given my current predicament, that was probably true. Wait a second.

I blinked. I hadn't said anything out loud and it had responded anyway. The message vanished as quickly as it had appeared. That was an odd system message as well. (Implying that there were normal ones? Amazing how fast you can adapt to the unimaginable.) It sounded almost conversational.

"System, are you sentient?" I asked. Even though it clearly had access to my mind, it felt better to talk out loud.

No answer.

"System, what are your operational parameters?"

No answer.

"System, grant root access."

No answer.

"System, enable power-user permissions."

Nothing. Worth a shot. I racked my brain.

"System, print ("Hello, world!")."

Nada. Hmph. If it was a computer of some sort, it wasn't parsing Python. Alright, System, keep your secrets. But know this: They're not safe from an engineer!

<Your tribe has increased to 3 members.>

I looked down from the tree. Below, two blue, fuzzy creatures with bulbous heads, flat noses, and wide, floppy ears were carrying what looked like the mangled remains of the dead canine over their shoulders. I looked at the mess I'd made of its jaws, blowing the mandible completely off with that fruit. Jesus, that could have been *me.* Then I looked at the wide-eyed goblins. They had rough hide wraps and skull masks of strange creatures, but they were unmistakably the same species I was. Both of them paused, shook their heads, and started clawing at the air in front of them and chittering. *Huh,* I realized, *they're looking at System menus.*

"Hey!" I yelled. "Get me down from here!"

The pair squawked in surprise, dropping their prize to stare up at me. They started panicking for a few moments before running off into the brush.

"Come back! I thought I was supposed to be your king!"

I hung in the tree, arms limp below me, and sighed. So much for royalty.

<Your tribe has increased to 9 members.>

I lifted my head. The first two goblins had returned, bringing with them another handful of the little blue fuzz-balls in skull masks and rough hide cloaks. Some of these new ones were carrying long sticks between them, while others carried shards of flint and shale. They dropped their equipment and set to a frenzy of work, banging rocks together and gnawing on the wood so fast it sounded like putting a board through a table saw. Within a few minutes, they had a set of stone knives and poles that, I had to admit, were quite a bit straighter and more sturdy-looking than mine had been. The ones with knives began stripping bark from the tree and uprooting vines to convert to cordage.

Well I'll be damned. They were using the goblin technology I'd unlocked. Just by virtue of being in my tribe, they'd gained access to the simple skill of converting tree bark to string that I'd unlocked. And, as much as I was loath to admit it, they were better at it than I was.

I don't know how they selected their champion to get stilted up. Goblin communication seemed to be almost completely nonverbal. When they did make a unique sound, it seemed like their language consisted entirely of grunts, sudden physical assault, and onomatopoeia. One might make a chewing noise to indicate that they wanted a pole trimmed, for instance, while simultaneously striking their intended trimmer with said pole.

It was a lot like communicating with partners during undergrad group projects, if I'm being honest.

Still, once they got one of them strapped up with stilts, they hoisted him up with great aplomb. He wobbled closer, windmilling his arms as the other goblins cheered him on. Unfortunately, he still couldn't reach me, and I still couldn't free myself from where I was wedged in between the tree branches.

"Come on, come on!" I called down. "Just a bit higher!" My new tribesmen chattered and wrapped their hands around the stilts, hoisting their fellow into the air. He squawked and pitched back and forth, suddenly unsteady. But he was still out of reach.

One of the goblins seemed to have a bright idea. He jumped, letting go of the stilts and dashing off into the brush. The others, now unbalanced, teetered in a chittering mass, and the one on stilts wailed as he toppled over, plowing into the ground face-first. I winced.

"Well, you tried," I said. I racked my brain. "Don't worry, guys. This is just the first iteration. We'll adapt, iterate, and test again. As your new king, I promise you, we will figure out a solution to this problem!"

My new tribemates got to their feet and started cheering. Huh. "Can you all understand me?" I asked. Several of them bobbed their heads in what was clearly a nod. Even being completely nonverbal themselves, it seemed they had no issues understanding my words and ideas. Strange. But then, so was a pseudo-gestalt tech tree propagating through a seemingly omniscient, omnipresent System. Heck, for all I knew I wasn't even speaking English anymore. Maybe I never had.

I caught a hint of movement out of the corner of my eye as the goblin who had previously departed returned. When I saw what he was carrying, even being upside-down, I felt like all the blood must have drained out of my face. The little guy hoisted one of the rotten fruits above his head, making a noise like a bomb going off. The rest of the tribe squawked in alarm and scrabbled to get away. They weren't fast enough—especially the one still with over-long stilts strapped on.

"Wait, wait!" I said. But it was too late. Not known for their patience, apparently. The goblin proudly hurled the fruit straight at the tree I was stuck in.

The blast, if anything, was even more powerful than the first.

<Your tribe has decreased to 7 members.>

CHAPTER 4

REGULAR LOSSES

At least I was out of the tree. I had completely forgotten that transferring my goblin technology skills to the tribe transferred *all* the skills and knowledge—including ones that weren't exactly safe. Those explosive fermented fruits had just killed two of my nine followers: the one who had thrown it, and the much-celebrated stilt-walker they'd elevated in a doomed attempt to reach me.

Still, I was alive and back on the ground. One by one, the survivors poked their heads out of cover and came to regard me, crouching down and pointing out various things about me to one another. Mostly my legs—or lack thereof. Before I could even ask them to do it, they were back at work fashioning a set of poles to use as primitive prosthetics and hoisting me up so that they could be affixed to my legs. I wasn't sure if this was a result of knowledge transfer from myself, or if they were simply far more clever creatures than their appearance and primary (and aggressive) method of communication would suggest. But once again, their versions seemed more effective and practical than my initial, rushed attempt with the dry wood.

"Thanks, guys," I said. They all grinned and looked at one another beneath the skull hats. Two returned to the dog creature and set to the task of hoisting the limp carcass between them. I pinched my chin.

"Hold up. Bring me one of those poles and some of the vines. I can make that easier."

My seven remaining tribesmen rushed to be the ones to fulfill my request, resulting in two separate fistfights and one goblin getting bitten. But they managed to get the wooden pole and the improvised cord over to me. I set to work tying the feet of the carcass to the poles, and then indicated that one goblin should lift at each end. They did so, and their eyes widened in wonder.

<Goblin Technology Unlocked: Dinner Poles>

They cheered, and several of them tried to muscle in on the pole to be the one to carry it. I struggled to walk alongside them, and three of the excited goblins approached me with another pole and some rope.

"No!" I said, holding up my hands. "Freight only!"

Still, I could barely walk through the rough underbrush on the improvised prosthetics. Thankfully, my new goblin body was super light, or I wouldn't have been able to stand on them at all. I considered, then pointed at the leftover wood.

"Trim those down and leave the ones on the edges longer, then lay them side by side and tie them together."

One frenzy of activity later, I had a reasonable approximation of an old-fashioned stretcher. I eased myself down onto it, then pointed at two of the goblins. "You and you, pick it up by those handles."

With specific goblins designated, there was less fighting to be the one to carry me. The two I'd chosen managed to take their positions with only minor blows traded over who would be in front and who would take the rear. Once that was sorted, they hoisted me off the ground.

<Goblin Technology Unlocked: Improvised Litter>

So the goblins could unlock technology on their own as well. That made sense. It was, after all, the *Goblin* Tech Tree. I could literally see the understanding sweep across their faces as the technology skill spread. I didn't know the mechanism—was this some sort of in-built goblin magic? Were they low-level psychics in some sort of goblin gestalt? Or just natural empaths?

"Alright. Let's take it nice and easy. Back to the village, or wherever —woaaah!"

Goblins apparently have no sense of pace, which matched their general lack of any form of chill or caution. Anyone not assigned to the pole or the litter was on bushwhacking duty, and they shouted as though charging into battle as they cut through terrain almost as fast as they ran, using just teeth, claws, and their simple stone knives.

The litter bearers ran at full tilt behind them, and I held on for dear life as they made their best effort to bump me off in their mad dash. Somehow, I stayed on. But I felt like fried rice being tossed around and flipped above a wok. I was going to need a better way of getting around.

The upside was that we made great time, and we weren't attacked by any forest monsters. I assumed few of them wanted to be caught in the path of forest goblin pathfinders, lest they be cut apart and trampled like the foliage. God knows the goblins weren't shy about making their presence known.

We reached the base of a sharp, rocky bluff, and the goblins surprised me by not slowing down much at all as we hit the cliff face and started climbing. I held on for dear life as the litter bearers somehow managed to balance the weight of the litter and their new king while ascending.

The climb was harrowing. But, as far as the general location went, a bluff was a sound spot for a village. Elevated, isolated, with enough trees for shelter. Plus, it had a commanding view of the nearby woods and was easily defensible from the top—save for one slope that looked slightly shallower than the rest. But something like that could be walled off and guarded. I'd have to survey the opposite side later. Looking out, I could see other, similar bluffs, and I wondered if they also held isolated goblin villages.

I didn't have much time to enjoy the view. After a moment's breather, the convoy returned to their frenetic pace and charged through the brambles straight to the goblin village.

While the bluff was impressive, the village atop it was less so. It was more of a tamped-down copse of trees with a lot of mud, a heap of bones, another heap of droppings, and a stagnant, scummy rainwater pond distressingly close to both of the previously mentioned mounds. I had a feeling I'd be putting that immunity to most toxins to the test sooner rather than later.

As we broke out of the new trail we'd carved in the underbrush, the litter bearers ground to a halt. I, having not yet invented seatbelts, continued forward. Luckily, I landed on my head and bounced. I tumbled into the center of the village.

<Your tribe has increased to 32 members.>

The litter bearers, having realized their mistake, squawked in distress and carried the litter over, trying to wedge it back under me.

"I'm good, I'm good!" I shouted, waving them back. "We're here, right?"

Several more goblins were present in the village. They all ogled me with open amazement as the earlier members of the tribe proceeded to mime the entire process of my discovery. Several ran off and returned with stones and sticks and bones and set to work crafting themselves basic stabbies of their own. Others quickly wove together a crown of bones and then presented it to me.

"Uh, thanks, I think," I said. I lifted the crown and fit it onto my head.

<Goblin Technology Unlocked: Boney Brow Crown>

The eyes of the tribe glazed over for a moment, and then several of them began cheering. Wow. The knowledge really did propagate just through proximity. I panicked and grabbed the nearest goblin.

"Make sure no one brings any of that rotten fruit in here. I don't want to blow up the whole cliffside, got it?"

The goblin made an explosion noise and spread his hands apart.

"That's right, no bada-boom. You see anyone trying to bring one of them in here, you bite them. Got it?"

My first guardsman gnashed his teeth and grinned, then began to scrutinize the other members of the village, who were themselves more interested in the corpse of the canine they'd brought back. They fell on the thing, ripping and sawing at it, pulling out soft innards and shoving them directly into their wide mouths.

I thought it would make me sick, but my stomach actually started to growl and my mouth to water so profusely that drool started dripping down my chin. One of my new subjects tore off a haunch and ran it over to me, a length of intestines still in his mouth. He slurped it up like a spaghetti noodle as he handed me the haunch. Red meat must have been the choice cut, if they were giving it to me.

The goblin in me wanted to tuck in, but enough of the human remained that still thought meat ought to be cooked first. Unfortunately, I didn't actually know how to build a fire beyond the basic theory. I'd never even gone camping without a lighter and a bag of charcoal briquettes. I was beginning to realize how much work I really had to do, and how much I would have to learn to even get to the point where I could start working on *technology* as I had always understood it. I shrugged and sank my teeth into the raw haunch.

It was *delicious*. Something about the texture bothered the still-human part of my brain, but the goblin was all about raw meat. My jaw started to work on its own, buzz-sawing through tough meat, tendon, and gristle until all I had was a picked-clean leg bone. My stomach bulged. I must have eaten a significant percentage of my own body weight in just a couple of minutes of frenzied feeding fugue.

My eyes started to droop. Something about the full belly and the dappled light filtering through the canopy conspired to convince me that speed-running civilization was a *tomorrow* problem. I looked around the clearing, seeing that many of the goblins were wavering on their feet and looking lethargic.

I supposed a nap couldn't hurt. But I wasn't sure where I was supposed to sleep. Did the goblins have beds of leaves and grass? Or did they just curl up wherever they got tired? How did they stay warm?

A pair of hands wrapped me from behind, and I was tackled to the ground. I tried to struggle, but a second goblin threw himself on top of us, and then quickly, a third.

"Betrayal!" I shouted. "I thought I was your king!" I thrashed out, trying to work my way free as more goblins leapt upon me, forcing me back down to the ground. I kicked out, and I'm pretty sure one of them bit my arm.

Several more of the goblins belly-flopped on top of the growing pile, which quickly became a cage of slender limbs and bulbous heads and . . . *snoring*? I stopped fighting and twisted my head around. Two of the goblins in the pile were fast asleep, and it sounded like the rest were well on their way. I guess a fed goblin was a happy goblin. Now that the sudden shock of being driven to the ground and dog-piled was beginning to wear off, the fatigue returned, and I found myself drifting off in the warm buzz of the goblin mound.

CHAPTER 5

SPEED-RUNNING CIVILIZATION

I awoke to a general panic among the sleeping pile and a tangle of flailing arms and feet. At first I thought we were being attacked, but then I felt the drops of rain and understood why the goblin sleeping mound was becoming a churning tangle of fleeing, frightened creatures.

I watched as they all sought shelter under trees and limbs, holding their smelly rawhide cloaks above them for cover. They had no concept of housing or umbrellas to keep the rain off—despite that being wet seemed to agitate them. I'll admit, it was an unpleasant sensation, having wet fur. But, having spent significant time on the water in college, I was able to grin and bear it. I pushed myself up and wobbled over to the scummy pond, cupping my hands and bringing the water to my mouth. It was only slightly better than the aftertaste of raw sewage. I thought back to the impromptu meal.

Part of me definitely found the texture of raw meat distasteful, even if my goblin taste buds relished the flavor. But cooking didn't just improve texture. It also released and preserved nutrients, allowing food to be kept longer and eaten more safely while providing more benefits to health.

I looked back at the village of goblins, who watched me from the shelter of bushes and trees. I spotted two slightly smaller goblins without the curious skull masks. Even as I wondered how to call up the System menu to check if my tribe had grown, it appeared before my eyes.

<Current tribe size: 34>

I'd gained two more members overnight. Well, the racial traits had mentioned that more goblins could spontaneously appear close to existing goblins. I hadn't expected that to mean that they'd appear nearly full-grown, though. That was how they kept from going extinct, I supposed, despite having next to no concept of language, invention, housing, or self-preservation. I doubted they'd be much for child-rearing—especially seeing as their heads were *at least* twice as wide as their narrow hips. If there was some sort of god watching over this place, he surely had a soft spot for keeping the little guys around despite all impracticality.

"System, can you provide me with custom notifications?"

<*Define parameters.*>

"Every time I wake up, define the current tribe size and delta from the previous tribe size notification."

<*Custom notification defined.*>

I took a seat near the closest tree and started to ponder the monolithic task ahead of me. Lofty goals like getting to this world's moon were well and good. But I had stone knives as a starting point, advanced space flight as the end goal, and a whole lot of fill-in-the-blanks in between. I was reasonably assured of being able to create, say, a simple aircraft powered by a two-stroke engine—provided I had aluminum, steel, and the ability to mill cylinder heads, pistons, and a prop shaft. Oh yeah, and fuel refined enough to power and lubricate the whole thing. But how to acquire metal as versatile as aluminum and shape it into panels? How to find and process oil into usable fuel? How to build a spark plug? And all with a nonverbal workforce.

I was getting ahead of myself. The goblins, as they were now, were living in a pure subsistence society of hunter-gatherers. They had no concept of anything but how to live for the next few minutes. They had no safety net, no permanent shelter, no food storage other than their own bellies. The existence of the cliffords proved they had natural predators as well, easily capable of picking off isolated members of the tribe. And what about larger predators? Forest dwellers? Hell, there might be humans in this world, and I'd seen enough movies to know that humans and goblins rarely got along. The tribe's only safety was in numbers, and being able to spontaneously reproduce was their ace-in-the-hole that let them maintain the population. Thanks to that, they were hanging on. *Barely.* Thirty members was not a sustainable number for a community that wanted to enter industrialization.

That's where I needed to start. Before I could start tackling advanced concepts like metallurgy and chemistry, I had to make sure their basic needs were met in order to expand the tribe. They needed to be able to know where their next meal was coming from, and that they'd have a roof over their heads so that the next rainstorm wouldn't leave their fur drenched.

Food was most important. I selected a party of six goblins at random. "Go hunt something for tonight's dinner," I said. The six of them raised their knives over their heads and raced off into the forest, screaming a war cry.

"*An animal!*" I shouted after them, shaking my head. Lord help whatever was in their path. Death by a thousand cuts awaited. Hopefully the hide would be in decent enough shape so that I could use it to figure out how to process leather.

I needed two things for that: tools and raw materials. You could do a lot with wood, stone, and string. But there were still limits. Luckily, the existing bone pile would be a convenient source of small, precise tool parts like needles and hooks and pins. Other raw materials were plentiful as well, and I was sure the forest would provide if I could figure out where to look. If we were going to kick-start construction and manufacturing, I had a few priorities that were, as yet, unsourced.

I needed material harder and sharper than shale for cutting tools. Obsidian would be the sharpest, but I knew that had something to do with volcanoes. It was also too brittle for things like saws and axes. Flint would be best. I was pretty sure it was more common and workable in relatively simple ways.

The three other basic materials my tribe currently lacked, according to the survival shows I had binged in the hospital, were clay, adhesive, and leather. Of the three, clay was the most important to primitive advancement. Clay meant containers and weatherproofing, and it was both easy to acquire and easy to work with. You could make tools and molds from clay, and even complex devices. Once you found a natural clay deposit, you harvested it, mixed it with sand, dirt, or water, depending on what you wanted to do with it, and then you shaped it just like clay you'd buy in a craft store. You needed fire or a lot of time in the sun to fully cure it, but considering how damp everything in the forest was at the moment, fire would have to wait.

Adhesive shouldn't be too difficult, either. We had sticky sap from the trees. If I could find some pine trees, their resin would be extremely effective—but storage and transportation of it came back to clay. I needed containers.

Leather came from animal hides. I'd seen them make it on a survival show, once, and it involved scraping the animal skin as clean as possible and then stretching it and rubbing brains on it. Which seemed pretty morbid. I wasn't sure why you needed the brains. Was there some fat, oil, or enzyme in brains that aided the tanning process? Either way, all the basic requirements were already in camp—including the mostly intact hide of the red canine from the night before. And the skull. Since clay would have to be found and transported, and I doubted the goblins would be keen to go out in the rain and hunt for it, I set that task aside.

I waved a couple of them over. "I need stabbies, string, and a wooden square, about yay big," I said, gesturing. The goblins mimed my motions and looked at each other before running off. Others handed their new knives to me—point-first, I should mention. I gingerly took the sharpest one and looked down at what remained of the canine—which, admittedly, wasn't much. The thing had been torn limb from limb and eviscerated in the goblin feeding frenzy. There was a decent patch on its back that only had a few bite marks with enough hide to maybe make a small shawl or cloak.

I'd never skinned an animal before, so I cut along where the least damaged part of the pelt was and pulled it back, resisting the very goblin urge to just stuff everything in my mouth by the fistful. I dug and scraped wherever it caught as I pulled, and eventually it came away in my hands. The back of it was slick with connective tissue.

About that time, the goblins who had run off came sprinting back with the makeshift frame, and I took the offered rope. I pursed my lips, looking at it, and then pointed to the bone pile. "Bring me a small bone."

The goblins raced off to do as I said. They came back with a selection of bones I didn't recognize, but then, I'm not that kind of doctor. I picked what might have been a bird's rib bone and ground a small eyelet into it with a knife, then threaded the smallest of the cord I could find and punched it through the hide.

<Goblin Technology Unlocked: Boney Sutures>

I pulled the cordage through and tied it to the corners of the frame to stretch it taut over the opening.

<Goblin Technology Unlocked: Sticky Framing>
<Goblin Technology Unlocked: Skinny Tanning>

I stopped. *Wait.* Boney sutures and sticky framing and skinny tanning. It took everything I had not to smack my wide goblin forehead. This whole time, I'd assumed the *sticky* in all the sticky goblin tech referred to the sap clinging to the bark-weave cordage. Did it instead refer to the *sticks*? Heaven help me if this technology tree was full of puns.

Handing the knife back to its original owner (I think; I was still having trouble telling individuals apart), I indicated the hide. "Clean this as best you can, then rub its brains on it."

I had barely turned around before I heard a splash and turned back to see the goblins smacking the whole kit and caboodle into the pond.

"Not like that!" I said, waving my arms. "Scrape it clean with the *knife*!"

The light of recognition passed over the tribe, and they waded back out of the pool and went to work cleaning the rest of the gristle and tissue off the clifford skin. I left them to it and turned to the rest of the village.

While they worked, I noticed several of the other goblins hacking poles together in various shapes, and realized that *sticky frames*, as the System called them, weren't just an end product, but a material on their own. Good. That meant they could be used to make more advanced things, like shelters. I found sticky frames being worked on that were vaguely triangular-shaped, and I had their owners hold them upright while I spent a few hours lashing a few crossbars and weaving vines into a lattice until I got the technology window to flash again with *<Advanced Sticky Frames>*. By the time I finished, the rain had stopped and the harsh afternoon sun was starting to beat down. The moon would eclipse it soon enough, with the totality lasting a couple of hours, if my judgment was correct. It seemed total solar eclipses were a near-daily event in the world.

Since I hadn't noticed a moonset or moonrise, I also had to guess that the moon was tidally locked to this hemisphere, though it did trace a slow circle in the sky during the hours that I spent working, going from about forty degrees from the horizon to directly overhead.

<Goblin Technology Unlocked: Sticky Shelter>

Now we were cooking. I looked around. Suddenly, half the village seemed to be reworking their projects. Good. They'd refine their frames, and then I could show them how to apply foliage and grasses for insulation. In the meantime, I returned to the hide, which the tanners were already applying the brains to.

<Goblin Technology Unlocked: Red-Hide Tanning>

With all the brains used up, the goblins left the hide and went to work fashioning what was left of the skull into a mask for one of our newest members.

Good. Things were proceeding well.

<Your tribe has decreased to 32 members.>
<Your tribe has decreased to 30 members.>

What the hell?

CHAPTER 6

STICKY STONE POKIES

I stopped, looking around the clearing. Most of the goblins were busy with small projects, hammering rocks to make tools, straightening poles, or winding cord.

The hunting party.

I looked off in the direction they'd charged hours before. I'd had thirty-four members in the morning when we'd all piled out of the mound. What had I been thinking, sending them off to hunt wildlife with *knives*? And only six of them. My desire to multitask for efficiency had just cost the lives of four of my tribesmen, and the fates of the remaining two were unknown.

If I was going to be their king, I couldn't be the kind of king who just took advantage of his people. This was going to need a rescue party, and I was going to be on it. And we weren't going in with simple stone stabbies. I took the poles, the knives, and the cords that the goblins had been working at and made my first advanced weapon by splitting the pole and wedging the knife in, before binding the whole thing with cord.

<Goblin Technology Unlocked: Sticky Stone Pokies>

Within a few minutes, we had fifteen of the simple spears, so I split the remaining tribe in half and took fourteen members while leaving the rest to gather more raw materials. I would carry the final spear. But, looking down, I wasn't sure of my ability to fight on these ramshackle prosthetic legs. I pulled two more goblins to act as the litter carriers and decided I would be moral support and shout orders from the back. That was kingly, too, right?

This time I brought extra cord and tied it around the litter to act as a restraint. I had wanted to improve this simple vehicle with a true seatbelt today. But now it was an emergency, and there was no time.

"Onward!" I ordered, pointing my spear in the direction the hunting party had left. It wasn't difficult to follow the hunting party's progress. Hell, the National Park Service could have used a batch of these guys in every forest in North America to keep the trails clear. We charged out, following their trail (and expanding it with our passing). What I hadn't realized was that while goblins are great at climbing *up* cliffs, they don't bother to climb *down*. Our charge carried us directly over the cliff face in a perfect parabolic arc. And this time, I was screaming right along with the goblins.

<*Good thing you're immune to fall damage.*>

Shut up, HAL!

We crashed down into a valley, landing headfirst to break our falls. Once we were upright again, we retrieved the litter from the tree where it had stuck. Then we pulled the spears out of the ground (OSHA would have had a fit) and we were back on course. We turned right and twisted around for a bit before settling on a path vaguely in the direction of the moon. This part of the woods was so crisscrossed with goblin trails that I never would have found the right one. I just had to trust that my goblin friends knew where they were going.

We passed by a small, startled pack of some sort of creatures that looked like a cross between a boar and a skunk and then shocked a flock of large birds to flee. I noted for later where some of the feathers fell, but we were past in a flash.

This time, when we reached our destination, I managed to hold on to the litter. We stumbled over a creek and into a clearing where I spotted our two surviving goblins up a tree, squawking what I had to assume were the goblin equivalent of profanities down at . . . well, I'd never seen a creature like that. Its facial markings and long, hooked claws reminded me of a three-toed sloth, but that's where the similarities ended. It had a squat face with sharp teeth in a protruding snout, and what looked like an armored hide covered in a stoney material that covered from the top of its head down to its wide, stubby tail. It snarled up at the stranded hunters and scrabbled halfway up the tree before falling down and rolling back to its feet. Of our fallen brothers, there was no sign except for some blood and tufts of blue fur on the foliage.

<*Careful.*>

"System? What do you know about this thing?"

<You might want to let this one go. It's level 10.>

Never!

It dwarfed us, but in reality, it was probably the size of a Great Dane, or maybe a small black bear. Besides, we were armed.

I waved my spear forward. "Attack!" I shouted. "Spears forward, stay together!"

I had pictured the goblins marching in rank, stone spearheads leveled as they closed in on their foes. I don't know *why* I thought that, given the evidence. As one, our company lunged forward, spears waving overhead as they screamed.

The stone-hide sloth thing turned at our war cry, locked eyes with me, and snarled before charging in. Seeing me up on my litter, it must have thought I was the biggest threat (or the most delicious meal). Suddenly this seemed like less of a rescue party and more of a suicide mission.

It was faster than its size and bulk (and slothy features) would have suggested, and before I knew what was happening, the first wave of spears was airborne, knocked aside by those long forearms. The second wave at least got their spears down, and one even had the brilliant idea to throw his. But stone met stone, and the spears bounced off as the diminutive goblins didn't have the strength to penetrate the thick hide. Still, the stone sloth came on. Shoot. Maybe the System had been right!

"Plant the butts of your spears!" I said.

The last row of goblins stuck their spears in the ground, squawking as the stone sloth leapt at them. My litter bearers panicked and dropped the litter in favor of hiding behind their own stone knives, and I toppled to the ground.

<Goblin Technology Unlocked: Sticky-Stone Pricklanx>

I rolled over and pushed myself upright. The sloth had thrown itself over the last rank, not understanding or not caring about the spears. Which, to be fair, did not seem up to the task of penetrating even the underbelly. But its weight had bowed the spears in almost double. Even as it struggled to reach the last rank of goblins with its claws, its hind toes left the brush. Almost as one, the spears straightened, snapping back to their original position.

<Goblin Technology Unlocked: Sticky Flex-A-Pult>

Unfortunately, physics dictates that an object in motion retains its trajectory. The stone sloth's rebound sent it straight over the heads of my company, and it was flying toward me at an alarming speed. Its arms windmilled through the air and it opened its mouth in a surprised howl.

I'm sure I screamed myself. I fumbled for the spear and hoisted it upright, turning my face away and clenching up just as the stone sloth fell. By God's grace or sheer luck, the spear was at just the right angle to wedge itself in the stone sloth's open mouth and the creature's bulk did the rest of the heavy lifting. Blood splattered across my face, and then the entire weight of the creature fell on me.

<Your tribe has decreased to 29 members.>

Had I not been a goblin king, that impact would have killed me. But while passing fatal damage might keep me alive (at the cost of another member of the tribe), my Head of the Snake skill did not transfer *pain*. I wheezed as the bulk of the thing crushed me, flattening my head against the forest floor in a most unpleasant way. Every bone in my body felt pulverized, and I heard multiple snaps. Which, I realized thankfully, were just my prosthetics. Small mercies. Well, not for the poor unfortunate who took my fatal hit. With the tribe down to twenty-nine members, thus far I'd been a net *negative* on their well-being.

My rescue squad wasted no time rolling the stone sloth off of me and helping me up to a sitting position. I couldn't stand without prosthetics, but I was content to watch as the goblins celebrated, hooting and hollering at the sloth's body. They kicked and punched at it, cheering, and then hoisted me up. Even by sheer accident, I'd dealt the killing blow.

"Hell yeah! Looks like meat's back on the menu, boys!" I raised my arms up to cheer with the rest of the rescue squad but then winced. I was still a bit tender from my near-death squashing. "Let's take this thing back to the village."

A rustling in the tree the stone sloth had been trying to climb took my attention, and I saw the face of a badger poke down from the foliage. I stared at it, and it stared at me. Did badgers typically climb trees? It seemed odd to me.

"How did you get up there?" I asked.

It stared at me a moment in shock. "Holy Rava! A talking goblin!" he replied, clearly startled.

"Holy hell, a talking *badger*!"

The badger disappeared back into the tree, and then a pair of squat, wide legs in leather trousers dangled down. Apparently, the thing was only badger from the waist up. Below that, it was . . . I hesitated to say *human*, because the thing was only half-again as tall as I was, and several times wider. But it dropped down holding a large, leather satchel, which slung around its shoulder.

Some of the other goblins approached, to which the badger-man flinched away, but I gestured them back. "Be good. I don't want you biting our new friend. He's not food."

The badger really surprised me then by pulling out a pair of small brass spectacles and peering through them at me. So, someone in this world had metalworking *and* crystal grinding. That was important to know.

"Oh dear. You really *are* a goblin! And no mask at all," he said. He reached into his satchel again and withdrew a small, bound journal, licking his finger and thumbing through the pages. "You would not happen to be a goblin *king*, would you?"

"Who wants to know?" I asked.

The badger shut the book and bowed deeply at the waist. "I'm terribly sorry! How rude of me! I'm called Rufus, level twenty scholar, free-trader, and Fae-touched. May I have your name? Do you *have* a name?" He raised his snout, suddenly excited. "I could give you one for free, if you'd like."

I opened my mouth to say *Chris*. But *was* I still Chris? Chris had died on that rocket, reaching toward an unattainable goal—an opportunity only made possible by the untimely appearance of a billionaire's genitals. Nah. Chris was dead, and this time we really were going to the moon. And we'd do it without NuEarth, and *with* goblins. I needed a name befitting a pioneer.

"Apollo," I said. Classic. Smooth. "Of tribe . . . um . . . Apollo . . ."

Not so smooth.

"And yes, I am a goblin king. Though I haven't been one very long." I thought for a minute. I hadn't heard another human's—well, you know—voice in almost two days. I didn't realize how much I missed it. "Would you like to come to the village for dinner? I promise you won't be harmed."

Rufus pushed his spectacles up his snout. "I daresay I'd not be much of a scholar should I refuse! Besides, the stoney devil tried to eat me! It only seems fair I should return the favor."

I grinned.

CHAPTER 7

RUFUS

It took a few minutes for the rescue squad to get poles and cordage sorted out. Eventually, they realized they'd need two poles and eight goblins to lift the stone sloth. But the heavy creature significantly slowed our progress back to the village—slow for goblins, anyway. It was still a breakneck pace by any measure. Curiously, we didn't reuse the trail we'd made coming down. The pathfinders just cut a whole new trail wherever they pleased. Rufus traversed along with us, sometimes on two legs, sometimes loping on all four. I could tell he wasn't used to the pace, but slowing down seemed to be the one instruction my tribe couldn't understand. Goblins only had two states: asleep and *gotta-go-fast*.

We made it back to the bluff by late afternoon, just before the sun slipped behind the huge moon. I'm not sure how the goblins managed to get the stone sloth up the crag—despite actively watching them do it. Rufus managed on his own as well, so I suppose badgers could climb after all. Once he'd climbed fifteen or so meters, though, he was completely winded.

He took in the hilltop copse and once again donned his spectacles. "Fascinating. I must say, there are few who are privy to the inner workings of a goblin crag. At least, few enough who don't end up split between those two piles, I imagine."

I followed his gaze to the bone and scat mounds, and then beyond to a village quite different from the one I'd left that morning. The goblins who had remained had transformed the clearing, processed a great deal of the raw materials on their own, and scattered the results with little regard for organization or structure. The lean-to shelters that dotted the bluff were facing every which way without regard for direction or spacing. One of them had even been woven *through* that of a neighbor.

Most of the goblins had also started using needles and thread to repair their own clothing. A few had gone out hunting with the new spears and brought back small game. Their ability to adapt to new changes in the tech tree was nothing short of astounding. And, despite my orders, I spotted one of the plump little bomb fruits sitting next to one of the shacks.

"It's not much, but it's home." I looked Rufus up and down. "I have to say, for such a dangerous situation, as you'd describe it, you seem quite at ease."

Rufus looked down at me. "I know a learned voice when I hear one, and a learned companion does not kill without cause. Besides that, you have already saved my life once. I'm not sure how I can serve to repay you. But I am well-traveled and have tales of many places." He pulled out his journal again. "And this is your tribe, yes? I had thought goblin kings were myths, yet here you stand. And all the myths agree that the king has the absolute loyalty of his tribe. Where all myths agree, there is truth, wouldn't you say?"

"Perhaps," I said. "You've been lots of places in this world?"

A glimmer in Rufus's eye struck me then, and I realized my mistake. I'd as much as admitted I wasn't from around here. And talking to someone like this made me realize just how much I actually missed conversation. I'd never been the type to sit on the periphery in life. I wanted to be in the action, in the show, making an impact. Goblins were good company in their own way. But most of the friends I'd made over the years were like-minded, driven students and later engineers and other astronauts at NuEarth. People who put their learning first and thought like puzzle-solvers. People who would challenge me to be more than I was, and who wouldn't think I was any less because of my legs.

"Aye. In *this* world, yes. I've seen the Crystal Halls of the Deep Dwarves, the Other-wood where the Fae play cruel jests, and the cities of men from which ships sail to the horizon and beyond."

"What's beyond?" I asked.

"You are. I've come to the newest frontier to uncover its myriad mysteries."

I eyed the badger-man's satchel. "Well, Rufus, if you've got something in there that can start a fire, we can talk over a haunch of your would-be devourer."

Rufus did indeed have something. Two somethings, in fact. Two small bottles that when their contents mated on a stack of firewood, a flame appeared. Interesting. Not least of all the vials—glass, again. That meant furnaces and glassblowing. As for the fire itself, that wasn't anything super mystical. There were a number of two-part chemical reactions that would cause instantaneous combustion on Earth. But, considering the makeup of the bomb fruits and the fact that I'd been reincarnated into a goblin body, oh, and that one of the tenets of the Goblin Tech Tree was the apparent ability to disregard physical laws goblins found inconvenient, I had to assume the local periodic table differed somewhat as well. But there were at least people who knew it.

Rufus coaxed the flame to a decent burn that would eventually reduce down to a bed of smoldering coals. In the meantime, he glanced at the dubious pond, then pulled a round bottle out of his satchel. More glassblowing. He uncorked it, and the sweet-sour smell of beer wafted out. Distillation, fermentation science. He took a long pull and seemed to recover much of his stamina. He offered the bottle.

"Not a fan of warm beer, but thanks all the same," I said. Besides, I knew one of two things would occur: either this body would be the lightweightest lightweight that ever got smashed off one drink, or the anti-toxin ability of the goblin race would negate the alcohol entirely.

While we waited, two of my goblins presented me with a stitched poncho, what was left of the hide from the clifford. I pulled it on to much cheering and directed the other goblins to mount the skinned stone sloth carcass on a spit and frame it over the fire where it could be turned. Since the goblins would be too short to turn it normally, what with the size of the fire and the size of the sloth, I set up a sort of crossbar, so that a goblin could jump, grab hold, and his weight would draw that section vertical, to which he would then slide off and the next goblin would jump and grab the next bar parallel to the ground.

<Goblin Technology Unlocked: Sticky Cooky-Spit-Spinner>

Rufus watched me with curiosity, taking notes in his journal, as well as some rough sketches. He seemed comfortable enough on the ground, but I sent a pair of my goblins to gather leaves and moss to begin lining the floors of the shelters.

When I retook my seat next to him to watch the stone sloth cook, I was the first to break the silence with an admission.

"I know little of this world," I said. "I was born only days ago, and though I was born with the knowledge of many things, none of it pertains to the land in which I live. If you feel you want to trade for saving your life, then trade me honest answers."

"A dishonest answer is no answer at all, but a lie," said Rufus. "I feel I play a dangerous game, treating with a goblin king. My curiosity gets the best of me, but the myths all agree on something else about you."

"What's that?"

"That your appearance heralds a time of strife and danger. Goblins present little danger in the grand scheme of the world because they each pull in whichever direction strikes their fancy. A goblin king has their loyalty and can point them all at a common goal. He is a unifying force with a powerful tool that, left unchecked, has the potential to be a blight upon the land if he sets his eyes on the world at large."

"I assure you, my designs are entirely self-centered and I have no desire to be anyone's blight."

Rufus slapped his thighs. "Ah, well, since that's settled, what of our world do you wish to know?"

CHAPTER 8

OF OUR WORLD

"You really don't want anything in trade for this information?" I asked. "They say knowledge is power."

"Ah," said Rufus. "But a question *is* an answer. You cannot take without first giving. I have a skill that tells me if your question is genuine or meant to mislead."

That was some Philosophy 101 stuff right there, but he was right. Every question I asked revealed my ignorance of something. And when I started asking of things of which I should have no knowledge, which I intended to, well, that would reveal something else entirely. If he was telling the truth about that skill, it told me two things: other people had access to this world's skill system, and I should definitely not lie to Rufus in case he had other skills to separate truth from falsehoods. I decided to start small.

"How is it we're speaking the same language?"

Rufus tilted his head. "All people of this land share a common language. Though some also have a language they choose not to share. It wouldn't do for people to be unable to communicate, would it?" He nodded his snout to a pack of goblins who were wordlessly argued about something—a debate that almost immediately devolved into physical blows.

"Good point. What's the name of this world?"

"Depends who you ask," said Rufus. He nibbled at the sloth haunch and withdrew a small brick from his satchel. He rooted around for a moment, but I handed him a stone knife and he used it to scrape what I presumed was salt onto the meat. "Rava. That's what the dwarves—my people—call it."

"You're a dwarf?" I asked.

"Wilds-marked. Fae-touched, if you prefer. The sign of the wanderer. But yes, my countenance is that of a beast—though I am not one, unless you get a few more of these in me." He lofted his bottle. "We come and go as we're driven by whim, one foot in the wilds and one in civilization. We're seen as lucky by some, oddities to others."

"You mentioned dwarves before. You also mentioned humans."

Rufus nodded. "Humans call the world Enclova, which translates to *Skyclad.* You see, they only view the world as the surface. The dwarven word, Rava, acknowledges the world below, as well as above. But you should hear what the orcs call it."

"What do the orcs call it?"

"Kelembog. It means *to be trampled beneath our feet.*" He nudged me with an elbow. "Tells you all you need to know about orcs, doesn't it?"

"I suppose it does." I had little desire to meet one. I watched as the fire popped and fizzled, considering how to phrase the important questions. And then I just decided to go for broke.

"Are there computers in Enclova?"

Rufus tilted his head down. "Computers? Those who practice arithmetic and figures?"

I waved my hand in a circle. "Not people, *things.* You might call them thinking machines, or logic engines."

"If there are, they are surely the demesne of wizards, who are not to be trifled with."

I nodded. I had less desire to meet a real wizard than I did to meet an orc. "What about internal combustion engines?"

Rufus's furry brows climbed. "My word, what a horrific thought!"

"No, no," I said. "It's a way to turn heat and pressure into motion using fuel that burns rapidly. It can be used to turn a wheel, or move a plow, or even push a ship without masts or sails."

"In all my travels, I've not heard of such a thing," said Rufus. He tapped his lips with a claw. "Though I once saw an eastern contraption that used the steam from boiled water to spin a puppet."

"So, steam power?"

"I suppose that would be one term for it, yes. I have seen artifices of wound spring as well."

"Clockwork?"

"Clocks were the least of it."

This was not entirely unexpected. All indications pointed to this being a pre-industrial land. "How about flying machines?"

"How hard can you throw?" laughed Rufus. "Apollo, if the Gods want a person to fly, they mark him with wings."

"What shape is the world?" I asked next.

Rufus pointed to the prodigious moon. "The same shape as Raphina. As round as a potbelly."

Raphina. My final destination. Fine, I knew about a few technologies already, like glass grinding and shipbuilding. There were a few others that might become important. "Firearms, grenades, cannons, and explosive powder?"

"I'm afraid I've never heard of such things, except for a trip across the sea where I watched a powder that burned swiftly and in strange colors." Rufus made a show of thumbing through his journal. "It seems as though I should be the one asking you questions. I am not living up to my end of the bargain, I fear you will feel."

"No," I said. "It's important to determine what means and methods are available, as well as what aren't. The land is called Rava, but where are we *now*?"

Rufus flipped through his journal to a rough sketch of an island. Though, since I couldn't tell the scale, I couldn't say whether it was the size of Hawaii or Australia. "Lanclova," said Rufus. "Shadow-clad. The untamed land under Raphina's watchful eye. Many nations have laid claim because there are fortunes to be made here. Natural treasures, remarkable plants, new knowledge, strange natives, and fantastic creatures abound. Its enticing mysteries are eclipsed only by its myriad dangers. Few are equipped to penetrate its depths."

Definitely Australia, then. Or, at least, this world's version of it. "But you can?"

"Badger," he said, as though that should be explanation enough. "Allow me a question as well. How do you know of sciences that have not yet come to pass?" asked Rufus.

"Like I said," I added somewhat dishonestly, "I was born with the knowledge of many things. Much of what I've just mentioned I will eventually build. But to do that, I'll need time and tools."

Rufus narrowed his eyes. "True enough. But not the *whole* truth." Then his eyes grew large as he thought about what I said. He laughed and slapped me on the back. "You will build a machine that *flies through the air*? I do not mean to sound rude, O King. I am sure you believe it. But you are sounding quite like a wizard yourself, with these claims. And even goblin kings cannot work magics."

"Your doubt is fair," I admitted, looking at the village. A small sleeping mound had already formed from the goblins who took their sloth rare. The rest were waiting for dinner and working, since my technology skill had passed them the benefits of cooked meat. The goblins were slicing it off a bit at a time as the exterior cooked, like shawarma. There was no way my tribe would have the patience to wait for the whole thing to roast through. "But I claim that not only will I fly through the air, I'll stand upon the surface of Raphina."

"A bold claim, indeed! But it will take more than claims to impress me. I've been all over this world and seen much of its mysteries—and peered behind the curtain of many of them."

I whistled for two of my goblins and pointed to the carcass. "Bring me the claws."

They moved to obey and went to work sawing and pulling until they'd worked the large, hooked claws out. They brought them to me. I held them up to Rufus. "What do you see when you look at these?"

Rufus took one and examined it. He applied twist and flexed it to check its strength, then handed it back. "Sturdy. Flexible. Light. Perhaps it would make a good knife."

What I saw was opportunity. An opportunity to make something this world, let alone my new half-badger friend, had never seen. "Let's make a wager, Rufus. You're a trader, yes? Return with some essentials to trade. If you're not impressed with what you see then, I'll give you whatever you want for those supplies. Any price within my means."

"And if I should lose this wager?"

"A free brick of that salt would go a long way, and perhaps some jewelers' tools."

Rufus scraped his claws across his furry chin. "Jewelers' tools. You're not wanting to set gemstones, I am thinking. Very well. I'll make a trip to Habberport, five days northwest of here at the coast—that is the port of a human prince's expedition. In ten days' time, I'll return and see the truth of your words. Or not." He raised one eyebrow. "You know, I could always lie and say I'm not impressed, even if I am. This is not a good bargain for you."

"I don't think you're the type to do such a thing," I said. "But even if you are, perhaps in ten days, the reappearance of a friendly face would be worth it on its own."

"It's lonely at the top," said Rufus. He gestured around. "Metaphorically *and* vertically."

He pushed himself off his haunches and dusted off. "Well, if I'm to return in ten days, I should walk through the night. I suppose I'll take my leave."

"You don't want to stay and rest?" I asked.

Rufus offered a sheepish grin. "Perhaps I'm not ready to trust the rest of your tribe. Not yet. But badgers are nocturnal, didn't you know?"

"I did not," I admitted.

"Aha! Perhaps there are some things I know that you do not, after all!" He looked up at the sky through his spectacles. "You'd do well to learn of the day and the night in Lanclova. Each holds its own danger."

I called for my litter bearers, since I hadn't had time to repair my legs. Once I was secured in the litter, I directed them toward the north-facing slope, which was shallower, but still too steep to descend unassisted. I called over for some cordage to use to rappel down the mountain and was only slightly surprised when the two goblins holding either end of the rope careened over the side, snagging a tree behind them. If goblins could blush, I probably would have had the reddest face watching Rufus record what he saw in that leather-bound journal. The two goblins reached the end of their sides of the rope, and rather than letting go, they swung inward and collided with each other.

<Technically, it counts.>

<Goblin Technology Unlocked: Gobby Counterweight>

Oh my stars. How was *that* a technology? But as soon as I thought about it, I realized the applications were nearly endless. Goblins were natural climbers, and what was weight at the top of a bluff if not a bucket of potential energy waiting to be utilized? They were certainly willing enough to hurl themselves off of any precipice at the slightest excuse.

But that would have to wait for another day. Rufus took the rope in his hand and eased himself down the slope. The goblins at the bottom switched to the other line, and since Rufus outweighed both of them, he was able to slide down while the goblins rode the line back up, grinning and hooting. The badger-dwarf waved when he reached the bottom, and I waved back along with the two counterweights.

Once my newest friend was out of eyesight, I returned to the village. Ten days. There was a lot of work to be done. But first, the tribe had eaten, and lethargy was starting to take over.

CHAPTER 9

PERKS

<The majority of your tribe is well-fed for the first time.>
<The majority of your tribe is sleeping comfortably for the first time.>

I squeezed my eyes shut, not exactly remembering how I'd gotten to the bottom of the pile yet again. But the window persisted.

<Procreation bonus granted. Your tribe has increased to 35 members.>
<Increasing your tribe size has unlocked a new goblin variant. You may select one of the following:
Hobgoblin Sentry: A larger, stronger, nocturnal goblin skilled in defending the village
—or—
Goblin Taskmaster: A speech-capable goblin capable of supervising independent tasks and transferring skills to assigned goblins.>

The taskmaster, obviously. Scale early, scale often. More efficient workers early meant more realized gains over time. Plus, speech-capable? I might not have to wait for Rufus to come back to talk to someone after all. Maybe some more martial goblins would have been smart for the added security, but sometimes you gotta risk it for the biscuit.

<Unsurprising. 2 taskmasters have been added to your tribe.>

I dug myself out from under the sleeping pile and pulled on the new pair of sticky-stilts I'd had the goblins make for me last night. That done, I walked to the edge of the bluff to relieve myself. There's something satisfying about whizzing off a cliff. When I returned, most of the other goblins were dragging themselves out and waking up, scratching their bare bellies and meandering around the village in their typical morning stupor. I spotted two who were slightly larger than the others, with a bit more cunning in their eyes. I whistled and waved them over.

"Oy, boss," one of them grumbled. The other said nothing, though she had the subtle wider hips that I think denoted female goblins—the only indication of sexual dimorphism I'd spotted, in fact.

I looked between them. "Shouldn't you both be able to talk?"

They shared a glance. The first one spoke again. "Oh, she can talk. Jus' not the type to yak on."

The first taskmaster had an accent right out of a bad British crime movie. "I see. Alright, well, I suppose you'll need names."

"Wossat?"

"Something to call you by, to set you apart." I pointed to the first. "Buzz," and then to the second, "Sally."

<Goblin Technology Unlocked: Names>
<Don't get too attached.>

Buzz raised his hand in a sloppy salute. "Right, boss. Wos onner agenda today?"

I sighed. There was so much work to do, it was hard to prioritize. But having two independent thinkers would go a long way toward making sure I wasn't spread so thin. I wondered what other industrious variants would be available as the tribe continued to grow.

"Buzz, you're on fire duty. I want you to have a few goblins mess with friction fires. Spin sticks against a piece of wood 'til it makes a glowing coal, then blow on it and add dried grass. Iterate on what works."

Buzz cocked his head toward the other taskmaster. "Wot about Sally?"

"We need to hunt more of those stone sloths, but spears aren't going to cut it. I want to start collecting bomb fruits and storing them at the base of the ridge. Dig holes for each one, so that if one explodes it doesn't trigger all the others."

Buzz looked at Sally, then back at me.

"You sure she's the same variant as you?

"Sally's onnit, boss. Trust."

"Good," I said.

I left them there and went to the supply pile. Knives and spears were all well and good, but they weren't the only tools in an engineer's arsenal.

What I wouldn't give for a 3D printer.

After sending out another two hunting parties, I sat down with the three primary materials for sticky-stone tools and started to make the essentials. It looked like there was actually some new rock mixed in with the shale that was harder and sharper. Flint, I had to assume. I started knocking off chips and soon got the hang of it.

<Goblin Technology Unlocked: Twisty-Cord>
<Goblin Technology Unlocked: Sticky-Stone Spade>
<Goblin Technology Unlocked: Sticky-Stone Hammer>
<Goblin Technology Unlocked: Sticky-Stone Auger>
<Goblin Technology Unlocked: Sticky-Stringy Driver>
<Goblin Technology Unlocked: Sticky-Stone Hand-Saw>
<Goblin Technology Unlocked: Sticky-Stone Cleaver>

Twine was the simplest compound invention. Really, just twisting two of the homespun strings together made them many times stronger. I needed the extra robustness for the abuse the rest of the tools would likely suffer during their use. I made new versions of the spade, the cleaver, the saw, and the auger as well.

The stringy-driver I was especially proud of. It was technically a belt-driver for manually powering rotary tools, with a loop of string attached to a small bow. When wrapped around a sharp stone that could be pushed into a surface and spun, well, that was a simple drill with infinite uses. I'm pretty sure this was close to a fire-making method as well, just with a piece of wood spinning in place of the stone auger.

It wouldn't be long before that technology propagated through the tribe. But I was still missing a major primitive material crucial to the upcoming projects I had in mind: clay. With clay, I could make molds for reproducing complex parts. But I also needed some way to transport it. I pulled together a collection of smaller, flexible sticks and set to building a lattice.

<Goblin Technology Unlocked: Sticky-Wicky Basket>

Thankfully, I had minored in underwater basket weaving in undergrad.

CHAPTER 10

THE CLAY WARS

With my basket complete, I got carefully to my new feet and waddled over to the main part of the village. Buzz and Sally had taken most of the tribe to work on their tasks. I could see Buzz's goblins all working at a variety of variations on the vague instructions of *rub two pieces of wood together*. Some were downright worrying, as a pair of them were sawing a pole back and forth against the trunk of a tree. A fine game for kids having a bit of fun, but goblins are so go-go-go, I think they might have actually been able to saw through the thing, given enough time.

One or two of the projects actually had a small bit of smoke rising from them. Well, that's how development works. There's a lot of trial and error, and the more you can iterate, the more you can discard failed solutions and focus on narrowing in on the right answer. I needed more tribe members to unlock things even faster.

There were about ten other goblins still left in the village, idling or scraping at the stone sloth hide. Though with that heavy, stoney skin I wasn't sure what we were going to use that hide for. It was much too heavy for a goblin to wear.

I threw some poles and twine and small bones in my basket and took the rest of the goblins with me. Together we threw ourselves down the cliff. It wasn't so bad, if I could convince myself I was skydiving. Unfortunately, that did little to soothe every human instinct that clung to my new body telling me I was about to die.

My legs managed to stay on, which came as an immense relief. I was starting to get the knack of securing things with the homemade cordage, and I'd taken the time to retie them with the improved twine.

Once we picked ourselves off the ground, I gathered the goblins around. "I'm looking for clay. It's like mud that stays wet, even when everything else is dry. It's soft, pliant, and sticky. Usually near water."

One of the goblins squawked for my attention and began to chitter. He picked up his spear and headed out into the forest. With the second-generation sticky-stilts, I was able to keep up a little better, even though the goblins had traded their knives for flint cleavers that they used to whirlwind through the underbrush like ninjas on cocaine.

We tore through in the meandering trail-blazing fashion I was growing accustomed to until we reached a clearing that had a wide, slow bend in a creek. And there, just behind the trio of stone sloths, was a patch of pristine, red clay.

Wait a minute.

Before I could tell them to wait, the entire group of ten goblins charged in, weapons waving. The largest stone sloth took both notice and immediate umbrage. It roared and charged, bowling through the collective of goblins and swiping its claws, snapping spear shafts and shattering cleavers.

<I bet a pair of hobgoblins would have been handy right now.>

Shut it, System! I need to think about strategy.

<Your tribe has decreased to 34 members.>

"Retreat!" I shouted.

The goblins began to fall back, the large stone sloth snapping at their heels. Luckily for me, he seemed more interested in staying between us and the other two than pursuing a meal. Family group, perhaps? Matron and cubs? Patriarch and mate plus offspring?

We made ourselves scarce in the clearing and I waited until I was sure the bane of goblin existence wasn't following us before I called a halt.

The remaining goblins panted and wheezed with the effort of the escape. Several of them keeled over face-first into the dirt while I considered.

"Does anyone know of any *other* clay deposits?" I asked.

Forlorn eyes turned toward me, and I put my little furry hands to my temples. That was it, huh? All right. "Wait here," I said.

I crept back through the woods alone, since stealth was apparently a foreign concept to goblins. When I caught sight of the clearing, I climbed a tree to try and get a better view. It was definitely a sloth lair. I could spot a crack in the rocks where they were coming in and out. Not only that, but the creatures made frequent trips to the clay pit in order to slather the material on their own hides, which made me think that the material on their backs wasn't stone or calcified skin at all, but long-cured clay.

This was a problem. It meant the stone sloths' (clay sloths'?) natural habitat involved clay deposits. We had barely scraped by against one of these creatures, and it had killed half a dozen goblins in the process. I had hoped they were rare creatures, but it seemed like clay might also be rare, and it also seemed reasonable to assume these beasts likely staked their claim on deposits.

I sat in the tree and watched them for a while. Eventually the largest one wandered off, but the second-largest stayed to watch the cub. The clearing was never deserted.

Climbing back down from the tree was noisy and haphazard, and I only realized at the bottom that I could have just thrown myself off of it. Still too much of those human instincts. I didn't know if that was a bug or a feature of this new life, but I'd have to overcome it if I wanted to utilize the full breadth of the few benefits granted to permanently level 1 goblins.

I wanted that clay. But three stone sloths and goblins don't mix well—at least, not well for the goblins. I needed time to plan.

<Goblin Technology Unlocked: Sticky Fire Spinner>
<Goblin Component Technology Unlocked: Multi-Goblin Carousels>

That sounded . . . terrifying. I tried to imagine the implications of Buzz putting together various combinations of the tools I'd unlocked in the morning to come up with paired devices of those names, one of which apparently produced fire. But the number of tribe members didn't drop, so as long as the village was still standing, I'd consider it a win we desperately needed.

Clay would have to wait for now. I didn't like that that was the case. Clay opened up a lot of possibilities—the least of which was making reusable molds to mass-produce parts. But we at least had fire. Progress was progress, but I needed rapid iteration. And I needed a plan to deal with the sloths.

CHAPTER 11

ALTERNATE CALORIC SOURCES

I didn't want to militarize the tribe. I wanted to industrialize it. But it seemed like goblins weren't high-tier in a fairly hostile world full of things that wanted to eat *them*. In fact, it seemed like, individually, they were the weakest creatures on this new planet aside from bugs and small fowl. And the biggest thing I needed, even more than clay or fire, was *more goblins*. Plus, there were other sentient races to consider. I'd found Rufus during lucky circumstances, but a half-dwarf, half something else was far from the norm, I was sure. Would goblins be so welcome in a human settlement? The snarling, biting little creatures weren't exactly diplomatic aces.

According to Rufus, there were human kingdoms, presumably the kind with soldiers and standing armies that would sweep aside a small village of goblins without breaking a sweat. The only saving grace was that most of them seemed to be across an ocean. So, we were remote enough and unimportant enough that it probably wasn't worth the logistics effort to come clear the forest of goblins this deep in the continent. Yet. If we did fight armored foes, we would need more than stone spearheads. And what would happen when the time came? Could I realistically kill a human? Above all else, I was a scientist, an engineer, and an explorer devoted to the betterment of all mankind through the progress of aerospace technology.

We had to get numerous enough to deter attackers without violence, but we also had to be ready when we were finally noticed. The best guard against violence is a big stick, after all. That meant defending ourselves through technological ingenuity, if not through strength of arms. Poles in hand, I took my cadre downstream.

There were definitely fish in that stream. One of my highest priorities for the tribe was finding a source of protein that didn't also eat goblins.

Fish would be a valuable food source if the village kept growing, which it would have to do. I had the group fashion a few stone spades using the poles I'd brought and use them to dig up some worms and grubs for bait. With the long poles, one goblin jumped on the end of the spade to bury it in the dirt, and another took a running leap at the top to turn up the soil, using leverage and momentum to make up for their lack of strength.

Despite spending a lot of time on the water, I'd never been fishing. I had a vague idea of what you had to do from pop culture. I arranged my goblins along the bank, each one with a pole and a small bone hook with a rock weight tied to the base. I went down the line and baited each hook. I had to pull the hooks out of the mouths of two goblins that couldn't resist eating their own bait before I got everything sorted.

<*Goblin Technology Unlocked: Sticky-Fishy Poles*>

Excellent. Understanding passed rapidly through the chittering bunch, and they started casting. After a few minutes, one of our goblins had a bite. He started to pull and was promptly yanked off his feet with a squawk of alarm. Whatever he'd hooked—all I saw was a long, dark shadow beneath the water's surface—dragged him through the river at high speed, and the rest of the goblins dropped their poles, chasing after. He was quickly gone from sight.

<*Your tribe has decreased to 33 members.*>

This time I assigned two goblins per pole, making sure they knew to *let go of the pole* if whatever they hooked managed to shift both of them.

Since there was an odd goblin left, I took him and went looking for the spot I'd noted northwest of the bluff where I'd noted feathers on the ground. It took some luck and doubling back over a few crisscrossing goblin paths, but I found the spot. I collected all I could find, and then I climbed the tree to see if there were any eggs. As luck would have it, there was one in a nest. It was a bit smaller than an ostrich egg, which made me wary. A bird big enough to have laid this was definitely a bird that could make a snack out of a goblin. So much for being bigger than local fowl.

I stole it anyway and climbed back down. Calories are calories.

<*Your tribe has decreased to 32 members.*>

I didn't have to wonder what had happened for long. A distant crack echoed across the forest. One of Sally's goblins must have accidentally ruptured or dropped one of the fruits. The things were dangerous, to be sure. A plan began to form in my mind, but I didn't have everything I needed just yet.

We returned to the fishermen to find a modest pile of fish and a suspicious pile of fish bones. I gave a few goblins the evil eye, and discovered they had zero poker faces. But at least we knew fishing worked. Still, I wanted a plan to catch whatever river monster had dragged my goblin into the depths. I wanted to get out on the river, too. But boating wasn't an immediate priority.

"Bring back any fish you catch before dark, we'll fry 'em up."

I probably didn't need to say that. The goblins put a lot of stock in all being back in the village before nightfall. I'd been awake at night, so I knew it was plenty bright enough for them to still function—especially with the huge moon overhead catching the light of the sun at low angles. Which made me think the woods must be even more dangerous at night.

CHAPTER 12

GOBLIN-GO-ROUND

I returned to the village with my egg to find several fires going and Buzz looking quite pleased with himself. The fire carousel ended up being basically the reverse of a traditional fire drill. Instead of spinning a stick against a piece of wood on the ground, they'd stuck a pole *in* the ground, and several goblins struggled to stay balanced as they spun a second piece of wood on top like a merry-go-round. Unsurprisingly, the whole thing teetered off balance and sent goblins flying every which way.

By then, the tip of the pole had been ground down to a smoldering red ember, and the goblins scrambled to pull it from the ground and touch it to a bed of tinder while two others puffed at it. Soon, they had a small flame. The whole process took a half-dozen of the little goblins.

In the engineering world, it's common knowledge that you can't solve problems simply by throwing more bodies at them—though the government still tries to do just that. In fact, it generally slows progress down. Well, with goblins it seemed like it was just the opposite.

"Once we got a couple o' us onner, we figured things out," said Buzz, nodding along. "Though, truth told, Sally's more fer tinkerin' with gizmos."

"I'll keep that in mind," I said. "What would you rather be doing?"

"Partial to buildin', meself. Village needs work, yeah?"

"I've got some projects in mind."

I watched the goblins working at their carousel. When I'd unlocked the goblin counterweight, I hadn't expected it to be a technological prerequisite for starting a fire. Maybe they just didn't have the weight or arm strength to tackle the problem the way a human would.

"I'm impressed," I said to Buzz. I held the pilfered egg out to him. "Think we can get this bad boy cooking?"

Buzz took the egg and dropped it whole onto the tinder bed. Well, I guess that was dinner sorted. Fish and eggs, not exactly an appetizing combo without some flour to make batter and some potatoes to go with it, but things were a bit austere.

I kicked around one of the older fires and found a small stick with a decent char at the end, then rooted around for a wide piece of bark. Then I sat down to sketch while I waited for the rest of the goblins to come back.

Sally brought her team up to the village just before the sun slipped behind the moon. The fishermen returned shortly after that with a sticky-wicky full of small fish that were put on poles to lean over Buzz's fire.

By the time dinner was ready, I had a decent—well, *rough* sketch of the parts I needed. I called Buzz and Sally over as I gnawed at a charred fish and showed them the drawing.

"Ideally, these would be made from clay or ceramics. But do you think we can carve these parts out of wood?"

Buzz looked at Sally, then turned back to me. "Sally reckons she could get it done, boss."

"Good," I passed over the sheaf of bark drawings, which Sally took eagerly. I gave Buzz a look. "Can you understand the other goblins without speaking?"

"Of course, boss. Innit a bit weird you can't?"

"This whole thing is a bit weird," I admitted. I took a few minutes telling Sally how to interpret the drawings, and how the parts should be made. The goblin nodded along. Her eyes bugged wider with each drawing. I don't know if her enthusiasm was for the opportunity to make some mechanical bits, or if it was based on no longer being on bomb fruit detail. Either way, it was one more step toward walking on that moon.

One small step for goblinkind.

The lethargy started to take me.

<Your tribe has decreased to 31 members.>
<Your tribe has increased to 37 members.>

It was a net gain, since I'd only lost three goblins the previous day. Still, it seemed almost as though at least a few were bound to go the way of the dodo at the slightest breeze. It just went to highlight how vulnerable goblins were, and how royally screwed they would be if their reproductive method wasn't as effective as it was mysterious. I pulled myself from the bottom of the pile of twelve or so goblins and stretched.

Buzz and Sally came to see me with another goblin in tow.

"This'n saw sommat come inner camp 'n' drag off 'is friend," reported Buzz.

"I see," I said. I considered. If we were going to grow, we couldn't lose goblins to predation. I'd have to see to the village's defenses.

"Put five goblins on building a wall of poles on the shallow side. Hopefully that will keep out curious beasts. Pick fifteen to go hunt and fish, and the rest to processing some thicker poles."

"Got it, boss," said Buzz. He meandered off while Sally held up the drawings from the night before. I noticed that she'd tried to make a few of her own, mostly of things like birds and bugs, but one or two of spear-heads, and one of a spear with a stone crossbar with two stick-figure goblins holding it together.

"We'll make an engineer of you yet, Sally," I said.

Sally beamed.

"Pick whoever is best with tools to help you make these parts. I'll be working alongside you in the village today."

Sally nodded enthusiastically and dashed off to collect her team of engineers, mostly by a combination of shouting, biting, and hitting them over the head *with* the designs. Perfect project manager material.

CHAPTER 13

STICKY-SPRINGY STILTS

For my part, I went to work on a different project. One a little closer to home. There were plenty of tools around. Goblins left to their own devices seemed to love tinkering and crafting things now that I'd introduced technology to the tribe. I picked up a selection of small knives, a saw, and an auger. From the wood pile, I grabbed two promising-looking bits of wood that were roughly the same size, and slightly larger around than my leg remnants.

Next, I retrieved the stone sloth claws from the bone pile, as well as some leftover gut-string the goblins had made from its intestines. I tested a claw against the ground, seeing how pliant it was, and how it had connected to the knuckle with a knobby tab.

I went to work, using the knife as a chisel to hollow out two depressions in each of the wood pieces until they were about a hand's span deep. Then, I flipped them over and drilled two holes in the underside with the auger, which was more complicated to use than I thought it would be. Once I had that, I checked the size against the claws and started making small adjustments with a knife.

<Your tribe has decreased to 36 members.>

Damn. I looked up. It was barely midmorning. The rest of the goblins were going about their business. It must have been one of the hunting party members. My heart thudded in my chest while I waited for a string of tribe-size messages to come in. After a few more minutes passed without additional notifications, I went back to work. I had to get in the mindset that I was going to lose tribesmen no matter what I did.

I'd figured the System was just being cold and callous when it warned me not to get attached. But Tribe Apollo might as well have had a revolving door. Goblins could die and be replaced with new, fully-grown goblins daily. My taskmasters would get names, to set them apart from the rest of the tribe. But the rest would never even have names, unless they started giving them to one another. Soon there'd be far too many for me to keep track of, and most of them couldn't speak names anyway.

I got the long, curved sloth claws fitted into the holes I'd drilled for them, then went to work smoothing the interior of the cups and packing them with down that I'd collected from the bird's nest, and some fur clumps from the bone pit. I cut a long, thin wedge out on the front and back of the cups so they could be tightened, then gouged circular grooves near the top to hold lacing.

Around midday, the sun dipped behind the moon, and I took off the sticky-stilts and tried the fit of my new prosthetics. On Earth, I'd had a sleeve go over my residual lower legs, and they'd laser-scanned my residuals to print me a perfect fit for the prosthetics. Here, I was just eyeballing it.

The hunting party returned around the same time, climbing over the edge of the bluff with a couple of carcasses in tow. At least one was a mangled clifford that had *definitely* been hit with a popper, but they also had a few fat birds and one small mammal that might have been something close to a beaver. And, sure enough, they had one less member. I wondered if it was the clifford, the beaver, or the bomb fruit that had done it. Half of them set to skinning the kills, while the others worked at getting a fire going using Buzz's fire carousel method.

I went back to my work. The left one fit decently enough, but the right was too tight. I took the padding out and shaved the sidewall down a bit more, then re-packed it and pulled it on. Better. Finally, I took the gut-string and used some of it to secure the claws in their notches, and the rest to wrap around the grooves and tighten both sockets around my legs.

<Goblin Technology Unlocked: Sticky-Springy Stilts>

I hoisted my new feet into the air and twisted them around, looking at the angle. These were certainly heavier than my old running blades. But the flat, wide claws of the stone sloth had a remarkably similar profile and not all that dissimilar flex profile.

<Goblin Technology Unlocked: Whirly-Wheels>
<Goblin Technology Unlocked: Toothy-Gears>
<Goblin Technology Unlocked: Cranky-Cranks>
<Goblin Technology Unlocked: Sticky-Axles>

Those ones hadn't been me. I guess it was time to take a look at what Sally's team had accomplished. I pushed myself unsteadily onto my feet and tested the strength and balance of the sloth-claw prosthetics. They had a bit more give than I was used to, but they were worlds better than teetering around on poles tied to my lower legs.

I took a tentative jump in place and was surprised when the springback flipped me ass over teakettle right into the bone pile. The other goblins started to take notice and stopped to watch and point. A few even laughed. Couldn't say I blamed them.

Not to be deterred (every great scientist and engineer was laughed at in their time), I got back to my new feet again and took a few tentative steps. It was almost like walking on a trampoline, or maybe those old bouncy shoes that looked like death hazards.

I got the hang of it pretty quickly (so quickly I had to wonder if that was a feature of the Goblin Tech Tree) and picked up speed around the village.

The goblins were still laughing, but now I thought they did so out of excitement and amazement. Several of them chased after me, hooting and hopping. This time, they had trouble keeping up with *me*. No longer would I be a burden if we had to beat feet.

What was more, I could run again. Not hobble, not waddle, not crawl, but *run*. Not fast, or I'd lose control, but still. The two years of rehab after my accident had been the most excruciating time of my life, not because I was in constant pain from surgeries and recovery, but because I didn't know if I'd ever walk again, let alone run, row, or bike. Anything that let me move fast made me feel alive. I had refused to give up. Refused to let myself be bound to a chair. Slowly, I'd gotten my life back. And I hadn't realized it, having been in pure survival mode, but my new goblin life wasn't complete until I had that feeling once again.

This, more than anything else, convinced me that I *could* figure it out. I could survive here, build my tribe, master the Goblin Technology Tree, and reach the giant moon, Raphina. Sure, there were a lot of steps along the way. But like I said, I like to move fast.

CHAPTER 14

STICKY-FLICKY SLINGERS

After my brief jaunt, I headed over to Sally to see how her team had come with the parts I'd given her to oversee.

The majority of it was garbage. It wasn't that the goblins weren't diligent, especially under Sally's constant percussive encouragement. They just struggled to understand the engineering schematics as thoroughly as I'd have liked. They'd managed to produce gears and levers and cranks, but many of them had irregular teeth or oblong shapes. But as I walked through the village, I noticed that other goblins not assigned to the task had also started adding gearing to make simple machines. The first place I saw them employed naturally was on the cooking spit, so that the chefs no longer had to leap into the air to turn the spit. Instead, they'd grasped the idea of angular transference and now had a system wherein two of them would push around a gear on the ground that connected to one on the spit. I examined the handiwork, and other than the strangely oblong gears, I couldn't find fault with the design. Impressive for creatures that hadn't known what gears were the day before. While they weren't great inventors, they were seemingly very clever at implementing applications for the technology I unlocked for them in ways that greatly complemented goblin physiology.

I had to sort through the parts in order to find what I needed. Sally watched curiously, even as she continued to administer her unique brand of leadership on anyone she thought might be slacking. By mixing pieces and parts, I was able to connect a pair of laths to a long body with a runnel going down the length, and a hooked bit of wood through a slot to make a lever. After that, I secured a string across the lath and fed it through a sort of sled that fit along the top rail. Finally, I fit one of the crank levers to the top and used it to push back the sled until it locked. Yes, since I know you're wondering, I made a crossbow. But not one for shooting stone arrowheads.

All eyes were on me now. Even Sally had paused mid-blow. I kicked around on the ground until I uncovered a smooth rock about the size of my little blue fist. I fit it to the sled, aimed at a nearby tree, and pulled the release.

The entire thing exploded in my hands. The body snapped in two, and the laths shattered practically into sawdust. It knocked me back on my ass, and the rock and the sled bounced off my forehead.

Luckily, it hadn't been lethal damage, because I didn't get the System message that another goblin had died in my place. I set the wreckage aside, ignored all the laughing goblins making explosion noises to one another, and went back to the parts pile while some of my tribe laughed so hard I thought I might lose a goblin from asphyxiation.

Prototype, test, iterate.

That was the name of the game. I went to work assembling the second prototype. This time I chose parts that were a little heavier, but sturdier. I couldn't shoulder the crossbow, so I had to pinch the back end between my elbow and side as I lined up the shot.

The release took more effort than I was expecting, but once it slipped, that sled rocketed forward like something to come out of the NASA's Jet Propulsion Lab. The laths straightened in an instant, and the stone shot out of the sled, whipping forward to impact the tree with a serious *thud*. Bark sprayed from the impact.

Every goblin in the village dropped what they were doing and came to marvel at this new invention.

<Goblin Technology Unlocked: Sticky-Flicky Slinger>
<Goblin Technology Unlocked: Simple Stoney Bullets>

Those seemed apt descriptions. I spotted Sally among the onlookers and handed the crossbow and crank over to her. "This is what you've achieved today," I said. "A shot to the noggin on one of those cliffords or stone sloths and they won't be looking to munch on any goblins until they stop seeing double."

She looked down at the bow, then back up at me.

"You want to build more inventions, Chief Engineer Sally?"

Sally swallowed, then opened her mouth and uttered one word so softly I wasn't even sure she had said it.

"*—yes—*"

Good. *Good.* I grinned and watched as Sally cranked the sled back and loaded it with a stone. The bow held, and the rock flashed out, sailing past the tree that I had aimed for and over the edge. I had thought about, and subsequently dismissed, the idea of simple bows and arrows for the goblins. The fact was, they simply weren't strong enough to draw something with enough weight to pierce the hide of anything larger than a clifford, and probably weren't patient enough for the hours upon hours it took to get good with a traditional bow. But crossbows use force-multiplying levers to reset, and you can aim them somewhat accurately with just a little practice.

Well, you know how goblins are. The technology spread across the village, and suddenly every furry Jones had to have a sticky-flicky slinger of their own to hang above the fireplace. Over the next hour, the village became a hailstorm of stones as goblins lined up at the impromptu firing range for practice. Small stones actually started to become scarce on the hilltop, which gave a few goblins an excuse to fling themselves off into the forest below to collect more.

There were a few more critical failures. The worst of them resulted in an amputated leg, but the other goblins were quick to cap his stump with a sticky-stilt, effectively staunching the bleeding entirely. Amazingly, that goblin went right back to tinkering as soon as he was able to stand. He came and stood next to me, showing off his new leg as if to demonstrate for the rest of the tribe that he had more in common with me than they did. More than a few jealous glares made me worried that there might be a few more "accidents," but it appeared that even goblins weren't crazy enough to deliberately maim themselves for a bit of perceived status (however inclined they were to accidentally maim themselves notwithstanding).

The target practice continued into the afternoon eclipse. Individual goblins weren't accurate with the things. But they didn't have to be. We had numbers on our side. And by the next day, we'd have even more. I had one more plan to try and get that clay without a fight. But if it came down to it, these crossbows could really tip the odds toward the tribe in battles with the local beasts.

I watched the practice a bit more before ordering everyone back to their assigned tasks.

Buzz waved me over so that I could check the progress of the palisade on the shallower side of the bluff. It looked good, but it was burning through rope faster than the craftsmen could make more. We were going to need a more reliable source of cordage. I added it to the *to be worried about later* pile. But it was clear the wall would take several days to complete, just on the one side. And when an early afternoon rainstorm sent the tribe scurrying for their shelters to work on smaller parts and projects, I had to wonder if one side would be enough.

One other thing that bothered me was the predator taking goblins in the night. The way goblins surrendered to an involuntary lethargy after eating meant we were easy pickings overnight. I had attempted to explain the concept of a watch. Even with trying to loop Buzz in as a mediator, he hadn't understood.

<*You know who stays up late? Hobgoblins.*>

Shut it, System! Even if I could go back and choose again, I'd take taskmasters ten times out of ten.

<*As long as you're happy.*>

Still, the System had a point. I'd have to consider that the next time I hit a milestone that granted a new goblin variant for my tribe. Which would have greater benefit to the tribe in the long run? A variant that increased work efficiency? Or a variant that reduced attrition through security?

In the short term, I decided to double the number of goblins assigned to the wall project. But goblins apparently didn't work in the rain. Not that I blamed them, as the sensation of wet fur was distinctly unpleasant. And the *smell*. Woof.

It didn't stop until almost nightfall, and shortly after, the hunting party returned with fish and small game, including a few more fat birds.

Buzz came over to my fire while the catch of the day was strung up above the fire to smoke. He looked agitated, fidgeting and twitchy. "The lads in the woods spotted tracks of javeline rutters."

"That some sort of pig?" I asked.

Buzz settled down and poked at the fire. "Half pig, half dwarf."

I tried to picture it. "Like Rufus?"

"Wrong half, boss."

Ah. So, like a pig version of a centaur, then. What would you call that? A boar-a-taur? A jaballero? Well, I suppose calling it a javeline rutter was good enough. "Bad news, I take it?"

"When ain't it?"

Fair. Wild pigs had a hell of a temperament. If their dwarven half inherited it at all, then I could see how that would be problematic for something like a goblin. Back home, wild boars had invaded Texas, where NuEarth was located. The CEO took weekend trips to hunt them in his personal helicopter, according to the company-wide emails he blasted out Monday mornings. Not that I was jealous of his helicopter. Real aircraft have wings.

"Alright. We'll put even more hands on the wall project. That north slope is our weakest point if someone wants to attack the village."

I thought Buzz would return to his workers, but he just laid down in place and went to sleep. Exhausted from the construction, probably. He might have been the first, but the dogpile was quick to form and I swear it gave off almost as much heat as the fire. That must be how they managed to survive winters in this world.

Luckily, it stayed dry enough in the shelters for small fires, and we managed to only burn one of them down. That was alright. I'd soon have the shelters built to a higher standard. But the priority was still building the wall and getting a hold of some clay.

I looked at the stone sloth hide, still intact and curing. Hostile nighttime predators, resource-bogarting carnivorous sloths, and now a race of intelligent boar-dwarves. I didn't think I'd get lucky enough for them to have Rufus's open mind toward a goblin king, either. I needed to move quickly. Tomorrow, I was either going to get that clay or lose a heap of tribesmen.

CHAPTER 15

FRUITS AWAY

<Your tribe has decreased to 34 members.>
<1 goblin taskmaster has been added to your tribe.>
<Your tribe has increased to 40 members.>

More nighttime predation, and double the frustration. I'd lost two goblins this time instead of one. Either the creature had been hungrier, or it had brought a friend. Whatever the case, I couldn't have nighttime attrition eating a third of my population growth. If I was going to be king of this tribe, then it was on me to protect them. We needed better sleeping quarters.

The problem was, we also needed hunters out looking for food in great enough numbers to sustain the tribe, we needed bodies on the wall project, and we needed Sally's team making crossbows. Not only that, but I still had to impress Rufus on his return in a few days.

At the morning taskmaster palaver, Buzz and Sally were accompanied by a third goblin. One of the new arrivals was an additional taskmaster, which would let me further delegate work in the tribe. I decided to call him Neil.

"Are you the talkative type?" I asked.

"Yeah," said Neil, and didn't elaborate further.

I looked at him for a minute, waiting to see if he'd say anything else, but he just stuck his finger in his nose and rooted around.

"So . . . what do you like to do?"

My newest taskmaster tilted his head. "*Like?*"

"Yeah. Sally's got her testing and production, and Buzz enjoys construction projects. If there's something you think you'll be good at, I can put you in charge of it. So what do you like?"

Neil thought for a minute. Then his pupils dilated. "I think I like *hunting.* And *knives*," he said. Then he considered for a moment longer as a manic grin spread across his face. “Explosions, too. I think I *really* like them, boss.”

I grinned back. “Ordinarily, that would be worrying. But, boy, is it your lucky day,” I said.

Rather than making more crossbow parts, I demonstrated to Sally’s team to start mixing mud with dry grass and forming it into bricks to dry. Making actual hardened structures required a great deal of resources we simply didn’t have, and the majority of our lumber was going to the fence and reinforcing shelters.

Today, I gave each member of the twelve-strong hunting party a crossbow. I had Neil get all the goblins down the north slope, in hopes of keeping as many crossbows as we could intact. Then I grabbed my own supplies that I’d prepared, as well as the stone sloth skin.

Two of the goblins still managed to break their bows, so I passed each of them a wicker basket. Each one was lined with moss and grass to make the inside as soft as possible.

“Congratulations,” I said. “You’re on bomb fruit detail. Each of you go get ten fruits from the pits Sally dug and keep those baskets far enough away that you won’t blow up the rest of us—or each other—if they go off. Understand?”

If the goblins were upset about being assigned explosive ordnance detail with the unstable fermented fruits, they gave no indication. They took the baskets and dashed off at top speed, squawking and making explosion noises as they went. One of them tripped and nearly lost the basket as he rolled but raised it over his head triumphantly when he came to a stop. The rest of the hunting party cheered him on.

We were all going to die.

When they returned (thankfully moving much more cautiously), I had them maintain a safe distance while I took the hunting party back to the clearing near the clay deposit. Ideally, we weren’t even going to have to fight the sloths. I took the hide, and then motioned over to the nearest goblin.

“You want the front or the back?”

The goblin looked at the stone sloth hide, and I swear his fur turned a paler shade of blue. He shook his head vehemently, but I proffered the skin, and with a reluctant look, he draped it over himself.

<Goblin Technology Unlocked: Skinny-Sneakers>

I had each of the goblins take a bomb fruit and carefully place it on the ground about ten meters apart from the nearest fruit. Then, I had them stand far enough apart that they should be out of the blast zone. Finally, I gave Neil instructions on what I wanted, took the empty wicker basket, and crawled under the sloth skin with my unfortunate partner.

It was hot and muggy under the hide. My visibility was limited to the two holes where its eyes had been. The thing was heavy, too, with the clay the former owner had used to armor itself. Maybe if it came down to it, that armor might protect us.

Yeah, right.

Slowly, we crept forward toward the clearing until the two stone sloths came into view. Papa sloth must have been out hunting or foraging, because I didn't see any sign of him. We shifted the heavy hide forward, inching toward the clay deposit near the river. I kept my eyes on mama sloth, making sure she didn't get any ideas. She spotted us, and eyed us warily, but didn't charge. I guess she must have mistaken us for a very ugly member of her own species. We passed the closest point to them, then started to move away toward the clay deposit.

I could see the older sloth physically relax, lowering her posture and returning to rooting around in the dirt with her claws. We got the hide over the clay, and I picked up a handful and squeezed it between my fingers. It was rich and red, with a little bit of grit and a smooth consistency. If I was lucky, the color was an indication of high oxidation and iron content, and the grit would be silica. I started to pack the wet material into the wicker basket. My partner helped, making the work go quickly. It was working!

We filled up the basket and left the clearing. The hunting party came into view, and a few of them raised their crossbows before Neil stopped them from firing. Maybe our costume was a little *too* good.

"Nice work," I said to my partner under the hide, who was a little wobbly at the knees. I traded the full wicker basket for the other empty one. "One more trip and we'll have all the clay we'll need for the time being."

Neil raised his goblin eyebrow, as though shocked I would willingly go *back* in. But when we made it back into the clearing, the bigger stone sloth ignored us completely. We headed for the clay deposit and started loading up the second basket. Things were going well until I heard a cold, wet sniffling, and looked down to see the stone sloth cub had gotten curious and come over to take a sniff of the new arrival. It had poked its head entirely underneath the skin. I stared down at it, and it stared up at me.

Before I could figure out what to do, my partner looked up from the wicker basket and squawked.

"No, wait!" I hissed. But it was too late. He balled up his tiny fist and planted it straight in the nose of the cub.

The cub, having gone from curious infant to victim of goblin brutality, scrambled back, whining in a high-pitched cry that was obviously some sort of distress call.

"Go, go!" I said. "Get the basket!"

As soon as I heard the older stone sloth's ferocious roar, and the answering call from deeper in the woods, I knew we were hosed. We hauled the basket between the two of us as fast as my new legs could carry me. The older of the two stone sloths had pushed the baby behind it, and its hackles were up. It growled and grunted at us and stamped the ground. Then, it lowered its head and charged.

Surprisingly, the hide of the stone sloth actually did absorb a lot of the impact. The matriarch hit center mass, which meant she actually hit the dead space between us two goblins, and all three of us went down in a tangle. The hide ended up draped over the charging stone sloth, which let my partner in crime and I make a break for it with the goods while the cub screeched at us and the older one flailed.

We put on a little extra speed. From the north, something began to crash through the brush, and I looked back to see the patriarch shredding through foliage to get to the clearing. It took one look at the situation and charged us.

"Drop it and run!" I shouted.

The other goblin didn't need further encouragement. He let his side of the wicker basket drop, spilling clay onto the ground. A distressingly few number of seconds later, the adult stone sloth trampled the wicker underfoot, dashing the clay in all directions. We sprinted through the trees, and this time Neil was ready. I had to watch my footing carefully, not only because of the primitive prosthetics but also lest I step on a bomb fruit. But that let the stone sloth close the distance. And like I've mentioned, despite their superficial resemblance to the slow, peaceful Earth creatures, these things could really move. If I hadn't had the sloth-claw prosthetics, it would have been on me.

Neil waited until I was clear of the field before he gave the order to shoot. Rocks began to fly past me. One or two were aimed at the charging stone sloth, because it's hard not to shoot at an enormous charging predator,

I suppose. But most of them were aimed at the bomb fruits on the ground that we were not quite out of range from.

"I got it, boss!" shouted Neil, raising his crossbow with what looked like a handful of small pebbles. He fired at us, and I had to cover my face against the rain of debris that sprayed against me. One of the stones struck home on a fruit, though, blowing up maybe five meters behind and to my right. The blast picked me up off my feet and sent me flying. Luckily, I landed on my head and bounced. My ears rang, and my vision swam. Something heavy landed beside me, and I was pretty sure it wasn't my partner.

Another explosion went off, sounding muffled and far away, then another. I heard a shriek and tried to regain my bearings.

<Goblin Technology Unlocked: Popper Trap>

I heard the tromp of goblin feet on the ground and saw several diminutive figures rushing past me. Sound was starting to come back, and I could hear the collective war cry of the hunters and the *snap* of crossbows going off. The goblins were *cheering.* At least, until one of them put a foot wrong—

BOOOOM!

CHAPTER 16

REVENGE OF THE SLOTH

<Your tribe has decreased to 38 members.>

The cheers turned to shouts of alarm as the goblins realized they'd chased their quarry back through our own minefield. Rather than slowing down and carefully picking their way out of it, they panicked and scattered in all directions at breakneck speed—miraculously not triggering a second accidental explosion. Neil came over to help me to my feet as things calmed down.

"Did we win?" I asked groggily.

Neil grabbed me by the shoulders and turned me around. The first thing I noticed was the fine mist of blue fur drifting in the light. Well, those would be goblins thirty-nine and forty. Or what was left of them. The second thing I noticed was the two halves of the matriarch, separated by about ten meters.

"Oh."

The third thing I noticed was the claw and wrist of the patriarch, which was the heavy thing that had landed near me. The beast must have been reaching to slice me with those long claws.

"We did win!" I shouted.

The goblins all started cheering again, fallen comrades mourned and moved on from just as quickly.

Neil came to stand beside me. "Wot's next, boss?"

To business, then. I brought the hunting party carefully around the minefield and into the clearing. Our wicker basket had been crushed, but there was no sign of the larger stone sloth, which meant we had free access to the clay. I had each of the goblins start weaving something to carry it with while I looked over the clearing.

On the east side, there was a crag in a large boulder where I was pretty sure the stone sloths had been nesting. When I peeked inside, that was confirmed. There were also bones. *Goblin* bones. I spotted at least one shattered skull, and several small, humanoid limbs. As soon as I saw *that*, I felt a lot less bad for killing the two adults just to get at some clay.

The cub was there, huddled against the back wall for safety. It was, to my goblin body, about the size a medium dog would have been to me as a human. Of course, I knew it would grow to several times the size and weight of my goblin body. Still, it didn't seem right, leaving it here. Chances were, it would die without its parents.

Neil came up beside me and peered in the crag. "Good eating," he said.

"Barely any meat on it," I said. "We got that whole sloth in the minefield to munch on. Let's take this one back with us."

Neil gave me a skeptical look but was quick to turn around and delegate the task of retrieving the infant. Two goblins managed to hoist it between them, and the thing was too stunned by its circumstances to really do anything about it.

Clay, cub, and carcass in tow, we headed back to the village. I hated to take materials away from the wall project, but I planned to borrow enough poles to create a simple pen for the cub. If nothing else, maybe whatever predator had been infiltrating the village would go for the isolated animal instead.

Neil was leading the way, but he stopped suddenly in the middle of the trail and held up his fist. He looked back. "*Make scarce, boys!*" he whispered.

The hunting party was a frenzy of activity as we took cover off the path, in the thickets, behind trees, and behind roots. I watched as Neil worked the crank on his bow to set a stone in place and peered at the path.

A four-legged figure pushed through the unbroken thicket onto our trail. It had a pig-like lower body, but a stocky, wide upper body and a battered iron helmet covering its face. This must have been one of the creatures Neil had warned me about. What had he called them? *Javeline*? It had a spear in its right hand with an iron spearhead.

Metallurgy, I thought to myself. The javeline had a source of iron in the forest somewhere. I wondered how they were collecting it and refining it into a usable form. *System, what level is it?*

<8>

Well, that wasn't so bad. Lower level than the stone sloth, actually.

The rutter stamped at the ground, and then reached down to brush its hairy fingers over our tracks before straightening. It tightened its hands on the haft of the spear, looking around at the surrounding forest. It let out a low, reverberating whistle that seemed to bounce through the trees and almost made the leaves vibrate. Two more of its kind joined it from the forest. One of them was *massive,* broadly built with a barrel chest and thick arms. A mane of black hair and a bristly, braided beard draped across his shoulders.

<16 and 12>

I didn't have to ask which of the new pair was the higher-leveled one. *System, can you superimpose levels above individuals?*

Floating numbers appeared above the heads of all three rutters. A cumulative thirty-six levels against a group of fourteen level 1 goblins. I didn't have to be a tactical genius to understand these odds. The javeline exchanged words, though it sounded more like the low rumbling of a landslide to my goblin ears. Then, they moved off along our trail, back in the direction we'd come from. *They heard the bomb fruits,* I realized. They were investigating. And thanks to the robust method of goblin pathfinding, they knew a tribe was also in the area. Well, they'd find the battlefield and see what was left of the stone sloths, too.

I had hoped we'd be able to find a diplomatic solution with these creatures. But it didn't look like that was in the cards.

Something snapped farther along the trail, and the rutters dug in their hooves and set off at a gallop toward the noise, spears raised. They were surprisingly fast on those little pig legs. Much faster than any goblin not being propelled by the blast of a bomb fruit. If it came down to it, they would run us down in the woods before we could make it back to the safety of the tribe.

We waited in our hiding spots until long after the javeline left—longer than I would have. But, when I made to rise, I felt a small fist against the back of my skull, pushing me back to the ground. I looked over at Neil, who was still watching the direction the javeline had moved off in. "*Not yet, boss!*" he hissed. His other hand was wrapped around his cleaver, keeping it at the ready. Neil kept my head down until *he* decided it was safe to move. As he was now the taskmaster of my hunters, I decided to trust his judgment. I may have a fancy degree and know about things like machines and rockets, but Neil was a natural-born goblin. He had access to instincts I would never possess.

The return to the village was a much more somber affair after our encounter with the rutters. We'd avoided them, this time. But what would happen if we weren't so lucky the next time? Would they be interested in negotiating with a goblin king? Or would they slaughter the entire tribe out of principle? Or *sport*? I didn't know anything about them, and we were better off not learning firsthand, for now. We needed time and more goblins. We needed better fortifications. We needed a leg up. We needed something better than *stone* at the end of our spears. And I had an inkling of how to get it.

Sally had set a few dozen raw adobe bricks to dry in the sun, and I'd need them tomorrow, along with a lot of wood.

<Goblin Component Technology Unlocked: Raw Icky-Brickies>

I thought for a moment. *System, can you track available resources like bricks and wood?*

<Define measurement parameters.>

Numbers for bricks works fine. Hmm. *Can we do kilograms for wood and bone and other resources?*

<Kilogram is not a recognized unit of measurement on Rava. I recommend utilizing the "choom" as a standard weight, length, and volume metric.>

What's a choom?

<Approximately the weight, surface area, and volume of an individual goblin's head.>

Lovely, let's go with that.

<Parameters defined. Tribe Apollo has the following resources:
Raw bricks: 54
Bone: 12 chooms

Timber: 24 chooms
Finished poles: 22
Scat: 15 chooms
Water: 4,201 chooms>

Convenient. On Earth, I'd needed a manually updated spreadsheet to keep track of inventory. Here, the System could handle tracking all that for me.

<*You're welcome.*>

Oops. *Thanks, System.*

CHAPTER 17

SKIPPING THROUGH THE AGES

<Your tribe has decreased to 37 members.>
<Your tribe has increased to 45 members.>
<Goblin Technology Unlocked: Dirt-Dobe Brickies>
<Goblin Technology Unlocked: Clay Thing-Holders>

Only one goblin taken during the night, and a good amount added. We woke to find a decent-size hole worried in a weak corner of one of the enclosed shelters where one of the goblins had apparently been dragged away in its sleep. The others were starting to get restless in the mornings. While they didn't seem to lament the loss of any single goblin, they also didn't like the idea of getting picked off in the night.

Somewhat selfishly, my primary concern was that it might happen to one of my taskmasters, whose specialty of keeping other goblins on task and making them better at their work contributed hugely to my ability to multitask. Still, we'd added eight additional members. I'd been doing some tracking, and it seemed like the increases were loosely based on the amount of sleeping mounds. Goblins would only form a mound with a minimum of twelve members and no more than about twenty. Each independent mound would produce one to three goblins per night, which meant we'd gotten pretty lucky by getting eight goblins out of three sleeping mounds. I decided to rework the shelters for max efficiency. If each mound could only hold about fifteen goblins, that would ensure distribution to the maximum number of mounds, which should optimize reproduction without resulting in undersized piles.

With forty-five members total, I could split the tribe evenly between my three taskmasters. There was safety in numbers, after all, and fifteen goblins with crossbows, spears, and cleavers would be much safer than just ten or eleven.

I checked on the juvenile stone sloth as well, and found it still asleep in its new pen, untouched by whatever was preying on the goblins. I got the feeling that a lot of predators wouldn't think the juice of dealing with the clay-reinforced hide of the sloths was worth the squeeze. Goblins were level 1 and practically defenseless.

Buzz brought Sally and Neil over for the morning roundup. I sent Neil off right away with the hunters, who took their assorted slingers, wildlife disguises, and fishing poles. I had them go west, away from where we'd seen the javeline. I wasn't going to mess with the boar-men quite yet. I also wanted them to bring back more hides for tanning. Buzz had his wall project, though his eyes got a bit greedy when he saw the stack of bricks Sally had cured.

"Sorry, Buzz," I said. "I need those for another project. But we're going to be making more. *A lot* more. In fact, I want you to send two of your crew over to the pond and just have them make as many bricks as they can."

With just Sally left, I pulled out another set of charcoal sketches I'd whipped up the night before while the stone sloth roasted. My chief engineer's eyes got as big as dinner plates when she saw that I had drawings, and she just about snatched them out of my hand. She looked through, eyes keen as she absorbed details of the structure. She chittered for her crew, and started squawking and directing traffic as they scrambled to arrange lumpy, misshapen bricks into a tower about two meters high and slathered them with muddy mortar. In the meantime, I tinkered with a design of my own using a few of the gears and a crank, along with a stretched hide and a stone drill.

When the last brick was put on top of the tower, the engineering crew busied themselves loading the bottom with fuel and tinder and carefully tossing in coals from last night's fire.

<Goblin Technology Unlocked: Fumey-Furnace>

Not exactly an accurate description. Really, it was a forced-air kiln. You see, fire requires two things—fuel and oxygen. You add more fuel, you get a bigger fire. But if you add more oxygen, you get a *hotter* fire.

Sun-dried clay is useful for cups, bowls, jars, and other containers. And I had a couple of those drying the previous night, which had finished by the morning. Primitive cultures on Earth had used clay for a huge number of applications, even for things like recording history. In fact, the earliest known recorded message was a business transaction, for barley, if I remembered my Econ 101 class. Which reminded me, I would need to consider some fermentation science eventually if I wanted my goblins to *really* celebrate my rule.

But I digress. One of the interesting properties of silica clay is that if you fire it in hot—like, *ridiculously* hot—temperatures, it turns into something between a glass and a crystal, called *ceramic.* You need a lot of air for this, and a lot of fuel, because forcing oxygen through that fire causes it to devour fuel like your fat uncle at Thanksgiving going through the sweet potato casserole.

Ceramic is brittle, sure. It can shear somewhat easily along its crystalline structure. But you can plan around that. And once you do, you suddenly have a material that can be harder and sharper than steel, easily shapeable until it's fired, doesn't need to be mined or smelted, is incredibly heat resistant, and has just a few simple ingredients that you can readily find in a mountainous forest area like the one the goblins were native to. Eventually ceramic would be critical to the moon mission, since that's what heat shields on reentry vehicles are made of.

<Goblin Technology Unlocked: Sticky-Skinny Impeller>
<I think you skipped a few steps, King Apollo.>

You're damn right, I did. We were skipping bronze and iron, and going right to pre-industrial. We'd need metal eventually, but ceramics were like a cheat code for primitive cultures. I whistled for Sally and had her assembly team start making raw clay parts based on my designs while the fire warmed up. They went to work shaping clay, making blanks for a few different designs. Knives, spearheads, arrowheads, ball bearings, connectors, pulley parts, hooks, fasteners, scribes, scalpels, fine hooks, and gears. Everything a budding goblin village needs to speed-run industrial parts manufacturing.

While the goblins worked on the first clay prototypes, I showed two goblins how to work the impeller. Two cranks spun spindles on either side of the kiln's air intake, and small wooden blades on each one forced air directly below the fire. It was a bit like a bellows, but with a constant supply of air to the fuel source.

It was hard work keeping the fan blades spinning, but Sally's goblins had energy to spare for any new toy. The fire underneath the kiln roared, venting out of the top of the furnace in a shimmering column of superheated air. We had a decent supply of fuel from the days of idle goblins collecting sticks and sawing down small trees that turned out to be inadequate for the wall project. But the kiln would take every branch we could feed it. The heat coming off the bricks was immense.

Before the interior could get too hot, Sally's team inserted the thin adobe plate with the first of the ceramic pieces. Then the second and third plates went in, and I pushed the door back shut. My fur was matted with sweat already. The fire team's fur was singed in places. We needed gloves and protective aprons for this, really.

The goblins on the impellers cranked and cranked, trading off in shifts as the fuel team swept out spent ash and put fresh fuel in. Being king comes with certain privileges, so I sat back and watched the glowing oven.

The kiln was really my first major contribution to the well-being of the tribe. We'd had to fight for the clay and had lost goblins in the process. But the tools and weapons that came from this kiln would give this tribe a much-needed leg up in this forest full of things that wanted to kill and/or eat its members. This was what would allow us to grow. It was the biggest step we'd taken toward moving from a survivalist hunter-gatherer society to one of industry and craftsmen.

We kept the fire going into the evening, even after Neil and the hunters returned with fish and fowl and hides and started to cook dinner. A few goblins even tried holding roasting sticks over the kiln output, but when the first and second birds burst into flames, the effort was abandoned. Even after Buzz finished the wall and sent his goblins out to replace the dwindling fuel stock, we kept the fire going. Sally's goblins worked in shifts on the cranks and at the fuel, making sure the kiln stayed red-hot into the evening. Finally, as the catch of the day was done cooking (now with containers ready to catch and store the oil and grease for later use), I called for a stop. Sally came over, fur so streaked with soot and grime she looked a bit like Rufus with his black-striped badger fur.

It had taken a whole day to make our first batch of ceramic parts. It would take the entire night for them to cool off enough to remove from the kiln. It was incredibly time, resource, and labor intensive to produce ceramic parts. The morning would tell if it was worth it.

CHAPTER 18

APEX PREDATOR

I jolted awake. It was still dark, and not the dark of the bottom of the sleeping mound. It was the dark of full night. The first time I'd woken up at night since coming into this new goblin body.

I felt an immediate sense of danger. We'd completed the wall and closed up the shelters. There shouldn't have been anything able to get in and trouble us in the night this time, but something wasn't right.

I pulled myself to the top of the pile and looked around. Plenty of light from the moon bathed the hilltop well enough to see most of the village through the slats in the shelter. I couldn't see any movement. I rolled down from the pile and pressed up against the poles that comprised the shelter's wall for a better view.

A scraping noise behind me drew my attention, and I whipped around to the other side. I scrambled back up onto the pile, disturbing a few of my moundmates in the process. I looked through the poles on that side. I could see the sloth cub's enclosure, still undisturbed, and the curled form of the infant inside, dozing off its dinner of scraps from the fish and fowl.

The scraping, again, behind me.

This time, I looked *up*.

Bright yellow eyes stared down at me through a hole in the roof of the shelter. A long, hooked beak worried at the opening, prying loose the weave to enlarge the hole. Whatever it was, it was big enough to block out the moon, and had small hands at the ends of bat-like wings.

I won't lie, I screamed. The goblins below me rolled over, annoyed, then saw the bat-thing and *also* screamed.

The beaked creature screeched in alarm at having been caught out, and that woke up the rest of the goblins. It beat its wings against the shelter, enraged, as the group inside became a hive of frenzied activity.

"Kill it!" I shouted, horrified. The silhouette of this creature, the light of its eyes, and the curve of its beak all triggered very deep, primal fear responses in my goblin brain that my human mind was powerless to stand against.

"Kill it, kill it, kill it!"

The shelter capsized as most of the mound threw themselves at the wall to get as far from the creature as possible. This thing had already been responsible for at least five goblin deaths, coming to haunt the tribe night after night. I'd never considered that it might be something that could *fly*. The wall was useless, and our shelters were only marginally better. What was worse, the System superimposed the level over its head—*18*.

The night-haunt thing's wide tail lashed at the air as it flapped backward. The entire hilltop was awake now. All forty-five members of the tribe were pushing out of their shelters and running for crossbows and spears, or even just simple clubs.

With the building now open, the creature dove in among the goblins from my shelter, snapping one up in its beak and shaking its head violently. It flung the goblin away.

<Your tribe has decreased to 44 members.>

The bat-thing pounced on another as he tried to flee, pinning the unfortunate goblin to the ground with its hands and digging its hooked beak into my tribemate's back.

<Your tribe has decreased to 43 members.>

This high-level creature was swatting down goblins like we would swat down flies. I didn't know if having goblins that talked made me more empathetic, or if I'd just grown closer to the tribe. But I now felt a fierce protective instinct over my little blue companions. I didn't want this creature to keep killing them. It turned its eyes. I followed its gaze and saw Buzz coming with a spear. He raised it high, but the thing pounced again, sweeping aside the stone spearpoint.

"No!" I shouted and threw myself at it. "Buzz!"

Its head snapped to the side, and its beak caught me around the middle. It squeezed. It squeezed so hard I thought I would *pop*.

<Head of the Snake activated.>
<Your tribe has decreased to 42 members.>

I screamed from the pressure and pain of the fatal blow that had passed to another goblin. The creature readjusted its bite, and the pressure tightened around my chest. I couldn't inhale. Claws raked at me. Hateful yellow eyes stared down, confused at why I was still alive. It let go of my chest and drove its beak into my midsection.

<Head of the Snake activated.>
<Your tribe has decreased to 41 members.>

Buzz was up, and Neil with him. Fitting, I supposed. They both had ceramic-tipped spears, and they drove them into the creature. Neil put his spear into its side, while Buzz pinned one of its wings to the dirt. It shrieked with pain, so loud half the goblins on the hilltop dropped and pressed their ears flat against their skulls.

Neil let go of the spear, still in the thing's gut, and pulled out two flint cleavers. He jumped up with a manic laugh, and then dove out of the way as the nighttime terror of my tribe snapped at him. He lashed out, and the creature recoiled, blood spurting from two jagged cuts.

"Boss!" shouted Buzz.

I turned, and scrambled out of the way as Sally and her team of engineers readied their crossbows. The crack of fifteen bows going off at once sounded more like a gunshot than a bowstring. Several shots went wide, and one bow exploded in its owner's hands. But the majority of the stones struck home on the bat-thing's side and head. It staggered, hurt and clearly dizzy. Neil saw his opportunity and dove in, cackling as he swung both cleavers into the creature. By that time, most of his hunters had found their courage *and* their spears, and they were menacing the thing from a distance. The night haunt curled around Neil, claws raking and beak snapping.

"No!" I yelled. I bounded in on my prosthetics, pulling the knife from my belt. One of those big yellow eyes was in front of me, and I drove the tip of my knife straight through it. The creature tensed, shrieking. It tried to pull back, but I leaned in and pushed harder, wrapping my hands around its head. My prosthetics slid through the mud as it thrashed and pulled at me. It howled in pain and panic, trying to throw me off as I held on for dear life. But it slowed, finally stilled, and then went completely limp.

"Get off him!" I shouted, beating at its side. I turned to the rest of the tribe. "Help me!"

Several goblins came over, and together we rolled the carcass of the flying creature off of Neil, who was curled in a ball, bloody from several deep scratches, missing an arm, but alive. I breathed a sigh of relief.

I sent goblins for mud and moss to pack the wounds and staunch the bleeding while I tied a tourniquet with cordage. Luckily, I didn't have to worry about infection since goblins were immune to toxins and germs.

<Goblin Technology Unlocked: Stringy Tourniquet>
<Goblin Technology Unlocked: Dirt-Daub Poultice>

The missing arm would mean he'd struggle to fight or hunt in the future. But Neil was a hero goblin. Even when I'd cowered in fear, he'd leapt in without hesitation. The rest of the tribe seemed to recognize his bravery too, because they hoisted him up and carried him in a lap around the village, cheering and hooting.

I didn't join them. I was watching the sky, where I saw other winged forms circling, along with the glint of yellow eyes.

This was just the beginning.

CHAPTER 19

COMPOUND PENALTY

<Your tribe did not sleep. No new goblins were born.>

The cost of the night haunt's attack was much more than just the multiple goblins it had killed in its rampage. It had also prevented the birth of at minimum four more, and as many as twelve.

In a cold sort of calculus, it might have been better to let the monster take one or two goblins if it meant the strange goblin reproduction cycle continued uninterrupted. I'd hoped to have more than fifty goblins at the start of the next day. Now, we were even further from that goal than we had been yesterday.

And to top it all off, a goblin who hasn't slept is a pretty useless goblin, it turns out. I was no exception. The tribe's lethargy resulted in almost no work being completed, other than processing the night haunt and laying its meat among the smoldering coals. Neil claimed the skull, which he'd taken as his new mask. But no hunting party went out, no wood was chopped, and Sally's team barely formed a handful of adobe bricks.

I didn't blame them. It was like a veneer of gray film had been pulled across my eyes and leaden weights attached at my ankles and wrists. My head hurt like I'd gone on a three-day bender. I barely mustered the strength to pull open the door of the kiln and remove the trays of fired ceramic parts.

<Goblin Technology Unlocked: Fire-Clay Tools>
<Goblin Technology Unlocked: Roly-Poly Bearings>
<Goblin Technology Unlocked: Rope Puller-Upper>
<Goblin Technology Unlocked: Tiny Fired Pokey>
<Goblin Technology Unlocked . . .>

About a dozen more notifications flooded past too fast for me to read them. It was the single largest influx of new goblin technology that I'd seen, and I could barely even read half of it. The chain reaction of the rest of the tribe internalizing the new technology was like a slow breeze rippling across the surface of a still pond, but forcing them to think in this state seemed to cause tangible physical discomfort as many of them clutched their heads and moaned like a horde of living dead. Having only seen these goblins in a state of either frenetic energy or deep slumber, this malaise was almost hard to bear.

The fact was, I was very attached to my goblins. Expendable as this world may have conditioned them to be, they were diligent, creative, energetic, and possessed of a strange sort of optimism. Every task was a new adventure, every new technology a world of possibilities.

I hated the night haunts for stealing that from them. But there was no denying that the day was ultimately a wash. At least we had food in our bellies from the night haunt itself. Maybe the others that I'd seen circling would be wary of approaching after the last one they sent didn't return.

The lethargy came swiftly and suddenly as soon as the sun passed behind the moon for the daily eclipse. Normally, the tribe would have no problem staying awake until after sunset, but in this state, it looked like the artificial twilight brought on by Raphina's shadow was enough. We barely had time to pull the shelters together before the entire tribe passed out.

<Your tribe has increased to 47 members.>

I woke up to the morning sun peeking over the horizon. We'd slept at least 75 percent of the previous day, but there had been no attacks during the night. Maybe the carcass of the night haunt had been enough to deter any other would-be visitors looking to make a snack of goblins. Maybe they'd tried their luck at another village.

Buzz didn't even come to the morning staff meeting. He just took his crew and set them to task with renewed vigor. A few of his goblins went around to the shelters, retrofitting roofs with sharpened poles to discourage nighttime visitors from above. The majority of his workers immediately started making as many bricks as they could. Buzz had expressed interest in the ones we made for the kiln, and he was smart enough to realize the scale of production we'd need for actual construction with the things—although that raised a problem. The pond, which was our primary drinking water supply, was rain-supplied. It wasn't large enough to also be our primary source of water for forming bricks. There was also limited space atop the bluff to lay out the drying mud.

Sally, surprisingly enough, had already come up with a solution. Apparently, she'd been teaching herself to draw. She grasped the possibilities of the ceramic ball bearings immediately in multiple applications—the most practical of which was a goblin-powered freight lift.

Granted, goblin engineering sketches aren't exactly easy to parse—her linework was akin to their bushcraft in that it simply went wherever it wanted. But a log hanging over the edge of the cliff with a larger ring around it and a load slung opposite several stick-figure goblins wasn't exactly difficult to divine the purpose of. If we had heavy lift capabilities, we could form and dry the bricks down at the river where there was more space and more material, and then bring them up to the village.

"Nice work, Sally. Add some grease to the moving parts, and I don't see why it wouldn't work." I called Buzz over. "Buzz, go ahead and move the brick-making operation to the river. We'll have a way to bring them up soon."

My chief engineer beamed and ran off. Sally especially was starting to show a propensity for anticipating problems and implementing solutions.

Neil had fit most of his hunters' spears with the new ceramic tips from the first batch in the kiln. As an experiment, he drove the end one through the stone sloth's hide. It stuck into it, rather than simply deflecting off as the stone and bone spearpoints had. He nodded his appreciation. "This'll do it, boss! Just wait 'til the next one thinks it can mess with Tribe Apollo!"

"Got one thing before you go," I said.

I had some of the goblins bring over the beak and mandible of the night haunt we'd killed the night before, and they lifted it on a pole atop the largest of our wooden shelters. I got a hoist up onto the edge of the roof with a sheaf of bark under my arm and whistled for attention.

The rest of the goblins stopped what they were doing for a moment and gathered around, pointing up at the totem and clacking their jaws in a reasonable approximation of the night haunt's beak snapping.

I held the bark over my head and raised my voice. "This is a symbol of defiance and resistance! We will not surrender to creatures of the night, no matter how hideous or hungry. No one is hungrier than a goblin! Let any monster who looks upon this cower in fear!"

The goblins cheered. Now, admittedly, I'm not much of an artist. I'd drawn a simple, circular frowny face with goblin ears and angry eyes. I looped it around the skull pole.

<Goblin Technology Unlocked: Totems. Erecting totems will convey temporary skill bonuses to goblins who admire them.>

<Goblin Technology Unlocked: Night Haunt Totem. Enhances goblin skill with piercing weapons and slightly increases night vision quality.>

Interesting. I would need to build more totems. I looked over at Neil. "Jab that carcass again."

Neil pulled back, leapt with a war cry, and thrust his spear again. This time, it went entirely through the outermost layer of the carcass hide. I grunted. Even the hook hand didn't seem to slow him down. The totem really did work.

Neil pulled it out and examined the tip with a critical eye. "Good stuff, boss."

"Be safe!" I called, as the hunters took a running leap off the side of the bluff. "Or, well. Never mind."

As for me, I had another project. The goblins mostly gave me space as I worked on things by myself. They'd come to realize that when I got to tinkering, it translated into a significant leap forward for them. Or, I thought as I looked down at my prosthetics, for me. Though I didn't know what progress or technological advances any of the other goblin tribes in the region had made on their own. For all I knew, each one had a rival king that had taken their tribe to metallurgy and steam power already, and we could soon be facing goblins with firearms or dirt bikes or what have you. I had seen smoke rising from one or two bluffs in the distance, so at least a couple of them had discovered the secrets of fire-making. Were other goblin kings common? I had to think not, since Rufus had commented how we were almost a mythical creature in this world. But there was a chance I wouldn't be unique.

Well, if he thought we were mythical before, wait until he saw what I was cooking up now. I took the lightest, most flexible poles in the stockpile and the sturdiest cord. I began sketching out a design and then shaping the poles into a frame. I also collected the rest of the stone sloth claws, and some of the bones from the night haunt, as well as its hide. The wings were made of a fleshy membrane that had cured quickly, and it was both light and durable. But we lost two more goblins out in the world while I worked. I didn't know if they belonged to Buzz or Neil.

I didn't know if the hide was worth all the goblins the night haunt had killed, but I was going to do my best to make sure it didn't go to waste. I stole a few of Sally's engineers to help with the tedious work of securing them to the wooden frame. Then, we stretched the thin night haunt hide over both claws and frame and used ceramic needles to sew it in place.

By the time the hunters returned, we had a reasonable frame and the sloth bones created the perfect rigid structure for the top of my new device. But it still needed work. The next few days would be quite interesting, indeed.

CHAPTER 20

SPEED FREAKS

<Your tribe has decreased to 51 members.>
<Your tribe has increased to 59 members.>
<Increasing your tribe size has unlocked a new goblin variant. You may select one of the following:
Hobgoblin Wrangler: A larger, nocturnal goblin skilled in animal handling
—or—
Noblin Tunneler: A larger goblin capable of tunneling, excavation, and earthen works.>

It had taken another three days to get the tribe up to the point where the System had given me a second variant. If anything, this decision was harder than the first. Tunneling and excavation meant we'd be able to mine ore and quarry stone, which would make developing engines and power generation easier. Eventually it would be critical to locate a source of copper and iron, and this noblin thing could be it.

But before that, the tribe's security was compromised. The night haunts had returned. It seemed the larger the tribe grew, the more the nocturnal predators took notice. We'd lost out on another night of sleep and growth due to one attack, and in turn, a day of productivity. And we hadn't even managed to kill the beast this time.

As much as we needed metallurgy, I had to put the security of the tribe first. I chose the hobgoblin wranglers. Even if they weren't going to jump-start my tribe's animal husbandry (which I hoped they would), having nocturnal sentries might deter the night haunts from breaking into the shelters at night.

<5 Hobgoblin Wranglers have been added to your tribe.>
<1 Hobgoblin Wrangler has been promoted to Taskmaster.>

System, show me the hobgoblin wrangler skills.

I watched as the window populated with the list of capabilities my new hobgoblins were born with. During the malaise brought on by the second sleepless night in a week, I'd been too disoriented to complete the fine work required for the glider I'd started with the night haunt hide. I'd taken the opportunity to interrogate the System and see what it could and couldn't show me. It seemed this world ran on a hyper-specific set of governing rules, much more high-conceptual in nature than the fundamental physics that ruled Earth. The System could show me the stats and specialties of every goblin in my tribe, if I asked it, as well as a host of other, more niche features. I used it to move several of the members around to better suit the talents of my individual taskmasters.

<Hobgoblin Wranglers
Hobgoblin: This advanced goblin can speak and reach level 3.
Nocturnal: These bad boys like to stay up late and get into trouble. Their eyes are tuned for low light. The downside is that they sleep until midday.
Thick-Skinned: Whether teeth, claws, or harsh language, wranglers will shrug off slashing damage from creatures.
Animal Kinship: Not much better than animals themselves, wranglers share a sort of understanding with the beasts of the world.
Daredevils: Wranglers love anything that gets the blood pumping and the wind through their specially tuned hair. Wrangler senses and reflexes are increased at high speeds.>

It was the perfect mix of traits to kick-start our animal husbandry program. We were growing as a village, and there was only so much hunting, fishing, and foraging could do to support a population without either livestock or agriculture. It was simply an issue of the resources in a given area being able to provide for X goblins who consumed Y chooms of food each day, and the inefficiency of traveling farther from a central hub without effective means of transportation. We were going to need a cultivated food source almost as much as we were going to need metal and electricity.

With four taskmasters, the tribe could be split almost completely evenly at just under fifteen goblins per. The only problem was, my fourth taskmaster was sleeping in, so his goblins would spend a good deal of the morning idle or working on their own tasks. That was fine. Let them.

Neil took the hunters northwest. They had the dual objective of watching for Rufus's return and making sure the javeline rutters didn't find him first. I don't know that they'd have attacked him on sight, seeing as both he and they were part dwarf. But I didn't want my first friend in this world falling afoul of them. In the meantime, I worked on the control surfaces of the version-one glider.

The design wasn't all that dissimilar to a glider concept I'd submitted to a NASA design contest in college, oddly enough. The controls allowed the user to subtly change the shape and angle of the wing in order to modify the glider on the fly (no pun intended) for high-speed and slow-speed flight—which I could now realize, thanks to the stretchy membrane of the night haunt wings. This was the design I'd had in mind when I fired up the first batch of ceramics, and the design used bearings and flanged joints that wouldn't have been possible with wood or stone. Ironically, the casualties taken during the first airborne attack were indirectly going to give us our first shot at unpowered flight.

As the sun reached its zenith, a quartet of shadows approached from my rear.

"Whatcha got there, boss?"

I turned. All five of the new wranglers had woken up, finally. They all wore the customary goblin trousers, but these had patched vests as well. They also each had a wedge of longer hair along the top of their skull, like a natural mohawk. Unlike the other goblins who wore skull half-masks over their eyes and crown, these ones opted to tie loose jawbones from the bone pit over their mouths like handkerchiefs on old-west outlaws. One of them had also apparently liberated the stone sloth cub from its enclosure and was tickling its belly.

"Flying machine," I said. "Well, *gliding* machine. Flying comes later."

"Sounds swell. Can I try it?" asked the largest of them. He must have been the taskmaster of the wranglers.

I had expected these guys to have thick Cockney accents like Buzz and Neil, but they sounded more like they were from the American Southwest. Though I read a long time ago that the southern American accent is actually closer to what Victorian English would have sounded like.

"Slow down, Chuck Yeager," I said. I cocked my head. Hmm. Good a name as any for a natural-born would-be flying speed freak. "It's not quite ready yet. I'm trying to finish it today."

"Just so long as *I* get one," he said.

I stood and dusted off my sloth-claw legs. “Make you a deal, Chuck. I’ll make sure you get to fly through the air, but you’ve got to figure out some way to cover terrain faster on the ground and fight a four-legged foe.”

Chuck grinned. “Give me some of the lads to work with and a few hours’ daylight to burn. We’ll do you proud.”

“Take the ten idle goblins with you,” I said.

My newest taskmaster whistled, getting the attention of several of the goblins milling about the village. “You lot, you, and you. With me. Grab your kit. We’re headed south.”

South. Out of the woods and onto the plains, then. I looked out over the bluff. “You want to jump down? Or would you prefer to try the new launcher?”

“You have to ask?”

I led Chuck and his new cronies to the southeast side of the bluff, where Sally had erected, of her own accord, a flex-a-pult to, as Buzz put it, *not waste time falling straight down*. We had two, so far, and she was working on a third, as well as a second freight crane. Even as I watched, two of her engineers were pulling a load of bricks onto the bluff with hooked poles while a handful of goblins balanced on the beam as a counterweight.

“The big reason you’re here,” I explained to Chuck, “is the night haunts. They’re eating goblins at night, and worse, disrupting sleep for the whole tribe. Whatever you need to deal with them—spears, slingers, axes, nets—it’s yours. They’re the biggest threat we face.”

“Leave it to the hobbies, boss-man.” He winked at me. “Hobgoblins own the night.”

I liked Chuck already. And I’m pretty sure when he saw the flex-a-pult, he fell in love. He stopped and stared at the contraption. We’d unlocked the technology the day we’d fought the first stone sloth, but I hadn’t thought much of it at the time on account of being in the middle of a pitched battle. But my chief engineer hadn’t let it go. She’d made an arrangement of poles that could be weighed down by her engineers until the poles bowed, and then released to fling an impressive load. Usually, that load was *goblins*.

Sally had also combined the flex-a-pult with the ceramic pulleys I’d made in the first firing and the ceramic gears. We’d managed to get it to the point where two goblins could crank the whole thing down. Sally was turning into an ace at seeing applications for simpler parts to service compound machines. Honestly, I think she’d have fit right at home in the robotics lab at NuEarth—though most of those guys were closer to trolls than goblins. Chuck climbed into the basket along with five others, and I stood clear.

Everyone still in the village took a break to watch the flex-a-pult launch. It was basically Apollo Tribe's national sport. The goblins lined up and hooted and hollered as Sally's operators finished cranking and transitioned to the release lever. I'd tried to teach the tribe to do a joint countdown, but goblins were as numerically challenged as they were verbally. What I *had* been able to teach them was *the wave*. From one end of the cliff to the other, my entire tribe screamed at the top of their lungs and threw their hands in the air.

"*THREE!*" I shouted.

The wave started at one end, hit the other end, and started coming back.

"*TWO!*"

The tribe had practically worked itself into a frenzy. Two of the goblins couldn't take the anticipation and leapt over the edge themselves. There was always at least one, where the flex-a-pult was involved.

"*ONE!*"

The wave reached a crescendo and lost complete coherence as my tribe lost their collective minds. Sally's operators put their weight into the lever, and the mechanism released. Chuck and a half dozen other goblins went airborne, *EEEEeeee*ing out over the southern forest toward the plains. The rest of the goblins assigned to Chuck scrambled to reset the flex-a-pult for their turn.

All in all, if I couldn't prevent goblins from simply jumping off the side of the bluff, I could at least help them along their way. Thanks to the height of the bluff, the flex-a-pult sent goblins at least five hundred meters horizontally, depending on the position of the moon. That was one of the other things about Rava that I'd noticed. Gravity was definitely not accelerating all objects at 9.8 meters per second, and it changed slightly throughout the day as Raphina made its slow circuit in the sky.

Plus, the little daredevils just loved being launched. They *wanted* to be airborne. I could relate. Who was I to deny them the simple pleasures in life?

<Your tribe has decreased to 58 members.>

Yikes. Well, maybe there was such thing as too much pleasure.

CHAPTER 21

RUFUS RETURNS

"Ahoy, Apollo! You'd not believe the journey I've had, O King!"

That was a voice I hadn't heard in almost ten days. While I wasn't terminally lonely anymore thanks to the talkative taskmasters joining the tribe, Rufus also brought critical knowledge of the outside world.

I put down the finished glider and went to the north slope, where Rufus was ascending in one of the freight baskets. The operators for the lift hooked the rope and pulled it over to the bluff where I helped Rufus from the basket. He looked down at my new legs. "His Highness is a good deal more mobile than last we spoke. I see the stone-hide sloth lives on with you. But I hope this was not meant to be your idea for trade for salt and tools."

"Just the appetizer," I said. "Come on, let me show you around the new and improved Tribe Apollo Village."

He marveled at the crane for a moment before we walked through the woods to the rest of the village, where he froze. "I say, you've certainly been busy these last ten days."

<Your tribe has decreased to 57 members.>

The sticky shelters had been replaced by adobe huts made from dried bricks—though we still had night haunts coming in through the thatch and clay tile roofs. Several miniature versions of the lifts were also present, with Buzz's goblins scrambling back and forth along the top arm to act as counterweights to lift the building materials. We even had impact hammers now, lifting logs on pullies with several goblins hauling and letting them drop to hammer terrain flat and drive poles into the ground.

It was actually a fascinating thing to watch a glorified goblin seesaw and maypole used to perform heavy construction. I had joked about it, but goblins really did make fantastic counterweights thanks to their climbing abilities, their keen sense of balance, and their immunity to falling damage when those first two qualities inevitably and spectacularly failed. We had started to develop multilevel structures with wood floors, creating discrete levels for sleeping mounds. Which was good, because space atop the bluff wasn't infinite and I wasn't ready to risk housing goblins down at the base of the bluff. That would be just as bad as offering them up to the night haunts.

Beyond that, we'd been drying more pottery to store things like raw clay, oil, grease, and even grubs for the fishermen. Cordage of various thicknesses and materials sat in coils under a rain shelter, and next to that was an assortment of other raw materials. Goblins took what they needed, and other goblins replaced the stockpiles. It was becoming a neat little operation, though not without systematic deficiencies that needed to be addressed.

"Yeah, we've been getting after it," I said.

"Quite the feat," said Rufus.

He caught sight of one of the flex-a-pults and went to examine it. He must have surmised its purpose fairly quickly, because he immediately retreated to a safe distance. "You know, humans use a device like that to throw rocks, not *themselves*. I think you'll need more than that to reach the moon, my friend."

"That?" I said, waving him off. "That's just a time-saver. Besides, I have no humans I need to throw rocks at. Come on, take a load off and let's catch up. How was the coast?"

Rufus allowed me to take him to what had become something of the village square, where most of the goblins gathered for dinner at night around the primary fire pit. The trader eyed the kiln curiously as we passed it, still smoldering from its second firing. Not all the parts we'd tried to make the first time had survived the process, after all. And not all of the ones that had, had worked. Ceramics were an exercise in persistence and the law of averages.

At the square, I'd had a squat bench made with Rufus's rough proportions in mind, and he dropped onto it with a sigh and a creak of distressed wood. "Your tribe found me a league north of here and were quite insistent that we divert west. Why is that?"

<Your tribe has decreased to 56 members.>

I poked at the coals for a moment, wondering if I was losing hunters, speed freaks, or both. Hell, even being in the village wasn't particularly safe. Several goblins had been squashed in construction over the past few days, and Sally's engineers often fell victim to catastrophic failures and injuries. Sometimes it seemed like a race between the two factions on who could accumulate more peg legs and hook hands. But prosthetics didn't seem to hamper their productivity, nor their spirit. I don't think *rehabilitation* was a word anywhere in the Goblin Tech Tree. "We've been tracking a band of javeline that don't seem friendly. I didn't want you to run into them by misfortune."

"I see." Rufus sat pensively for a moment and poked at the old coals from the fire. "Misfortune would be the correct word, when it comes to their ilk. I wish you well. I take it they are the reason for the fortifications?"

"Not exactly," I said, glancing at the night haunt totem. "In fact, we've had no direct contact. But I did see that they have metal tools, so I had considered trying to offer a trade."

"I would advise against such an act. And not simply because I stand to profit greatly from my exclusive friendship and monopolistic trade policy with Your Majesty, mind."

"Of course not. But speaking of profit. Did you bring things to trade?"

"But of course," said Rufus, swinging his large pack down and opening the top of the ruck. He pulled out a bottle and passed it over. "That's not to trade, O King, but to lubricate the negotiations."

I unstoppered the bottle and pressed it to my lips, taking a swallow. I pulled it away, coughing. "Stout."

Rufus grinned his badger grin and took a sip of his own before stopping the bottle and wiping his muzzle on the back of his arm. "Blackberry wine. Cheap *and* strong, and easily able to survive sea voyages thanks to its foul taste and tendency to remain at the bottom of cabin chests. Now, let's see what I have for you . . ."

He reached back into his bag and pulled out a small, bound book. "I thought I might pack heavy, this trip, with the weight of knowledge. There are few things a learned creature covets more than more learning." He handed the book over, and I opened it at random, not even sure I'd be able to read the words. But they appeared clear as day, and I flipped back to the introduction and read it out loud.

"*A treatise on the practice of harvesting and processing iron nodules in peat bogs in northern Baleron.*" I looked up. "Where's Baleron?"

"About fifteen hundred miles east as the crow flies, across the sea and up in the foothills," said Rufus. "That's why I got such a good deal on it in Habberport."

"I didn't know you could find iron in bogs," I said. "I thought you mined it."

"Ah-ha! We find another fact the goblin king did not already know! We're off to a much better start today." Rufus slapped his thigh and laughed. "It can be mined as well. Harvesting it from bogs is a somewhat antiquated method, but quite effective. Would you like to see the others?"

"You brought more books?" I asked, trying to hide my excitement.

"These are quite heavy, you know. I hope you have something good to trade."

I barked a laugh. "There's always these," I said, unlacing the prosthetic and handing it over for Rufus's inspection. He turned them about. "Or at least the designs for them. These ones are fitted to me. They're stronger and more flexible than wood. You can run, jump, and climb in them. I assume this world has soldiers, or those who were victims of illness or accidents that lost limbs."

"Hmm, more than meets the eye, then. Quite a trade for a simple book. And what would you want in return for such an imbalance?" asked Rufus. "A tool? A sack of pepper?"

"Just knowledge, and the promise that you'll share this with those who need it. I'm not ready for the world to know who I am, but I won't sit on the knowledge of advanced prosthetics, either." I ran a hand through my fur. "Pepper, you say?"

Rufus reached into his bag and withdrew a journal. "Kindness, then, is what you ask."

"I'll take pepper, too."

"Will you draw and describe them in here in exchange for a local bestiary? And, yes, perhaps a bit of pepper."

I accepted the journal, as well as my leg back, and sketched a few diagrams of the simple mechanics of the prosthetic. I tried not to let it show on my face how valuable a bestiary would actually be. It might hold secrets to defeating the night haunts, or point us toward a creature that would be useful livestock. It might even tell me more about the javeline rutters. I'm pretty sure Rufus saw through me instantly. He did have skills for that, after all. Which I needed to ask him about later. I pulled the bladed prosthetic back on and reached into my own bag that I kept tied at my hip. "I have something else for you," I said. I pulled out a small palmful of the ceramic balls we'd fired and handed them over. Rufus held it close to his eye and rolled it between his fingers.

"This is quite round. I may not know artifice, but I know perfectly smooth spheres are of some rarity and value. Is it clay?"

"Not quite. Try to break it."

Rufus squeezed the bearing between his fingers, then pressed it between his palms. Finally, he got to his feet, put the bearing on the log bench, and ground at it with his boot heel. He picked it back up and furrowed his brow. "Not a scratch!?"

"We can make them by the dozens, all as strong, smooth, and as round as that." I whistled to get my tribe's attention. "Hey, Sally! Bring over one of those finished bearings," I said. I waited for her to bring over the small device, which she did before casting a shy glance at Rufus and making herself scarce. I held the ball bearing out for Rufus to see. As he watched, I spun the outer part of the bearing, which rode smoothly on the ceramic balls inside. "And from what you've told me, I don't think there's many people in this land creating *these*."

Rufus took the bearing, twisting the outer layer back and forth. "I'm afraid I'm not a . . . what would you call someone who uses these?"

"A machinist," I said. "Sally uses them to operate the lift that brought you up to the village."

"That, a machinist," said Rufus. "I can't tell you what the true value of this is. But I know artificers who might be similar to your *machinists.* There are those in a city to the south, beyond the plains and deep in the desert, who create brass marvels and brook with strange contraptions such as these. If anyone will recognize the use for such a trinket, it is they."

I was sure they would. Ball bearings were only the fundamental development that enabled complex moving parts for the entirety of the modern world—arguably one of the most important inventions in history. Along with gunpowder, internal combustion, and electric power generation.

"Keep that one, then. You don't have to trade me anything for it, just find me a customer who will trade for more."

Rufus tucked it into a pocket of his coat. "And what would you want in exchange for more, should I come with an order?" he asked.

I thought about it. "Copper wire," I said.

"Not silver or gold?"

"Just copper. And magnets, if you can find them. I imagine these artificers might have some."

"Magnets?"

I put my palms together. "Special stones that push or pull on each other from a distance."

"Ah, lodestones."

I unrolled a set of precision ceramic instruments next and laid them out for Rufus to examine. "Doctors and artificers might both find use in these."

The half-badger picked up one of the small knives and tested the edge. He hissed when his finger came away with a spot of blood and stuck the digit in his mouth.

"Ah, yes, should have warned you," I said. "That scalpel is sharp."

"*Sharp,* he says. It sliced through fur and skin as though they weren't even there! Is this the same material as the spinning ring?"

I nodded. "It's a hard material, difficult to scratch. But it can be brittle, especially large pieces. They used it for armor where I came from. A plate of this will stop a crossbow bolt."

"Indeed!" said Rufus. "*That* I could certainly find customers for." He pulled out a small pack that turned out to contain the jewelers' tools I mentioned I wanted. I'd completely forgotten that I asked for them, and I felt a bit guilty when I saw them.

"Ah, I, uh, yeah . . ." I said, running a hand through my blue fur at the top of my head. "Yeah, I suppose I don't really need those, now."

"And after I hauled them all this way," Rufus chided, winking. "Though others will certainly want your version. I know several chirurgeons and a dentist in Bale's Landing who came to Lanclova in search of exotic medicinals. They surely have contacts on the mainland who could move these. Make more, and I will sell them for you."

I smiled. Despite his animalistic appearance, Rufus was an easygoing fellow with an easy-to-like attitude. I hadn't realized how much I'd missed him since our first meeting. "I'm glad you came back," I said, surprising even myself.

"A unique oddity such as yourself certainly brooks a second visit, I should say," said Rufus. "Begging your pardon at referring to you as odd. That aside, we had a wager. And despite the curiosities you've shown me, I feel as though I'm going to win it."

I grinned. "That's because I saved the best for last. This one isn't up for trade. Follow me."

CHAPTER 22

MAIDEN FLIGHT

"Are you tanning a skyena hide?" asked Rufus, when he saw the prototype glider sitting on the launch rails.

"We've been calling them night haunts," I said. "And no. This is something I guarantee you've never seen before, no matter how far you've traveled." I checked the frame, the membrane, the connections, and the security of the wicker cradle before settling down into it on my belly. I worked the left wing and the right, making sure the surfaces had free movement and no binding. Thanks to the ceramic bearings from the second kiln firing and some fish oil, everything slid with minimal friction.

"Attention!" I shouted out. "Operation: GERONIMO!"

A wave of excitement coursed through the village. Almost everyone dropped what they were doing and came over. Several goblins fought over the ropes that had been laid out next to the simple wooden rails, but realized the lines were long enough to share. That was fine. The more goblins on the ropes, the better this would work. Hopefully.

Rufus watched, perplexed but polite, as I ran through my final checks and looped the line around the hook on the nose of my improvised aircraft. If there was one thing they drilled into us during my private pilot training, it was to always check your aircraft before a flight.

I'd never gotten the technology unlock for the glider, so I had to assume the System was also watching in suspense to see if it worked. Which reminded me.

"Hey Rufus. You're able to converse with the System too, right? The thing that tells you your skills and abilities?"

"Of course," he said. "Everyone can hear the voice of the Empowering Spirit."

"Interesting."

"Do you not have one where you're from?"

I shook my head.

Rufus crossed his arms and nodded. "Hmm . . . I believe you. My grandfather told me, as a boy, that *his* grandfather remembered a time before it began to speak and show visions. Before that, skills were something you *built*, not something that granted you power when given. The voice began as a pale whisper that has grown louder over the years. For as long as I've been alive, the spirit has spoken to everyone and its will shapes the very fabric of the world according to its own patterns. But it also empowers monsters and various evils. To what end, only the Gods know."

"You don't consider the System itself to be a god?"

"It insists that it is not and punishes those who persist in worshiping it. What god would insist upon its own disbelief contrary to clear evidence of its presence? The Empowering Spirit simply *is*."

"I suppose I see your point," I said. So, it hadn't been here forever and seemed to be gaining more influence over time, imposing rules and these strange *skills* that conflicted with the natural order I was used to on Earth. That was an interesting development. I had to wonder what Earth would have been like if there was an all-powerful, semi-sentient program that both empowered and was accessible to its users. If simulation theory was correct, and it seemed at least *plausible*, given my "reincarnation," then somehow *this* simulation could be breaking down and showing the man behind the curtain, as it were. The locals interpreted it as a spirit speaking to them. But they'd never seen a computer program. Or *The Matrix*, for that matter.

<Were you going to launch that death trap or not?>

Right. I supposed I'd better get back to it. I secured myself in the glider and looked up at Rufus. "I hate to leave you like this, my friend. But if all goes well, I should be back before dinner."

<Your tribe has decreased to 56 members.>

As long as enough hunters are still alive to bring dinner back. The attrition today seemed higher than average.

Most of my goblins were at the end of their patience anyway. The ones on the ropes had been edging closer to the cliff face the whole time, and I was a little surprised that none of them had just flung themselves over early.

Goblins must have evolved from lemmings, because there were few things they enjoyed more than a good cliff and a sudden drop.

"Hold on, Apollo," said Rufus, stiffening. "This is a jest, yes? You can't possibly mean to—"

The goblins, no longer content to wait, instead began to *weight.* They took a swan dive off the edge of the cliff with the rope. Oops. The others, not to be outdone, followed suit, and suddenly the force of a dozen of my tribemates falling pulled against the hook at the nose of my glider. With a jerk, the whole contraption slid forward on the greased rails, building speed alarmingly fast. My stomach jumped up into my throat as I hit the ramp, pulled by the towline. The hook slipped, and before I even had time to register what had happened, I was soaring through the afternoon sky.

I'd always loved flying. I'd built a kit ultralight together with my roommate in college that was probably more foolhardy than safe to fly. But then, what's life without the challenge of risk? I'd been part of the soaring club at the local airfield since my sixteenth birthday. I can't describe to you how it felt being back in the air, wind blowing across my face as the airfoil rippled overhead. The sky was in my blood, and my tribe had just given it back to me.

<Goblin Technology Unlocked: Sticky-Skinny Airy-Wing Thing>

Oh ye of little faith, I thought to the System. As though chagrinned, a list of notifications began to scroll across my window.

<Goblin Component Technology Unlocked: Basic Airy-Knotics>
<Goblin Component Technology Unlocked: Basic Airy-Foils>
<Goblin Component Technology Unlocked: Goblin Launch-o-che>
<Goblin Component Technology Unlocked . . .>

Technically, I felt like most of the unlocked individual concepts and components that had gone into the glider should have unlocked as I was building the thing. The principles were sound from the get-go. Rava's governing system just wouldn't admit that it didn't think I'd actually be able to fly. It did conveniently bring up a small window that displayed my current airspeed and altitude in *chooms.* Okay, I take back some of the mean things I thought about it. Today, anyway.

I did a quick control check to make sure all my surfaces were articulating correctly. My left wing flex was a bit soft, but nothing I couldn't compensate for by shifting my weight in the cradle. I leaned into a shallow bank and verified my target to the east-northeast.

Today was about more than just flying for fun. Those other bluffs I'd seen in the distance were nearly insurmountable journeys for someone of a goblin's stature traveling over the ground. But as the crow flies? Well, that was another matter. I just had to make sure I was back before the night haunts (skyenas?) started coming out. Despite what the System had said, part of me still held up hope that Dave and Sandy, my NuEarth companions, had made the jump with me. If they had, maybe they were goblin kings as well, leading small tribes on bluffs of their own. It was time to find out.

The goblin counterweight launch system had given me a huge boost in speed, but now I needed one in altitude. Gliders can fly for hours by catching thermals and updrafts, and I'd made sure to prepare one ahead of time. Sally had fired up the kiln with the third batch of ceramics, but that waste heat all rose. I was able to angle into it, and I felt myself grow heavier in the cradle as the hot air caught the underside of the glider's wings and my altitude figure started to climb. Once I leveled off again, the bluff looked more like a small rock hundreds of feet below me. I couldn't even see individual goblins anymore.

Even with the reduced gravity of Rava, that kiln had lifted me far more effectively than it should have been able to. The Goblin Tech Tree must have been greasing the wheels of physics in my favor. Well, any advantage I could get, these guys needed.

With my course set and my altitude stable, I relaxed for a bit. For the first time since I'd come to Rava, I was completely alone. Rufus had said the human name of the world meant *skyclad.* Well, now I truly was clad in that sky. I was one with the winds, riding on the gentle currents swirling across the horizon. I had brought this with me. I had brought *flight* to Rava. And it was one of the critical stepping stones to reaching Raphina.

On Earth, it only took seventy years between the first powered flight and the first moon landing. And NASA never even had the loyalty of a goblin tribe or the absurdity that was the enigmatic internal logic of the Goblin Tech Tree. I didn't plan on taking seventy years. I didn't even plan on taking *seven* if I could keep iterating through the ages and skipping the biggest technological pitfalls and dead ends. The benefit of modern knowledge could be a huge force multiplier when applied to primitive tools and materials. But for the moment, I put all that aside and simply reveled in being wrapped in the sky.

CHAPTER 23

REMNANTS

It took about an hour of flight and one additional thermal to the east (off some natural hot springs, judging from the smell of sulfur wafting on the draft) for me to make it to my destination. One of the bluffs I'd seen smoke rising from came up in the distance, and as I drew closer I could definitely see signs of habitation from the air.

I soared wide, banking back and trading altitude for speed. I swooped down toward the thin trickle of smoke rising from the bluff and swept over the treetops, head angled down to look for signs of fellow goblins. It only took me about a minute to fly over the village.

It was completely destroyed.

What little mud hovels they had once had were crushed and trampled, and I saw raw materials scattered in a hurry. The source of the smoldering was a pile of spread ashes and a scorched frame that I think had once been a wooden structure—possibly once the pride of their village. Now it was barely a grave marker.

I curled my lip in distaste, feeling a shock of grief. While I'd grown somewhat inured to the loss of any *single* goblin, the destruction of the collective of another tribe sickened me. It churned my stomach. What had done this? Night haunts didn't start fires.

Reluctantly, I banked and headed south. There was another bluff I wanted to check. It was slightly closer to our own. I hadn't seen smoke, but if there were goblins there was a chance they hadn't discovered carousels yet.

<Your tribe has increased to 61 members.>
<A Hobgoblin Scrapper has been added to your tribe. Hobgoblin Scrapper is now an available variant.>
<A Hobgoblin Scrapper has been promoted to Taskmaster.>

What?

I banked so that I could look down at the ground. Through an opening in the trees, I could see four small goblins, whose fur was slightly greener than that of my own tribe. They were jumping and pointing at my flying machine, but then they locked up and went rigid. I realized it was the trance of technology—everything I'd unlocked was flooding into the survivors of whatever cataclysm had befallen their village. I leveled out and made a buttonhook turn, hoping to find them again. But the four had moved back into the trees.

So, they weren't all dead. That was good news. Great news, even. Plus, apparently finding different goblin variants would unlock them for my own tribe, much the same way unlocking technology did. The potential for more specialists upped the urgency of discovering additional tribes. Scrappers were probably useful, too. I wondered if they specialized in breaking down tech into component parts and cobbling it back together. I grinned and leaned into a turn to catch the hot-spring thermal again and then headed south.

The moon had passed overhead, and its pull had a noticeable effect on the performance of the glider. I was holding altitude longer, but once the eclipse passed over the clear areas, I would lose the benefit of those thermals.

The whole time I was flying, I felt the distinct impression of attention on me. At first, it made me paranoid. There were, after all, myriad predators interested in goblins. Some of which fly. And I couldn't think they'd look kindly on me making a flying contraption with their buddy's desiccated hide. But the presence wasn't hostile. It took me a little while to figure out that the extraneous presence I felt was the System itself devoting extra attention to my efforts.

"System, are you watching me?" I teased.

<Always.>

That was honestly more than I expected to get from the recalcitrant entity. I had always imagined it as a chubby CS engineer typing out snarky replies to me from the other side of a keyboard. This was the first time I felt it as a tangible presence in the world.

<What does it feel like?>

"Flying?"

<Yes.>

I huffed a laugh. *Can't you just read my mind? You're psychic or all-knowing or something, right?*

<I always know your thoughts and memories. I do not always understand your emotions.>

I thought for a moment. Even though the System could hear my thoughts, I still answered out loud. "Like distilled freedom. Like all the worries of the world just become so small as to not matter. Up here, it's just you and the air currents." I squeezed the handles of the control system. "I always preferred gliding over powered flight. The wings are like a part of you. It's amazing. It's always *been* amazing. And it will always be."

The System didn't answer me. I did feel the presence lift somewhat, though not disappear entirely. I supposed it had other tasks and couldn't afford to spend all its processing power on one little goblin glider, no matter how novel to this world. If this was some sort of alien simulation, maybe the bug-eyed gray alien administrating the whole thing had dreamed of piloting a UFO one day before he settled for a life of computer nerd-ism. I could relate. For a long time, I never thought I'd get my chance to go into space. Fate had conspired to give me that opportunity, then taken that opportunity away from me not once, but twice—first in the accident, and later in the explosion. Some *other* force had intervened to give it back. Not right away, and not without a mountain of effort. But that was a mountain I was willing to climb, and as far as I knew, I was the only person on this entire planet with the will and knowledge to do it.

It took about an hour to reach the other plateau to the southeast, near the border of an arid, badland area. I'd earmarked it for survey, betting that the sunbaked desert would give me enough thermal lift to easily make it back. I was delighted to find that an active goblin village thrived on the bluff, and there was a frenzy of activity. I dipped down for a lower pass over their plateau.

The frenzy of activity turned out to be a war of sorts between the tribe and a large type of pale, frilled lizard. The goblins were holding their own, but they were doing so with sticks and thrown stones. Once the shadow of the eclipse passed, the lizards retreated, scaling down the shaded face of the cliff on the side that blocked the sun.

I banked and followed the lizards from the air. They were quick little devils. They were only level 1, just like the goblins, but there were a lot of them and they moved as a pack back to a dry, dusty area on the plains with lots of cracks and crevices. I lost them there as they slithered into tight burrows and disappeared. I made a note of the area and rode the thermal coming off the baked ground of the plains in a large circle, surveying the land. There were large creatures on the badlands. I spotted herds of small leaping animals, as well as solitary behemoths that must have been the size of an elephant. I wanted a closer look, but I'd regained enough altitude to return for a low pass over the village in peril and reluctantly turned back toward the forest. They spotted me instantly, and pointed and shouted. Two of them threw rocks that fell hopelessly short.

<Your tribe has increased to 73 members.>

That was the biggest single jump I'd seen yet. So, the warring tribe had only twelve members, currently. They lost at least two fighting with the lizards, which I had seen get carried off the cliff. Without enough goblins to replenish losses, they would lose the war of attrition. Especially if the lizards came at night as well as during the eclipse. I saw several of them go rigid as my Goblin Tech Tree unlocks unfurled in their minds.

As much as I wanted to stay and see how the next battle played out, I was losing light, and with it, the thermals. I still had to make it back to Village Apollo. If nothing else, the twelve remaining goblins on this bluff now had fire, spears, and other technology to give them a slight edge. Who knew, if the lizard skin was photosensitive, the fire alone might be enough to deter them.

I angled back toward the hot springs I'd passed over earlier. Even with the sun dropping, they should give me the boost I needed to make it back to Village Apollo. But my mind kept wandering to what I'd just seen.

I was so lost in thought about how I could help the goblins on the bluff that I didn't see the shadow pass over me.

CHAPTER 24

A MISSED ENGAGEMENT

I didn't know if night haunts had a skill that let them paralyze prey with their screech, or if that was just a part of my goblin physiology. But when I heard the noise directly behind me, I locked up.

I'd never seen the night haunts around the village before full dark, but apparently, they began patrolling the skies near dusk. Or maybe this one saw me from its roost and flew into a rage at seeing one of its own converted into a glider. Either way, it tore a gouge in my left wing on its first pass.

The glider bucked and dipped to the left, having lost a good portion of its lift on that side. I cursed and tried to level out, looking around for the night haunt. I spotted him gaining altitude off to the north, preparing for another strike.

I pitched down, trying to build up speed so I could get low and fast over the treetops. The glider was completely defenseless against the aerial predator. Out of the corner of my eye, I saw it tuck in its wings for a stoop and come at me again. I yanked back on the controls, exposing the underside of the wings to the buffeting wind and slowing drastically.

The night haunt overshot and ended up in the trees. I leaned my weight forward and banked to the right—but my turn was sluggish. And I now had a huge problem: My glider no longer had the energy to make it back to Village Apollo.

I saw a clearer stretch of woods off to my right and leaned into a turn. With my left wing struggling to maintain lift, I lost a lot of altitude adjusting my heading. The tops of the trees started to slide past, and I flared off high to avoid impaling myself on the tallest branches. Unfortunately, the wind in my wings tore the left membrane further, and I started to spin left.

I shouted and braced for impact, but the tail caught on a branch, and I was ejected from the glider with a *snap* of the cords tying me down. I shot straight ahead, bounced off my head, and dug a head-width trench in the dirt when I landed again.

Right. Fall damage immunity. A crash like that back home would have been immediately fatal. I gave silent thanks for my new goblin body and pushed myself over onto my back and propped myself up on my elbows. Looking down, I immediately took it back.

One of my prosthetics had come off. A single running blade doesn't do much good on its own. I thumped the back of my head into the dirt and groaned. I was going to have to make a sticky-stilt and hobble all the way back to Village Apollo. It had looked at least five or six kilometers away when I'd been struck by the night haunt. That's a long trip through untamed lands as a healthy, adult human. As a goblin? Well, for all our wanderings, we'd never gone more than about three or four kilometers from the bluff. The woods were just too dangerous. If anything, I was closer to the first bluff I'd visited with the completely sacked village.

That wasn't a comforting thought. Village #3 was at war with lizards. I still didn't know what had destroyed Village #2. I had my guesses, but this land was full of so many threats to a tiny goblin tribe that it's a miracle any survived at all.

A crash on the other side of the brush drew my attention, and I saw a pair of bright yellow eyes in the dimming light. The night haunt pushed its way into the clearing, and I scraped at the ground, trying to pull myself away.

I might not be able to die while members of my tribe were there, but I could still feel *pain*. I didn't much think being torn at with the long, sharp beak and claws would feel great. And there was nothing saying I couldn't lose *more* limbs.

"Look," I said, scrabbling. "I didn't mean to make your friend into a glider. It just sort of worked out that he was there and I had the tools and needed an airfoil. No hard feelings, right?"

The night haunt crawled forward on the claws at the ends of its wings. Its head was low to the ground, and it growled. Its tail was poofed up like a startled cat, and it approached me in a serpentine, pacing back and forth as it drew closer.

"Nice monster . . . *niiiice* monster."

I could see the muscles in its haunches bunch up. It snarled, dug its claws into the turf, and then flinched as a spear embedded itself into the ground between its front paws. It yowled, hissed, and began to back away into the foliage.

My blood went cold. Goblins didn't scare night haunts. Which meant it hadn't been a goblin that threw that spear. That thick, heavy spear with a metal crossbar. I rolled my head back, fixing my eyes on the broad, bearded forms of the javeline rutters that had come out of the woods. Three of them came into the clearing, and the System helpfully put their levels at *7*, *8*, and *11*. One looked down curiously and nudged my remaining prosthetic with his spear. Another went to retrieve his own spear. The last started poking around the remains of the Mk 1 glider.

"Hey," I said.

The one with the spear pointed at me stumbled back, drawing the attention of the other two. "It talk!" he said. His voice was a low rumble.

"So what?" said the one at the wreckage. He picked up my other prosthetic, looked at it for a moment, and then discarded it. "It vermin. Kill. Take tongue."

"Wait! I'm not—*hyurk!*"

The pig-man standing over me thrust his spear down into my chest. It was like lightning zapped through my heart. Every bit as painful as the accident that took my legs, and then some. I could feel the blade going into my lung.

<*Head of the Snake activated.*>
<*Your tribe has decreased to 72 members.*>

The rutter pulled the spear out. I gasped, rolling onto my side. I pressed a hand to my chest, and it came away bloody, even though the wound had transferred to another member of Tribe Apollo. That didn't lessen the pain, though. Tremors shook through me, and I had trouble drawing a breath.

The one at the wreckage stomped back. "I say kill, Mitri! I have highest level. You listen me."

"I *did* kill, Rotte! Look!"

The one called Mitri held his spear up, where wet blood glistened in the moonlight. The others looked at it. Rotte, the one that seemed to be the leader, rolled me onto my back with his hoof, looking down at my chest. He grunted, angling his spear down.

"No, please!"

He brought the spear down and I screamed as it bit into me again.

<Head of the Snake activated.>
<Your tribe has decreased to 71 members.>

The pain was a searing, white-hot rod. I'd already died once, and now I wanted to do it again. Would they just sit here and keep stabbing me until they killed every member of my tribe and *then* me?

I couldn't bear it. Buzz, Neil, Sally, Chuck. I couldn't lose them like I'd lost Dave and Sandra. I couldn't take any more loss, and I couldn't take any more pain. There'd been too much already.

"System!" I gasped. "I renounce my job! Make me not a king anymore!"

<I'm sorry, Chris.>

The spear fell again.

CHAPTER 25

JAVELINE HOT POTATO

"We take it," Rotte growled. "Kill later."

Mitri reached down and scooped me up, throwing me over his shoulder. I winced. The pain of the javeline spears was still fresh. But the bastards trussed me up like, well, like a prize pig, and cantered back into the woods.

We didn't go far. They must have seen the glider from the ground, just as the night haunt had, and come to investigate. I started to smell sulfur and feel humidity dampen my fur, and I realized we were heading toward the hot springs that I'd flown over. We broke into a small clearing with several steaming pools and a campsite nearby. Their camp was small and disorganized, with three small hide tents and some supplies. They'd left a fourth, smaller rutter to guard it and cook dinner, by the looks of things. He had a metal cook pot hanging on a hollow iron pole. The tender looked at me curiously.

Mitri tossed me down onto the ground, knocking the wind out of me. "Tie up."

The smaller boar-man went to the packs and retrieved a length of chain—real metal chain. Not the rough cordage we were working with. God, the things I could do with a metal chain. They looped my wrists with the chain and then strung the whole thing around a branch, hoisting it to where I could barely sit.

"My tribe will come for me," I said.

Mitri looked up at the last of the fading light and made a rude noise. "Is night. No goblin come."

He was right. Goblins are chaos personified until about an hour after eating. When they crash, they crash *hard*. The javeline disregarded me for the time being, busying themselves instead with scooping whatever stew they'd brewed out of the cook pot into wooden bowls, which they slurped from, slopping half of it down their bristly flavor-savers. That finished, Rotte trotted past me into the woods, and a few minutes later, a stench wafted out that made even my raw-meat-eating goblin throat clench up and gag.

Rotte came back into the camp, trailing the stink along with him. He huffed a laugh. "Was bad one," he said, and then went to the cook pot for seconds. Disgusting creature. Once the hunting trio had eaten their fill, they sat back on their haunches and began to joke and laugh while the camp tender ate what little burnt scraps clung to the bottom of their pot.

After a few hours, the third javeline, the one that had scared off the night haunt, got bored or restless and wandered over to me. He prodded my sloth-claw blade with his hoof. "Is truth you talk?"

I debated staying silent. But I had a feeling it would just lead to me getting the business end of a spear, again. "Yeah," I said. "I talk." I looked up. "My name is Apollo. What's your name?"

"Muthus," said the javeline rutter.

"Why are you keeping me prisoner?"

The javeline shrugged. "Is strange, goblin that talk. Don't die. Maybe is worth sell."

"We don't have to be enemies," I said. "If you take me back to my tribe, we could trade. You have metal. I'm sure we have things you could use."

Muthus shook his head. "We trade goblin *for* metal. For spear. For pathfinding needle." He stuck out his tongue and pulled his ears. At first, I thought he was just being rude. Then I remembered what Rotte had said at the crash site. *Kill. Take tongue.*

I shivered. "Why would anyone want goblin ears and tongues?" I asked.

Muthus rubbed his belly. "Tongue is good to human for cure poison." He flattened his hands and raised them up. "Ears to elves for make potent."

"Make . . . make *potent*?" I asked. Then I realized. "Oh . . . *oh* . . . Oh, no."

Muthus squatted down on his haunches. "But goblin that talk like man? Goblin don't die? Worth ears of twenty goblin. Maybe ten and twenty."

"Is this what you do?" I asked. "Hunt goblins for a living?"

Muthus shrugged, getting back to his feet. "Hunt what need hunt. Goblin good. Goblin *vermin*. No one miss."

No one miss. Again, I was reminded just how alone goblins were in this world. How dismissed and discarded they were. Elves were huffing our powdered ears before sexy-times to raise their pavilions. Javelleros rounded us up for sport and profit. Lanclova was a harsh land, untamed and coveted by jealous eyes. If I was to have any hope of achieving my goal, or even living long enough to have a chance at it, I had to secure Tribe Apollo's place in these shadowed lands.

The javeline retired to their crude tents. I pulled at the chain, but the branch held firm and the chain just rattled loudly in the night.

"*QUIET!*" Rotte shouted from his tent.

I settled back, thinking. The tribe would be fine. For now. In the morning, they might come looking for me. Javeline were strong, and if I interpreted the situation correctly, they could gain levels through this world's System—unlike goblins, who were perpetually destined to be the weakest creatures. We were the joke, the speed bump for adventurers on their way to the real challenge. Well, there were seventy of us, and only four javeline. We may not have had levels, but we were legion.

The only problem was, how would I get them to come find me? Where would they even start looking? If the javeline broke camp and moved out early enough in the morning, they'd simply outpace any goblins on foot, even with the benefit of flex-a-pult assisted launches and wranglers. No. I had to do something.

CHAPTER 26

GORN IN SIXTY SECONDS

I tried everything I could think of to get loose, even gnawing on the chain. Goblin teeth were tough, but not chomp-through-iron tough.

Even with the imperative of escape looming over me, there was nothing I'd be able to do if I couldn't get free.

The sun dropped well and truly behind the horizon, opening Raphina's eye over the camp. I heard rustling in the brush and froze. The nocturnal predators of Lanclova were many, and I wasn't safe at the top of a fenced bluff.

The rustling grew louder. Could it be one of those photosensitive lizards had followed *me*? Maybe the night haunt the rutters had frightened off had come back for his stolen snack. I clenched up.

A goblin tumbled out of the brush. He came to a sitting position, slightly dazed, stared at me, and then pointed and opened his mouth to shout. A pair of thick hands reached out of the brush behind him and clapped over his mouth.

The hands were thick and knobby, with large, furry knuckles. The hobgoblin they belonged to was also thick and knobby. Whereas Chuck and his wranglers were lean and wiry, this one was built for power. His fur was darker, too. Closer to navy blue than the electric blue of my tribe. He had a hide cowl wrapped around his face, and a pair of flint cleavers tucked into a corded belt. He was level 5, which was higher than the wranglers.

"*Quiet!*" he hissed. "*You tryin' to rouse the porkbellies?*"

The smaller goblin got the message, because when the hobgoblin removed his hands, the smaller one clamped his own in their place. With a glance at the hide tents, the hobgoblin dropped to the ground and low-crawled to my tree. Past him, I could see the moonlight glinting off two other sets of eyes in the bush.

Since I hadn't acquired any new tribe members, I had to assume these were the four survivors I'd flown over.

"*You still wiv us, King?*" asked the hobgoblin, who must have been my very first scrapper. He sounded like he spoke around a mouth full of gravel. The scrapper motioned for one of the other goblins, who crept out of the bush holding my missing prosthetic above his head.

I nodded and held the chains out of the way as the scrapper slipped the socket over my stump and started to lace up the clamps. A regular Prince Charming, this one. The metal clinked slightly as I shifted. "*Can you get me out of these?*"

"*Inna pinch.*" The scrapper licked his lips and carefully began to pull the chain loops. But the sound of metal grinding against metal was too noisy.

"*Stop!*" I whispered, looking at the hide tents for any sign of movement. I heard something shift inside one of them, and the scrapper ducked low. The movement stopped, and he issued a low growl. "*Even if we do get these off, they'll come after us in the morning,*" I warned. "*And they're faster.*"

"*Bad news, that.*" The scrapper cracked his knuckles quietly. "*I could take one of 'em if I got the jump. But four's aft o' too many,*" he said. "*We need somethin' to even them odds up. Got any more o' your contraptions like what popped in our heads?*"

I thought. A few of the rock slingers would have evened the odds a little. Or some of the bomb fruits. But there was no way the four of them would be able to make slingers without first crafting a set of tools, and that would take too long—hours to navigate through dangerous terrain and retrieve bomb fruits just to most likely blow themselves up on the return trip when they stumbled over a root in the dark. Projectiles or other distance weapons would be ideal. But the javeline didn't carry bows or crossbows that we could steal, and their spears were much too heavy for myself or the other small goblins. Shame we didn't have the slingers, because there were plenty of small, smooth stones on the banks of the hot springs.

One of the other goblins wrinkled his nose and waved his hands in front of it, sniffing.

The scrapper noticed and shushed them. "*Rutters like to camp wiv the springs 'cause they're the only things wot stink more'n they do.*"

"*That'd be the sulfur,*" I said. "*Smells like rotten eggs where the—*"

I stopped. *Sulfur.* I looked at the softly glowing coals of the dying rutter fire. *Charcoal.*

Hmm . . .

I had no idea if the chemical reactions of this world bore any resemblance to that of Earth in my home universe. It stood to reason the periodic table would have differences in a world where magic and rule-enforcing omniscient systems existed. But chemistry had never been my forte anyway. I hoped a little Goblin Tech Tree grease would smooth over the gaps.

Everyone's got an episode of a TV show that was always on whenever they were channel surfing. For me, it was a certain episode of *Star Trek* where the captain got stranded on the planet with the weird, diamond-eyed lizard. Now, I know what you're going to say: *He's an astronaut, of course he's a Trekkie nerd*. But the truth is, I was always more of a *Battlestar* guy. I've barely even watched *Trek*. Except for that one episode, which seemed to always be on, and which has lived rent-free in my head for fifteen years.

If it was the same episode for you, then you've probably already figured out where this is going.

I motioned the goblins closer. "*We're going to need a few things*," I said. I looked at the first goblin. "*By the springs there should be some yellow, stinky mineral. I need powder from it. Can you scrape some off and bring it to me?*"

The goblin pulled her knife and lifted it overhead, keeping one hand over her mouth to stifle her own excitement. She vanished back into the brush.

I pointed to the dying fire. "*I need some of the charred wood from that fire. Make sure you don't grab anything glowing!*"

The second goblin nodded enthusiastically and dropped to a low crawl, serpentining his way into the rutter camp. I looked at the remaining small one. "Sorry to do this to you. But I need some of the javeline scat from their latrines."

I pointed, and the goblin wilted, looking at me with an expression of pure betrayal. But he stomped off into the forest. It wasn't hard to tell where the latrine was. It was the only thing smelling worse than the sulfur.

"*Wot of me, King?*" asked the scrapper.

"*The rutters had hollow poles holding up their cookpot. I need those poles.*"

The scrapper looked at me skeptically until I explained to him what the goblins were going to do with the poles. Then the hobgoblin grinned. "*Oy, sounds like a proppa' lark.*" He turned as if to leave, then hesitated. "This *name* fing, boss. I fink I want one."

The first name that came to mind, looking at his muscled frame, was, of course, *Armstrong*. But I'd already named one of the goblins *Neil*. Ah, so what? I feel like the first man to walk on the moon deserved a twofer. Besides, the goblins all had single names anyway. Like Cher, or Zendaya.

"*Armstrong*," I whispered.

Armstrong flexed his ample biceps and grinned. Arms like that would have been right at home on the rowing team. I watched as he dropped to his belly and snaked into the camp. The tubes had been stowed with the rest of the cookware on the far side of the clearing after the camp keeper had cleaned them. He went slowly, taking his time and staying as quiet as possible. He was oddly stealthy for a goblin. I pulled up his info in my System menu as I watched.

<Hobgoblin Scrapper
Hobgoblin: This advanced goblin is capable of speaking and can reach level 5.
Nocturnal: These bad boys like to stay up late and get into trouble. Their eyes are tuned for low-light. The downside is that they sleep until midday.
Scrappy: These hard-knuckled bruisers love a good fight—especially if their opponent doesn't know they're in one. Scrappers have a bonus to surprise attacks.
Sneakers: These light-footed goblins are capable of getting in and out of tight spots without detection. They have a bonus when using camouflage.
Track-em: These goblins excel at following trails left by other creatures.>

I'd been expecting a machinist when I'd heard the term *scrapper*. But this guy was basically the goblin equivalent of a special forces commando. Of the two, this was exactly what I needed. *Thanks, System.*

The goblin with the scat returned first, carrying the pungent droppings on a flat rock. Then came the goblin with the charcoal, and lastly the one with the sulfur. Now, I didn't know the finer details or ratios of making black powder. Rocket fuel? Sure. But I was never a gun person, and never even considered joining the Army. But I knew the basic components. The only one I wasn't completely clear on was saltpeter. But I remembered that they used to get it from bat guano in the Civil War (thanks to Mr. Clarkson's tenth-grade field trip for history that I never thought I'd use). I figured the rutter scat was probably foul enough to explode on its own, so it might have some of that third ingredient or something almost as good. Fertilizer had phosphates in it, and fertilizer had been used for bombs in the past.

My newest tribe members used sticks to mix the concoction into a big, smelly mess. By the time Armstrong returned with the tubes, we had a weird, greasy putty that looked like vomit and smelled like pure death.

I had them break it up and feed it into one end of the tubes, and then take rocks and pebbles and feed them down the other end and tamp them down with sticks. Goblins, being what they are, got immediately overexcited and missed the mouth of the tube entirely. A rock pinged off the iron exterior, and we all froze as the metal rang like a tuning fork. Armstrong lanced out and grabbed the pole, stopping the ringing. But the damage was done.

The rutters began to stir.

CHAPTER 27

BATTLESTART GOBSPLATICA

What is noise?" yelled Mitri.

"Oy! Told ye shut it!" Rotte shouted from his tent.

Armstrong hooked two of the goblins in the crooks of his elbows and melted back into the brush. The third started to run, then grabbed the putty-smeared rock and made scarce. I sat stock-still, donning my best look of innocence.

The three rutters emerged from their hide tents, and boy, let me tell you, they're even uglier with their helmets off. All three had thick, hairy jaws with oddly protruding tusks that I'd assumed were fixed to their helmets and not their *faces*. Above that, they looked about like uglier versions of the dwarves you'd see in a movie. Least of all because I'd interrupted their beauty sleep. But if any of these things were to get enough of that to look pretty, they'd be a shoo-in for a fairy tale of their own.

Rotti and Muthus grabbed the spears from beside their tents before they trotted up. Mitri just cracked his hairy knuckles.

"I warn talking goblin!" said Rotte. He lifted his spear and thrust it toward me. I squawked and dove out of the way, wrenching my arms on the chain but narrowly avoiding being impaled. This just made Rotte mad, though the others chuckled. He thrust again, and once more, and I managed to barely get out of the way. By now, the other rutters were laughing openly.

"Mitri!" Rotte snarled.

Mitri trotted forward and grabbed the chain just above my wrists. He yanked it up, easily lifting me off my feet, and sank a heavy fist into my gut.

<Your tribe has decreased to 69 members.>

Really? That's all it took? Granted, it hurt like the devil! But were goblins really that paper-thin?

<Your tribe has decreased to 68 members.>

No. I didn't get the Head of the Snake notification. Something else was happening. Something back home that I wasn't there for. Night haunts? The wranglers should have been protecting the village against them. But I had more pressing concerns. Mitri wound up and slugged me again. I gasped for air, kicking my feet helplessly.

"Something odd," said Muthus.

The others ignored him. Rotte lifted his spear again. "Hold it still, Mitri. This one no miss."

Mitri moved to the side to be out of the path of Rotte's spear. Beyond the spear, I saw several shadowy forms creeping in from the other side of the camp. Coal light glinted off rough iron in their hands. Armstrong and the others were still getting into position. I had to buy them more time.

"Rotte!" insisted Muthus. Rotte started to turn back, but if he did that . . .

"Wait!" I gasped. "You were facing me this whole time? I thought I was talking to your backside!"

Rotte snapped his attention back to me, face reddening. Foam started to trickle at the corners of his mouth.

"You were prettier with the helmet on."

"I make goblin sorry," seethed Rotte. He gripped the shaft of his spear so tightly the wood began to creak under his fingers. Behind him, I saw my improvised riflemen plant the butts of their poles in the glowing coals and angle the muzzles toward the trio of rutters.

I hadn't wanted to do this. I hadn't wanted to introduce firearms to this world along with all the horrors that came with them. I certainly hadn't wanted every goblin in my tribe to be running around separated from a boomstick by a few bowel movements and a bath. I would have liked to skip every conceivable variation on a gun that I reasonably could on the way to securing my tribe's path to the moon. But now I was looking at my first formation of goblin riflemen. And I hated myself just a little bit for its necessity.

"Did goblin have one leg before?" asked Muthus.

"He has no legs, idiot!" barked Mitri. He looked down. And stopped. I looked down as well.

Oh hell. Armstrong and his pals had tracked us here from the glider wreck, and they'd brought my other leg. The rutters had brought me here with only one.

"How he get . . ."

Rotte spun around, raising his spear and hurling it at the fire pit. One of the goblins squawked and dropped his pipe, diving to the ground to get out of the path of the spear. But Armstrong and the other two held steady.

Mitri dropped me to the ground and charged alongside Muthus. I didn't know how long it would take the fire to heat up the putty in the tubes, but I had to—

<Goblin Technology Unlocked: Icky-Sicky Boom-Putty>
<Goblin Technology Unlocked: Basic Goblin Rocket-Tree>
<Goblin Technology Unlocked: Basic Goblin Blastics>
<Goblin Technology Unlocked: Goblin-Guided Payload>
<Goblin Technology Unlocked: Single-Stage Rock-it Boost'em>
<This is going to be interesting.>

We must have tamped the stones in the tubes down too hard, because they didn't explode out the front end like scattershot. It was the back ends that blew, the ones in the fire. They exploded in a shower of sparks and a shrill, mounting whistle. And it didn't launch the detritus in the business end. It launched the whole kit and caboodle—goblins included.

The first one to go was the one that had been dropped in the fire. It fizzed, ignited, and careened skyward where it popped in a burst of yellowy sparks.

<Goblin Technology Unlocked: Goblin Signal Flower>

Everyone in the clearing stopped and stared. Especially the goblin that had dropped the pipe, now clinging gratefully to the ground. The two goblins that had held on to their pipes rocketed forward on plumes of sparks, screaming and holding on for dear life. They impacted Mitri and Muthus before the pair had time to register what was going on.

<Your tribe has decreased to 66 members.>

A cloud of blue fur, thankfully shielded from my view by the unfortunate javeline, erupted at the same time about a half-meter of iron pipe sprouted from the dwarven backs.

I hadn't invented guns. I'd invented *missiles.* Goblin-guided missiles. As incredible as they were terrifying.

Armstrong was a heavier payload. When his missile ignited, he looked more like a witch riding a flaming broom as he screamed and flew toward Rotte. The blood- and fur-covered javeline rutter stared and then tried to dive out of the way at the last second. The pipe missed him, but Armstrong hit him. The hobgoblin was made of sterner stuff than the average goblin. He bowled the heavier rutter over and the two went rolling. And if that didn't count as a surprise attack for the scrapper bonus, then I don't know what would. The final eastern bluff survivor, the one fortunate enough to not be carried off by his own gun, yowled in rage and chased after them.

With them fighting, I worked at my chains, no longer caring about the noise. In fact, my little goblin ears were ringing anyway. I managed to get the loops off just as I saw the camp tender emerge from his hiding spot. He took one look at the tableau and ran for Mitri's spear.

"Armstrong!" I shouted. Having cast the last loops of chain off, I dashed over to the tussling trio. The hobgoblin had a pair of cleavers tucked behind his belt. I pulled one out and started to hack at the flank of the javeline, for all the good it did. I just wasn't strong enough to get through his thick hide.

The thunder of hooves sounded, and a spear took me in the back.

<Head of the Snake activated.>
<Your tribe has decreased to 65 members.>

The force drove me into the ground, and the pain took my breath away. I was dragged through the dirt and the foliage as the camp keeper kept his charge up. Every meter became a fresh hell.

<Your tribe has decreased to 64 members.>
<Your tribe has decreased to 63 members.>

He was killing me over and over. My arms were useless by my sides, and both of my prosthetics came off.

<Your tribe has decreased to 62 members.>

Some snarling creature brought the javeline rutter to a screeching halt. He dug in all four hooves, kicking up a wave of dirt and dead leaves. My own momentum kept me going, sliding off the end of the spear and tumbling through the dirt and brush at high speed. Through my spinning vision, I caught a glimpse of big red shapes charging toward me, and of the backside of the camp keeper as he threw the spear away and retreated.

A pair of feet thumped to the ground near me, and hands wrapped my shoulders to pull me upright.

"S'alright chief, we got yer back."

The spinning had made me sick, and I heaved what little was in my guts—which wasn't much, since the javeline hadn't fed me. Good thing, too. If they had, I'd have likely been too lethargic to mount an escape.

I finally managed to look up at the hobgoblin with the mandible mask. "Chuck?" I asked. "What are you doing here?"

"Rangin'. We knew there 'bout where you went down. But not where they took you. Least til we saw yer signal," he said. He pointed to the sky. The first pipe gun had gone off like a bottle rocket and detonated in the sky. You could still see the yellowish smoke. But that was still miles from Apollo.

My vision cleared enough to see the other wranglers, and my jaw dropped. They were *riding cliffords*, the red canines from the savannah that had tried to eat me on my first day in Lanclova. Each wrangler had a tight grip on their clifford's mane in one hand and a spear in the other, while a second goblin balanced on the back haunches with a rock slinger. Even now, the goblin riding behind Chuck struggled to control the beast, but they didn't have the animal handling skills of the wranglers.

Chuck tried to help me to my feet, and then realized my lower legs were missing. Instead, he picked me up, punched his wayward mount on the nose to remind it who was boss, and then slung me over the back of its haunches like a sack of potatoes.

I figured we'd be getting out of Dodge, but instead he spurred the clifford on toward the one javeline still fighting. We bounced and jostled our way back into the clearing. I struggled to get my arms between me and the clifford so that I could tilt my head up far enough to see what was happening.

Armstrong was up and clear of the melee. He was bruised and bloody, but hobgoblins are built tougher than us standard goblins. The rutter leader, Rotte, was sprinting off into the woods, looking a bit like a pincushion with all the wrangler spears sticking out of him. But it's not easy to kill a wild pig. I had no doubt he'd make it back to the rest of his kind.

Chuck dismounted again, and clasped wrists with Armstrong.

"Good lookin' out fer the boss," said Chuck. "Can't conscience where we'd be without 'im."

Armstrong put a hand behind his head, looking almost embarrassed at the praise. "Weren't nuffink," he said.

Where we'd be without him. Probably better off. I probed the already-closing wounds on my body—wounds that had passed on to another goblin elsewhere through means I didn't fully understand. Between playing sports, riding motorcycles, and flying, I'd been a bit cavalier in my last life. Always looking for the next thrill, the next challenge, until I could experience the ultimate one: walking on the moon. Now, here I was doing the same thing on Rava, sailing off on my own. My pop had always said his heart would give out watching me bungee jump or white-water raft. And then his heart had given out at a steak restaurant as he tried to eat a thirty-ounce T-bone in twenty minutes to get it 50 percent off. He'd been looking to put one foot in the grave ever since my mom had passed when I was in fourth grade. Maybe I get my risk-taking from him. But now, it wasn't me who would suffer the consequences of my actions. A handful of goblins had died tonight without even being here. Without even knowing *why*. Ironic. Now that I was practically untouchable, I had more to lose than ever.

The other goblin on our clifford helped me to sit up.

I looked at the other two rutters impaled on the poles. "Sorry about your friends, Armstrong. I wanted to save you all, but you ended up saving me instead."

The hobgoblin waved me off. "Big group o' rutters done for the ol' village. I fink me mates'd be proud wot to have done-in a few back." He grinned. "You see 'em? Were all *shwoooosh—Splat!* Proper scrap, that!"

The scrapper laughed, and it seemed his mirth was contagious as the rest of the goblins started making *shwoosh-splat* noises and howling with laughter.

I looked to the woods on the other side of the camp, where the rest of the wranglers were returning after having run off the final javeline. "Rotte is going to report this. If there's more rutters in the woods, you can bet they'll have their sights set on a goblin king before long. We need to show them that we're tougher quarry than some impotent elf's wallet is worth."

"Aye, boss," said Chuck. He patted the side of his clifford. "Ain't no helpless hands they'll be finding. Tribe Apollo claws back."

"That we do."

CHAPTER 28

MUTHUS WITH A SIDE OF MITRI

There's good eating on a javeline, it turns out. Once I got over my qualms about munching on the flesh of a sentient species (which my goblin side was frighteningly willing to do), I realized that being half pig made them the closest thing to a taste of home that I'd had since coming to Rava, and it was worth staying up a little past my goblin bedtime to roast. They went down especially well when seasoned with the block of salt and the pepper Rufus gave me in acknowledgment that I'd won our wager (*<Goblin Technology Unlocked: Sneezy-Seasonings>*).

<Your tribe has decreased to 61 members.>
<2 Hobgoblin Scrappers have been added to your tribe.>
<1 Hobgoblin Wrangler has been added to your tribe.>
<Your tribe has increased to 69 members.>

I awoke to the patter of rain on clay tiles, which left me blessedly dry. Buzz was already up and checking the waterproofing on them, evidently satisfied with his work. I pulled myself off the pile and whistled up at him.

"Welcome home, boss," he said. "Figured you'd want a good roof once Chuck fetched you back. I'd have come with, but I'm not much use in a scrap."

"That's okay," I said. "Neither am I, as it turns out."

Buzz dropped down and grinned at me. "Kings ain't s'posed to fight. That's why you got us an' the hobbies, yeah?"

I sat in the shelter and watched the rain fall for a bit. The prior day had been rough on the tribe. We'd lost a lot of goblins between regular daily attrition and the fight with the javeline rutters. The night haunts hadn't gotten into any of the new improved structures, as far as I could tell. But that meant the lizard war had continued with the tribe to the southeast. They were now my top priority.

Rufus woke up a short time later and extricated himself from the mound of goblins that had decided the half-badger made a better bed than the straw and moss flooring. The disheveled trader pulled on his boots and fished through his bag for a drink. "Any o' that pork left?" he asked.

I pursed my lips. "Don't you see any moral qualms about eating a javeline? They're intelligent beings."

Rufus raised a bushy eyebrow. "You've met them, yes?"

"Unfortunately."

He moved to the fire and started sifting around the stone grill for morsels. "And you still think they're intelligent?"

"They're self-aware, free-thinking beings," I said. I sighed. "In my world, eating another intelligent being is one of our ultimate taboos." I paused for a moment. "Did you know they were cutting off goblin ears and tongues?"

Rufus hesitated. That told me everything I needed to know.

"My friend . . ." he said carefully. "Until you got me down from that tree, I admit I thought of goblins as little more than a nuisance—best ignored if not avoided outright. I don't brook with the trading of such snake oils. But I admit, I never gave the practice much consideration . . ."

"Until now," I finished. The rain petered off, so I walked closer to the fire pit and sat near the beast-kin.

"Until now," Rufus agreed. He licked the grease from his fingers and came and sat down beside me. "The last ten days have given me many reasons to see things in a new light. I fear you will not be looked on kindly by those seeking to exploit Lanclova. Your ears and tongue will be the least of your worries."

Rufus pulled his pack over and fished out his journal. He thumbed through it, reaching the pages that I assumed pertained to the scholarly details he'd gathered about myself and Tribe Apollo. He tore them out and laid them on the smoldering coals. They caught quickly, crisping in the heat. I watched them curl and char, until the ashes rose on the breeze.

"I could have just held onto those for you," I said.

"Ah, yes, but then what of my grand gesture?"

I huffed a laugh, and then sighed. "I'm not a fighter," I said. I cradled my head in my hands. "I'm a scientist and an engineer. I never even joined the military—never raised a hand in violence against anyone until I came here. All I ever wanted to do was go to space and explore."

The badger-kin trader straightened from the fire and cast a look over his shoulder. "I sense no deceit in what you say. In the quest for knowledge, you share more with me than those who seek to exploit the land beneath Raphina's watchful eye. Perhaps it's folly to cast my lot with a goblin king. Yet here we are. I will go south. I will speak to the artificers. Try not to die before I return."

Most of the goblins were up and milling around now. Not all of them were early risers like Buzz. The hobbies would sleep past midday, of course. But there was still work to be done.

I looked up at Raphina, the tidally locked moon that hovered over this land. With the sun in the sky, her eye was closed—a void in the morning starlight made of the daily new moon. She was waiting for me. And it didn't matter what it took. I'd walk on her surface. But first, there was work to do.

I called over some of Buzz's builders. "Bring me the javeline heads."

CHAPTER 29

MULTITASKING

<Goblin Totem Unlocked: javeline. Goblins who appreciate this totem temporarily gain resistance to slowing and demoralizing effects.>

The effect was near instant. The goblins seemed less impacted by the effect of the rain on the village, continuing to work—if slowly—instead of huddling inside the shelters until it stopped.

I found Sally at the edge of the bluff, hard at work with a charcoal stick and a sheaf of bark filings under a lean-to. She'd woken up with the new knowledge passed down through the Tech Tree in the wake of my ill-fated attempt at making explosive black powder. Well, black *putty*, at least. Instead of powering simple firearms, I'd made something close enough to what this world considered rocket fuel to unlock the basic concept of rocket motors. As I expected of my chief engineer, she was busy combining new and old concepts into amalgamative technology to further her own understanding.

She passed some of the sketches over, and I looked at the primitive schematics, nodding, equal parts impressed and appalled by her ideas.

"We're going to need more sulfur," I told her. "And clay. And hides." I scratched my head. "I hope the artificers can get us refined copper wire. There's so much we need."

Behind me, I heard cheering as several of the goblins loaded into the flex-a-pult. They had new contraptions with them that I hadn't seen before. As soon as the flex-a-pult launched the first five goblins, they unfurled mini gliders that caught the wind and launched them skyward. They floated in circles as the next several windsurfers loaded up and got a boost. Only one of them lost hold of their glider and plummeted into the forest at the base of the bluff.

I watched the lazy floaters taking enjoyment from the sheer act of soaring, and I couldn't help but smile. These little astronauts in the making—though they didn't know it yet—were fearless in the face of heights and willing to embrace change at an unheard-of rate. Two weeks ago, a smooth rock had been the height of their technological prowess. Now they were conquering the skies. Millennia of human innovation had been squeezed down into a fortnight. But we needed more. If I was going to rescue the remaining goblins on the southeast bluff, I needed the hobgoblins, and I needed something that could carry them.

"Have your team make more of those gliders," I said. I took one of the bark scraps and a piece of charcoal and began sketching out a modification of the stubby-winged design that extended the wings out, added winglets, and made it better for soaring.

I left her to find Neil, who hadn't yet set out with his hunters and fishers.

He looked up at me from where he was greasing the rails of his slinger. He'd fashioned a loop on the bottom of it that he could feed his hook through to keep it steady for shooting and reloading. Next to him was a pile of down that he'd been using to line the sled for some reason. "Yes?"

I sat down next to him. "Got a special task for your boys today. Javeline left their camp in a hurry. I need the supplies they left. Tents, poles, tools, anything they can carry back. I'm sure they had food, too. See if you can salvage anything from the crash site. Also, we need sulfur and rutter scat for putty."

Neil tilted his head. "Ours works near as well," he said.

"It does?" I asked, looking at the overflowing latrine pit on the edge of the village. I'd been planning to use it for fertilizer once we started an agrarian tech path. But apparently goblins were little phosphate factories who literally shit components for primitive rocket fuel. Which meant, the more goblins, the more icky-putty. As if I needed more reasons to grow the tribe.

Neil nodded. He set down his slinger and held up a small, round clay jar, then tested the fitting in his sled.

"What's that?" I asked.

Neil giggled and made the goblin pantomime for an explosion. Good God. The little psychopath was turning my rock slingers into grenade launchers. I took the jar. It was about the size of my hand, which meant it wouldn't be much of a payload. But it would certainly ruin the day of whoever or whatever got hit with it. The javeline might think twice before running down goblins if every wrangler on a clifford had a goblin with a slinger riding shotgun packing a few of these things. I looked around and saw several of his hunters working on other clay jars to set out in the sun to dry. The First Apollan Grenadiers Division. Yikes.

As loath as I was to condone the creation of explosive weaponry, I had to admit it was at least safer for the tribe than the bomb fruits. And we desperately needed to defend ourselves long enough for the tribe to grow and develop more variants. But I worried about putting too much destructive power in the hands of a collective who immediately gained an innate knowledge of its functioning. The standard goblins weren't as skilled at specialized tasks as the variants, but they were skilled *enough* to be dangerous—to our side as well as any enemies.

Neil collected his hunters and loaded their equipment and folding gliders into the flex-a-pult. They launched off toward the southeast toward the hot springs—no longer falling straight down after the apex of their parabolic launch but catching the wind and pulling away. These new gliders massively extended the range of the flex-a-pults when launching goblin-based payloads. Which, in turn, expanded our own rapid response territory from just a couple of kilometers around the bluff up to about five kilometers. That encompassed the hot springs, as well as the edge of the grasslands to the south. To the west? Well, to be completely honest, I hadn't given much thought to the west yet. There were other bluffs on that side, but they were much farther than the ones to the east and through thickly forested and swampy terrain that offered few spots for thermals to form. No bones about it, we'd need powered flight to reach them.

To the north, humans were a ten-day round trip for a half-badger across the forests and foothills of a mountain range. But how much territory did a half-dwarf beast-kin cover in a day? I should have asked Rufus. We just knew too little.

I worked with Sally and her crew until midday. They were busy with the new glider pattern, while I had my own task. We wouldn't be able to finish the gliders until we had the canvas from the javeline tents that I'd sent Neil to retrieve. Canvas was something our aeronautics program needed, but maybe I could substitute more wing membranes from night haunts. Of course, that required hunting them during the day, which would almost certainly cause casualties. A better solution would be to set traps to lure them in at night and take them by surprise with hobgoblins. I threw my project over my shoulder and went to see the resident experts on nocturnal dealings.

The hobgoblins woke up about the time as Raphina's eye, stumbling from their shelters bleary-eyed and yawning. I had jobs for both the scrappers and the wranglers.

Chuck and Armstrong came over first thing.

"Armstrong. Did your village ever have contact with the one south of you?"

"I seen 'em," he said, looking out to the southwest. "Small like. No hobbies. Never caused us no grief. Recluses, boss."

"They're at war with pale lizards that don't like sunlight. Or, it would be more accurate to say, they're being predated upon in the same way the night haunts are attacking us. Think your boys can give them a hand on the war front so they can start making gliders instead of spears and head this way?"

Armstrong looked around. "Getting cozy up here, boss."

"I'll deal with that."

The scrapper cracked his knuckles and grinned. "In that case, we can do for some lizards."

I clapped him on the arm. "Good. I'll send support your way as soon as we get the new gliders built."

Armstrong rounded up his unruly rabble of scrappers and trotted off to the eastern flex-a-pult.

I turned to Chuck. "Nice save with the cliffords last night. How did you manage to get them following your orders?"

Chuck shrugged. "Just an understanding, boss. Best to raise 'em as cubs. Then you don't gotta remind 'em who's boss as much. Hard to hold on when they get to bucking and biting."

I hefted the leather on my shoulder. "This might help with that. Where are the kennels?"

CHAPTER 30

BOGGED DOWN

<Goblin Technology Unlocked: Skinny Saddle>

I carefully looped the under-strap and ran it through the cinch beneath the clifford's muscular belly. I didn't know much about riding, but I'd seen western movies. Saddle on top, bridle in front, straps below. Right? How tough could it be?

I backed up as the clifford snapped at me, but Chuck dipped in and popped the red canine on the nose. Properly chagrinned, the beast settled, and Chuck was able to swing up onto the hide saddle. He wiggled around, then gave a nod. "It'll do, but I still want my glider."

"It's coming. Neil should be back with the canvas and sulfur before midnight. In the meantime, I want to get a lay of the land *from* the land. It's hard to spot resources from the air, and there are a few we still really need."

It didn't hurt to project our power out a bit, too. Once we had the numbers for it, I intended to have regular patrols by both ground *and* air so nothing could sneak up on us. It would take a few more reproductive cycles, a lot of work, and a lot more hobgoblins to be able to cover the territory, though.

Chuck held the clifford still while I clambered up onto its back. Someone handed me a slinger and a small sack of stones. The rest of the wranglers mounted up with their goblin gunners in tow. They looked at our saddle with jealous eyes, and I had no doubt that all of them would have their own by the next morning.

Each of the hobgoblin wranglers had a small hide holster on their back with two short spears. Between the spears, the slingers, and the cliffords themselves, this was about as well-armed as I'd seen my tribe. But I still only had six wranglers, and there was a lot of ground around the village to cover.

"Where to, boss?"

"Northwest, I think," I said. "Rufus said the closest settlement was humans to the northwest. I want to see what's out in that direction."

Chuck reached back and smacked the flank of his clifford, and we were off before I could squawk with surprise. Cliffords, it seemed, shared one trait with goblins: They only had two speeds. Standing still and *complete mania.* The canine dug its claws in and launched into a sprint, barking and bounding through the woods. Despite being a savannah creature, it seemed well equipped to traverse the dense forest. It changed directions quickly by jumping up and kicking off tree trunks, and surmounted foliage by simply barreling through it while Chuck ducked low and I held on for dear life. I got the impression he was more *suggesting* directions than steering it, but the way the wranglers and their gunners hooted and hollered while the cliffords barked their heads off made it seem like everyone got max enjoyment out of the experience. I'd never ridden a horse on Earth, but I'd ridden motorcycles. And this scratched a similar, if bouncier, smellier, more manic itch.

I suppose it was a bit closer to a motorcycle club in rowdiness than any kind of horse-riding club. At times, the hobbies were leaned so far forward I wasn't sure how the cliffords didn't topple ass over teakettle. Unlike the peaceful soaring of the glider, this close to the ground the sensation of speed was almost overwhelming. As fast as I thought we were going, when we broke onto one of the goblin trails, Chuck *really* gave the dog its head and the thing tore down the straightaway, tongue lolling out to the side like a pennant and claws kicking up sprays of dirt. A look back through the canopy and I could see the bluff. We must have covered four or five kilometers already, which was not bad for creatures only about a meter tall.

Chuck finally slowed us up near a stream so the dogs could drink and the goblins could grab some wild onions from the bank. I knelt down at the bank and ran my hand through the water. The water was red-orange in color—much like the clay had been. Upstream were some higher hills in the distance, bordering on mountains. I thought for a moment, then cupped my hands and took a drink. There was definitely a metallic taste to the water. I ran a hand through my fur, considering.

"Chuck, where's the river dump out?" I called.

He was ruffling the muzzle of his clifford, who was growling and chomping the air. Clearly the pair had built something of a bond, even if the dog got a firm punch on the nose whenever the chomps got a little too close to Chuck's face. He glanced over at me. "Downstream," he said.

Well, *obviously.* I headed back over. "You been there?"

"Not yet."

I headed over to the hobbies and the dogs. "Let's check it out."

I climbed back up on the haunch of the clifford and waited while the rest of the crew got situated. Chuck pointed the dog vaguely southwest and gave it a smack to get it going. We tore down the riverbed, scattering some critters and birds. I spotted a splash in the water and several fish jumped out on diaphanous fins—only to be snatched from below by a long-snouted reptile. My eyes went wide. I wondered if that was what had gotten the goblin the first time we tried fishing. It certainly looked big enough to drag one of my fishermen out into the water and then make a meal of it. Note to self, postpone the swimming lessons.

I noted a possible pocket of clay along the way—based on a resident stone sloth that we outpaced as it charged after us. The cliffords seemed to need no extra encouragement to avoid the large, clawed creature. It was, by far, the biggest one I'd seen yet, and had a high level to reflect its stature. A volley of rocks from the slingers might have been what discouraged it from following us too far, but I suspected it just hit the edge of its territory. The stream started to level out, and I caught a whiff of more stagnant water up ahead. I didn't know if it was my new goblin nose or simply being away from the smog of the cities and roads back home, but my sense of smell had definitely sharpened. The trees got shorter, and then turned to tangled vines and twisted shrubbery.

Chuck called a halt, and I hopped down from the back of the clifford and rubbed my backside. While fast, the bony canines weren't exactly the smoothest ride. My blades sank about five or six centimeters into the turf, and I could feel the resistance of moving through water. Chuck swept some foliage out of the way and hissed.

"Bog," he said. "This what you wanted to see, boss?"

"Sure is," I said. He and one of the other hobbies held back branches to let me and a pair of slinger-toting goblins scramble out into the bog. I was quickly in water up to my knees, pushing through the vegetation. The bog was wide and mostly open, with just a few large trees offering little cover from the heat of the day that turned the air into a humid mire. I could see the spot where the stream emptied out, as well as other slow flows on the other side. The water ran slowly through the bog, and the entire thing was covered in a layer of mossy, mulchy vegetation.

Was this peat? I had only a vague idea of what *peat* really was. I hadn't had a chance to read the book Rufus had left on collecting iron from the bogs, but this seemed like a sound place to start looking. I reached down and pulled up a handful of the loose, fibrous turf. It was soaked through, matted, and woven together.

Once I got about waist-deep, something startled a flock of birds across the bog, and I watched them take flight. Underneath them, several of the mounds of peat—at least, what I *hoped* was peat—slid and slipped on ripples of something entering the water of the bog. Something *big.* I hadn't read Rufus's bestiary, either. I slowly backed away, unable to see what had slid into the bog. If it was anything like the river monster that had snatched the flying fish, I didn't want to tangle with it.

I kept my eyes forward for any sign of the creature, but I should have been watching where I stepped. An angry buzzing and snapping brought my attention around in a hurry.

"Boss, freeze!" shouted Chuck from the bank.

A small cloud of *big* bugs flew out of a hive in the peat that I'd apparently disturbed. I stood as still as I could, looking at the flying insects as they flew around, searching for something to take their aggression out on. They looked like some sort of wasp, except they each had two stingers. And as I watched, a tiny arc of electricity climbed up between the stingers like a miniature Jacob's Ladder. They were like some sort of lightning bug, except in a more literal sense. Mentally, I dubbed them *tesla wasps.* One of the two goblins who had accompanied me into the bog squawked and dropped his slinger in the drink, jumping and grabbing his backside.

I heard a buzz mount behind me, and then a *snap.* A jolt of electricity arced through my little goblin ass, causing my leg remnants to spasm and dropping me face-first into the stagnant water. The thing had stung me *and* shocked me! I didn't know what being tased felt like, but I had to imagine it was pretty similar. I flailed around and let out a cry that bubbled underwater. I completely panicked when I saw a pair of luminescent eyes coming toward me in the murk and burst back above the water in a cloud of the agitated tesla wasps. Their disposition hadn't improved. My splashing attracted their attention, and I'm sure the volley of stones from the goblins on the bank of the bog didn't calm things down.

Several of the tesla wasps swooped down, narrowly missing me with their sparking thoraxes. They came close enough for me to hear the *snap* and *pop* of the electricity between their stinger tines. Another one scored home high on my back and my right arm spasmed, luckily knocking aside another that was diving in on me—but then my arm went completely numb.

Something big burst out of the water near me with a snarl, and I looked behind to see something vaguely crocodilian, but with four eyes and a thick, bulbous tongue. The System didn't even bother assigning it a level, just a vague "*??*" over its head—probably its way of telling us we were completely outmatched. The goblin next to me saw it, too, and leveled his slinger at it. He sent a stone arcing forward, but it sailed above the bog lizard's head and skipped off the surface of the water.

Turns out, the croc-thing had a similar trick. It opened its mouth. The tongue shot out like it was spring-loaded, and I barely got out of the way. The slinger goblin wasn't so lucky. The tongue had a knobby bit on the end, and it impacted the goblin's forehead with a *crack* like an egg against a frying pan.

<Your tribe has decreased to 68 members.>

The goblin dropped below the water with a splash as the croc roared.

Luckily, the wasps switched to the bigger, louder target. They swooped down on the snarling bog monster with the *hiss* and *pop* of discharging voltage. That just made the thing angrier, and it thrashed about with tail and webbed claws while I made my escape with the remaining slinger goblin, who would win no badges for marksmanship. I got stung/shocked twice more before I reached the bank of the bog and stumbled onto sort of dry ground. I gasped, fur dripping.

Chuck helped to stand, though I was shaky on my prosthetics since my butt was still numb. "You had enough, boss?"

"Not nearly," I said. I looked over my shoulder as the bog monster retreated beneath the water. "This place is *awesome*!"

CHAPTER 31

READING MATERIAL

Back at the village, I started looking through the volumes that Rufus had left. The first was the iron harvesting and smelting guide. From its descriptions, it sounded like the bog we'd found would likely have unharvested iron deposits. But then, the book also said that the iron was fermented by the presence of "good humours" in the water. I had to remind myself that this primitive world might have people in it who didn't know what they were talking about. Then again, maybe in this world that *was* how iron formed. Still, I would need to get some goblins down there and figure out how to get the iron. The good news was that, thanks to the river feeding fresh iron into the bog, iron was a renewable resource. The bad news was that it took about a generation to restore. And a human generation was about a hundred times longer than a goblin generation, judging by the average lifespan of creatures who willingly flung themselves off cliffs. Once we'd harvested all the iron and fired it into steel, we'd have to find a new source.

I needed steel. It was a necessity for internal combustion, for space flight, for rocketry, and though I hated admitting we would need them, for firearms. At least, if I wanted the goblins to be properly equipped against larger-scale threats in Lanclova like the javeline and, ultimately, the ones who had sent the pig-men to collect ears and tongues. We still needed to do something about predators and nuisances in the bog. The croc-knockers were nigh-insurmountable problems for a species whose technology did not yet include things like *nets* or *helmets that weren't other creatures' skulls.*

The bestiary was, if anything, even more unscientific than the iron guide. At least, I hoped it was. It depicted four different species of dragon, six hostile wild cats, several creatures from Greek mythology I'd learned in school but which sported new names, and only a rumor on night haunts as "local lore of a predatory, amber-eyed bird." It did mention the croc-knocker, the river monster, the javeline, and the stone sloths.

Of goblins, it simply said "Inedible and primitive. Best avoided."

We were barely a footnote. It didn't even mention our tongues or ears, which meant this publication must have predated the dubious discovery of snorting goblin ears to raise elven banners. Or maybe those were just as unscientific as they sounded—this world's equivalent to rhino horn and ginseng.

In the late afternoon, I spent time helping Sally design a snare for the wranglers. It was basically a hollowed-out wooden pole with a loop of cord, similar to what you'd see a dog catcher use in an old-timey cartoon. But enough of them looped around the throat of a night haunt should let the wranglers bring it down and finish it. After sawing a pole in half, we scraped out a hollow and fed the loop of cord through. Then we sealed the pole back together with resin and more cordage.

<Goblin Technology Unlocked: Hollow Sticky-Stringy Snatcher>
<Goblin Component Technology Unlocked: Hollow-Stickies>
<Goblin Component Technology Unlocked: Stringy Snares>

A few minutes later, Chuck rode up the lift and jogged over, eyes wide. I held the prototype out for him, and he admired it, working the loop. I'd designed it with notches in the back and knots in the cordage, so that the loop could be pulled taut and set with the notches.

"Fantastic, boss! This'll make roundin' up more rides a breeze. Might even get one or two o' those meat pens occupied."

"That's not all they're for," I said. I measured out the pole. It was half as long as a hobgoblin. "Long enough to keep away from a night haunt's claws, yeah?"

Chuck grinned, bouncing on the balls of his feet. "Tonight's the night, then?"

"Make sure each of your wranglers has one ready."

"Got it, boss!"

I wanted to make sure every wrangler had these tonight. We needed more night haunt hides for gliders. Especially since I'd crashed the first one.

Just then, Neil came back to the village with dire news.

"Fish at the bank ain't bitin'," he said. He held up the meager catch the fishermen had managed to take—which might feed a dozen goblins. On a day when half the hunters had been sent to retrieve javeline supplies and sulfur, that was hugely worrying. Not only that, but I'd lost five goblins to attrition already, bringing the tribe's total back down to seventy-one.

"We might have overfished the river," I said.

"Still fish," said Neil. "Just deeper."

Hmm . . . That wasn't an impossible challenge. The solution was simple, really: boating. I should have created boats for the goblins right after I made fishing poles and lures. The fact that we, as a civilization, had invented gliders before boats would have been unheard of on Earth. But since goblins had no recourse against aquatic predators, I had wanted them safely on land. And since goblin bodies had very little mass, despite their oversized heads, it made them ideal pilots for unpowered flight. Especially since their fall immunity meant they wouldn't even need a parachute to bail out. But gliders weren't going to keep a growing population fed. Fish was a staple until we could get livestock. To get livestock, I needed more wranglers. I already had Buzz's crew building simple fenced paddocks at the base of the bluff for the wranglers to use, but so far they just contained some cliffords (who couldn't climb or abide heights, according to Chuck), while the stone sloth cub still had its enclosure at the top of the bluff when the wranglers weren't carrying it around and coddling it with bits of cooked meat.

"Alright. Bring me Sally."

Neil motioned to one of his fishers, who bounded off in the direction of the engineering division.

I sat down to sketch out some designs on bark. By the time Sally came by, I had two designs for platform boats with pontoons that would allow goblins to get to deeper water and be stable enough for several of them to fish off of. I also had an addition to one of the glider designs that got Sally extremely excited.

"Split your team, half and half. These are the priorities," I said.

Sally took the drawings of the boat and pointed down and to the north. I nodded. "Yes, we'll have to assemble these by the river. I'll go down in the morning to do this personally. You work on these gliders. I want two of them ready to launch as soon as we have wing material. Do we have enough ceramic parts?"

Sally nodded enthusiastically, so I sent her off to decide which of her team would accompany me in the morning. We'd take some of Buzz's construction crew as well, to speed up the raw materials processing. Thinking about it, if I wanted the iron, I'd also have to have them build an outstation to keep the iron harvesters safe during the night. The bog was far enough away that goblins couldn't reasonably traverse the distance, work, and return home by nightfall. They also needed a way to deal with the predators *in* the bog. The high-level croc-knocker would probably devour goblins by the dozen if left unchecked.

Speaking of nightfall, it was almost sunset before the rest of Neil's goblins returned with sulfur, food from the javeline stores, and canvas from their tents. The engineering crew worked tirelessly with what light remained while the hunters and wranglers enjoyed the windfall that came from having chased off the rutters.

Still, with the fishing growing more challenging and the tribe growing, I had to wonder how many more nights the tribe would go to bed with full bellies. I made sure every wrangler had a snatcher and an extra goblin who hadn't fed to stay up and assist them. Though my stomach growled and twisted at the smell of roasting fish and actual *bread*, I held off so I could stay awake, too. The night haunts were critical resources. Their ribs were even better than the stone sloth claws for framing airfoils, and I wanted to make sure we didn't end up losing half the wranglers trying to bring one down tonight.

CHAPTER 32

HAUNTED

<Your tribe has decreased to 67 members.>

Keep behind me, boss," whispered Chuck.

I could see the twin yellow eyes circling high above, nestled in the winged shadow silhouetted against Raphina's open eye. In my hands, I clutched a slinger with one of Neil's poppers nestled in the sled, hoping for all the beans that it didn't explode the instant I pulled the catch. Every goblin in the tribe had gone to sleep with dirt and moss stuffed in their ears so that the poppers and night haunt shrieks wouldn't wake them and cause another panic. Goblins woken early didn't produce more goblins, and right now a lack of variants and warm bodies was our biggest bottleneck as a tribe.

The last time I'd interrupted a night haunt during its night haunting, it had dealt me lethal damage three times, on top of killing several other goblins outright. When I thought about it, even though I couldn't gain levels, the tribe itself was still something like my health bar from some sort of video game, getting bigger as the tribe expanded. That was a very sociopathic view of the situation, but a potentially exploitable one. As much as I didn't want to be responsible for the deaths of loyal goblin followers, the fact was that I lost multiple goblins a day just due to them *being goblins.* Attrition and replacement was an in-baked element of their species' strange reproductive practices, meaning the loss of a single forest goblin was almost a trivial thing in the grand scheme of even such a small tribe. When needed, those lives were another important resource to the tribe. And just as consumable as hides, or meat, or icky-putty.

You might think it difficult to justify, and if I'm being honest, I hated thinking about my goblins in that regard. Well, let me put it in perspective. There are two kinds of astronauts: those that become astronauts doing everything by the book, following every rule to perfection, and exemplifying the ideal mentor to aspire to, and those that do whatever it takes to get what they want, letting no obstacle or shortcoming stand in their way. I was going into space without legs, so I'll let you do the calculus on which set I fall into.

"*Easy lads, 'ere he comes,*"

I squeezed my slinger tight, watching as the dark silhouette slowly spiraled down to the village. It was nearly silent on those wide wings. Its shape against the moon triggered fears rooted deep in the goblin parts of my brain. Being outside when these things were in the sky was not a survival trait for this species. Not yet, anyway.

The thing came in for a glide, finally stretching out its talons and landing upon one of the shelters with barely a whisper, despite its size. And it was a big one. Level 14, as the System labeled it. It looked around, swinging its beaked muzzle to make sure it hadn't been noticed landing on the clay roof tiles—but we were well concealed. Then it put its eye to the roof, looking for cracks and weaknesses as it shimmied around on narrow claws. Finding none, it went to the edge of the roof and found the new shelter we'd laid out.

Ten goblins slept in a dome woven from flexible branches, blessedly unaware of the predator among the village. The night haunt jumped down from the roof of the shelter and padded toward the dome. It could see the goblins sleeping inside through the loose weave, but the lattice of the shelter was too tight to get its claw through. The tips of its talons came just shy of the nearest goblin's shirt. Frustrated, it began to climb the shelter, toward one of several circular openings in the lattice wall that looked just large enough to allow a night haunt's arm and shoulder.

What the night haunt didn't realize was that the inside of the hollow was a trap of flint chips on a concave funnel. When it tried to pull its claw back out, it ran afoul of the one-way opening. It tried to pull back, then screeched in pain, and seemed to realize what had happened.

"Now!" shouted Chuck. He and the other wranglers jumped out from behind the materials stockpiles. Three goblins erupted from the bone pile with slingers of their own. Two of the "sleeping" goblins inside the dome stood up and grabbed spears concealed in the bedding.

The night haunt howled, enraged. It was smart enough to know it had been tricked, and smart enough to realize what a precarious position it found itself in. It stopped trying to free its hand as the goblins inside the dome started to thrust their spears through the lattice. But that was just a diversion.

Chuck and his wranglers moved forward with the snatcher poles, loops extended. The night haunt still had back talons that were more than sufficient to disembowel a goblin, and a muscled tail that would crack bones. It lashed back and forth, lifting one of the wranglers off his feet and tossing him careening through the bone pile.

I kept my slinger trained but held off on the release, lest the explosive go through the lattice and into the sleeping mound. I also kept my eye on the sky in case the terrified shrieks of the night haunt called any of its buddies down for the assist. It was tough to tell, but one of them might have descended some.

One of the wranglers darted forward and managed to get his loop around the back claw of the night haunt, digging in his heels and pulling against the beast. That put pressure on its trapped arm, and it shrieked and kicked, trying to pull away again. It only had one avenue of escape, and it was one I hadn't considered.

With beak and claws, the night haunt tore open the trap wide enough to get its entire body through, although not without taking a dozen small wounds from the branches and flint. Its heavy body thumped to the floor, twisting as the snatcher pole hit a fulcrum. The thing about night haunts is that they weigh substantially more than even a hobgoblin. So the one that refused to let go of the pole soon found himself airborne, flying *over* the enclosure as the pole snapped.

He never hit the ground. A second night haunt snatched the unfortunate wrangler out of the air with its back talons and disappeared over the edge of the bluff.

<Your tribe has decreased to 66 members.>

Damn! The night haunt had brought friends. Spears and snatchers turned skyward as swooping shadows swung low over the village. Chuck managed to jump and get his snatcher around the neck of a haunt, bearing it to the ground with the help of another goblin. His remaining wranglers moved in with their own snatchers as two of the regular goblins were picked up and carried off by winged shadows.

<Your tribe has decreased to 66 members.>

Not only that, but the night haunt inside the lattice dome had become enraged, and the once-safe spearmen inside were now the entire subject of its attention. It pounced, rebuffed only by the ceramic tips, and climbed up the inside of the dome to prepare for another attack.

"Gunners to the dome!" I shouted. I hefted the slinger and ran to the lattice, angling my laths to make sure the projectile went through a gap and didn't explode in my face. I pulled the catch and the laths snapped back into place, launching the jar directly above the night haunt. It burst against the roof of the dome with a *pop* right where the creature had been holding on. The night haunt lost its grip and fell directly on the sleeping pile, scattering the mound of diminutive creatures.

Other slingers thrummed, and the *pop pop* of bombs left behind an after-odor somewhere between an outhouse and the Fourth of July. Rudely awakened goblins were tossed against the inner walls of the dome by the concussions and went from zero to panic without hitting a setting in between.

As one, they scrambled for any weapons stashed inside the dome. The night haunt, maybe triggered by retreating prey, maybe more than a little concussed itself, pounced unsteadily, stumbling and crushing two goblins against the wall of the dome—not enough to kill them, but I could see their squishy goblin faces deforming through the weave as though their skulls were rubber. More yet picked up spears and cleavers.

I reached into my bag for another icky-sicky jar and stuffed it into my sled, working the lever to reset the catch. The goblins inside the dome now stood shoulder to shoulder, creating a small thicket of spears pointed at the night haunt. Shoving the end of the slinger up to the lattice, I called out again.

"*Volley two!*"

Pop, pop, pop!

<Your tribe has decreased to 63 members.>

Unfortunately, one of the slinger goblins had made the mistake I'd taken pains to avoid. His jar smashed straight into the lattice and blew up in his face, sending the goblin flying and setting the lattice on fire as the thick, burning putty coated it. It splashed over one of the unfortunate spearmen in the dome, as well, who dropped his spear and panicked as his fur started to smolder.

Behind me, the night haunt the wranglers were tangling with yowled. I risked a glance to see that two of its limbs were caught and Chuck was atop it, driving a spear down into its back. A lot of its blood was on the ground, and the wranglers on the snatchers were pulling as hard as they could to make sure it couldn't find any purchase to fight back.

More of the cage started to burn, and I whistled for attention from all the goblins not already fighting the howler with the wranglers.

"To me!" I shouted. I still had ten panicking goblins in a structure that was now at risk of burning down. I put my back against the dome, gripped the lattice, and lifted as hard as I could. Prosthetic legs aren't really built for lifting heavy loads, though, and they started to slip out from under me. Luckily, the rest of the goblins rushed to my side and combined what meager muscles they had to hoist up one edge of the shelter high enough for the goblins inside to scramble out.

Within a few moments, all that was left inside were two goblins with spears and the night haunt, who saw the small opening we'd made. It darted toward the lifted wall and I made the decision.

"Drop it!" I shouted.

The edge of the shelter thumped back into the dirt just as the night haunt's front claws raked at the base, scrabbling to get under and get out. Several goblins thrust spears through, dissuading the beast, who finally turned, coughing and sputtering from smoke, and dashed toward a different side. The goblins raced around the outside perimeter to continue keeping it away from the walls, and the wranglers joined in as well with longer spears.

Finally, the night haunt abandoned its goal and turned its attention to the two goblins still trapped with it. I turned away as it pounced, intent on getting its last meal before the execution. Even while choking and dying from the smoke and the myriad small wounds inflicted by the spearpoints the goblins were thrusting back through the lattice, it persisted. They are nothing if not spiteful creatures, it seems.

<Your tribe has decreased to 61 members.>

CHAPTER 33

DEEPER WATERS

<2 Hobgoblin Scrappers have been added to your tribe.>
<1 Hobgoblin Wrangler has been added to your tribe.>
<1 Goblin Taskmaster has been added to your tribe.>
<Your tribe has increased to 75 members.>

I could still smell the smoke when I woke up. The survivors of the night before had tucked in immediately to devour the night haunt, and we seemed to have avoided the lethargic stupor that came with not getting enough sleep. Good. I couldn't afford to waste a single day.

Luckily, I seemed to have gotten a good roll on the new goblin births overnight. Thirteen new goblins off of five sleeping mounds was, as far as I could tell, near the max possible. That was good. We needed a real win after the previous night's quite literal Pyrrhic victory. I also decided to stop considering the question of goblin reproduction as a scientific one, and start thinking of it like an engineering one. That is to say, it was fine that I didn't know how it functioned as long as it continued to do so.

Buzz was up early, as was his usual habit. His crew was clearing away the remains of the cage and hauling the second dead night haunt over to the tannery to be processed. He waved me down, and I headed over. His entire crew were now wearing gloves, which they'd stitched from leftover small hides the hunters had brought back.

"Didn't go quite as planned, eh, boss?"

I looked at the ash trails. "Not quite. But your trap worked great. Think you can rig up another?"

Buzz pulled a scrap of bark from his pouch with a nub of wrapped charcoal in it. "Have one done by nightfall with six o' the lads bangin' it out."

"Good, I'm going to get a few more under your team. I want that other project started today as well. Like I showed you in the book."

Buzz nodded excitedly. "The lads are on it, boss. Trust. Be up to your specs. Other priorities?"

We were interrupted by a loud *whoosh* accompanied by a scream. I looked over at the spiraling smoke trail and the goblin who was almost managing to hold on to his booster.

"Houston, successful stage-one separation," I said as the goblin lost his grip and fell somewhere in the forest to the west. "That one wasted no time. I need to invent locks so we can lock up the sulfur."

"Sounds like a Sally job. Wot about my boys?"

"Fuel," I said.

Buzz's eyes slid over to the scat mound.

"*Fire* fuel. I want to run up the kiln again soon. We're going to need a few things in order to start getting iron out of that bog."

"Chuck wants more space on the west side for his cliffies. We'll pull timber from there."

I slapped Buzz on his shoulder. He dashed off to relay the news to his crew. While he did that, I pulled up the System menu and assigned half the fresh goblins to his team and half to Neil's hunters. Sally's team suffered the fewest casualties, since they rarely left the bluff, so I kept her with the same roster. Though they did have a tendency for projects to explode in their faces. On second thought, I gave her one extra.

The new taskmaster found me while I was sifting through the new arrivals to see which were best suited for which teams. She dashed up, skidded to a halt, and stood rigid like a soldier.

"*Sir!* Ready and able to tackle any and all challenges!"

I'd already looked at her skills in the System, so I knew what she was good at. I dismissed the window and looked at my newest taskmaster.

"Eileen. You ready to fly a test flight?"

Eileen practically vibrated with anticipation. She had high stats for agility, perception, and mechanical operation—which was a trait I hadn't yet seen. It must have been a side benefit of starting to unlock various simple machines on the Goblin Tech Tree. So, any goblins I put under her should get a bonus to operating machines as well. "Always, sir!"

I pushed off my chair and folded my hands behind the small of my back, strutting like a general. "I'm putting you in charge of the tribe's air delivery wing. Assemble your crew and report to the east launcher at midday. Until then, help Sally with her preparations. She'll brief you on the plan." I stopped pacing and considered what I'd just said. Was Sally more talkative around the other taskmasters? If not, the brief would be *very* brief.

Eileen saluted and dashed off.

I'd have loved to stay and help with that project, but I had boats to build. Neil had all his hunters staged on the north side of the bluff with sets of tools, in addition to their usual assortment of slingers, spears, and cleavers. Two of his group also hoisted one of the ceramic impellers that we used to force air through the furnace.

Everyone threw themselves down the slope except for the ones lugging ceramics, which I made sure took the lift down, so they didn't shatter the implements before we even got to the river. I still wasn't keen on the vertical approach to travel. I took two of Sally's engineers and two of Buzz's builders over and loaded into the flex-a-pult with a handful of the rare mini-gliders to start prepping everything we needed.

Neil's hunters split off to look for game, but he accompanied me to the river with the fishers. The goblins buzz-cut their way through, crisscrossing previous trails until we hit the bank of the river. It still mesmerized me how the goblins moved more like a rolling wave than a group of individual creatures, tumbling over one another and crashing against obstacles until they were battered or bitten out of the way. The area northeast of the bluff toward the old stone sloth den and clay deposit had been crosscut so many times it looked a bit like a checkerboard. It was, by far, our most trafficked area outside of the bluff itself.

We came to a slow bend in the river where a few of Buzz's goblins were already cutting logs to size and Sally's engineers were weaving cordage from vines. Some of the fishers went to trawl the banks for small shellfish and large bugs while I set the rest to task shaping structural poles into a platform and lashing them together. We started to make a shallow draft boat according to my sketches, with a pair of pontoons to hopefully keep it stable enough that excitable goblins wouldn't capsize the whole thing at the earliest opportunity. The space between the wood was packed with pitch and chewed bark on the outside, while the inside got another layer of sap and then the canvas from one of the javeline tents. I had another pole mounted on bearings, to which I added the impeller and crank assembly near the back. And on the forward end of the boat, I added a second column, with a long crossbeam and ceramic winch assembly to pull a flexible pole under load, and secured it with the crossbeam.

I looked up at the sun slipping toward the edge of Raphina. "We're losing daylight," I said.

"Best fishing time," said Neil. "Trust."

The javeline rations (and the javeline themselves) had been a nice one-time windfall, but I had to make sure I could keep the tribe fed when the night haunt haunches ran out—which they would. I had left them smoking over the coals with some salt, but they'd last the tribe two, three days at max. And my hope was now that we'd killed two of them, the rest would be more reluctant to attack the village.

Just as the sun slipped behind Raphina, we carried the boat to the water and pushed it down the muddy bank into the river bend.

<Goblin Technology Unlocked: Sticky-Skinny Boats>
<Goblin Component Technology Unlocked: Wet-Jet Steering>
<Goblin Component Technology Unlocked: Basic Hydro-Planes>
<Goblin Component Technology Unlocked: Sticky Water-Slappers>
<Goblin Component Technology Unlocked: Basic Nautics>

It sank immediately.

"Well, that's disappointing," I said, watching the bubbles rise to the surface. With all the time I'd spent on the water, I thought I'd be better at building a decent boat. At least the technology had been unlocked. I sent two goblins wading into the shallows to retrieve the ceramic parts we couldn't easily replace.

It took us a couple of extra hours (losing the eclipse in the process) to rig up a second one, with Sally's engineers making multiple adjustments. This time, when we pushed the assembled craft into the water, it wobbled, but didn't sink.

Neil's fishers looked at one another excitedly and redoubled their pushing. I had to take a running jump to make sure I actually got on board. And let me tell you, stone sloth claws are not meant for walking on the uneven surface of a wooden boat. The fact this thing was watertight at all was nothing short of a miracle of Goblin Tech Tree engineering.

Several of the goblins helped me to my feet, including Neil. Others had already set trawling lines or were rigging bait to poles. Two more clambered onto the impeller cranks that I'd set up like bikes using the javeline chains that had once bound my wrists. They started pumping away with their little legs and the water at the back of the boat churned. I had to stumble over and grab the steering ring to get them spun around to the right direction before they could ground us on the bank.

Rather than forcing air through the impeller, the goblins were forcing water. It was much less practical than a direct drive propeller, but it was smoother and caused less chop in the water, which I figured would be better for a fishing vessel and less likely to tangle in the river weeds. As soon as we got to the deepest part of the river bend, I had the goblins hop off the impeller cranks and help me kick a bundle of rocks over the side to serve as our anchor. We drifted a bit with the current, but the line drew taut and I secured it to the gunwale.

Two of the fishing teams got quick bites and pulled in their fish. Both of them needed extra help wrangling the bigger catches from the deeper part of the river onto the boat. I nodded to myself as I watched. By any measure, this wasn't an impressive vessel. It would have struggled to keep three or four humans afloat. But it easily held more than a dozen goblins. And it was just the first (sorry, *second*) prototype. I had no doubt the fishers would iterate and improve the design, as well as work on things that hadn't even occurred to me. Getting boats into the tech tree was overdue. If everything hadn't been such an emergency since I'd been reborn, this would have been much earlier on my to-do list. But it would become an emergency soon enough if I put it off any longer.

"Boss," said Neil, from the aft end of the boat. I walked over and joined him. He pointed to a shadow in the water about thirty meters back from where we trawled. It was about as long as three goblins laid head to feet, and several fish were leaping out of the water ahead of it.

River monster.

The bestiary had sketches of multiple aquatic predators. The one specific to rivers and moving waterways that preyed on humanoids was an amphibious predator that looked like a cross between a salamander and a barracuda, long and lithe with powerful jaws, a finned tail, and a set of stubby limbs. It veered away from the boat, for the time being, and Neil relaxed.

I walked up to the forecastle of the boat and kicked off a thicker line attached to a boom, baited with a special bundle that included offal so vile that even the goblins hadn't wanted to eat it. Then, I sat back to cast my pole along with the rest of the fishers for an hour or two of just casting and pulling while I listened to the river and the bugs and the birds and, for some reason, the occasional explosion. Being back on the water was almost as good as being back in the air. And really, this is what reincarnation should have been about: sailing and soaring and working on engineering projects. Not getting stabbed by pig-men and fighting for my life against beaked bat monsters. In the face of powerful predators, tenacious hunters, and sometimes just the goblins' seemingly absent sense of self-preservation, protecting not only myself but also the goblins who looked to me for leadership, seemed like a monolithic challenge.

One of Neil's fishers hooted and yanked in his pole, aided by his partner. A sizable fish flipped out of the water and smacked another fisher in the face. The three of them fell in a tangle of punches and bites and ended up tying themselves in a knot with the fishing line.

And yet, if I couldn't protect these guys, I'd never walk on the moon. Even if I hadn't grown attached, they would still be worth every squawk, squabble, and scrap. The goblin side of me, of course, just wondered if it could somehow sneak the fish out of the tangle while the rest were distracted.

The sound of cliffords barking drew my attention to the riverbank. Chuck and a few of his wranglers bounded through the trees, pulling up just shy of the water. He stood up in the saddle and shaded his eyes. "Bossman, you over there?"

I put my foot on the gunwale and cupped my hands. "Yeah, I'm here!"

"Sally says she's almost ready. Wanted me to come bring you back."

I whistled and pointed to the impeller cranks. Two of the goblins not currently casting bounded over, clambered up on the assembly, and began pumping. A few others helped me reel in the anchor. We started to move, and I twisted the ring to get the impeller pushing us toward the bank.

"Boss, this one's stuck," said Neil, from over by the bow.

I looked over as he tugged on the line. "Careful with that one, it's loaded to the . . ."

The line thrashed in the water, nearly pulling Neil overboard. Two goblins dove over and grabbed his feet, keeping him from dropping into the drink as the boat dipped toward the bow.

The thick cord drew a perfect line to a dark shadow writhing beneath the surface.

The river monster had returned.

CHAPTER 34

FLEXIBLE FISHING

The impeller came completely out of the water, goblins tumbling off the crank assembly and rolling toward the bow. Several goblins hoisted spears and ran to the front of the ship. But that just made the list worse as we started to move on the line.

"No, no! To the stern! *The stern!*" I shouted.

Some stayed to throw spears at the thrashing shadow in the water. But enough listened to my orders that we got the back of the trawler down in the water and I started working the impeller myself, cranking as hard as my little goblin legs could pump. Neil joined me, pumping his legs and panting so hard his tongue lolled out the side of his mouth. I reached out and turned the ring with one foot, angling the vector of thrust to keep us steady in the water.

The river monster pulled against the line, and wood creaked. My feet splashed in the bilges from where the bow had dipped so low it started to let water in.

"Boss!" shouted Chuck from the shore, pacing his clifford back and forth. "I think you got somethin'!"

"*Ya think?*" I muttered. Another goblin came up, and I traded places with him and stumbled my way to the bow. In the water, the river monster had swallowed the offal bait, helpless to resist the siren song of javeline tripe. It gnawed and clawed at the line. But I still hadn't forgiven it for the goblin it had dragged off our first fishing day. I locked eyes with it as I gripped the lever built into the forward assembly and yanked.

The retaining bar on the flex-a-pult built into the bow of the ship slipped out of its bracket, and the pole under tension snapped taut, yanking the river beast out in a perfect parabolic arc. It soared above the staring goblins and had just enough line to strike the rocks on the shore. *Hard.*

Angular momentum is a harsh mistress. The back two-thirds of the river monster turned to instant puree with a sound like a gunshot, splashing fish guts over everything within five meters—which included the wranglers and their cliffords. The dogs leapt back, yelping in surprise and fear at the noise and sudden movement. And then leapt *forward* as they realized lunch was served. The wranglers tried to rein them in, but eventually they just dismounted and joined in eating before the dogs ate all the best bits.

The front third of the river monster still gripped the offal bait with teeth and claws. It had held on better than the goblin rocket jockey from earlier that morning. I looked at the shocked expression on its fishy face—which, I suppose I'd be surprised too, if I'd suddenly accelerated at twenty-plus G's and come to a terminal stop.

Wait . . . ugh. I couldn't believe I was commiserating with one-third of a fish.

"Wicked," said Neil, surveying the damage as the boat drew closer to shore. "Lunch is on, lads!" he shouted. "Truss some up to take back!

The goblins all abandoned the boat in a frenzy of blue fur and flashing teeth, reducing the few recognizable parts of the salamander in a few minutes, stuffing their faces with some and wrapping the rest in leaves and stowing it in baskets for the evening meal.

I watched the carnage, shaking my head. "They'll be useless all afternoon," I said.

"Waste not," said Neil. Not one to mince words, but one for minced meat. I clambered up on Chuck's clifford, which only growled at me this time. Chuck finished chewing what I think was half a liver and swung back up into the saddle. He offered me . . . I'm not up on my fish organs. But my stomach growled. I sighed and took it. When in Lanclova.

We wheeled around and bounded south, back toward the bluff. I heard another *shwoosh . . . POP!* and looked up to see a starburst in the sky at the end of a spiraling rocket trail. I wondered if this goblin had remembered to let go.

<Your tribe has decreased to 74 members.>

Guess not.

I shook my head. Definitely needed access control on the sulfur. With how much the goblins enjoyed a free launch, I felt like about two thirds of the tribe would willingly go full Major Kong and ride a rocket all the way to the big goblin graveyard in the sky. Then again, with what I had planned for the rest of the day . . . well, maybe I was the one that ought to be worried.

We reached the bluff just as a net full of bricks was going up the lift. Chuck ground to a halt so suddenly I tumbled over him and my leg caught in the netting. Chuck leapt from the back of the clifford and latched onto the net next to me.

"You're not slated to go on this run," I said, confused.

He barked a laugh. "You think I'm going to let you out of my sight on this thing? I'm launching right after you. Besides, you owe me a glider."

"That I do!" I gave him an upside-down salute as the goblin counterweights passed me headed in the other direction. Truth told, I was glad for his presence. Of all the verbal goblins, Chuck was the one I trusted the most. The hobgoblin was capable, clever, and hard-working. His crew had rescued me, brought down a night haunt on their own, and now he would be watching my back. Once up, I waited for the minders to hook the load and pull us over onto the bluff before dusting myself off.

Most of the tribe still on the bluff was gathered around the eastern cliff, where I'd launched the glider from the greased rails to go explore the other bluffs. Sally had the prototype heavy glider mounted up, and Eileen waved at me from the front where she was strapped in. Six of Sally's engineers were attaching long wooden tubes to the underside of the glider just outside the rails.

"Just in time, boss! You want to take the reins for this one?" asked Eileen. She'd adopted a skull mask of just the orbital bones and a rough hide cap, which made the bones look a lot like a pair of old-timey flight goggles without the lenses.

"Nope!" I said. I moved over and climbed to the netting on the glider. "I need to make sure you can function without my micromanagement. I'm just here for the in-flight movie."

"Good, I'd have fought you."

"You'd have fought your king?"

"And won!" She reached over and grabbed a pair of semaphore flags. "Preflight checks!" she shouted. Her crew assembled and took their places as she hoisted flags and watched their responses. Satisfied, she called out, "Passengers aboard!"

Almost a dozen goblins climbed aboard, including one of the two new scrappers. Each of the goblins had a basket strapped to their back. I joined and fixed myself in place with the available cord.

"Safety disengaged!" Eileen shouted.

I looked around for Sally. "You included a safety?" I asked.

She lifted one hand and wiggled it about. *Sort of.* One of her goblins unhooked a rope from the rear of the glider. Two more approached with hot coals. I tightened my grip on the frame. Just like the first time I'd flown, I started to feel an invisible pressure that I'd come to recognize as the System's direct attention. I wasn't sure why it was so interested in flying, as compared to hunting or fishing or whatever any of the civilized peoples of Rava were doing. But then, from what Rufus had said, no one on the planet was doing anything as interesting as experimenting with flying machines—not that he'd seen, anyway.

"Begin launch sequence! Step one!" shouted Eileen.

The two engineers held the coals to the ends of the rockets. One of them didn't get out of the way fast enough as its motor caught and blasted fire back. The goblin went up in a bright burst of glowing blue fur.

<Your tribe has decreased to 73 members.>

The other motor caught as well, and the flames became a torrent that lurched us forward. Two of the passengers lost their grip and fell off the back of the glider, which solved my concern about adding my weight to the flight. I held on for dear life as the roar mounted and we slid along the wooden rails toward the ramp, our teeth chattering from the vibration. This takeoff was going to be at a much higher speed than my first flight with the glider. The aircraft rattled so badly I thought it might come apart in the violence.

But then we were off the rails, into the afternoon sky, and still accelerating on the icky-sicky rockets.

<Goblin Technology Unlocked: Rock'em Assisted Airy-Knotics>
<Goblin Technology Unlocked: Multi-Crude Aircraft>

"What's step two?" I shouted over the rush-roar of the rockets.

"There is no step two!" Eileen shouted back.

CHAPTER 35

MULTI-CRUDE AIRCRAFT

The rocket boosters burned for several more seconds before the flames fizzled, and the two rocket pods fell away from the soaring aircraft while my ears rang. The nose started to pitch down, and Eileen raised both flags over her head. The goblin at the back of the aircraft hauled on its cords, raising the elevator until our pitch stabilized. Then, she thrust one flag out to the side, and the goblin at the end of the wing lifted its aileron. The wing dipped on that side and we established a gentle bank to the southeast. The glider was too big and too heavy for one goblin to control it alone. Eileen needed her whole crew operating the individual control surfaces that kept the aircraft aloft.

I heard the *shwoosh* roar of another launch behind us and twisted around to see a smaller glider riding up into the sky behind us. That would be Chuck. I wish we had radios to communicate with each other. But at least if we went down, he'd know exactly where to bring the rescue team. And I'd have a scrapper with me from the start. I looked at the burly hob-goblin holding on with white-knuckled fervor. She wasn't quite as solid as Armstrong, but I had no doubt she would throw herself at any threat with the same ferocity.

The rockets burned for less than a minute, but they had gotten us almost a third of the way to the bluff already. As we passed over the hot springs, three of the goblins bailed out, *EEEEeeeee*ing down to the forest canopy below. They'd be harvesting more of the sulfur that we needed for the primitive rockets.

We kept going, getting lift off the heat still rising from the pools. The bluff was coming up, and Eileen was doing a good job managing the glider's energy. I lowered my head for a closer look, and it seemed like the lizards were already swarming out of their desert holes and moving for the village. They weren't high-level, but there were a *lot* of them. With the sun behind Raphina, they were taking their opportunity to raid the village.

The village itself was in much better shape than when I'd come by in my first glider. A palisade had been erected on the southern side, and goblins stood atop in helmets made from lizard skulls, equipped with long spears and slingers. Traps and weighted pendulums dotted the rampart and the cliff face. I spotted several goblins, much bigger than the rest, moving along the wall and getting into position as the lizards hit the base of the bluff and started to climb. Armstrong waved at us as we soared overhead.

Eileen raised one of her flags, and we dipped to the left, angling over the village. All but the crew bailed out, free-falling down. Builders, engineers, and fighters for the war effort against the lizard menace—including the newest hobgoblin scrapper, who shot me a grin and a thumbs-up as she fell toward the village. I wouldn't abandon these goblins. I didn't want to abandon the bluff, either. It was an important expansion opportunity. I didn't have to be a military genius to know castles were built on high ground for a reason, and the plateaus were the highest ground short of the mountains to the northeast. Rather than evacuating, I would fortify this village, just as I'd fortified Village Apollo in my war against the night haunts—a war we might actually be winning, despite the obvious level disadvantage.

"Payload's away, boss!" shouted Eileen. "But we got another surprise for them, don't we lads!"

"Yeah?" I shouted up. "What have you got kicking?"

With most of the weight off the glider, our performance improved dramatically, and Eileen directed us in a wide loop, coming even with the side of the bluff where the lizards were starting to climb.

Eileen stowed her semaphore signals and crawled back to where I sat in the middle of the fuselage. The goblins at the wings and tail locked their control surfaces and made their way to the middle of the aircraft, where they uncovered a wicker basket full of small clay jars padded with moss and straw.

"Are those what I think they are?" I asked.

Eileen handed me one of the small pots, grinning with a mouth full of sharp teeth—so wide that I thought her head might just come right off. "Compliments of Neil, ya know? I wanted bomb fruits, but he said these would be safer, so I had the lads whip some up: bomb fruit juice mixed in with the icky-sicky. Best be quick! She won't hold steady long."

"That would explain the explosions this morning," I said. So, Neil had figured out a way to get the explosive juice from the fruits. Though, based on the number of explosions, it seemed like it was far from a sure thing. Probably why Neil was fishing when they'd tried it.

My master hunter had a keen thought, there, in mixing it with the putty. The vibration from the rocket-assisted launch would have absolutely set off a bushel full of bomb fruits, no matter what you tried to cushion them with. I briefly wondered if there was a safe method of stabilizing the juice in liquid form. But that seemed like a dangerous line of thinking, especially when goblins were prone to drinking nearly any liquid they encountered. I passed the popper to the next goblin, who passed it to the next, until we'd distributed two to the entire crew of the glider. The side of the cliff loomed, and just a few meters from us, the lizards scaled the sheer face of the plateau.

"Let 'em have it!" shouted Eileen as she reared back and hurled her icky-sicky popper. The rest of her crew followed suit, and I tossed mine as well, one after the other.

The clay jars hit the cliff face, and small explosions rippled against the surface of the stone, dislodging lizards and sending them plummeting down the side of the wall. They reached and scrabbled for purchase but found none as they disappeared below the treetops. An entire wave of the beasties came off the cliff face and fell to their deaths, and falling rocks accounted for several more. But the battle was far from won, and the glider was losing energy.

Cheering from the top of the bluff reached us as Eileen returned to the front of her glider and the rest of the crew took their positions at the control surfaces. A shadow passed over us, and I looked up as Chuck did a hairpin turn, knife-edging along the cliff wall and slashing one lizard nearly in half with his cleaver. Others snapped at him as he passed, but the wrangler was too quick to be caught. He pulled his glider out of the dive and overtook us with his lighter craft. I waved to him as he soared on ahead toward the nearest thermal.

<Your tribe has decreased to 73 members.>

Behind us, more lizards flooded up the cliff. Some were knocked away by the simple traps and hazards, but the first few had reached the spears and cleavers of the goblins and hobgoblins. The beasts seemed to be without number. But in a war of sheer numbers, I got the sense that you shouldn't bet against goblins. Not ever.

Not when there was a goblin king in town.

Ahead, Chuck abruptly deviated to the north. Eileen watched the wrangler's sudden turn and looked back at me. "Should we follow, boss?"

"Can we afford the detour?"

Eileen checked her surfaces, tested her speed by licking a finger, and gauged her altitude by tossing a pebble off the side and counting the time it took to reach the trees. "I think so."

I had the System's helpful window showing me all that information the easy way, which made me curious.

System, can Eileen not access the flight data window?

<*She has had it active throughout the duration of the flight. But she is what I believe you would call an "old-school aviator."*>

Not bad, Eileen. Trust your instruments, but back up your findings. I could respect that.

"Get after him, then. His eyes are better than ours. Let's see what he spotted."

Eileen raised her flag, and we dipped into a bank that carried us toward the mountains to the northeast. We crossed the river where we'd launched the first of our fishing fleet, and I saw the vessel back in the middle of the river, though we were too high to see the individual goblins crewing it.

We continued on, passing over thick forest with open stretches, and stopped to circle over a sun-baked patch of ground to ride a thermal up for some extra altitude before continuing on. The terrain started to rise into the foothills, and Chuck began to circle. Eileen directed our heavy glider over to the area, and I looked down.

A horde of javeline moved through the woods—at least fifty—in what must have been the main war band that sent off detachments like Rotte's group of rutters. Some of them looked up and pointed with spears or slung rocks from leather straps that fell laughably short of the aircraft. Given the general direction they were headed, it looked like there was a bluff farther east that they had their eyes on. But they'd come for us eventually. I scowled. Goblin ears and tongues, eh? Well, we'd give 'em a welcome.

"Hey, Eileen. We got any more poppers?"

She flashed her wicked grin and signaled her crew to lean us into a slow circle. I moved to the armory basket and pulled out a pair of munitions. There were still five left. The javeline watched us with wary curiosity, probably wondering if we were some sort of large bird. I wound up and hucked the first two poppers, then grabbed two more and threw them as well. Baseball was never my sport. I'd always been a rower and a runner—give me a twelve-kilometer shaded course and an EDM soundtrack at 170 beats per minute and I'll choose it over a diamond and a bat any day. But I could get the jars close. Luckily, the two situations in which *close* counts are horseshoes and, well, hand grenades.

The javeline maintained their disinterest until the first poppers exploded in their midst, shocking and scattering the pig-men. The rest fell in quick succession, wreaking havoc among the ranks as the rutters scrambled away from the danger. But I'd knocked down a few of the half-bacon bastards and they'd had no idea what happened. I could see at least two of the rutters down, and another half-dozen dazed or limping from the sharp fragments of the clay casing.

I hoped one of them was Rotte. But there was no way I'd get that lucky.

"Alright," I said, putting the cover back on the empty basket. "Let's go home."

CHAPTER 36

SUBTLE PROGRESS

<2 Hobgoblin Scrappers have been added to your tribe.>
<3 Hobgoblin Wranglers have been added to your tribe.>
<1 Goblin Taskmaster has been added to your tribe.>
<Your tribe has increased to 124 members.>

"Alright, test flight number nine. Go for launch," I said.

Sally pulled the lever to drop the rock load, and the glider shot forward on the rails. I watched it hit the ramp and then take to the air as the scrapper onboard pedaled furiously. His pedaling went to a direct drive wooden propeller at the back of the aircraft that started to spin.

For about thirty seconds, it looked like he might manage to keep it up. But the nose started to dip, and no matter how much the scrapper tried to correct, the prop just wasn't generating enough thrust to keep smooth airflow over the wings. The whole thing tipped, and the scrapper came out of his seat. Both pilot and plane plummeted to the terrain below the bluff without even reaching the tree line. I winced as the sound of the wooden frame splintering reached us on top of the plateau.

"This ain't it, boss," said Eileen, standing next to me with her hand on her chin. "We're going to need another solution if we want to save on sulfur."

I sighed. Even the scrappers weren't physically strong enough to maintain powered flight that overcame the added weight of the prop assembly. Even with the reduced gravity from Raphina directly overhead, and even launched directly into the wind, a goblin-powered aircraft just didn't seem feasible. We were going to need either gas envelopes or internal combustion to maintain powered flight. And right now, both were still out of reach due to material constraints.

Getting the lighter-than-air gas for airships was surprisingly easy. My most recently born taskmaster, Javier, had stitched a test balloon that was hovering right now—directly over the latrine. It turns out that goblin scat, in addition to making a great base for primitive rocket fuel, puts out an *insane* amount of methane that could either be trapped in an envelope to create lift or burned to create hot air. And the solution to needing more fuel was the same as the solution to most problems as a goblin king: *get more goblins*. I'd managed to stay out of trouble the past few days and enhance our progress on all fronts except this one, which had given the tribe some breathing room.

The problem with gas-envelope airships was a materials one. Even with the square-cube law on your side, you needed *a lot* of surface area for an envelope capable of lifting people—even people as small as goblins. Lizard skin would only go so far. I needed a source of canvas or other textile. Internal combustion was a more mechanically complex solution that required metal—which was on the docket anyway—as well as liquid fuel, lubricating oil, and a stable source of ignition. A simple, self-lubricating rotary engine had only a few moving parts and could take a hell of a beating. I could build one out of ceramic. But when it failed (and it *would* fail), it would do so catastrophically and most likely explosively.

I sat at the western edge of the bluff as Eileen and her team ran over to the east side to set up for the day's transfer of supplies and personnel to Village Canaveral—what I'd named the bluff beset by the lizards. There seemed to be no end to the lizards, and reinforcing the village had only brought them out in greater numbers. Even with the enhanced fortifications and a dedicated taskmaster with a militaristic skillset (John) heading up Canaveral's defenses so that I could give Armstrong some much-needed rest at Village Apollo, an end to the war was nowhere in sight. Which had, ironically, become a huge boon as I needed fewer hunters and fishers to support the tribe. The lizards were the closest thing in Rava to DoorDash. Every glider we sent to Canaveral with fresh goblins and raw materials, they returned filled with lizard meat and hides. But all the rocket-assisted launches would put a strain on our sulfur reserves.

Below, the open land had started to stretch where Buzz's timber team had cleared area for Chuck's paddocks. Rather than a single herd animal, the wranglers had brought back a hodgepodge of grazing savannah creatures and thrust them together to figure things out via spaghetti testing. Essentially, they had thrown the entire biome at the wall and were seeing what stuck in the goblin equivalent of animal husbandry. It had started to attract predators, but Chuck had let the stone sloth cub have the run of the enclosures like a sheepdog and it kept most other nasties away. It was growing incredibly quickly as well. The cub now weighed as much as a hobgoblin, and I knew it would only get bigger.

Far beyond that, iron waited for me in the peat bog, and that consumed the lion's share of my attention and planning. Metal was the answer to most of our immediate bottlenecks. But it was a long way to travel on foot. A couple hours' ride on a clifford meant at least two days' walk as the goblin bushwhacks. And goblins wouldn't—couldn't—survive on the ground at night without the safety of a bluff. So, we were going to bring the bluff with us. But that would still be a multi-day trek through dangerous terrain with heavy supplies.

I'd started inventing wheels, wagons, yokes, and even gravel roads to haul everything in preparation. Luckily, a large enough group of goblins basically carved their own freeway as a matter of course when moving from place to place. Roads were a simple matter of paving over that cleared brush with gravel from broken or discarded construction bricks. When I was going to grad school, they'd shut down one lane of the main stretch outside my apartment for six months in order to repave two miles of asphalt. Give me a dozen of Buzz's builders and I'd have had it done in three weeks.

I sat for a while, considering that iron and the threats in the bog. We'd been there all of ten minutes and encountered two major dangers—and who knew what else lurked there. I wouldn't send the iron expedition unprepared. Weapons, leather and ceramic armor, fortified building supplies, and munitions were all going. I worried that the expenditure of personnel and resources might not be worth it if the bog bounced us back as brutally as it had the first time. At least I also didn't have to worry about things falling apart in my absence.

Thanks to my supervision, the tribe was running like a well-oiled machine—or at least a stack of spinning plates kept aloft by a well-oiled stage magician. Logistics were a matter of raw materials available versus collected versus consumed, and I'd specialized in closed-loop systems in my engineering classes. My expertise was surprisingly as applicable to the primitive tribal management as it had been at NuEarth. At least until the next crisis occurred. And it seemed like goblins lived in a near-constant state of one crisis after another.

<Your tribe has decreased to 123 members.>

Case in point. The javeline and night haunts were still out there as well. I'd seen smoke rising from a bluff in the direction I'd last seen the rutters moving and had to assume they'd wiped out another tribe before I could get to them. I *needed* powered flight in order to rescue the more distant villages.

I brought up the System window and checked the rosters. Looked like Buzz had lost one of his construction crew to some sort of accident.

I dismissed the window and pulled myself to my feet. The sloth claws were holding up well, but I couldn't help looking forward to the day I'd be able to augment this design with steel springs and blades. And it was coming. I was certain of it. No pig-men or croc-knockers or lizard swarms could slow me down for long.

CHAPTER 37

FRIENDLY FIRE

A glider soaring over the grasslands spotted Rufus coming up from the south. The wranglers went to meet him on cliffords and escorted the trader to the freight elevator.

He looked around, mouth slightly agape at the differences in the village.

"It looks a bit different, I know," I said. We'd replaced all the sticky shelters with stone and adobe versions—as high as three stories tall. But Rufus fixated on the tallest building in the village.

"A bit," he said. He pointed to the square tower on the east side. "What are they doing?"

I followed his gaze to a pair of Eileen's goblins atop the tower waving hide flags. "Directing traffic," I said. After a moment, a scout glider came in to land on the narrow strip, skidding to a halt on the dirt path that passed for a landing zone. The pilot scrambled out, then went over to the pond to scrub the bugs off her face. On the launch rail, a small rocket booster ignited, sending the replacement scout craft rocketing into the air.

"So that's what I've been hearing for these two days past. I thought it was earthquakes and thunder, yet I saw no lightning and never once felt the ground quake."

"The tower was really a prototype," I said. I took Rufus to the central courtyard of our developing little city, where a ring of shaded pavilions and long tables circled the fire. This was where the tribe ate after sundown, as well as where Sally's team did most of their work during the day. Two dozen of her engineers were currently tinkering with various projects or manufacturing parts, or scribbling incomprehensible new designs. "The internal part of the tower has sleeping room for thirty goblins, and the top can be expanded for more. I wanted to try building one here to see how many bricks it would take before we made one down below. But it makes for a great air traffic control station."

"Air traffic," Rufus said, and laughed. "Tabun'Quo'Horal are not going to believe this."

"Tabun' Quarrel who?" I asked.

Rufus unslung his pack more delicately than I was used to seeing him treat his things. He pulled out a spool of copper wire, the bearing I'd given him, and a few other trinkets. At last, he withdrew a small brass jar and a roll of gauze. I looked at the jar. It was *capped*, with the first indication I'd had of threading on this world. "Liquor from the artificers?"

"If only," he huffed. "When I showed the City of Brass the things you gave me and described what I saw here, they insisted on sending a representative in person—so to speak—to confirm things for themselves before agreeing to any long-term trade agreements. The fact they were willing to do so speaks very loudly, Apollo. They leave their city rarely, and only at great risk to themselves."

"When should I expect this representative?" I asked.

By way of answer, Rufus unscrewed the stopper on the brass jar. At first, nothing happened. Then, tendrils of pale blue flame began to creep through its neck. The tendrils felt around as I watched, fascinated. They lit upon the gauze. But, instead of singeing the sheer cloth, as I expected them to do, the wraps billowed and the bottle rattled as fire flowed out of it and the wraps assumed the loose shape of a humanoid half my own height, which stood up on the table and bowed to me.

"*Good king*," it said. Its voice sounded like the whisper of wind through the forest. "*We are Tabun' Quo'Horal of The City. It is our honor to meet you.*"

"You're kidding," I said, looking between the badger-kin and the new arrival. "The artificers are magic lamp *djinn*?"

<*Technically Ifrit.*>

What's the difference? Still, no wonder they were so reluctant to travel out of their city. If they traveled in bottles, practically anyone could promise to take an Ifrit one place and then move them somewhere else altogether. If there was value in goblin ears and tongues, a creature of living flame must have demanded a pretty penny indeed.

"*We are familiar with this word*," said Tabun. "*Djinn. It is a crude, reductive term. We dislike it. Almost as much as we dislike when the newcomers term us demons.*"

"Newcomers?" I shot a look at Rufus. He caught my implication immediately. *Others like me. Sandra and Dave, maybe?*

The half-badger shook his head. "Humans, elves, and other outsiders. Lanclova was long-deemed too dangerous to explore."

I looked back to Tabun. "I see. So you're not demons or djinn. How do you call yourselves?"

"*We are Ifrit.*"

Alright fine, so there is a difference.

"Sorry about that," I said. "I meant no offense. Ifrit it is."

The Ifrit bowed again. "*Your humility honors us,*" it said. It walked across the surface of the table, toward a pair of gawking engineers who were putting together a set of ceramic gears for a winch. It touched the gearing and part of the gauze wrapping deflated. The winch began to spin in one of the goblin's hands, much to the creature's shock. It squawked and dropped the piece. The Ifrit flowed back into its wrappings.

"*Interesting application of gear ratios. This allows one of your goblins to lift something greater than his own weight, yes?*"

"That's one of the potential applications, yes, Tabun."

"*Tabun' Quo'Horal. To call us simply 'Tabun' diminishes the union of Quo and Horal, whose voice you now hear. I am acquainted with the fleshling habit of familiar brevity. If you must shorten our name, please call us Taquoho.*"

So there was more than one entity inhabiting those wraps. Made sense, really. I mean, as much as anything in this world did. Clearly these were magical creatures in some way, and this was the first hint I'd seen of magic's actual existence other than the explicit denial of it to goblins by the System that had indirectly implied its presence. Still, several fires can join to become a single blaze, right? "Sure thing. Taquoho. I'll try to remember it."

Taquoho bowed again. "*When our honored friend Rufus told us of you, we must admit we thought it some strange jest or poison of the mind. It is our great shame that we thought you so. The City has not encountered a goblin king in many years, and the last one was certainly not inclined to trade or practice artifice. This hardened silica material you've created, we believed it was some machination of the newcomers. We are glad it is not, because we greatly desire to see more of it.*"

They moved on to the next station at the tables. A pair of Sally's goblins there was assembling an impeller. Taquoho again diminished and flowed into the device. The impeller was much larger, and the Ifrit was able to squeeze the entirety of their body into it. The gadget vibrated on the table and started blowing back the loose skin of the engineer's face like he was a dog leaning its head out the window on the highway.

A voice issued from the ceramic shell, echoing in the hollow chamber. "*Fascinating. Less mechanically efficient than bellows or a fan blade, yet compact and contained. It impresses us what you have achieved with such primitive means.*" Taquoho flowed out and filled out the gauze wraps again. "*If we provide you with a schema, are you able to produce parts in your ceramic material?*"

"Hold up," I said. "Did you just possess my impeller?"

"*That is a crude, reductive description. But accurate.*"

"Can you possess larger devices?"

Taquoho stopped. I got the feeling of ephemeral eyes on me. "*It is the basis of our culture. We craft vessels that let us interact with the world in ways the True Form cannot. It is the reason many of the newcomers assume us to be demons. Ever, we seek to better our vessels. Please provide an answer to our query.*"

I'd gotten so excited so fast that I'd forgotten the Ifrit had even asked me anything. I thought back. "Yes. I can produce ceramic versions of parts you provide. How large an object could you possess?"

"*By what frame of reference?*"

I looked around at the projects Sally's engineers were currently working on and pointed to a new iteration of the goblin-powered propeller. I pointed to it. "Could you move something like that?"

The Ifrit leaned over, peering at the assembly. He did his vanishing trick again, and the prop began to turn, *slowly*.

"*I'm afraid it is much too heavy and tiresome for us to move with alacrity. Perhaps a stronger union might. Pray tell, what is this device for?*"

Rufus glanced over at me. "Are you going to tell him?"

I shrugged. "Easier to show him." I stood on the table and whistled up at the tower. "Eileen! Prep the heavy!"

Taquoho filled out their gauze wraps again. "*You have a working of artifice for us to view?*" they asked, not quite hiding the excitement in their voice.

Rufus barked a laugh. "You could call it that! Bloody death trap, it is. Impressive bit of machining, though."

"Aww, don't say that, Rufus," I said. "You're coming too!"

CHAPTER 38

ON THE WING

<Your tribe has decreased to 121 members.>

The wind blew through my fur as Eileen turned us into a bank. I had to be the one to hold Taquoho's bottle with its tiny questing flame cupped in my hand against the gale. Rufus was holding on for dear life.

"This model is just a glider. But I hope to have powered versions soon using that propeller assembly you just saw."

We flew south from the village over the grasslands where thermals were plentiful. Below us, the savannah stretched, and just beyond I could see the transition into a red, sandy desert. Could I make out a faint glimmer on the horizon? Was that the city of Ifrit or just a mirage?

"*How curious. How does it fly when its wings are stationary? What mechanism keeps this skycraft aloft? Goblins cannot use magic.*"

"Aerodynamics," I said. I pointed to the wings. "It's all about airflow over that surface creating a negative pressure area above the wing, which pulls the glider upward against gravity. The more air over the wing, the more lift. Right now, the only way we can get airspeed is by trading altitude. That's why powered flight is so effective."

"*We are not familiar with this natural philosophy. And it is controlled by pushing and pulling on those cords?*"

I nodded. "Raising the aileron puts us in a bank, changing the thrust vector of the lifting surface."

"I'm going to pretend I understand all this!" said Rufus. "In hopes that understanding it will make it less terrifying!"

I laughed. "Believe it or not, there are places where flying is one of the safest forms of travel."

"And how many gliders have crashed as a result of your attempts in Rava?" he asked.

I grit my teeth. That question depended on whether he meant the refined glider attempts, or the small single-goblin hanging gliders that were more like jumping off a cliff with an umbrella than soaring. But I doubted he'd like the answer either way.

"If you're so frightened of a hard landing, why did you join us?"

"Badger!"

Of course.

"*We take it your attempts to harness the meager might of goblinkind were unsuccessful in this endeavor of powered flight, and you are seeking alternate means.*"

"That's right," I said. God, it was nice to talk shop to people who could follow science, even if they didn't quite understand (at least, in Rufus's case). "There are two main ways to get powered fixed-wing flight—electric motors and internal combustion engines."

"*Have you not considered clockwork?*"

"Too heavy. It's not an efficient store of potential energy in terms of strength-to-weight ratio for flight. No. I could make a basic internal combustion engine with more metal and a fuel source. But I could also make a basic electric motor with the magnets and copper wire you sent with Rufus. Except, I'd also need a battery to power an electric motor."

"*It harnesses the elemental primal of linear lightning to spin a shaft? How curious. I can conceive of numerous applications.*"

Sounded reductive and crude. But of course, I didn't say that. "Close enough. Batteries are chemical and mechanical in nature. I know of several types, and how to build battery cells. But I have no way of finding the chemicals in question without an online order—erm, without a chemist. That would be lithium, nickel-cadmium, or lead and copper and an electrolyte like . . ."

I trailed off. *Sulfuric acid.* This whole time, I'd had a viable electrolyte in the sodium- and sulfur-rich water at the hot springs. My heart began to beat faster. Rechargeable batteries were in sight if I could secure more lead and copper. That meant electricity. Probably not enough voltage to get us to another bluff without the battery being too heavy for an aircraft to lift, but it was a start to an idea.

Taquoho had gotten more comfortable on the flight, and their questing tendril stretched downward. I lowered the jar, and they began to flow out of the jar and into the glider.

<Goblin Technology Unlocked: Pilot Flames>
<Goblin Technology Unlocked: Fly-by-Fire Controls>

Really? Back-to-back puns? They're not even a goblin.

"*We can feel it. The air, the . . . lift. It is exhilarating. This new type of body fascinates us. So few moving parts, and yet such freedom of movement. The Spirit is querying—it has offered us new skills.*"

New type of body? Huh. I guess for an Ifrit, it sort of was. I could see why primitive humans would consider them demons bewitching objects and devices. The glider shuddered and rocked gently from side to side as the flight control surfaces began to work on their own. Eileen started hurling abuse and threats at her crew, but I raised a hand to her.

"Let them cook," I said. She calmed down, and her crew backed off their control surfaces.

In a few moments, Taquoho infused the entirety of the glider. They may not have been strong enough to spin a heavy propeller at speed, but they could certainly move ailerons and elevators. They brought us into a gentle bank, entering a thermal. The upward momentum pushed me down against the frame as we rose in a slow, wide loiter. It seemed Ifrit, with their inclination to inhabit mechanical devices, were natural pilots. Pale blue flame trailed behind the craft at wingtips and tail.

Rufus was squeezing his crossbar so hard I thought the wood might shatter under his claws. Eileen looked more snubbed. She was the flight captain, after all, and she'd just turned her machine over to a lamp flame.

We flew for almost ten minutes before I heard Taquoho's voice again.

"*We tire.*"

I signaled Eileen, who pretended not to notice at first, feet kicked up at the fore end of her captain's station at the nose of the craft. But eventually she shot me a grudging glare and moved her crew back in place to take over the flight.

"Tired of being an airplane?" I asked.

"*Only in the sense that we require recuperation. But I do not know that we could ever tire of flight.*"

You're not the only one, I thought to myself. Every time I flew, the System focused on the endeavor to such a degree that the attention was palpable. What made it so curious about flight in particular?

Maybe it was just the strain of simulating complex flight physics. I still hadn't ruled out the possibility that this was all an elaborate computer program and that my existence was some cruel code base in an alien computer. Maybe I could crash the System by forcing it to simulate too many aircraft flying at once. If I somehow *did* do that, what would happen to me?

<Your tribe has decreased to 119 members.>

But then, the complex physics that governed every perceivable part of this world were much more complicated than aerodynamics over an airfoil. Hell, you could make a basic flight simulator to calculate lift over a wing in a few days with a decent knowledge of Python or C++. Maybe the System was simply curious. I had no idea why such a thing might spark the intrigue of a worldwide computer, but then again, I also had no idea why the System had been programmed with such a petulant sense of humor.

<You try listening to the inane babble in the head of every megalomaniac with delusions of grandeur.>

Case in point.

Hey, wait a minute.

I narrowed my eyes and waited to see if the System had anything else to add. It refrained.

Taquoho poured themselves back into the bottle in my lap while Eileen and her crew resumed their positions.

<Your tribe has decreased to 115 members.>

What the hell?

"Back to, erm, the village now, I presume?" asked Rufus, hopefully.

"Yeah," I said reluctantly. I was losing goblins with the sun still out, so it would probably be smart to make sure they weren't getting into trouble. Within a few minutes, we were off the plain and back to the forest with Village Apollo in sight. They already had the dinner's cookfires going. I could smell the smoke drifting on the air.

Then I heard the *pop, pop* of explosions, and I realized it wasn't cookfires I smelled. It was *fire* fires. Several of the thatch roofs were burning, and I could see a flurry of activity on the northern wall.

"Eileen, bring us around to the north," I said.

Eileen dipped the aircraft around, taking us in a wide circle around the bluff. As we got to the north side, the scene at the wall came into view. A small army of eight or twelve javeline was at the brick wall with pikes, torches, heavy hammers, and crossbows. These ones weren't bare-chested and garbed for scouting like the rutters. These had armor across their shoulders, torsos, and flanks that looked to be working moderately well against even the ceramic tips, and more than a few chipped spears and cleavers were being swung down or waved about. They were more like, I don't know, *maulers.*

<Your tribe has decreased to 112 members.>

The maulers managed to pull down a few of the wall's defenders with long, hooked polearms, which accounted for the deaths. But with forty-some-odd goblins on the ramparts hurling stones, grenades, and abuse down at them, they were having trouble getting close enough to hammer down the wall. In the forest below, I caught flashes of red among the trees as Chuck and his wranglers harried them from behind with slingers and thrown spears. It was a difficult position for the javeline, but they were tough, hardy creatures, and difficult to deter.

What finally broke them was the sight of the aircraft, and its silhouette casting a large shadow over their formation. Some of them pointed skyward with weapons or fingers, and a pair of bolts punched up through the left wing from javeline crossbows. Yikes. I held Taquoho's bottle close so as not to drop it as Eileen maneuvered.

With our appearance, the javeline maulers made themselves scarce. Maybe they remembered us dropping bomblets on them from the previous flight. They withdrew down the steep slope on the north side of the village, leaving two of their own number dead on the slope.

We'd won the battle. But it didn't feel like a victory. In fact, I felt more vulnerable than ever. Eileen brought us around and into the wind. We set down on the cleared and level landing strip, and I jumped out, shouting for Armstrong.

My scrapper taskmaster, Armstrong, appeared, with a cut above his right eye and, despite everything, a grin on his face.

"What happened?" I asked.

"Ah, well, ye know," he said, working his shoulders. "Bit o' a scrap, boss. Nothing we can't handle."

"Yeah? And what if they come back at night?"

Armstrong had nothing to say to that.

"Neil!" I shouted.

The leader of the hunters stepped out of the crowd. He was cleaning his cleavers. "Boss?"

"Take every bomb fruit we have. Bury them on the northern slope. Before nightfall. If those armored javeline come back, I want to introduce pork rinds to the ionosphere."

A wide, excited grin spread across his face. "Trust."

"Good. Buzz, Sally!"

My OG taskmasters appeared.

"Wall, thicker and higher. I want a trench in front of it, and I want some scaled-up slingers on top of it, something that can launch a sled full of rocks."

Buzz glanced at Sally and then back at me. "She's already drawn up plans for it while we was scrapping. Tribe Apollo is onnit, boss. We know what to do."

"Good," I said. I looked around. Despite the deaths and the chaos, the village wasn't in a state of panic. Just me, really. My lieutenants gathered around me were calm—at least, calm for goblins. It struck me, then, that they really did know what to do. I'd set this village up to function without my direct intervention. If I'd been ten minutes later flying back, maybe those javeline would be inside the wall, and maybe they'd still be getting shoved off by Armstrong's boys. But I was in danger of becoming the very type of micromanaging supervisor dreaded by the engineers at NuEarth. "Very good. Carry on, then. I've got some negotiations to return to. I trust you all to do what needs doing."

And I did. I think my taskmasters picked up on that, because they left with chests just a little bit puffier than when they'd arrived.

CHAPTER 39

BODIES OF BRASS

"*A most unfortunate situation, King Apollo. We detest and dislike the javeline almost as much as we detest and dislike the newcomers. I am pleased to see that your town was not overrun.*"

Town. I looked around the central common area, at the buildings rising from the bluff. I guess with all the wooden and adobe construction with clay roofing tiles, it was starting to look less like a primitive village and more like a town. The goblin-powered cranes only added to that aesthetic with the ongoing construction efforts. There was also a chance Taquoho was playing to my ego. In which case, it was working.

"Thanks," I said. "I'm sorry you got caught up in the middle of that. I know you took a risk in coming here."

"*A risk well worth it*," the Ifrit insisted, bowing in their gauze wraps. "*Our friend Rufus did not exaggerate the marvels he beheld. This . . . aerodynamics. This rocketry. Your ceramic components. Your flying bodies. We are joyed to have found one with such a love for natural philosophies and artifice. The City will be joyed. There is much to gain from friendship.*"

"Not least of all, new friends," I said.

The Ifrit seemed to burn just a little brighter.

Rufus uncorked his bottle and opened his journal. "I'll drink to that. Shall we get down to brass tacks? Emotional gain from friends is all well and good, but I believe there's also much to gain, *monetarily*, from trade."

"*Yes, we forget ourselves*," said Taquoho. "*We were sent to evaluate the truth of your production and have seen it—and much more—for ourselves. It is not mere trinkets and bearings you can offer, but these flying bodies, this icky-sicky fuel which burns fast and hot. And your work area and tools and materials. It would be wise for our people to use them here.*"

Rufus nearly choked on his bottle.

"I . . ." I started. I glanced over at the badger. "You . . . want to move some of the Ifrit to Village Apollo?"

The Ifrit waved their stubby arms in what it must have thought was a calming gesture. "*On a temporary basis, only, I assure you. To ensure parts and components are produced to specification and perhaps to negotiate for winged bodies. Once we inform our king of what we have seen here, we are sure they will agree. We will account for our own sustenance and require only minimal space. In return, as fair rents, we can offer more than simple wire and lodestones. We can offer zinc, brass, piping, cog-work, springs, clockwork bodies, time-keepers, and bells. We can also provide goods from the newcomers at the southern shore, who we find not as detestable as others, and who we have brokered with on occasion through our friend Rufus.*"

I glanced at Rufus, who nodded enthusiastically. And I could think of a million uses for all of that stuff. Brass had its limits as a metal—it was useless for things like spears and knives, what with its softness. But pipes, springs, gears? Ho boy. We were talking about some pretty advanced mechanical possibilities. Plumbing, steam boilers, turbines, and more. But that wasn't what interested me most. The most intriguing part of the offer was the possibility of having the Ifrit themselves take up residence in Village Apollo. It would give The City a vested interest in the security of Village Apollo. But that wasn't all. These were beings that could possess and manipulate mechanical objects in a completely alien method without adding weight or drag. They could analyze and manipulate devices from the inside.

You know what else could do that? Computers and complex wiring through servos, solenoids, and hydraulics. The Ifrit were walking, talking ghosts in the machine. And I wanted to get every single one of them so hooked on goblin engineering that they never wanted to leave.

"I think we can support an arrangement like that," I said carefully.

"*We are pleased. But we are also tired from our journey and our learning of the flight body. I will trust our friend Rufus to compile the fine details of your prospective arrangement with our King of The City.*"

"Sleep well," I said. I uncapped Taquoho's bottle and held the mouth up for him.

The Ifrit emptied the gauze wraps and funneled back into the bottle. Rufus carefully folded the gauze while I threaded the cap back on the bottle and set it on the workbench, looking at the colored brass. I ran my hand through the fur on top of my head and considered.

"The more I see, the more I realize that I'm the stranger here," I said. "This place is so different than the one I come from. Things like goblins or the Ifrit or magic only exist in fiction there. The more I learn, the more isolated I realize I am."

"You have your tribe," said Rufus.

I watched a pair of goblins wrestling over a stick, which immediately broke between them, and each decided they'd rather have the half the other got. It quickly devolved into clubbing each other over the head.

"Doesn't exactly help with the weirdness. You mentioned that Taquoho traveled only at great risk. I take it that it's very rare for an Ifrit to leave the City of Brass," I said.

"Extremely rare," said Rufus. He opened his bag and replaced both bottle and gauze. "While they often welcome visitors, it is seldom that they travel beyond the safety of their walls. The insistence upon sending a representative with me—even one so low-ranking as Tabun' Quo'Horal—impresses upon me that I am perhaps caught up in affairs far beyond my station. The Ifrit are well-regarded for their wisdom and far-sight among the natives of Lanclova, if not for their physical prowess."

"So when he said their king would want to send several of them here to oversee their materials and components orders . . ."

Rufus offered a toothy grin. "I nearly fell out of my chair. I could not have known the Ifrit had records of previous goblin kings because they keep no written records. Nor how much they would become enamored over your . . . what were they called?"

"Ball bearings," I supplied.

"Yes, how much your *ball bearings* would impress them. They are not a people known for being easily impressed by others' artifice. In truth, I had thought they might find your ceramics and flying machines an interesting novelty. Not so compelling as to leave the safety of the Brass City and move several of their unions here."

"You say *union*," I said. "I'm still not sure I understand the Ifrit social-family structure."

"And it's likely you never will," said Rufus. He licked the tip of his quill and smoothed his journal pages. "Raphina has witnessed my dealings with them beneath her watchful eye for years, and I'm sure she's just as confused as you or I. If there are guiding codices or taboos in the City of Brass, they are unique to each Ifrit. What custom one union might insist upon, another might find . . ."

"Crude and reductive?" I asked.

Rufus roared with laughter. "Just so! A uniquely frustrating people. But fascinating, and earnest. As long as you learn to spot the ones with a penchant for trickery and avoid them, there's profit to be had."

"Speaking of profit. I'm wondering how you get your take in all this."

The quill began to scratch across the journal. "Simple. I'll mediate all trade between your kingdom and the king of the City of Brass. In exchange, I'll take one percent of the value of all trade in precious metals or trade goods, to be provided by the Ifrit."

"In both directions?"

"Yes. I don't know what value they will place on your ceramics or other technology. But the king is nothing if not fair. He won't cheat me because it's not in his nature, and you will not cheat me because I'm not charging you commission. Not that I think you *would*, but there is no one to hold you accountable if you reneged, you see."

"Savvy planning for a trader. What's to stop me from visiting the City of Brass on my own to broker deals?"

"High-level monsters in the badlands and the desert, mostly. Even your gliders wouldn't be safe from the sandstorms and the terrors that prowl the southern skies. The ground is even more fraught with danger if you don't know the ways. You could take a thousand goblins trying to reach the Brass City and you would lose a thousand goblins before ever you saw its walls."

I tilted my head. "How do you manage it so easily?"

"Badger," answered Rufus, as if that continued to explain everything. "But you should absolutely visit the city once you have safe means of doing so. It's a wonderful marvel. Now, what should I tell the king of the Ifrit that you would like his people to deliver when they arrive?"

"Canvas sailcloth," I said without hesitation.

"Making ships in the middle of the jungle, are we?"

"You'll see soon enough," I said. Textiles were still in short supply, and if the Ifrit were bringing a convoy, I didn't have to worry about making sure I asked for something small enough for one half-badger to transport. "And brass piping. And sealed brass casks, if they have them. Big ones." I held my arms as wide as they could go. "Plus nuts, bolts, a dozen baskets of coal."

Rufus scratched my words into the journal. "Oh, is that all?"

"Why, did I forget something?"

Rufus laughed. "Curious. I would have bet anything you would want their tiny cogs and clockworks for your artifice. You continue to confound me at each turn. Very well." He blew on the pages of his journal to dry the ink.

I stood and stretched. "Micro-engineering doesn't get me to my goals right now. I need quick, dirty solutions to technological leaps in the Goblin

Tech Tree, not refined, furnished aesthetic solutions. The Ifrit themselves may be a part of those technological leaps."

"That sounds ominous," said Rufus.

I shook my head. "I don't think they'll see it like that."

"Oh?" asked Rufus. "How will they see it?"

"As a wide menagerie of new and wondrous bodies, I hope."

Rufus stowed his journal and sighed. "I suppose I won't be staying the night this time, either."

"At least stay for dinner," I said. Across the square, the hunters were dragging the javeline that had been killed in the battle while the cooks cleaned their cleavers with greedy eyes. "Looks like pork ribs tonight."

"I suppose it would be rude to refuse. After all, it will take some weeks before I have cause to return from the coast. The Ifrit, as well, will take considerable time to consider this deal and whether they wish to send any unions to visit your tribe. You'll be on your own a good while yet."

"I'm never on my own," I said, looking out at the tribe going about their business. Never alone, but that didn't mean never lonely.

"True enough, my friend."

As Rufus tucked into his meal, I considered the possibilities the deal with the Ifrit might bring. Parts, sure. Allies? One could hope. Their ability to function as a replacement for electric control systems on devices with moving parts might be a key element to actually reaching the moon. But also the possibility for more like-minded people, deeply interested in science and technology. Even if they were some sort of fire elemental spirit. I just hoped I could get them as excited about the prospect of visiting Raphina as I was.

CHAPTER 40

CARAVAN

<1 Hobgoblin Scrapper has been added to your tribe.>
<2 Hobgoblin Wranglers have been added to your tribe.>
<Your tribe has increased to 133 members.>

I walked the north wall, surveying the upgraded fortifications following the javeline attack. Sally already had two of the scaled-up slingers on heightened mounts provided by Buzz. What was more, I saw several rockets as well, angled down toward the slope on bearings. The work crews were already digging the trench at the base of the wall by the time I woke up, and they'd made a decent bite in the terrain. It would be a multi-day effort—made worse by the fact I was taking half of Buzz's construction goblins with me today. This was the day we'd be making the trek to the bog to set up the remote iron operation.

Even with the javeline at the gates, though they hadn't attempted a second attack during the night, I couldn't keep delaying exploration in favor of defending one little bluff. Steel was a critical resource—possibly the most important resource we lacked. I intended to make our first battery-powered motor as soon as I got back. I'd soon have everything I needed.

The carts down near the paddocks had been strapped up to cliffords, who struggled to move the loads of adobe bricks and lumber that would form the base of the artificial bluff. With nearly thirty goblins assembled at the base of the cliff, plus Chuck and his clifford-riding escorts, we set off west toward the bog in a massed whirlwind of cleavers, claws, and paving stones.

I rode with Chuck on the back of his clifford, holding tight to the saddle as the forest flew by. We passed the river where two of our flex-a-pult fishing boats were casting off, goblins furiously cranking on the outboard impellers. We ranged ahead of the trailblazers, but never lost track of them, as you could hear the frantic assault on the forest from hundreds of meters away. We ranged most of the morning and into the afternoon until we hit the first roadblock.

"There he is!" said Chuck, pointing one of his throwing spears. I spotted the stone sloth we'd found on our first trip to the bog. It was a few kilometers outside the camp to the northwest, and we'd run through his riverside clearing so fast the first time that the beast barely had time to give chase. This time, it had ample warning that goblins were in the vicinity, and it wasn't shy. Stone sloths were incredibly territorial, in addition to being carnivorous goblin predators.

Chuck angled the wedge of seven wranglers in, and we spread out as the stone sloth charged. It was a big'un, with claws that would have been too large to use as prosthetics unless I really *did* want stilts. It was level 23, higher than even the patriarch of the family group we'd fought. How many goblins had it eaten to get that big?

I scanned the ground as we moved and spotted two large clay deposits near the river. *Perfect.* We were running low on the clay we'd extracted from the previous den we'd discovered to the northeast of the bluff, and another source was paramount to meeting the orders of ceramic the Ifrit were going to put in.

Chuck, of course, was focused on more pressing matters—like not dying. He yanked his clifford into a tight turn to avoid the grasping claws, not that his mount needed much encouragement. He tossed his spear at the same time, the ceramic tip piercing the thick hide of the beast. A volley of clay poppers followed, *popping* against the thick, clay-reinforced armor on its back. It roared and gave chase.

We held off on further provoking the creature. It chased us nearly half a kilometer before it finally slowed, winded, and returned to its den to lick the few wounds we'd managed to inflict.

"That good, boss?" asked Chuck.

"Yep. Let's tell the group: We're camping here tonight."

It took until the eclipse finished for the main convoy to reach the rest of us. But when I looked back on their progress I saw a wonderful sight: a road lined with (admittedly uneven) patchy stones and crushed clay bricks. It was far from straight, having picked up the goblin's customary windy pathing that occasionally even looped back on itself. But it was a road that could be traversed much faster the next time.

<Goblin Technology Unlocked: Rocky Roads>

We began to set up the night shelter—which probably belonged in a circus act. I tied the longest rope we'd made yet to the corner of a pair of stacked wooden lattices, and then put the rock into the sled of a slinger and fired it up through the trees. Two goblins dove out of the way as it came crashing back down, but it still bounced off one of their skulls as neither had actually looked at where it was descending. After recovering, both goblins immediately jumped on the rope and began trying to climb it, which had the opposite effect, pulling the rope—and the corner of the lattice—up into the canopy. I repeated the trick on the three other corners, and soon the whole structure was hoisted up about ten meters off the ground. All four corners were tied off, and then the second, smaller lattice dangled underneath.

Once that was done, a handful more goblins scrambled up a rope ladder and began installing some bearings at strategic locations. With that complete, ropes were fitted to the bearings and they began hoisting up food and provisions for the night, along with weapons, bedding, and slingers. The whole process took about an hour. All in all, we'd made good progress on the first day. The stone sloth den was about a third of the way to the bog, which meant that we stood a good chance of making it before nightfall the next night if we pressed hard. Most of the goblins were tired from the journey before they even ate their trail provisions, and once they stuffed their little blue faces, they passed out harder than ever.

The hobgoblins stayed on the ground with the tied-up pack cliffords. They'd be the night guards in two specially built armored wagons and would alert the rest of us if something attacked. I was willing to risk losing out on the reproduction of the sleeping mounds in the lattice if it meant maintaining the integrity of the caravan. But all that happened was a few of the fat forest fowl tried to make nests in the upper lattice.

<Your tribe has decreased to 129 members.>
<2 Hobgoblin Scrappers have been added to your tribe.>
<1 Hobgoblin Wrangler has been added to your tribe.>
<Your tribe has increased to 138 members.>

I woke up to bird poop splashing on the top of the goblin mound. So a low roll for goblin reproduction, *and* that happened. But there were nests with eggs in them on the upper lattice already, so that was breakfast sorted. A totally added and unexpected element of the mobile temporary goblin bluff.

The goblins at the bottom of the pile had matted fur in a cross pattern, making them look a bit like they'd been grilled. But at least they avoided the night droppings. The cliffords and the hobbies slept below with just enough goblins to make an effective pile.

Things were quiet. Well, quiet for a goblin morning. And it took me a few minutes to figure out why. This was the first morning I'd woken up in Rava without a palaver with my lieutenants. Buzz and Sally were back at the bluff with Neil and Javier (our clothier). Armstrong would be heading back to Canaveral to relieve John. Chuck would come once he and the other wranglers awoke, but for now, it was me and my silent (relatively speaking) partners. And it was going to be a busy morning.

"Alright, gang. Unpack the RPPs," I said. "Let's go get that clay."

The goblins scrambled to the back of a wagon set a decent way away from the others. They opened the back of it and withdrew several long, wooden tubes. It took two goblins to carry each one, which meant we could bring thirteen of them between the goblins we had currently awake. We also passed out special vests and the first of the ceramic skull masks.

We hauled the tubes to the edge of the stone sloth territory, and each pair planted one end in the ground while the other balanced a yoke on their shoulders. I surveyed the area and placed a few specialized slingers. I noticed more than a few wobbly knees and nervous, twitching ears as the goblins cast looks toward the stone sloth den beyond the trees. We weren't bothering with the skinny-sneakers this time. No stone sloth hide infiltration. I needed to show these goblins that their strength in numbers could take out much larger threats, even without the hobgoblins helping. That their power lay not in the individual, but en masse.

Of course, that was little help to the goblins sent to poke the bear—or, sloth, as it were. They were wearing the first of Javier's custom armor. It was more like modern ballistic armor than a suit of medieval armor, in that he'd made a vest with a front and back pocket, into which slid a single, slender ceramic tile. We were actually able to use the roofing tile mold to make them. The goblins already wore skull masks, which were a bit like helmets. From what I'd observed, things that hit goblins with enough force to crack the masks generally killed the goblin as well. So it had been a simple matter to upgrade the material—though the awkward shape took up a lot of space in the kiln. They shrugged off losing limbs almost as fast as you could produce prosthetics for them, so instead I'd focused on vital organ protection in the chest, to keep the tribe numbers high. An armless, legless goblin could still sleep in a mound.

In effect, the whole getup made them look like pint-size video game characters with skull faces and tactical armor. Something you'd see in a shooter game, maybe, more than something like a fantasy—except for the blue, furry, straw-thin arms and legs sticking out. Special forces muppets. Sesame Team Six, maybe.

The slingers were a bit short range, so the bear-pokers had miniature versions of the larger wooden tubes clutched in their claws. Time to go to war.

CHAPTER 41

WORLD WAR CLAY

I'd consulted the bestiary on the Lanclovan monsters Rufus claimed were so dangerous, and it said that some of them could get up as high as level 40 or 50. There were even *dragons* in the interior that were in the high sixties. Plus some sort of ancient skyborne predator in the deep desert that was presumed to be somewhere in the triple digits. Rufus hadn't been kidding when he'd said I could take a thousand goblins into the desert and I'd lose a thousand goblins. But I had to wonder how he and the Ifrit were able to travel the region safely, and what prevented these monsters from destroying the artificer city.

Eventually, we would have to face monsters like that. And the majority of the fighting force would be goblins. Goblins, as the System was often quick to remind me with floating numbers superimposed on my vision, were perpetually level 1.

But that was a problem for another day. Details on the bogs and waterways of the jungle described much more manageable threats of monsters in the teens and twenties. We were going to lose goblins trying to collect iron. Hell, we'd probably lose a few just to misfires and the unpredictable nature of the Goblin Tech Tree. But we also hadn't attempted to take on anything above level 20 before, and I had to believe that the monsters in the bog were at least that tough. A bigger, stronger stone sloth would be a good litmus test to see if we could conquer the challenges the swamp would present.

"Prodder team forward," I ordered.

The armored goblins hefted their device and trotted toward the stone sloth's den by the river. The other goblins waited, and I had to maintain discipline as some of them got bored or simply forgot what they were trying to do. Others had begun playing with the RPPs or chewing on the housing.

All the levity ceased when I heard a shrill whistle, followed by a distant *pop* and then an enraged roar. Shock and alarm rippled up and down the line, and I marched back and forth offering encouragement.

A few moments later, a pair of armored goblins ran screaming back toward the caravan.

"*eeeeeEEEEE!*"

An enormous monster followed hot on their heels, massive claws digging deep furrows in the turf as it gave chase. It was truly massive when seen from the ground, and not the back of a clifford. The stone sloth took a swing, which cut cleanly through a sapling and skipped off the ceramic back plate in the slower prodder's vest. The impact knocked him forward, and he tumbled like a wheel back toward our line while his partner squawked and ran even faster, knowing he was now the closest goblin to our foe.

"Hold!" I said.

One of the goblins must have thought I meant *fire*, because he ignited the sulfur striker on the end of his RPP, and smoke and flame gouted out the back end. The rocket-propelled popper launched out the other end of the tube, streaking across the intervening distance. It split the difference between the two prodders, then veered off hard to the right, where it exploded against an old stump in a spray of clay shards and ceramic bearings that pierced the canopy above. The stone sloth barely flinched. It had eyes only for the backsides of the goblins who had struck it with the smaller versions.

"It's still too far!" I warned, holding up my hand. "Hold!"

The rolling prodder reached our minimum safe area, and I dropped my hand once the second one crossed out of the kill box.

"*Now!*"

The rest of the goblins held tight to the housings as the gunners struck the rockets alight. Up and down the line, primitive rocket motors kicked to life, joining in a roaring crescendo. Only two exploded in the tube.

<Your tribe has decreased to 131 members.>

Ten rockets streaked out, with ten heavy poppers on the front. They exploded around, under, and *against* the stone sloth. The impact blasted the heavy creature off its feet, tumbling it to the side as the fragmentation warheads peppered it with shards of clay and ceramic. But the thing was tough, armored, and not about to be brought down by just a few goblin-sized rockets. Still, when it climbed to its feet, it was bleeding and disoriented.

"Stage one complete! Proceed to stage two."

The rocketeers dropped the empty RPP tubes and most picked up spears, huddling shoulder to shoulder as they leveled the ceramic-tipped business ends toward the sloth. The rest picked up slingers and fanned out. The stone sloth began to approach, but having its momentum killed made it less willing to charge directly into the wall of spears that had caused its predecessor to accidentally discover the flex-a-pult. It couldn't just bulldoze over the formation. The goblins squawked and menaced it, standing in close ranks to present a thicket of razor-sharp spearheads that began to circle up into a half-moon around the stone sloth, even as they gave ground toward an area marked on the forest floor.

"Work him back!" I ordered.

My goblins eased back. The monster struck out with its long claws, unable to get past the thicket of spears, though it did manage to tangle a few of them and yank a couple of goblins out of the formation. It opened its mouth wide and crunched down on one while the other was smart enough to drop its spear and crawl back under the phalanx. I had another spear waiting for him, and he took his place again.

<Your tribe has decreased to 130 members.>

Any time the sloth tried to move back toward its den, the slinger goblins that had circled around fired a volley of poppers into it, discouraging retreat. Its only avenue of movement was toward the phalanx.

"Good!" I said. "Now, begin *stage three.*"

Three of the goblins at the rear of the formation backed out, gladly putting more distance between themselves and the large predator. Instead, they picked up a trio of slingers that had been positioned earlier, loaded with rocks attached to cords, which were themselves attached to corners of a net.

The longest, most arduous part of this expedition wasn't creating the tools, or the mobile bluff, or the wagons. It was simply manufacturing enough cordage to make a net capable of holding such a large stone sloth.

<Goblin Technology Unlocked: Springy-Stringy Trap>

Each of the slingers angled their crossbows up and fired. The net sprung up from where we'd laid it out near the rockets. The launched slinger anchors drew the net taut against the wooden stakes holding it in the ground, and then draped it over the bulk of the sloth. It roared in confusion, pulling against the net.

"Stakers!"

The slinger goblins on the other side of the sloth dropped their bows and unslung mallets from their backs. They ran up and placed more wooden stakes on the far side of the net, hammering them down into the ground to secure the trap.

We'd done it.

Shouts of alarm drew my attention, and I thought the straining stone sloth might be strong enough to rip through the net. But what I saw was something else entirely. Several of the goblins had spotted forms in the trees across the river: a squad of javeline maulers, watching us with their thick arms crossed.

"Stay focused!" I shouted. "Stage four. Finish the job!"

I picked up one of the discarded slingers as the phalanx fanned out. I held it low, crooked in the corner of my arm as I made my way to the near side of the riverbank across from the armored maulers. Behind me, the stone sloth roared as the goblins pressed in from all sides and delivered death from a thousand cuts to the restrained monster.

The javeline prodded one another and pointed to my prosthetic legs. The largest among them, a level 18—nearly strong enough to challenge the stone sloth in his own right—stepped forward with his heavy spear and pointed it at me.

"You are talking goblin, yes? You make big fire and wooden bird and ride dog? Do not die?"

"That's right," I shouted back. "I'm the talking goblin. Who are you?"

"I am Hrott, brother of Rotte."

I narrowed my eyes. "Did you come to take my tongue and my ears, too?"

Hrott thumped the butt of his spear into the turf. "I am a taker only of *life*, little goblin. Prince of Habberport men make demand you come. So, you come talk man prince."

I had no interest in getting spirited away to a human city. I couldn't imagine that would end well for me in any scenario. A few goblins ran to join me, blood-tipped spears in hand. A glance behind told me the fight was reaching its end, and the clay deposit was as good as ours. The goblins at my side hooted, squawked, and hissed at the javeline, jumping up and down. A few pointed their own slingers.

I put on my best deep-southern drawl. "So what yer sayin' is, y'all are with the gov'ment?"

"What you say, little talk-goblin?"

I leveled the slinger. "Folk 'round these parts don't care fer gov'ment types. Y'all need to be movin' on."

"I not understand small goblin voice. Speak you me clear."

"This clear enough for you?" I asked as I pulled the trigger on my slinger. The jar shot out, arcing over to the other side of the bank, where it fell short. It was not a precision instrument, after all. But it made a nice little *bang* and covered the trio in mud. Hrott shied back, and then roared with rage and profanities. One of the others leveled a crossbow at me, but Hrott pushed it down. Not only did he want me alive, but it sounded like he knew from Rotte that the System kept me from dying anyway. A few other goblins let loose with rocks from their slingers, and one even threw his spear, which fell woefully short and splashed into the river. The spearman's compatriots rained blows on him by way of admonishment.

"This is being mistake, little talk-goblin! We will bleed you and then crush you."

I yanked the crank on the slinger to reset the sled and held out my hand, palm up. Another goblin dropped a new popper into it, and I fit it to the slinger and brought my sights up. "My only mistake was missing your head, porkbelly. And I'm not in the habit of repeating my mistakes."

The boar-dwarf growled within his helmet. But the goblins had finished off the stone sloth and were starting to bring more of their own slingers over. Maybe taunting the javeline was an error. But the sensation of Rotte's spear punching through my chest was still fresh in my memory, called to the surface with a visceral, sharp phantom. The most efficient way to wipe out Tribe Apollo would be to capture me again and then stab me 130 times until I was the only one left. For the sake of the tribe, I couldn't put myself in the clutches of the javeline again. And I would have to be a damn fool to give my well-being over to the care of these cruel brutes.

If this human prince wanted me, he could come out here and talk to me himself.

CHAPTER 42

BOG STANDARD

The clay at the stone sloth den would see to our immediate needs in supplying the Ifrit with ceramics. We'd already built the infrastructure to transport the clay, so it was just a matter of traversing our first road with a wagon, loading it up, and hauling the clay back to the bluff to be worked. The stone sloth, as well, had a good deal of the stuff slathered on its hide, cracked and dried like the desert. Water would loosen it up.

In the afternoon it started to downpour. But Javier's tailors had made us all cured hide cloaks with hoods for the expedition, so the goblins didn't even cease working when the rains came down.

With the time it took to clean and process the stone sloth and remove the clay on its back for transport, we lost most of the light. So I didn't bother to have the portable bluff broken down. We took the rest of the day clearing out the area, and then roasted sloth meat for dinner. Eileen's overflight reached us as we were getting the fires going, and several of the goblins rushed to the armory to be the one to get the signal rocket. I watched the small rocket climb skyward and burst apart. One rocket meant proceeding as planned. Two meant send additional backup. Three meant the goblins got overexcited.

Chuck took his wranglers back to make a report of our victory, after expressing disappointment that he had missed both the battle with the stone sloth and the haranguing of the javeline maulers. But hunting something much higher level with just your bog-standard, garden-variety goblin had been the entire point.

All in all, it had been a promising day. The goblins sat around the fires, watching the dinner roast as they banged sticks on rocks and chanted in a tuneless, singsong approximation of music. I'd tried teaching them some Queen, some Beastie Boys, and even some Taylor Swift, but the tribe was in desperate need of an autotune. Still, morale was up, and the goblins were fat *and* happy when they climbed up onto the mobile bluff. I was hoisted and thrown to the middle of the lattice and given the place of honor at the bottom of the sleeping mound, despite my protestations.

This was the first time since coming to Rava that I went to sleep feeling that life was good again.

<Your tribe has decreased to 124 members.>
<Your tribe's morale is unusually high. A one-time spawning bonus has been added.>
<3 Goblin Wranglers have been added to your tribe.>
<2 Goblin Scrappers have been added to your tribe.>
<1 Goblin Taskmaster has been added to your tribe.>
<Your tribe has increased to 148 members.>

Damn! Twenty-four new goblins overnight, and a quarter of them were variants. That was, by far, the single best night of spawning the tribe had experienced. Winning battles was good for the mysterious goblin libido, apparently. The mound I woke up in was noticeably bigger than the mound I'd gone to sleep in, as evidenced by the weight squeezing me against the lattice structure.

One of the new taskmasters had even spawned with us on the expedition, so I named him Hadfield (since Chris was technically taken). He pulled me out of the pile himself, extricating me from the late risers.

"Mornin', boss," he said.

"Morning. Welcome to the tribe. What's your poison?"

Hadfield tugged at his cheek fur. "Campin', explorin'."

"Boy, are you in the right place," I said.

He grinned at me. "The System provides! Why don't you relax while I get this beast movin'?" His eyes glazed over as he took on the look of someone navigating System menus. "I'll just go ahead and take the liberty of recruitin' some trail hands from the tribe, beggin' yer pardon."

Providence had put Hadfield on the road to the bog. So, he'd be the boss of the first remote outstation. *The System provides,* he'd said.

System, do you give me goblins based on what my tribe's needs are?

<Denied. All assignments and generations are random in nature. Perhaps you are lucky.>

Lucky. Right. So lucky my rocket blew up on the launchpad. *Soooooo* lucky!

<Luckier than your companions.>

Oof. That was the closest the recalcitrant entity had given me to confirmation that the two other astronauts aboard my spacecraft hadn't also been reborn in Rava. If I was the only one who pulled through, then Dave and Sandra really were dead. I had held out hope that the two had somehow also made the jump, and I might find them waiting on another bluff with tribes of their own. That was part of the reason I'd rushed to try and reach the other villages. Now? This was a bit much to think about before breakfast.

System, are there others in Rava from my world?

No answer.

At least having been at the bottom of the pile, this time I didn't have to clean bird poop out of my fur, for which I was quite grateful. More birds had made poor life choices by making nests on the lattice and filling them with eggs. We had to clear the nests anyway in order to break down the temporary bluff. Win-win, really. We were back breaking new trail by midmorning. A full day of travel would put us a stone's throw from the iron bog.

One of the wagons broke off, hauling back some of the clay for refining at Village Apollo. The rest continued on, bumping and careening down the fresh road as fast as the pathfinders could cut and clear it. The cliffords pulled at their harnesses like they had a grudge against the things—which it was quite possible they did. They barely tolerated riders. One of the wagons that carried adobe bricks carried mostly gravel by the end of the day, so we used it on the road.

By the time the sun started to drop in the sky, we were getting close enough to the bog to smell the stagnant water and a metallic tang. The book on peat bogs had said the iron was a result of "humours in the water," which I had to assume actually meant some sort of bacteria in the water that released iron as a byproduct of its natural processes. According to the book, the iron would collect as nodules on the underside of peat patches, so goblins would have to wade into the bog to get it.

I called a halt while it was still light enough to get the portable bluff up into the canopy. Hadfield took charge, running around in a hat he'd improvised from wetlands ferns until he could get a skull mask. The frenetic energy of the taskmasters got the shelter up in record time, and with only two goblins tangled in the lattice.

I'd lost eight goblins over the day elsewhere in the tribe, bringing me back down to 140 members total. The high roll had put me ahead, but I had a feeling we'd lose that and more in the bog striving toward our most important goals yet.

I surveyed the convoy of thirteen wagons. Some would take that number as a bad omen. Hell, just look at Apollo 13. That mission had been cursed. Not as cursed as my launch, I supposed. But still. Just to be safe, I had the goblins hack apart one of the wagons, leaving us with only twelve. Most of these would be scavenged for parts anyway. We wouldn't need all twelve to carry iron back. In fact, we were going to build the furnaces here.

I gathered up the handful of hobgoblins we had with us as the non-variants began to ascend the rope ladders to the portable bluff. They were mostly scrappers, plus a couple of wranglers to handle the cliffords. Since the hobbies stayed up late, they were immune to the lethargic effects of dinner, and still alert—if on edge. It wasn't hard to puzzle out why.

"Look," I said. "I know it's tough being away from the village overnight. Tomorrow we'll start building the permanent tower, and then we'll have a home away from home. This close to the bog, we don't really know what's waiting for us. So stay vigilant. I'm depending on you."

The scrappers puffed out their chests, proud despite their unease. The wranglers dug their fingers into the fur of the cliffords for comfort. They glanced up at the lattice.

"Don't worry," I said. "We'll be fine. Just keep an eye out for the cliffords."

CHAPTER 43

WELCOME TO THE JUNGLE

<Your tribe has decreased to 132 members.>
<1 Hobgoblin Scrapper has been added to your tribe.>
<2 Hobgoblin Wranglers have been added to your tribe.>
<Your tribe has increased to 148 members.>

What in the hell? I opened my eyes and looked through the open lattice below at the carnage that had been our convoy. Several wagons were demolished. They'd been torn apart at the frames. Of the cliffords, there was no sign. Which was a *bad* sign. I quickly realized the hobgoblins were gone, too. Which was a *really, really* bad sign.

I dragged myself out of the pile and over to the edge of the portable bluff, where Hadfield was kneeling, along with several of Buzz's builders and a scrapper.

"Well, at least one of you managed to survive," I said, looking at the bigger hobgoblin.

Hadfield shook his head. "He's new."

"Oh? Well, happy birthday." I sighed. "What a disaster."

"But, boss, we got a problem."

"Yeah," I said. I had to take control of the situation before it spiraled. "The builders are slacking off."

One of the goblins at the edge of the lattice squawked in indignation, then remembered who he was talking to and acted appropriately cowed.

Hadfield tossed a stick down into the clearing. "They don't want to go down in case whatever did that is still mucking about nearby."

"Understandable. I know of this animal that sometimes has to jump into water to hunt food, but they're never sure whether there's a predator underneath it waiting for them."

"How do they get sorted?" asked Hadfield.

I lifted my prosthetic and planted it in the back of the nearest goblin, knocking him over the edge of the lattice. He tumbled, *EEEeeeeing*, to the ground below, where he bounced off his head and ran for the rope ladder. It was still retracted from where we'd pulled it up the night before. He started hopping, trying to reach the lattice. It was about nine meters too high.

"Ah," said Hadfield. "Straight to the point." He raised his hand. "Slingers ready!"

The rest of the goblins ran to retrieve weapons, which were conveniently stored away from the edge of the platform. They readied poppers in their sleds and trained them down at the forest below. I had to yell at them to angle their payloads over the edge. If they managed to burn down the temporary bluff, we'd *all* be on the ground, and with no pack animals, hobgoblins, or wagons to protect us.

We waited for a few minutes until our experimental penguin stopped jumping and started trembling in fear so bad his knees sounded like maracas. When nothing came out to gobble him up, I relaxed and gave the go-ahead for the rest of the goblins to bail out. Once we'd picked ourselves up off the ground, I set to examining what was left of the campsite.

All the hobgoblins had been dragged off. Silently enough that whatever did it left only blood and tufts of blue fur behind. Of the cliffords, there was no fur or blood. Their leads simply ended in frayed cordage. But they hadn't raised a ruckus in the night, which was the strangest part.

We'd had most of the food supplies in the lattice with us, so even though the carts were smashed, they'd held mostly building supplies, which themselves were fine. Bricks, wood, cordage, tools, and parts to build portable lifts and cranes were strewn among the wagon wreckage.

I called over the scrapper that had been born in the pile the night before. "Sniff around and see what you can find. Report it back to me."

The scrapper saluted and unexpectedly dropped to all fours, sniffing at the ground as he started patrolling the campsite. I hadn't meant the instruction literally and was about to correct him when Hadfield stopped me. "He knows what he's about, boss."

"I'll take your word for it," I said. I raised my voice so the rest of the goblins could hear me, pointing out a couple of stragglers. "You six, go with him. As for the rest of you, we've got work to do! Unless you want to sleep on the ground tonight, let's get moving!"

Goblins might not be verbal, but their body language was expressive enough to tell when they were bothered. Honestly, they might as well have been wearing glowing neon signs with their emotions depicted by excited noble gases. My gaggle of swamp builders were terrified. As their king, I had to be brave for them. But the situation definitely worried me. What could get in, kill multiple hobgoblins and all the cliffords, and not make enough noise to wake the tribe?

The bestiary was in one of the wagons that hadn't been smashed, so I dug it out and thumbed through while our builders tore at the clearing with spades to get the area—if not level, at least slightly less lumpy. We weren't as close to the bog as I'd have liked, but I wanted to make sure we had hard cover tonight in case whatever had visited us could climb. Or worse, fly. Just because the night haunts prowled the heights of the bluff didn't mean they couldn't visit a swamp.

Our slingers now had small nets that we could launch skyward to trap night haunts. And I was now confident that we had enough goblins to take them on, even without variants. But this didn't seem like the night haunts' MO. Whatever had visited us had gone for the goblins on the ground instead of the ones elevated in the lattice, and the night haunts had only ever taken one or two goblins at night. Not five or more. They'd also never shown interest in other animals, like cliffords or the captive stone sloth, who had been easily accessible at the village. No, this was something else.

Rufus's bestiary was incomplete. And that was putting it generously. Lanclova apparently repelled most explorers, and the "newcomers," as Taquoho had called them, kept mainly to the coast because the interior of the continent was incredibly dangerous. This was a land notorious for powerful monsters enhanced further by the System. Lots of the entries were based on hearsay, native legends, and speculation. The only entry that made sense for where we were was an incorporeal night spirit that bewitched expeditions who ventured west of the mountains.

By midday, the bricks were stacked up almost four meters and continuing to grow. The scrapper found me as I was supervising the lifting of a flex-a-pult into position.

"Found somethin', chief."

I left the construction to Hadfield and followed the scrapper and the other goblins. We skirted the edge of the bog, close enough to hear the bellowing of croc-knockers in the distance. After going about a half-kilometer, the scrapper stopped and dropped down, pointing to the mud.

Multiple sets of tracks had come and gone. Small, webbed feet, with strange circular tracks irregularly placed alongside some of them, mixed with the larger tracks of a hobgoblin. The scent of blood mingled with the mud and iron from the bog and, curiously, burnt fur. I turned around, looking back at the campsite. You could just barely see the temporary bluff suspended in the canopy from here. I ran a hand through my fur, considering.

"Wotcha fink, boss?" asked the scrapper.

I took one of the spears from the other goblins and set the butt into the mud near the footprints. It was a perfect match.

"There's some sort of hominid in the bog," I said. "Did you find any tracks like this closer to camp?"

"Nuffink."

"And no sign of the cliffords or other hobbies?"

"A paw print here 'n there."

I took a deep breath. So whatever these tracks belonged to, they weren't what attacked us and stole the cliffords. But they had captured one of my hobgoblins. "Alright. Let's head back."

We'd planned for this. Well, not for losing all our hobgoblins and every animal on the first night. But we'd expected this to be a dangerous venture. Goblins were going to die to get us the iron in this bog.

When we got back to the camp, I began to distribute the rest of the armor we'd brought, as well as padded packs of poppers for the goblins to keep on hand. At the current rate of construction, it was going to take three days to finish the top tier of the tower, but I could start moving goblins into it tomorrow night. Until then, we had to survive another night in the lattice.

Croc-knockers, tesla wasps, some sort of ethereal spirit, and now a sapient, possibly hostile race were too big of threats to tackle with what we'd brought with us. I decided to push up our contingency plan. One of the wagons had a new experiment. I took the scrapper and two goblins with me and unpacked the balloon kit sewn from the hides of the eclipse lizards. It had needed thirty-two square chooms worth of frills, the lightest part of their hides, which equated to about sixty of the lizards. But it resulted in an extremely light, almost foil-like material that weighed very little and had decent stretchy properties.

I attached a clay canister to the bottom and used a coal from the previous night's fire to start a small flame on the scat contained inside. As the balloon started to expand from the burning methane in the goblin scat, I attached a banner to the tether that had been stained with charcoal. This was the first functional balloon big enough to lift a goblin, and it was prepared to do so by means of a small platform just large enough for a single goblin to sit on.

Whistling for attention brought a halt to the construction. "Who wants to fly?" I asked.

I might as well have been giving away free hotdogs at Fenway for the riot it almost caused. After the disaster of the morning's discovery, it felt good to reintroduce a little levity into the tribe. Goblins seemed to have memories similar to that of goldfish, because all thought of getting the shelter up gave way to the stampede of grasping arms and excited squawks. I had to hold the platform over my head to keep them from grabbing at it.

"Woah, woah!" I called. I picked one goblin at random and nodded to him. "You're today's lucky winner!"

The goblin roared in triumph and was immediately the target of concerted physical assault as he made his way to the front. Luckily, the armor he wore absorbed most of it. He stripped out of his plate carrier and shimmied up the rope to the platform. I passed up a hide flag that we'd stained red with berries for him to wave. Slowly, we let out the rope and the balloon began to lift, thanks to the methane flame heating the air within.

CHAPTER 44

GET ME OUT OF THIS JUNGLE

Believe it or not, the French invented hot-air ballooning many years before Orville and Wilbur launched the *Flyer* in Kitty Hawk. While the brothers were futzing with engines, French aeronauts had been floating over Burgundy under colorful canopies powered by the principles of air density for a century. But the Wright brothers had better marketing, so everyone remembers them.

The balloon lifted, and none too soon, as the first daily scout glider appeared in the air. It caught the glint of the reflective lizard skin and swooped down close enough to see the goblin frantically waving the red banner back and forth before turning back to the southeast toward the bluff.

We had four color codes. White meant the operation was continuing. Blue meant we were continuing and would need an air delivery. Red meant immediate reinforcement in the form of hobgoblins. Black meant the mission was scrubbed. I didn't want to have to heft the black banner.

"Alright," I said to the assembled goblins. "They saw it. Start pulling him down."

"*eeeeeeEEEEE!*"

Our aeronaut thumped head-first into the ground and rolled to a sitting position, rubbing the top of his head and grinning. The rest of the goblins cheered, and then looked at me expectantly.

<Goblin Technology Unlocked: Skinny-Floaty Dive Board>

I sighed. "Okay. One jump each, and then back to work." The tribe cheered and shoved and pushed to each be the first to shimmy up the rope for their turn at a swan dive. Some of them ran to the wagons for personal gliders to prolong their air time. I shook my head. Then I stopped and considered. I borrowed one of the gliders and shimmied up the rope myself. Climbing came naturally to me as a goblin. Even without legs, goblins could climb extraordinarily well. Climbing had never been my thing on Earth, since I figured if I wanted to go higher, I should work harder to become an astronaut.

Once I reached the top, I swung out onto the narrow platform under the balloon and unfurled the personal glider. The hide canopy caught the wind almost immediately and nearly pulled me off the platform. But I got the glider overhead, gripped the pole underneath, and tossed myself down.

The personal gliders the goblins fashioned for themselves weren't like the night-haunt-wing soaring aircraft or Eileen's heavy glider. They were somewhere between parasails and umbrellas in effectiveness. But this one still let me get enough airtime to make a decent circuit of our immediate surroundings. The bog that began due north about a kilometer as seen from the air actually stretched west and then south, as well, making our tower location something of a peninsula intruding into the marsh. The marsh itself was much bigger than I'd initially expected as well, stretching farther west where another river emptied into it.

One positive aspect was that I didn't expect we'd get attacked by a large force from this angle. If humans wanted to come down from Habberport, they'd have to either come through the foothills to the northeast or trek farther south to avoid the marsh, coming in from the southwest by skirting the edge of the plains south of the bluff land. The bog would slow down any substantial force, and they'd be inundated with hostile fauna the entire way. But it was also a blind spot from the air. A lack of thermals over the bog and thick, humid air made for poor gliding. If a force did chance the journey, we'd have no way to spot them early.

I circled west as I descended, careful to allow myself enough altitude to get back. Getting lower in altitude let me resolve a bit through the canopy, and through a break in the trees I spotted an island in the bog with several croc-knockers basking in the midday sun. If they knew we were here, they weren't making any effort to leave the bog to pursue us.

As I circled south, I caught a flash of red in the trees. I drifted closer and realized it was some of our missing cliffords running through the bog, I angled toward them for a closer look. If they hadn't been eaten, that meant they'd just gotten loose and Chuck might be able to round them up.

That was good news, as these ones were all trained up. Hell, maybe they'd just gotten spooked when something attacked the hobbies and I could lead them back to the camp.

<*Careful.*>

My breath caught. The System was not often quick or proactive to warn me of danger. I angled away just in time for the cliffords to look back at me and open their mouths. A black shadow, or mist, or *swarm* of something flooded out of them and resolved into a vaguely doglike shape that was about five times the size of the cliffords themselves. A low, reverberating growl filtered up from the canopy. I would have thought I was seeing things, except that the System was *very* quick to put an *XX* level above it, which was System's way of saying *not a chance in hell.*

Nope, nope, nope. I didn't want anything to do with it. I turned the glider all the way around and made for the tower construction as a spine-chilling howl rolled after me. Friggen' bestiary was apparently right on the money. I looked back to make sure the weird shade wolf thing wasn't following me. But it, and the cliffords, were gone. Somehow, that was more worrying. Something hadn't *eaten* our animals. Something had apparently *possessed* them.

<*Your tribe has decreased to 144 members.*>

It wasn't just us having problems. I had to remember that the bog expedition was just one arm of a multi-faceted plan to grow and advance the tribe. With the sun slipping behind Raphina, Village Canaveral would be fighting off lizards for the next few hours. The problems in the bog weren't insurmountable. Sure, the ghost-cloud-wolf-swarm-thing was an issue. But it hadn't affected any of the goblins on the lattice. In another day or two, we'd be off the ground and in a permanent tower.

I made a small circle of the camp before I landed. Sure, the bog seemed to be fraught with peril. But where wasn't? Maybe the Ifrit had more information about the dangers of the swamp. Once they made their way to Apollo, I could ask them. And I had my motor project, generator parts, rotary engine, and batteries to look forward to as well. We were going to eat this elephant, one bite at a time. But it all hinged on success harvesting iron from this bog. And that was the next step.

I helped with the tower construction throughout the rest of the evening, which seemed mostly about keeping the goblins from sneaking away for more jumps on the balloon. It was almost a blessing when it ran out of gas (literally) toward sunset and began to sag back down to the ground. None too soon, as rain started to fall and the wind began to howl. Chuck and his wranglers arrived not long after and swung out of their saddles.

"You sure you don't want me to stay overnight, boss?" he asked after I explained the situation to him. He ran a hand through his clifford's fur, almost protectively.

"I'm sure," I said. "We'll have the scrappers in the temporary lattice instead of on the ground in case anything goes wrong. I don't want to risk more cliffords."

Chuck relaxed and patted his mount on its muzzle. Despite his offer, it wasn't difficult to see he was relieved about not putting his personal good boy on the line.

"Besides, I need you keeping tabs on the javeline movements. How are things at Apollo?" I asked.

Chuck grinned. "They tried again, but they broke quick when they hit the buried poppers." He made an explosion noise and laughed, which spread throughout the village like a verbal meme. "Don't think they'll be back soon. Easier to hit other tribes first."

I nodded. It was troubling that the javeline knew where our bluff was. But at least it was well-fortified. We had explosives as long as we had regular access to the bomb fruit orchards and the hot springs—at least until we stopped being able to collect sulfur.

System?

<You have approximately 4 chooms of sulfur, and scouted nodes have 12 potential chooms of harvestable sulfur.>

It was a finite resource, and we were burning through it with daily air delivery flights. I could alleviate the need for it somewhat with rechargeable batteries. "We need to get to those villages first. Any sign of our Ifrit friends?"

"Not yet."

I hadn't expected there to be. It was likely Rufus wouldn't even reach the City of Brass to start negotiating with the king for at least another day or two.

"Alright," I said. "Best head back. Thanks for the supplies."

Chuck glanced at the rear seat on his saddle. "I could take you back, if you want. Sleep safe at the village."

I shook my head. "No. I'll turn the camp over to Hadfield once things are running. But I need to be here to deal with the challenges of the bog."

"Just keep a couple scrappers close," said Chuck, swinging back up into his saddle. He looked around, somewhat nervous. "Unnatural fer a goblin to nest on the ground like this."

The wranglers left. I had the expedition goblins drag the bags over to the lattice lift to haul anything edible up top. It was going to be a long night.

CHAPTER 45

IGNIS

<Your tribe has decreased to 139 members.>
<2 Hobgoblin Scrappers have been added to your tribe.>
<3 Hobgoblin Wranglers have been added to your tribe.>
<Your tribe has increased to 155 members.>
<Increasing your tribe size has unlocked a new goblin variant.
You may select one of the following:
Hobgoblin Hawkeye: A larger, stronger, nocturnal goblin skilled with ranged weaponry
—or—
Noblin Igni: A larger, stronger goblin skilled in fire-based applications.>

I wriggled my way to the top of the sleeping pile. *Noblins.* I'd never heard of that before. *System, do fire-based applications include things like internal combustion engines?*

<Additional information available upon selection of variant goblin.>

Does said information pertain to internal combustion?
There was a pause.

<Additional information available upon selection of variant goblin.>

C'mon, System. Give me something here.

<References to unresearched technologies in the Goblin Technology Tree do not appear in variant skills.>

Ah-ha! That was almost as good as an admission—not specifically about the variants, but that internal combustion was possible on Rava, despite the differences in the makeup of the world and its elements. If it was an unresearched technology, it was still present in the tree. But was there a way to see those offshoots?

System, show me the tree.

A wide window expanded in front of me, showing a vast number of interconnected nodes—a visual representation of the entire Goblin Tech Tree. Most of it, at least 95 percent, was still dark, and would likely remain so. I had very little desire to explore, for example, the *Flatula-Horn Rhythms* technology path the System had suggested as a follow-up research option to our basic jam sessions. Other illuminated systems were their own little islands, like glider technology and ceramics, where I'd skipped a number of interim steps by applying modern knowledge to take advantage of primitive resources.

The fire-making tree had quite a few branches coming off of it, just a handful of which had been discovered. I assumed that section contained a large amount of power-creation technology like steam, internal combustion, and possibly even nuclear fusion or fission (which was a terrifying thought, goblins with the power of the atom).

The igni were quite possibly some type of engineer-specialized goblin—what I'd originally thought the scrappers would be before they turned out to be commando goblins. If so, then they'd be important to breaking into the Industrial Age.

But hawkeyes . . . goblins specialized in ranged combat. Iron and steel would mean firearms. Even if I didn't do it for them, the ingredients would be there and the goblins would eventually figure out how to make this world's version of a matchlock, then a musket, and so on. Making sure those weapons were in the hands of goblins who actually knew how to use them might help secure the tribe when someone or something more powerful than a handful of javeline came knocking at the gates.

But who was I kidding? We were goblins. Accuracy was a metric of overwhelming volume, as far as I was concerned. The slingers already functioned in volleys, and how precise did explosives really need to be?

Give me the ignis, please.

<*Good thing you replaced the wooden structures with brick.*>
<*5 Noblin Igni have been added to your tribe.*>
<*1 Noblin Ignis has been promoted to Taskmaster.*>

I crawled out of the sleeping pile and looked around, excited. But my excitement waned when I realized none of the new noblins were with us. They must have been split between Apollo and Canaveral.

Just as well. I didn't need a pyromaniac setting fire to the wooden lattice that kept us off the ground while the tower was being finished.

Give me the deets, System.

<Noblin Ignis
Noblin: This advanced goblin variant is capable of speech and can reach level 6.
Flame Retardant: Igni are resistant to heat damage.
Armor Pro: Noblins are not encumbered by heavy armor.
Porcine: Noblins consume an extra choom of food per day.
Hot Hands: Igni gain a bonus to crafting speed and quality when using heat elements. The hotter the element, the higher the bonus.
Pyro: Igni gain a bonus to heat element weapons and technology.>

I considered. *System. Does heat-based weaponry include rocketry and firearms?*

<Rockets are considered heat-based. Details on undiscovered Goblin Technologies are not reflected in current bonuses.>

Fantastic. Heat-based crafting. That was as close as the System could get to screaming that these guys were natural blacksmiths and steel-smelters. And they could aim a rocket. And might not burst into flame the moment a spark looked at them.

I tapped Hadfield awake. He moaned, rolled over, and yawned. Then he sat up, clacking his teeth.

"Let's get a move on, comrade."

Hadfield kicked one of the goblins over the edge of the lattice, and we waited to see if she would be eaten. After a few minutes (well, moments, really—goblins aren't the most patient), the rest of the goblins bailed out of the lattice.

The first thing I noticed was that one of the wagons had been tampered with. Not by a wild animal or the shade wolf. Something had jimmied open a latch and rifled through the contents. Several clay jars that had held fish oil for greasing were gone. A bundle of rope was missing as well, along with a basket of spare ceramic spear tips, bearings, and other ceramic parts.

The hominids had paid us a visit during the night, clearly. I could see their webbed footprints, but they must have been pretty quiet to get in under the hobgoblin noses. Great. We were already at war with night haunts, javeline, and eclipse lizards. I didn't need to battle swamp people, too. Especially ones that had just armed themselves with ceramic spear-points. Well, at least we had ceramic plate vests. But there'd be no more thieving. I had the goblins unload the wagons and pack everything into the tower while the builders kept stacking bricks higher and higher.

Well, we did have something that might show them that we weren't a tribe to be trifled with. I had the head of the large stone sloth brought out. The goblins had already processed the skin, brain, and tongue, but it left a rather impressive skull that the builders hoisted up onto the side of the tower, along with feathers and other assorted bones.

<Goblin Totem Unlocked: Stone Sloth Alpha. Goblins who appreciate this totem gain a moderate bonus to piercing and impact damage reduction.>

Most of the goblins stopped and took a few minutes to perform their version of oohing and aahing. In this case, it was holding up three fingers in the shape of the long sloth claws and making a reasonable attempt at its roar, when multiplied by thirty goblins. Excellent. By the end of the day, the top of the tower base would be as tall as the lattice platform, and my tribe could finally feel secure in their home away from home. Midmorning brought a rainstorm, so the oil-cloaks went on and work continued. No slacking today.

But we weren't in this bog just to build towers. We were here to harvest iron. I took twenty standard goblins, plus all the hobbies, and headed for the peat bog.

CHAPTER 46

PEATY-PRILLING

When we got to the water's edge, the designated iron collectors swapped their skull masks for ones of reinforced ceramic, in addition to donning their plate carriers. We had spears, slingers, poppers, and even a few of the RPPs left over from the stone sloth alpha battle. This was everything but the kitchen sink. I just hoped it would be enough.

"Alright," I said. "Let's get to work."

I'd brought enough bricks for the tower, but the tower wasn't the only thing I intended to build here. Mud and grass were in ample supply, and I wanted anyone not working on the tower or geared for battle to be manufacturing additional bricks on the shore of the bog. We needed a bunker on the waterfront, storage, and room to expand as the expedition grew. Builders started hacking at the reeds with flint cleavers as others turned out mud with spades to be mixed and molded.

Strangely, even though the goblins all used identical molds (which I'd measured and double-checked), no two bricks came out the same size or shape. This contributed somewhat to the lumpy, uneven construction of the goblin structures that made them always look as though they were tired of staying upright. Everything the goblins produced had this quality, and I had to assume it was some sort of quirk of the Goblin Tech Tree letting them harness technology they didn't actually fully understand. Still, it was going to be a problem once we started developing mechanical devices with tighter tolerances.

The expedition had no guarantees. There was still a chance that all of this ended in disaster. We crept through the reeds at the bog's edge. I poked my head up enough to take a look down the shore to see if I could spot any larger predators. Waterfowl and bugs dotted the surface of the bog, and the goblins flushed out the occasional frog that would try to hop for its life only to end up stuffed down a goblin gullet. Perks of being on the work detail,

I supposed. Until one of the goblins didn't bother to chew, and started to ribbit every time his mouth was open—much to the other goblins' delight.

I spotted two of the crocodilians sunning on an island out in the bog, but there was no telling how many others lurked beneath the surface. I could now see the levels above the two: *25* and *26*.

System, are these ones smaller than the one that attacked us the first time?

<Adversary level display threshold increases as stronger foes are vanquished.>

Interesting. Taking out the stone sloth alpha must have bumped up that threshold high enough for the croc-knockers. They were only a few levels above the alpha—still much stronger than goblins, but stronger than *how many* goblins? Hopefully, we wouldn't find out today.

I ducked back behind the reeds and gathered the three scrappers I had with me. All of them had loose-weave net cloaks on, and I had them hold still while I stuffed reeds, grass, and moss through the netting until each hobgoblin resembled little more than a lump of peat themselves.

<Goblin Technology Unlocked: Beguiling Grassy Cloaks>

"Alright. Keep an eye on those crocs. They start heading this way, you give the signal."

"Onnit," whispered one of the scrappers. "Trust."

The sneaky commando goblins melted back into the reeds, and I actually had a hard time tracking them any farther than just a few meters away. They made barely a ripple in the water as they slid into the bog and slowly became one with their environment.

I had a couple of wranglers similarly outfitted, except those I had in reserve with their snatchers ready, to hopefully loop around predators and give the other goblins time to flee.

Now it was time to get the rest of the goblins to work. I sent them out in pairs: one armored goblin with a slinger and spear for each harvesting goblin with a basket and peat knife. The book had described a fairly simple process of carving the iron nodules off the bottom of the peat masses. The deposits accumulated over time and could grow anywhere from the size of a pea to the size of a fist.

I sent them out onesie-twosie at twenty-meter intervals so that a large congregation wouldn't draw the crocs out. Non-variant goblins aren't known for their stealth, but they at least sloshed more carefully than normal, knowing there were predators in the bog. This wasn't the natural habitat for base goblins the way the forest was. They meandered around, looking uncertain even though I'd explained what to do in advance. It took me a moment to realize: This was something I'd have to demonstrate myself. Well, any good leader should never ask their workers to do something they're not willing to do themselves, right? Otherwise I'd be no better than the useless middle-managers at NuEarth that bossed the engineers around while not knowing the difference between a servo and a solenoid.

I kept an eye on the crocs as I waded out with two of the goblins closest to me, blade in hand. I ended up in the team with the goblin who had swallowed the live frog, so I got to listen to the distressed *ribbits* from one of my partners. So far, neither of the croc-knockers had stirred from their basking, and the surface of the water was disturbed only by fish, frogs, and the large blue wading birds that speared them, which looked like herons with a row of hedgehog spikes down their backs. The birds themselves were only level 2, so they didn't pose much of a threat, even to non-variant goblins.

We headed toward a concentration of peat on the surface, and I slipped my hands underneath to feel for the presence of iron. Goblin hands are extremely dexterous—maybe even more so than human hands. I ran my fingers through the tightly woven plant matter until they lit on something small and hard. Pay dirt—er, pay *peat*. I slipped the knife underneath and carefully cut the nodule free. The other goblin held out his sticky-wicky basket and I dropped the piece of ore into it.

<Goblin Technology Unlocked: Peaty Prilling>

A shudder ran across the surface of the water as the concept propagated through the present goblins. The rest of the harvesters snapped out of their stupor and looked at the knives in their hands with new light. Teams began to get to work, fishing underneath for iron. I kept at it, pulling two more small nodules off the mass of peat.

It was working. The iron was in our grasp. So many applications that required metallurgy were going to open up because of this.

I got so absorbed in the work that I didn't notice the dark shadow that had crept up behind us until I felt something hard and sharp nudge me in the back of the head.

CHAPTER 47

FROGGED DOWN

I nearly squawked, spinning and waving the knife in front of my face.

The wading bird jumped back, wings flapping for balance as it looked down at me curiously. It tilted its head in one direction, then the other, to gander at me with each eye, as though it wasn't sure what it beheld. Maybe it wasn't used to goblins in the swamp, but it certainly wasn't afraid of us. The quills that had stood up when I surprised it flattened back down. It leaned forward and pecked at the bone crown on my head.

"Shoo!" I hissed. My adversary was not deterred. It looked down at me from the lofty height of about a meter and a half. Then it stepped past me and stuck its beak close to my partner. Our guard raised his spear, but I held him back.

"No! We don't want it making a ruckus. Maybe it'll go away."

My armored partner gave me a dubious look but kept his spear at the ready. The bird stepped closer to our companion, and that's when I heard it.

"*Ribbit.*"

The wader pushed its wings overhead, creating a shadow over the three of us as it stared down at the goblin who had swallowed the frog. It prodded its beak down around the water line, looking for the source of the sound.

"It's hunting!" I said. "It wants the frog!"

The goblin clapped his hands over his mouth, but not before another *ribbit* worked its way up from his depths. The water bird snapped its head up, realizing the source of the sound, and thrust its beak down toward the goblin with all the grace and subtlety of a drunken ex on New Year's. The goblin fell back, arms windmilling as he splashed and squawked.

"*Can it!*" I hissed. "*Get out of here, bird!*" I ordered.

Instead of obeying me, the waterfowl shoved his beak right into the mouth of the struggling goblin, an act that was as stupid as it was brazen. But man, I guess it really wanted that frog. It was like watching the worst game of Operation ever as the bird fished through my panicked partner's innards. He must have nibbled the little guy's uvula, because the frog, and everything else the goblin had eaten in the last twenty-four hours, came fountaining up right into the bird's face.

The bird trilled in outrage and alarm—doubly so when the frog made its timely escape. But the low whistle humming across the bog brought my attention over to the island where the two croc-knockers had been basking. An island that was now empty.

Uh oh.

"Out of the water!" I called. "Get the iron onto dry land!"

The rest of the goblins had stopped working to watch the show, some cheering for their comrade and some trilling like the water bird, presumably supporting its conquest. But they all heard my call and looked back at the now-empty island. All interest in the epic battle evaporated. Even the water bird took flight. A pair of frog legs dangled from its beak.

The shore suddenly seemed so far away. I pushed through the water, no longer as concerned with stealth. A cry of alarm brought me back around. The goblin guard was furiously thrusting his spear down into the murky depths when suddenly a fountain of bog water sprayed upward, carrying the guard with it. The long jaws of a croc-knocker followed, snapping shut on the goblin. His armor held out as the jaw muscles on the creature bulged and shook, but then the plates gave out with a *crack*, and the shouts cut off.

<Your tribe has decreased to 154 members.>

This wasn't the croc from the island. This one was bigger and still had the *XX* above it. Which meant the ones from the island were still out here.

Somewhere else along the line of harvesters, another croc-knocker struck—on an unarmored goblin this time, which meant any iron that he'd collected had just gone down the croc's gullet in a tragic loss.

"Poppers and spears!" I shouted, holding my own wicker basket out of the water. "Poppers and spears!"

The *pop pop* of the clay grenades began to erupt against the hard shell of the crocs, and they roared in anger. There were no tesla wasps to intervene this time. Just a dozen goblins with ceramic-tipped spears and minor explosives.

<Your tribe has decreased to 152 members.>

A pair of goblins on the shore angled one of the RPPs toward us, and I dove face-first under the water as they struck the primer. I could see the flare of the rocket motor pass over me before the explosion created a wave of water that knocked me almost to the shore. I held the basket tight to my chest as I broke the surface for air.

The croc reeled from the rocket-propelled popper but recovered quickly and opened its mouth. I could see the muscles bunch up before the hard knob at the end of its tongue shot out within a few centimeters of my head and conked one of the rocket goblins on the skull. Ceramic chips flew as the goblin was knocked off its feet. But I didn't get a notification for its demise. Thank you, ceramic! Thank you, stone sloth totem!

<*Your tribe has decreased to 149 members.*>

That didn't mean things were going *well,* of course. The crocs weren't just hungry, they were *angry.* Especially the one that had nearly hit me. It fixed its eyes on me, and there was more than ordinary animal intelligence there. It opened its jaws again and reeled back its tongue for another shot. As the knob passed me, I saw a red shine and realized: its tongue was wrapped around a piece of iron the size of my fist.

Iron tools! The damn crocs were already technically *in* the Iron Age! And they were clobbering us with it.

Well, I'd come here to get iron. And damned if I was leaving without it. I still had the hooked ceramic knife in my hand. Dropping the wicker basket, I reached out and grabbed the iron nodule, bringing the knife underneath the thick, cord-like tongue and yanking it back.

Ceramic is sharp. Unbelievably sharp. The croc's tongue resisted a little. But once the knife bit in, all that resistance evaporated and the tip of its tongue split away, along with the iron it clutched. The croc-knocker roared in pain, tongue whipping around with the released tension. It fixed its yellow eyes on me and barreled through the water. It ignored the closest goblin, the unfortunate frog-vomiter, and came straight on.

Maybe I hadn't thought this plan through all the way.

I sloshed my way toward the shore. Meanwhile, all the goblin builders on the shore had grabbed spears and were now shouting a rallying war cry as they charged toward *me* with the intent to protect their king. I passed the line, prize clutched in my hand.

<Your tribe has decreased to 145 members.>

More poppers went out, and another RPP fired from the shore at one of the other croc-knockers. But nothing seemed to deter the bog monsters. I even saw the wranglers launch the net at one of them, but the croc just dipped below the surface and gave it the slip before coming back up to crunch on another guard.

<Your tribe has decreased to 143 members.>

We were getting our collective butts handed to us. I reached the shore, dripping and gasping for air, with my prize pressed to my chest. Most of the other iron harvesters had made it to shore with their spoils as well. But at least half the fighters had been swept aside like detritus on the surface of the water. Still, it hadn't been as big a slaughter as it might have without the ceramic armor or the stone sloth totem boost.

I stumbled my way up the bank alongside the rest of the harvesters and what remained of the guards. We weren't even a threat to the crocs. We were *snacks.* Despite conquering the litmus test I'd set for us with the stone sloth alpha, we'd bounced off the bog again in glorious fashion. At least I'd gotten a little trophy. I couldn't imagine the iron ore we'd collected would amount to being worth the price of ten-plus goblins, but, where at first you don't succeed, iterate and test again. We'd learn from this and—

A growing cascade of squawks brought my attention to the two croc-knockers that had levered themselves up on the bank and begun stomping around the shore, chasing goblins carrying their baskets of meager takings back into the forest bordering the swamp. They caught sight of me and their eyes slid up to my bone crown, then narrowed. Oh hell. They could recognize me. Both bellowed deep, guttural growls and started dragging themselves toward me.

We beat a hasty retreat, not stopping until the tower was back in sight, along with the builders. The crocs had stopped chasing us at the tree line, and the scrappers in their bog disguises had caught up. But I wasn't going to risk getting caught out by the shadow wolf that had possessed the cliffords, either. Best not to stick around.

CHAPTER 48

CROC BLOCKED

The problem with the crocs was that ceramic-tipped spears and poppers might as well have been sticks and harsh language as far as the high-level beasts were concerned. Their hide wasn't just tough, it was also thick and scaly. Our weapons weren't penetrating deep enough to draw blood, let alone deter the monsters. I unpeeled the tongue from around the iron prill and folded it up, stashing it in my snack pack on my skinny hide belt in case I got hungry later.

System, how much iron did we collect?

<4.1 chooms.>

Please tell me that's in volume.

<Weight.>

Damn. Without the ability to deter, defeat, or distract the crocs, that was likely to be the result every time. So far, the only thing I'd seen be mildly effective against them was the tesla wasps, which were equally happy to zap us goblins. Weaponizing the bugs wouldn't just be a matter of finding and trapping them—if such a thing could even be done.

"Boss!" Hadfield yelled down from the tower. "You should come see this!"

I glanced at the other goblins and hurried over to the tower, where a rope pulley dropped down and two goblins counterweighted me up at lightning speed. As soon as I landed on the top platform, Hadfield pointed off to the east. A column of white smoke rose from Village Apollo, clearly visible from the bog.

"Oh no. What have the igni done to the village?" I asked.

Hadfield shrugged. "We're getting ready to loft the balloon. What signal do you want to send?"

I considered. The iron gathering had been a disaster. But it was always going to be messy, and I had a few more days before the new guests would arrive. "We're continuing. Resupply and additional personnel."

"You got it! Take a load off, lads!" said Hadfield, grinning. All of the goblins who had been with me in the bog slumped over, moaning. I needed to figure this problem out. They would follow my orders to their own detriment. At least, until their fear response overwhelmed all sense of reason in their little goblin brains, and then they'd break and run. But they would be most effective if they *believed* in my orders. Believed that, somehow, what they were doing was to their benefit. Ordering wave after wave of goblins to their deaths might eventually accomplish my goal, but it would be inefficient and wasteful as the entire workforce would end up paralyzed by fear.

I waited as the goblins set the balloon up and lit the fuel canister. Hell, say nothing of the goblins, *I* was feeling demoralized. I couldn't even go for a run to blow off steam because there were monsters in the forest. But I could at least go for a short glide. As the balloon began to ascend, I borrowed one of the personal gliders and hopped on the platform. The lizard-skin balloon strained against the extra weight, but thanks to the burning goblin excrement, the air slowly started warming enough to pull me off the ground. I rose up past the cheering goblins who'd stopped working on the tower to watch the balloon loft. They'd take a midday break in order to shimmy up the tether and dive off. Some of them would even have gliders. What pleasure the rest got out of bouncing off their heads, I couldn't say.

As the platform lifted above the trees, I got yet another kick in the teeth. The croc-knockers were now dozing in the reed area we'd cleared, next to our bricks that we'd set to dry. Well, they weren't bricks anymore. The crocs had smashed everything vaguely goblin-related in the clearing. They knew which direction we'd come from. Just one more problem.

The balloon reached full height none too soon. I spotted the glider inbound from the east and hoisted the signal flag. The light aircraft did a tight circle, hooking around the balloon and drawing close enough for me to see one of the wranglers lying prone in the harness. He recognized me and gave a quick tilt of his wings. I waved back, then grabbed onto the platform as a strong gust hit the balloon.

"Woah!" I said. The glider pilot seemed to be having issues of his own, as his aircraft nearly inverted. He wrestled it back on course and turned back east. Maybe a half-kilometer toward the village, his wings bucked and nearly folded in on themselves. A wall of wind hit his glider like a hammer, and it was all he could do to keep from being hammered down into the treetops below.

"Reel me in!" I shouted down.

The goblins below had no chance of hearing me. In fact, they'd formed a circle and started doing *the wave* in anticipation of me jumping. I held on tight to the balloon platform, wondering why, in my infinite wisdom, I hadn't thought to include anything like, say, a seatbelt.

When the wind hit the lizard-skin envelope, it nearly jerked the platform right out from under me. I felt the whole ensemble buck and pull against the tether. The glider went flying, despite my attempts to grab at it. Below me, the goblins panicked as the sudden windstorm kicked through the trees. Some of them had the presence of mind to grab the rope and start pulling down the balloon. But too many of them yanking on it at once while the wind pulled the other direction would stress the line. It wouldn't be long before—

Snap.

My stomach lurched as the balloon separated from the tether and spun in the wind. I prepared to jump, ready to abandon ship—until I saw what was under me. The wind had blown the balloon to the northwest at the end of its tether, to the point where I now hovered over the site of our unfortunate battle that afternoon. If I bailed out now, I would land right next to the two croc-knockers. The bastards were tripping me up again, and it wasn't even on purpose this time! I had no choice. I held on as the loose balloon continued westward. Unhelpfully, the System provided my airspeed/altitude window.

This was a disaster. I couldn't bail out. But I couldn't keep floating forever, either. The fact I was still gaining altitude was problematic as well. I reached up and bashed the fuel canister out of place. The fiery jar of goblin scat went tumbling down into the bog below. Curiously, when it hit the surface of the water, instead of snuffing itself out, the flame spread rapidly across the surface and flared for a moment near an island. That startled a flock of birds, who quickly flew up and nearly knocked me out of the balloon. I swatted at the little devils, but they had sharp beaks and boy did they let me know it. One of them succeeded in tearing a small hole in the gas envelope.

"Ah, hell," I swore. Looked like climbing in altitude wouldn't be a problem anymore. The balloon leveled out as the hot air began to escape.

I was still high enough to get a lay of the land from a bird's-eye view, so I focused on committing the terrain to memory. Navigation on Rava wasn't difficult. Between the moon and the mountains to the northeast, I always had a positive visual marker. Plus the several bluffs that dotted the forest north of the plains were distinct enough.

The bog extended west and north in this direction, though it was roughly the shape of a crescent moon hooked around a peninsula on our side of the wetland. The balloon was carrying me more west than north, and I wasn't sure what was on the other side of the bog. I hadn't taken a long-range glider out that far because the lack of thermals made the return journey uncertain. Go figure.

Over the next hour, I watched for a better spot to drop as the balloon slowly descended on its own. Somewhere with land, and not just a small crop of rocks that a croc-knocker could easily get onto. I didn't want to drop *in* the bog, but dropping on the other side of it would mean a long trek either through or around it anyway, and that might be even more dangerous than the croc-knockers. I had to at least get out of the croc-infested eastern shore. Every minute carried me farther from the tribe, but also farther from the clutch of croc-knockers that we'd pissed off.

I spotted an island with a bit of a hill to the west that my flight path was taking me *mostly* near. It wasn't quite steep enough to qualify as a proper bluff, but it might do in a pinch. Best of all, I couldn't see any crocs sunning on the waterside. On my current flight path, I'd pass within a few dozen chooms of it. It looked like my best bet would be to get out of the water quickly, and then I could work on getting back to the expedition. As the balloon floated over the island, steadily losing altitude, I wriggled out of the lines of the platform, reached up with my bogging knife, and sliced open the balloon. The whole thing deflated, and both I and the balloon began to free-fall.

The human part of my stomach still jumped up into my throat at the idea of such a suicidal fall. But, of course, it wasn't any threat to me as a goblin. I just had to make sure I landed headfirst.

Hitting the water felt like being slapped with a rock, but my head pushed through, and then buried itself halfway in the mud at the bottom. I beat at the base of the bog bed, trying to dislodge myself as my prosthetics waved in the air above the surface. Luckily, I'd loosened up the mud on impact, so I came out relatively easily and thrust my head above water for a breath. The balloon and platform had fallen somewhat close by.

First order of business: Get the remains of the ensemble to land.

A splash in the water somewhere behind me drew my attention. I turned around to see a ripple in the water headed my way.

Oh, no. First order of business: Don't become lunch. I splashed through the water, trying to stay ahead of whatever was coming. I was still a dozen feet away when a wide, spade-shaped head breached the water, along with a massive shell. It was kind of like a turtle from Earth, only this one was wide, flat, and horned with a crest of red, fibrous kelp growing on the back of its neck. Huh. I half expected it to start spitting fire and trying to kidnap princesses from Italian plumbers. It hissed at me.

I relaxed a bit as the System put its level above its head: *9.* We'd taken care of much worse. Only—I'd had my tribe at a time. No, no. My first instinct was right: Alarm was perfectly warranted. I resumed my panicked retreat as the turtle's head dipped out of view.

The ripples approached, way too fast for something that was supposed to be as slow as a turtle. I was never going to make it.

CHAPTER 49

MAROONED

The jaws of the turtle opened and lunged toward me, snapping and gnashing. They locked around my chest and squeezed so hard I thought I might come apart. It wasn't as bad as getting stabbed by the javeline spear, but it was damn close.

<Head of the Snake activated.>
<Your tribe has decreased to 142 members.>

Of course, I couldn't die unless I was the last member of the tribe. Instead, a random goblin would take the hit for me. I beat at the turtle's head as it tried to take another chunk out of me. This time, it forced me under the water and held me against the muddy bottom. I kicked and punched, unable to breathe. Its sharp jaws dug into my center, trying to get purchase.

<Head of the Snake activated.>
<Your tribe has decreased to 141 members.>

God, the thing was *strong.* It felt like pushing against a brick wall. Leading from the rear, I sometimes forgot just how weak goblins were as individuals. The turtle dragged me across the bottom. My lungs burned. Would drowning just start ticking down goblins?

I didn't have to find out, as the turtle whipped its head around and tossed me over its shell. I cartwheeled through the air, splashing back down into the bog water. Ol' boy was probably frustrated with the fact that I wasn't dead already, but it planned to rectify that situation presently. I got my bearings as quickly as I could and reached down to my hide belt. The turtle came back around, swimming just under the surface. This time, when its head broke the surface and made to chomp me again, I stuffed a popper in its mouth instead.

Startled by the audacity, the turtle reeled back and chomped down. I barely managed to get my fingers out of the way before its jaws snapped shut, as if the popper were a gumball. A bright flash shone through its nose and eyes, along with a gout of flame from its nostrils that singed my fur. The thing froze, blinked, and looked at me, bewildered.

"There's more where that came from," I warned as I backpedaled toward the island. "Just try it again. Actually, please don't try it again."

Smoke billowed out the thing's nostrils. Honestly it was a shock the popper hadn't blown its head completely off, but I guess the turtle was made out of sterner stuff than the low-level clifford that had chomped a bomb fruit my first day on Rava. Still, it glared at me with a wary eye, probably debating if I was a morsel worth the trouble. After a tense moment in which I held another popper out and ready, its internal calculus must have fallen on the side that there were less spicy meals around. It sank below the surface with a final glare. The ripples headed away, and I let out a breath and replaced the popper in my padded case. I only had two of them left. I'd have to make them count.

With the turtle gone, I was able to wrestle the wreckage of the waterlogged balloon up onto the shore of what looked like a large island. I dragged the wreck up higher, hoping that the croc-knockers wouldn't go farther from the shore than I'd seen them previously. They seemed to have a set territory, but they were clearly not our biggest fans, so they might make an exception for me.

In the grand scheme of things, I hadn't drifted far from the tribe. Two, maybe three kilometers. I could even still see hints of the smoke from the main camp through the canopy. But three kilometers on foot to a lone goblin might as well have been another continent. Every time I'd been isolated since setting foot on Rava, I'd immediately been under threat. And the bog wouldn't exactly be kind to a rescue party, either. If a rescue came for me. They would have to A) know where to find me, and B) survive the swamp themselves. We'd lost almost 10 percent of the tribe just trying to steal a little iron to smelt, so that didn't seem likely. No. If anyone was going to get me out of this situation, it was me.

While I pulled off my wet cloak and hung it on a low branch to dry, I took stock of all the tools and materials I had handy. I'd taken to carrying a hide cord belt with a few small bags on it and a hard case for a few emergency poppers. Of those, I had two left. I also had some cordage, my hooked bogging knife, and a set of ceramic precision tools. I had some dried fish and meat as well. It wasn't much. But, I wasn't being digested in a monster's stomach while my tribe slowly ticked down, so that was a plus.

From the balloon, I salvaged the lizard-skin envelope, the rigging, the heating cradle, and most of the platform. The hole I'd torn in the skin looked potentially reparable. I just needed cordage small enough to thread through, and fuel (or rather, more food than I had, in order to manufacture it inside my own body). And a favorable wind. I ran a hand through my fur. And to not be a borderline helpless, one-meter-tall goblin.

Enough of that. That was defeatist thinking. This was a setback, but I was *not* going to let it define me. I would *not* spiral, and I would *not* wallow in my misfortune. That wasn't me. I push forward. Always. And I never let anyone or anything define my limitations. I thought back to the footprints on the edge of the campsite. *Something* had figured out how to survive in this place, despite the carnivores, the insects, and whatever other threats lurked. Of course, that something *was* another lurking threat. But if I was going to make a list of all the things in Rava that could kill me, I'd die of old age before I finished.

It was time to go to work.

After a quick snack.

And maybe a nap.

CHAPTER 50

BOGLINS

<Your tribe has decreased to 138 members.>
<1 Hobgoblin Scrapper has been added to your tribe.>
<2 Hobgoblin Wranglers have been added to your tribe.>
<1 Noblin Ignis has been added to your tribe.>
<Your tribe has increased to 151 members.>

I woke up shivering in the oilskin cloak. Goblins typically nested for warmth and reproduction, but I'd spent the night alone, on an elevated platform that I'd pulled up into the crook of a low tree in order to put *any* amount of distance between myself and ground-based predators. I didn't seem to be suffering the malaise typical of a restless goblin night, so that was a plus—if a small one.

Plan A was to repair the balloon and float out of here on a change of the wind. But that necessitated more food than I had in order to produce the methane-rich goblin scat. Fish were my best bet for that. I spent the morning making a pair of flexi-pole fish traps—a combination fishing pole/flex-a-pult that would swing a hooked fish back onto the shore. I'd seen fish in the bog, including some that were big enough to eat *me*. I used what was left of my meat to bait the small hooks and the cordage from my pouch to make the lines, and then cast them out into the bog.

With the traps active, I set out to explore my immediate surroundings. I crested the top of the hill and looked out west, where a thick layer of brush spread out. I couldn't see any crocs on the shores leading down to the water. Maybe they were too steep, or maybe the beasts were still asleep instead of sunning themselves on the silt banks. Good riddance. I hoped I didn't see any all day. I did, however, spot—or rather hear—a nest of the tesla wasps nearby, by their telltale electric snaps and pops. And I did not want to run afoul of them, either.

I made it a couple hundred meters or so by midmorning, at which point I reached the western shore of my little island. I also heard the distant *twang* of the flexi-pole going off, so I decided to head back. Sure enough, there was a fish that had splatted against the rocks with a very shocked expression, hook still in its mouth. I collected the meat, reset the trap, and headed back to my meager camp to start a fire.

With the dampness of the bog and with no other goblins for a carousel, it would be tough to get a fire going. At least through traditional means. When I'd met Rufus, he'd struck a fire by combining a pair of liquids from a set of small vials. I didn't have those two chemicals, but what I did have was a trio of small clay balls filled with volatile juice.

I collected some kindling and sticks, as well as some creeping ivy from the trees, and sat down with one of the poppers and my ceramic precision tools. One was a tiny hand drill, and that's the one I went to work with. In my old world you might call it a pin drill, with a bit about 0.8 millimeters across, if I judged it right.

It took a few minutes, working slowly to avoid catastrophic failure, for the ceramic bit to auger through the hardened clay and penetrate the softer material within. I carefully tipped the opening toward my small pile of fuel. The bomb fruit juice didn't blend perfectly with the oily goblin scat and sulfur mix of the poppers. It took a few moments, but a bead started to form at the lower opening, growing to about the size of a pea before breaking off and dropping over the tinder I'd scraped together.

I quickly slathered a bit of mud over the opening to seal it, and then struck the wet spot in the tinder with the hilt of my bogging knife. There was a *crack* and a smell like the Fourth of July, and then a tiny flame nestled in the fluff.

<Goblin Technology Unlocked: Incendimal Fire-Starties>
<The igni are going to love that.>

Oh boy.

I got down on my hands and knees and blew into the budding flame until I had a decent fire going, then set the remains of the fish to roast on a piece of bark. As it cooked, I sat back with some vines from the forest and my knife to make a cord fine enough to stitch up the lizard-frill balloon. The crackle and pop of the fire kept me company as I worked, blending with the sound of the bog—which was mainly the sound of insects interspersed with the occasional croc-knocker bellow. So far, none of them had accosted me on this island.

I'd gotten so used to the noise of the village. The goblins were many things, but *quiet* wasn't one of them. Running around at top speed, chittering, biting, and just generally being menaces made the bluff sound a bit like a daycare from hell for most of the day. But it had become *my* daycare from hell. I didn't like being alone.

I heard the *twang* of the flexi-pole again, only without the *splat* that meant a catch. I sighed, getting to my feet. Fish had gotten lucky this time. I grabbed a few morsels and some fishbones to make a better hook. One small fish wasn't going to get me very far.

I trekked down the hill of the island to the coast, but when I saw what had happened, I stopped and dropped down to the ground.

Five small hominids stood by the water, examining the sprung fishing trap, while a sixth sprawled on the silt with a red welt running vertically up its ugly, fleshy face. I watched from my concealed position as one of them smacked the other fishing trap with the butt of its pronged spear, causing the contraption to go off. It somehow *also* managed to smack the one already prone on the ground. Judging from their spears and their fleshy, webbed feet, these had to be the same creatures that broke into the wagons and stole our supplies.

They looked like, well, they looked like *goblins*, albeit furless, fleshy, and fishy. It had to be a subspecies or variant. And if they were a type of goblin, then my ability to command them might work on them.

System, will these things defer to a goblin king?

<Yes. Boglins are a variant goblin capable of leadership under a goblin king.>

Perfect! Swamp-dwelling goblins! The System provides.

I stood from my hiding spot, striding confidently down the hill. I raised my hand in greeting and offered a big, toothy grin.

"Ahoy! I'm King Apollo!"

The boglins stared at me. Still not close enough, apparently. I kept approaching, waiting for the prompt to catch up and the System to tell me that the tribe had grown by another six members.

System, what gives? I thought these guys will answer to a goblin king.

<They do.>

I stopped, confused. I figured it out about the time one of the spears hit me in the gut. A lance of pain washed over my body. The world shook, and every muscle in my body lit up like it had been struck by lightning. As I toppled, I looked down at the spear embedded in my belly.

Huh, I thought, before I lost consciousness.

CHAPTER 51

KING RINGO

<Your tribe has decreased to 139 members.>
<Your tribe is dismayed from heavy losses. A spawning penalty has been applied.>
<Your tribe is distraught due to their missing king. No variant goblins were born.>
<Your tribe has increased to 142 members.>

"Boss, boss! Wake up!"

I came to with a wicked headache and rubbed the spot of blackened fur on my belly where the spear had singed me. I was in a loose cage woven from bog tree branches and vines. In an adjoining cage next to me knelt a hobgoblin scrapper who had a meaty hand on my shoulder. He looked a bit rough around the gills, but no worse than I felt.

"Where are we?"

"Boglin village," said the scrapper. He scowled. "Nasty snot-nosed boglins. Ain't even got fur wot like a propp'r goblin. Spotted 'em the other night. When the wranglers hopped on the cliffies to chase 'em down, they made scarce and some nasty cloud took over the puppers. The boggies caught me from behind with those zap-sticks and brought me back here."

I pulled myself to a sitting position, groaning. The sun was still up but dropping low to the horizon. I wasn't sure how far I'd been moved, but it must have been a decent distance because there was a village here, and not a small one either. I counted at least twenty goblins attending to tasks—with a diligence I recognized.

A group of six were working together to erect more wooden structures while another set shaved down poles. Yet a third group had strung up a neatly quartered turtle to bleed out into dried mud bowls. The turtle I'd seen had been level 9. That was no easy foe for rudderless goblins.

Something had moved their hands in the same direction.

"The boglins have a king, don't they?" I asked.

The scrapper nodded. "Seen 'im. *Ringo.* Big bloke, fish crown."

"Fish crown?"

The scrapper held his hands up at the side of his head. "Fish crown."

I sighed. "Looks like I need to have a talk with fish-crown Ringo, king to king."

Several of the boglins, drawn by the noise, drew close and gave us curious looks. They didn't move like the goblins of Tribe Apollo. They were slow, smooth, and almost sinuous, whereas forest goblins were manic, jerky, and chompy. The boglins moved like, well, the *bog*; in such a way that you might lose them against the background if you weren't paying attention. Their skin being the color of mud with pin-lines of light green that looked like peat moss only lent to that effect, as did the greenish-yellow fur that grew in patches on their heads, necks, and shoulders. But they could move fast if they wanted to. The one who had thrown the spear at me did so in the blink of an oversized eye.

One of the onlookers knocked the back of his spear against my cage. I backed away, and they undid the simple latch that I probably could have jimmied from the inside without much trouble. I think it was more to hold the door shut than keep me secure. The only problem was, I had nowhere to go. Even if I could get out of the cage (easy), past the native boglins (slightly harder), and off this island (harder still), I'd still be in the middle of the swamp filled with predators and a hostile goblin tribe (impossible).

So, instead of busting out, I waited for them to open the paltry jail and got to my feet. At least they'd left my prosthetics attached. They pointed at them for a moment, and I looked over at the scrapper.

"They was trying to decide wot yer legs were."

I saw a handful of small rocks change hands, and then I realized they were the scales of some creature. This tribe had developed currency—and gambling. Good God, the idea of goblins at a Texas Hold'em tournament . . . well, some things are too horrific to consider. That was one technology I didn't want Tribe Apollo adopting.

Slender fingers wrapped around my arms as two boglins grabbed me by the shoulders and pushed me out onto the loose mud of the village.

"Boss!" the scrapper shouted after me.

"Sit tight," I said. "I'll be back."

I managed to keep on my blades as they scrambled me up the hill. This was what passed for high ground in the bog, I supposed. I was surprised goblins were able to survive without a bluff here. But they'd clearly managed to avoid being wiped out by croc-knockers long enough to grow into a tribe of thirty, maybe thirty-five strong.

A wooden fort dominated the top of the hill, held in place by mud slathered against the base of the walls. Two boglins guarding the front of the fort moved a section of the wall out of the way so my escorts could shuffle me through the opening and into the apex of the bog tribe's village.

I smelled the king before I saw him. The unmistakable musk of old microwaved fish preceded him. He came out, legless and fat, carried on a chair supported by four boglins. Whereas the other boglins were patchy and mottled, the king had a mane of greenish hair that was slicked back with some sort of oil or grease. On top of that was what I can only describe, as the scrapper had said, as a fish crown. No amount of words could ever do this rancid thing justice. As if I needed more proof of his kingship, his ambulatorily challenged stumps waggled in the air as the four boglins struggled under the weight.

"It's true, then!" he said, pointing a stick toward my crown of bones. His chair bearers managed to get him mostly facing me, but every few seconds one or another would lose balance and he would have to twist his neck to keep me in sight as the raised chair tilted or rotated. "An invading king from the forest!"

I shrugged out of the grip of the two boglins and stepped forward. The king cringed, but I was clearly unarmed. Curious that he would be so skittish with thirty-odd tribesmen ready to die for him. "I'm not invading!" I protested.

"Ho-hum! You built your tower on my shore, floated your balloon of stitched skins as a threat, and attacked the 'knockers to show you had no fear. Strange way of *not* invading!"

"I'm not lying," I said. But I had to admit, from King Ringo's perspective, my actions could be read as very, *very* hostile. In a way, I was his javeline. I was the unknown force on his doorstep threatening his sovereignty and the safety of his tribe. He had no way of knowing that I had no ill intentions against him.

"I don't want to live in the bog, I just wanted to collect some iron ore! It grows on the peat moss, and even the crocs have it in their mouths."

The king looked down, and I noticed a scruffy-looking goblin somewhat smaller than the others.

"Erm, King Ringo, I believe he means the clangy minerals the croc-knockers use to incapacitate their prey. But this is impossible. No one would be foolish enough to pry open the maw of a 'knocker to steal their knob."

A talking variant, some kind of advisor boglin. Just what I needed, some crooked vizier figure.

"I know what *iron* is, fool!" The king shifted uncomfortably. "You're right, of course. You can't beat a croc."

I reached down, fumbling for my snack pack, which had been taken, along with my knife, the poppers, and my tools. "Where are my things? I can prove it."

King Ringo waved his hand. One of his goblins slinked away, and returned a few minutes later with my belt, my knife, and most surprising of all, the glider I'd dropped from the balloon. I was worried he would handle the poppers too roughly, but he showed adequate care with all my things. Rather than bring them to me, he took them to the boglin king, who began to root through with much less finesse. He fished around in the snack pack and pulled out the severed tongue I'd kept, throwing it on the ground as if it were a snake.

His advisor variant knelt down to examine it. "It is indeed as he claims. A tongue this size must have belonged to a full-grown 'knocker. Curious, Great King."

"It's not curious!" barked the king. "It's downright suspicious! As is the rest of this!" He pulled out my ceramic hook knife and waved it in the air. "Swamp Spirit, what manner of blade is this? Some sort of mud? And don't tell me *unknown* again!"

From his frustrated squawk, I imagine the System must have done just that.

"It's not mud, O King," I said, taking a page from Rufus's book. Flattery couldn't hurt. "It's clay, such that we find in the forest and bake or fire. It becomes hard enough to hold an edge."

King Ringo held it between his thumb and forefinger as his stumps wiggled. "You seek more of this in my land!"

"I've already told you, I just wanted iron ore."

The king snuffled as he dug through the rest of my pack. He pulled out one of the poppers, raising it up and testing it with his teeth. I moved forward, intent on warning him, but he recoiled, shrieking, and I felt the jolt of a hard rod hit my lower back. Lightning shot across every muscle in my abdomen, sending me to the ground, coughing. One of the boglins had hit me with his spear. Surprisingly, I felt no blood when I probed the spot.

After I recovered, I straightened. "What are you frightened of, King Ringo?" I asked. "You're a goblin king, are you not? You can't die while you still have a tribe."

"You'd like me to think that, wouldn't you?" he sneered. He leveled the knife at my chest. "But a king can kill a king. Were I not so noble, I could gut you here and now. I could take your goblins. Then, *I* could take *your* tribe, as you no doubt planned to do with mine." He settled back. "Lucky for you, I'm so kind and generous."

System?

<He's telling the truth.>

About the *kings killing kings* thing, at least. I swallowed. Even the javeline couldn't kill me outright—though they'd tried. This goblin held my life in his fat, webbed hands. "So what's stopping you?"

Ringo leaned back, reveling in his power. "Why should I? What use have I for blue-furred squabblers who can't even swim? Keep to your forests and trees. What care is it of mine? But my scouts told me you had a *fire*. The swamp is too wet to burn. You must carry it with you." He shook the popper. "Is it within *these*? You have knives sharper than flint and towers and floating sacks of skin and winged, whistling flyers. I want it all!"

"You want the secret technology of Tribe Apollo?" I asked.

"Yes! Give it to me!" He shared a look with his advisor. "Then I'll consider letting you go."

Clearly neither of them had any intention of doing that. But I didn't think the king would kill me, either. I spread my hands. "Well why didn't you say so? I'm happy to share."

The boglin king's advisor narrowed his eyes at me. "Sire, he must be lying."

"I know that!" said Ringo, kicking his stubby leg remnants. "Take him back to his hut and give me time to think."

The two boglins grabbed me again, and I struggled. "But I just said I'd give you what you asked for!"

"That's why it's so suspicious!" snarled Ringo. He tested the edge of my knife against his thumb. "No one *gives* a goblin anything. If I've learned anything here, it's that." He sunk his head into his shoulders. "Everything in the world looks down on goblins. If they don't eat us, they kill us for sport. Mark me, I'll wring the secrets from you yet. My tribe *needs* that knowledge. And you're not leaving until I get it."

CHAPTER 52

MIND-BOGLIN INVENTIONS

<Your tribe has decreased to 139 members.>

They put me back in the cage next to the scrapper, not even bothering to latch it this time, for all King Ringo's paranoia. I opened it and stepped outside, and took a second to unlatch the scrapper's door as well. My partner had spent the evening digging a hole in his cage, only to find that water quickly filled in anything he dug out.

"Not much of an escape tunnel," he admitted, settling back against the bars of his cage. "Wot you reckon, boss?" He made a noise like a rocket taking off and clapped his hands. "Make like with the porkbellies? A little rocket-tree action for King Ringo?"

"No," I said. "I'm going to escape. And then I'm going to help him."

"*Help* him? You know wot he's got us in, right now? A *cage.* We put night haunts in them. And you know what comes next."

"It's not even locked," I said, swinging the door open and stepping inside with the scrapper. I looked around at the rest of the island through the bars and sighed. "I don't hate this tribe—or Ringo, for that matter. I pity them. And it's true they need us more than we need them, but we can't start wars with everyone we meet. Not every problem can be solved by launching a rocket at it." I sat back, muttering. "Besides, we have no sulfur. You know how the icky-putty works."

The scrapper grunted and went back to his hole. I wasn't wrong, though. Ringo might be a half-mad swamp-brained buffoon, but we each stood more to gain as friends, and only stood to lose as enemies. I just had to somehow convince him of that. He wanted fire, ceramic, and ballooning. I could give him that and more. I could give him boats. I could give him armor. I could let him walk.

I stepped out of the scrapper cage and approached a pair of nearby boglins.

"I want to make a gift for King Ringo," I said. I gave them a list of supplies, and they looked at each other and departed. A few minutes later, the advisor boglin showed up at my cell. "What's this about a grift for Ringo? Are you trying to scam the great king and steal his hard-earned resources?"

"A *gift*," I said. "I want to make him something."

"You want to take his something? Spoken like a true thief!"

I smacked a fist into my palm. "That's a reach and you know it."

"Fine," he said, crossing his arms and sniffing. "I heard you true. But I still don't trust you! What are you planning?"

"First I want to give you a name. Ringo's got one. An . . . interesting one, at that. You're clearly important around here. Why don't you have one?"

The advisor hesitated. "My king has not seen fit to give me one."

"How about George?"

The advisor worked it around his mouth. "Gee-oor-jah."

"Close enough."

Despite his best efforts to mask his emotions, I could see the excitement in the boglin's tapping feet. "Very well. What do you want to give King Ringo?"

I lifted one of my legs. "I want to make him something like this."

The advisor looked down at the mechanical joint that connected my lower leg remnant to the sloth-claw prosthetic. "Hmm . . ." he said. "I shall take the idea to my king."

He left, and I turned to the scrapper. "See? They can be reasoned with."

The scrapper shrugged and kept digging.

Several hours passed, well into the eclipse, before George returned.

"He's not interested."

"What?" I asked.

George shrugged. "What need has a king of false legs? Being carried is the mark of true royalty, yet you are carried by no one. This is why you are a false king."

"Did you even really speak to him?"

"I may have got distracted by official duties."

I buried my face in my hands and screamed into my palms. Fugg me for wanting to walk and run and jump instead of getting carted around on a litter and thrown down cliffs, right? So un-kingly. The scrapper whistled and made an explosion sound behind me. I was beginning to agree.

It looked like I was stuck. Whatever I said, the boglins assumed I was lying—even if I expressly agreed with them! What frustrating people.

But they were still goblins. And it seemed like goblins in this world, above all else, needed to stick together. Even with what limited resources I had, I could probably kill Ringo and take his people. All I had to do was trick him into biting down on one of those poppers and *poof*, thirty to forty boglins added to the tribe. But I didn't want to hurt Ringo. I wanted more neighbors in Rava that I could trust—even if I could only trust them to think I was out to get them.

The advisor tossed a small sack down on the floor of the cave and stormed off, which looked to contain the cast-off bits of fish guts that even the other boglins didn't want. My stomach growled, and fire or not, I fell upon the offal with relish, chomping down on scale, bone, and meat. I had to make a concerted effort to stop my goblin side from devouring the whole bag, and passed half of it through the bars to the scrapper.

"Here. You'll need your strength."

"Aww, *King*," he said, taking the sack. He shoveled the rest into his mouth and spat a bone in the direction of the fort. "He may have their loyalty, but you got our *trust*. You're twice the king wot 'e is."

I felt the lethargy start to take me. This was a problem I'd have to sleep on.

CHAPTER 53

NEGOTIATING TACTICS

"You want to go into the bog?" asked Ringo. He raised one fuzzy eyebrow and leered down from his chair, center of gravity dangerously forward as the boglins struggled to keep it level. "I told you I want *fire*. I want *towers*. I want *flight*!"

"Yes, O King," I said. "The answer to those is in the bog. Fire lives in the water. I saw it as I flew over. I can give you fire, I can give you flight. But I won't give them to you for free."

The king shared a look with his advisor. "You wish to trade safe passage through the swamp for these secrets?"

I shook my head. "No, sire. I've decided to stay with the tribe voluntarily. I wish for us to grow closer. As . . . friends."

The advisor boglin, George, stood on his toes to whisper into Ringo's ear, but there was still so much distance between them due to the lofted throne that he had to whisper extra loudly and I could hear him quite clearly.

"*Sire, he's clearly planning to get close only to assassinate you!*"

"*I know that, fool! We will keep a close eye on him. Find out what he wants.*"

The advisor cleared his throat. "We are pleased you have finally decided to recognize the greatness of King Ringo. An exchange between kings ought to be a give and snatch. So what is it that you want from my gracious king?"

I bowed. "I wish to know how it is our king has kept his people safe from the dangers of the bog. My tribe is weak, and we have fallen victim to the aggression of the croc-knockers. How is it that you've kept them at bay? I'm sure that information is much, *much* too valuable a secret to trade, but I must try."

Ringo snorted a laugh. "Simple. So simple even a forest goblin could grasp it!" He held out his hand, and a pair of goblins came forward carrying a longer version of the boglin spear they'd used to subdue me. He grasped it and then thrust the tip down toward me. I flinched back, which greatly amused him. He chortled and chuckled. But while he did, I examined the tip.

The wood at the end of the spear had been split, and pinched between the bound tines was one of the tesla wasps! The two electric prongs stuck out several centimeters from the end of the rod. They were *shock* spears.

I had assumed the spear that hit me must have had some sort of fast-acting venom powerful enough to knock out even a goblin, despite our resistance to toxins and poisons. But this was an ingenious application. When I'd first encountered the crocs in the bog during my initial recon with Chuck, the only thing that had managed to deter them had been the enraged wasps. Well, a dozen goblins with wasps on the ends of sticks was almost as good as an angry swarm.

"How did you capture the wasps?" I asked.

"You don't *capture* them, fool," said the advisor. "You raid the nest from under the water and steal their eggs. You hatch them *in* the spear."

Genius. Maybe I hadn't given the boglins enough credit.

"Now, being as we're *friends*, now"—the king and advisor shared a *look*—"tell me how fire lives in the swamp."

I cleared my throat. "Very well, O King. As I was passing overhead, I dropped my own fire in the bog. But instead of the water dousing the flame, it caught and spread. I thought little of it at the time, until I saw that!" I pointed at the king's head.

He probed his face with his fingers. "My face?"

"Your hair. You've matted it with a black, greasy fluid from the swamp, yes?"

King Ringo dropped his fingers. "Indeed, a dark spring spurts forth a wonderful liquid. I find it gives my fur a dignified sheen. You seek the sheen? It's very kingly."

"King Ringo, I believe that spring holds the secret to swamp fire. If I teach you to trap it, then we can bring fire back to the village."

Ringo ran a hand through his hair. "Intriguing. What would you need to trap the fire?"

"Merely the help of my scrapper and a device I can fashion from simple hides and wooden poles." I patted my little leather shorts. "I had one with me when I fell, which would speed up the process. But I'm afraid I lost it.

I suppose I'll just have to enjoy your food and hospitality for a week or so longer while I fashion another from your generous supplies."

The advisor whispered up to the king. "*Sire, he's clearly trying to stall his side of the bargain while he mooches food and materials. We recovered the device he dropped!*"

Ringo turned to me. "My advisor says we can provide your capturing device. We will proceed *without delay.* Unless you think there is some reason we should not make haste?"

"Well, we should consider all approaches to this. One should never be—"

"Without delay!" decreed Ringo. He gestured with his rod, and the boglin guards grabbed me.

It took the king a few minutes to gather his personal guard, which consisted of half the boglins in his tribe apparently dedicated to no other task but his own safety. Ringo rolled deep. Honestly, I could learn a thing or two from ol' Ringo. If I managed to pull this off, I vowed not to get isolated from my tribe again. Maybe this sort of thing was fine in my old life, when there was no one to really suffer the effects of my loss. It'd been a high-profile launch, and my picture would probably be on TV for a while with a few moments of silence from people who had never met me. But almost everyone who had ever *really* cared about me left Earth years before I did.

But now, with a tribe to take care of, I had to acknowledge that my risky behavior had put me in compromising positions multiple times. In the interest of delegation and efficient application of resources and lack of delegation, I'd eschewed my own personal safety repeatedly. For the sake of my new friends, I had to take into consideration that mitigations had to be put in place—even if those mitigations were other goblins giving their lives to protect the good of the tribe by not allowing enemies to kill me over and over.

The scrapper was brought out of the cage and joined us, stretching his considerable muscles. "Thanks for springin' me, boss," he said. He leaned in. "*I got a confession. The tunnel weren't shite.*"

His cage hadn't even been locked. "*I've got a plan,*" I whispered back. "*But I don't know if I can get us both out. Are you with me?*"

"*I'm wiv' ye, boss!*" said the scrapper, nodding.

King Ringo hissed. "Stop that whispering! Conspiracy!"

I bowed. "Good king, you've caught me. I had thought to avoid your noticing. But your eyes see all."

"And don't forget it!" Ringo settled back into his chair. "Now. We go to this spring of the sheen-fur water with all haste."

I had thought the boglins slow and plodding, but once they hit the water it was like watching a school of tetras. These guys had a lot of maneuverability thanks to webbing between their fingers and toes, and all the energy in the water that their forest-born cousins did on land. The king's chair cut little white-water wakes as he struggled to keep his seat, and my boglin supervisors pushed me so quickly that my prosthetics rode up on the water like water skis.

Hmm . . . System?

<Fine.>
<Goblin Technology Unlocked: Floaty-Boaty Blades>

Hell yeah.

CHAPTER 54

ICKY SLICKY

It was actually somewhat marvelous, the way the boglins used their tesla wasp rods to zap the croc-knockers that came too close. A few of them still got potshots from range that killed two of our escorts and one of the throne-bearers, causing King Ringo to almost fly out of his chair in a most unkinglike way. But the king of the bog was clearly more willing to expend his tribemates than I wanted to be.

Rava had dealt him a poor hand, for a king. It was a miracle Ringo had even kept his tribe alive in such a hostile environment. Javeline and humans hadn't found him simply because no one *wanted* to go in the bog. He may have been paranoid, vain, and self-important, but he was also modestly successful in the face of an incredible challenge. I really did want to help these guys, if I could. King Ringo's goblins, with King Ringo in or out of the picture, deserved a fair shot at securing their future in Lanclova.

Much like the boglin king's fish crown, I smelled it before I saw it: the sweet-sour tang of petroleum fumes bubbling up through the swamp water. It wasn't crude oil, either. The slick rainbow sheen of film that spread out over the surface of the water was thinner and more pale than unrefined crude oil. This was something else—closer to kerosene, maybe. But unmistakably a hydrocarbon (or this world's equivalent). My heart began to race. I had kept the food bag from the night before, and I skimmed it across the surface with trembling fingers, careful not to get any of the substance on me.

"For my fur," I said to the boglins guarding me. This seemed to placate them as I retied the skin to my belt.

Ringo leaned down from his chair. "I've brought you to the spring. Now, tell me how it can be used for fire!"

"Do you see how the bubbles rise, O King?" I asked, pointing to the gases filtering up from the underwater well. Methane or natural gas would be my best bet—what would normally be burned off as a matter of course in the process of extracting oil. "They contain a strange, invisible miasma that burns like a tree touched by lightning, if you can set them to spark. It's actually what we're smelling right now. But it rises in the air once the bubble bursts, so we have to trap it with this device." I held up the glider.

The scrapper looked at me, confused. He knew well what the glider *actually* was. This part was risky. As I continued speaking, I held up two fingers, and then tilted my head subtly toward the oil slick. "If we collect the miasma from above the spring, we can take it back to the village and use it to make fire. With fire, we can make clay and ceramic—like the knife." I made a fist, as though I was gripping the knife, then flicked my eyes back toward the scrapper and opened it, in the forest goblin hand sign for an explosion. The scrapper looked confused for a moment, but then he put things together. His expression grew serious, and he offered the slightest of nods. Even trying to be subtle, the advisor noticed the exchange that passed between us, and the tiny boglin's eyes narrowed. George was a sharp one. I just hoped my scrapper picked up on the instructions as well.

King Ringo was getting excited. He rubbed his hands together. "It was here, under our noses, the whole time. Oh, yes, King Apollo. You're doing me a great service."

The advisor climbed up the goblin throne-bearers, and then the throne itself to whisper in Ringo's ear. The king's eyes narrowed, and he regained his composure enough to remember that he was supposed to be suspicious of me.

"And I suppose you'd like to collect it yourself, hmm?"

"Oh no, O King Ringo," I said. I raised the folded glider above my head. "The fumes must be gathered from as high as possible for the best potency. It should be Your Majesty himself, atop his tall chair, that does the gathering."

"As if I'd be foolish enough to fall for that!" snarled Ringo. "Invisible miasma? Fire boiling up from the bottom of the bog? He pointed at two of his goblins. "This is clearly dangerous work. You and you, carry King Apollo over the spring. Make sure he collects as much as possible."

The two boglins looked at each other. They reluctantly handed their spears off and one climbed onto the other's shoulders.

"King Ringo," I said. "At least let me use my scrapper for this. He's quite strong, and taller than a boglin."

Ringo's advisor hissed. "*Absolutely not*. In fact, keep him back. Spears!"

The other boglins leveled their spears at the scrapper, who stayed at the edge of the sheen with his hands up in placation. But he winked at me.

"Very well," I said. I clambered onto the shoulders of the boglin, who teetered precariously. "Alright, take us in."

The bottom boglin started forward, slow and steady, causing us to lumber toward the gas bubbles.

System, do the boglins also have blast resistance?

<If you want me to tell you this is a good idea, I'm not going to.>

The three-man tower teetered and almost toppled. I couldn't help thinking that all we needed was a trench coat to get into an R-rated movie, and had to fight back a laugh, lest the king's advisor find it suspicious. Ugh. *Keep it together, Chris.* If I took a dunk in the oil, this plan would go in a decidedly different direction.

We managed to make it directly over the spring. I unfurled the glider and held it overhead, angling it and trying not to let the breeze catch it and torque us over.

"It's working! Is it working? It's working!" said King Ringo, leaning so far forward that the goblins on the back legs of his throne were lifted completely out of the bog, swinging their legs in the air.

I nodded to the scrapper. He gave a series of indecipherable but very conspicuous hand signals, which the boglin next to him noticed. The boglin turned and squawked in alarm to the King's advisor, but as soon as he did, the scrapper punched him in the side of the head.

Scrapper surprise attacks were incredibly effective. The boglin skipped across the surface of the water, leaving his spear spinning in midair. The scrapper grabbed it, held it up, and threw it directly at the bottom boglin in our tower.

I barely had time to widen my eyes in surprise as the spear took him in the chest, and the shock traveled both down, and up the three of us. Every muscle in my body tensed with pain—but it wasn't as bad as when I'd been hit directly.

"*Betrayal!*" bellowed Ringo. "Kill them! *Kill them!*"

I had meant for him to tap the oil slick with the prongs of the wasp to ignite the surface. I don't know what mad goblin logic made him want to throw a spear at a goblin I was *literally riding on*. But then, if they were predictable, they wouldn't be goblins. Of course the boglin tower collapsed.

And of course I started falling toward the oil. My plan was about to go up in flames.

Then the arcing electricity from the tesla wasp skipped across the surface of the oil slick. And the water beneath me turned into a roiling ball of fire. My plan really *did* go up in flames, because my plan *was to go up in flames.*

<Goblin Technology Unlocked: Basic Icky-Slicky Combust'em>

The two boglins that had carried me were instantly incinerated. I felt a little bad about that. The rest of them recoiled from the spreading fire. But the gout of resulting hot air hit the underside of my deployed personal glider, and I managed to hold on despite the weakness from getting tasered by bug-sticks and getting the fur singed off the lower half of my body.

<Head of the Snake activated.>
<Your tribe has decreased to 138 members.>

The blast had still been enough to kill me. At least, it felt like it. I was scorched, and the heat was akin to dancing in the mouth of the forced-air kiln. It was unlike anything I'd ever experienced, and I'd been to a test firing of NuEarth's thirty-two-nozzle rocket motor that liquefied the concrete pad.

The glider bucked and jerked from the turbulent, rising air. I was climbing so fast I thought my arms might pop out of their sockets from the acceleration. My blades kicked helplessly in the air.

I looked back down at the spreading field of fire and the retreating boglins. I'd killed at least eight of them. A quarter of Ringo's tribe swept away like chaff, but they were now closing in on the scrapper.

As they reached him, he looked up and gave me one last salute before he was driven down by spears—ones tipped not with wasps, but with sharp ceramic points stolen from our own wagons.

<Your tribe has decreased to 137 members.>

I hated that it was necessary. Hated how effective it was, and how easily justified, and how willing the goblins were to throw their lives away for creatures like me or Ringo. They would take me to the moon, yes. But I would give them a *reason* to live for me—not just a biological imperative. I looked away, searching for King Ringo. I found him splashing in the water, his throne-bearers having ditched the chair in an effort to distance themselves from the fire. I locked eyes with him and shouted down over the roar of the fire.

"I've kept my side of the bargain, Ringo! *That's* how you make fire in the swamp! And this is how you flyyyyyyy!"

"*Beeeeeetttrraaaaayyyaaaaalll!*"

CHAPTER 55

SWAMPED

The glider carried me up and up, over the burning wellspring. I kept hold as I climbed in altitude, still in pain from the burning and explosion. The sounds, sights, and smells of the swamp faded away and I was just left with the sound of air rushing past. I'd come by air, and I was leaving by air—albeit this time I'd done so by burning myself at the outset in some sort of weird reverse-Icarus situation. Would someone eventually write mythology about me? Perhaps Earth and Rava would share Apollo as a mythical figure.

With the problems of the swamp beneath me, I got my bearings and got the glider pointed southeast, where I spotted a dot in the sky that soon resolved into another glider. It caught sight of me as well and angled my way, flying close enough that the goblin inside could recognize me—at which point it turned and ignited its booster back toward the bluff. Huh. So, Sally had been launching them with a rocket pod for speedy return. Smart.

From the air, it was easy to spot the finished tower on the jutting peninsula a few hundred meters back from the water's edge. I glared down at the croc-knockers basking on the beach as I passed over them. Now I knew their secret. All I had to do was find one of the tesla wasp nests, and we'd have a method of deterring the crocs long enough to get iron. And now I also knew there was oil—or the next best thing—in the bog. All the parts for internal combustion were within reach. We could have a working prototype in a matter of weeks, if the igni were worth their chooms at metallurgy. Yes, the bog was still dangerous. Yes, we'd lose goblins along the way. But progress always came with risk.

Hadfield had finished the tower and started a sprawling network of tree platforms connected by rough rope bridges, effectively turning the tower into a small village's worth of elevated terrain. Defensive emplacements lined the towers, and I saw two turtle shells from the large carnivorous beasts being used to collect rainwater—one for drinking and one for bathing. Though I imagined the goblins would forget which was which with alarming regularity.

The goblins on lookout spotted my glider coming in and raised a ruckus, shouting and jumping and pointing me out to their companions on the ground. Quite a few goblins were busy with tasks down there, including a kiln being worked by a larger goblin in a ceramic mask with a stack of ceramic plates and helmets next to him and a huge basket of charcoal nearby. It seemed like extra goblins had been brought in to aid the man—er, *goblin* hunt.

I angled toward the tower, where they'd apparently bagged another night haunt and put a new totem up. Bringing the glider in, I flared off for a landing. Before I could hit the wood-and-stone top of the structure, goblins flooded out of the opening and packed themselves tightly on the platform, such that there was nowhere to land but *on* my tribe and tilting the top of the tower to a worrying degree. It created a tangled mess as I fell among them, and they equal parts tried to catch me, embrace me, and loft me up like I was crowdsurfing at a metal concert.

I lost the glider in the kerfuffle, and then the whole gaggle of goblins rolled, surging toward me—which then had the effect of spilling a good portion of us over the side and onto the ground in a furry blue cascade of screaming, panicked goblins. Thank goodness for fall damage immunity, because we just ended up in a pile on the floor of the bog, a tangle of flailing limbs and gnawing teeth. Until a pair of strong hands wrapped around my leg remnants, hauling me out.

Even upside down, I recognized the two hobbies. "Chuck, Armstrong!"

"Good to see ye, King," said Armstrong, rotating me upright.

Chuck just looked somewhere between relieved and constipated. Fair, considering what I'd put my lieutenants through. I reached out and put a hand on his shoulder. "Not your fault. You can't be everywhere, and I made a stupid, rash decision that cost this tribe too much. I won't put myself at risk of being isolated again."

Chuck relaxed and looked away. "I just want to see us reach Raphina, boss. We can't do it without you."

Someone must have been cutting onions, because my eyes started to sting. I cleared my throat. "Armstrong! Put me down!" I ordered.

He placed me gently back on the ground.

"Armstrong, I am officially making you captain of my guard. Where I go, you go. If I try to go somewhere *stupid*, you have the authority to prevent me from doing so until I have time to get my head right."

Armstrong froze as a glazed look passed across his face.

<Goblin Technology Unlocked: Secretive Servants>
<Goblins assigned to your personal Secretive Servants can ignore your direct commands under certain circumstances.>

What circumstances?

<Secret ones.>

Haw haw, System. Very funny. I sighed. Oh well. Armstrong shook himself out of his stupor and flexed his prodigious biceps. "I won't let you down, King! Consider me your shadow."

I opened up the tribe hierarchy window and assigned a few goblins underneath him.

"As for you, Chuck," I said. The hobgoblin perked up as I continued. "From now on, in my absence, you have my authority. I want to know that if I'm not around, the tribe is in good hands: yours."

Chuck scowled. "Boss-man, if you're not around, I'm having the entire tribe out looking until I can drag you back."

I huffed. "I don't doubt it. Even if you lost half the tribe pulling me out of the fire—er, metaphorically speaking, of course."

We both glanced down at my singed fur and both elected to ignore it. But really, it was the logical choice. Between gliders and cliffords, Chuck was super mobile. He could be places I wasn't, and had good judgment—for a goblin, of course. Which was somewhere between the judgment of a toddler and that of a golden retriever given explicit instructions not to eat the bacon left on the table.

"Anyway, if croc-knockers are the only obstacle between us, it's not going to stop you much longer. Grab your wranglers. We've got bugs to catch. But first, I want to meet our new variant."

Chuck left to wrangle his wranglers, who I noticed were not on mounts. He must have figured out that whatever that strange swamp spirit was, it was taking all our cliffords. I walked toward the kiln, glancing up at the signal balloon currently being lofted with a goblin holding a flag—a yellow one this time. They must have expanded the semaphore codes while I was gone, too. I had no desire to learn what the yellow flag was dyed with.

Working the kiln was a porcine brute of a goblin with a fleshy potbelly protruding from beneath his furry blue chest. His thick sausage-fingers wrapped around a hooked pole that he looped around the front access for the kiln.

"You must be the new ignis taskmaster," I said.

The ignis tipped his mask to me with his free hand, which rather than a skull mask was one of the ceramic plates fitted to a leather hood with a small slit for his eyes and bulbous nose. "Aye, boss. Y'all had some strange notions on how to work this thing. I smoothed 'em out for you."

"Oh, you got the ceramic parts to fail less?"

He swung open the hatch and pulled out a rack, much to my amazement, of what looked like pork ribs.

"Well, yeah, that too, s'pose. The clay should go further now. Stronger plates, less exploding when you put it in cold." He set the rack down. "But that can wait. Reckon you must be hungry after being stuck in that bog. Javeline rib while you spin your tale of how you got back to us?"

"I think we're going to get along just fine, Prometheus," I said. Maybe I just had Greek mythology on the brain, but naming him after the man who had stolen fire from the gods seemed appropriate.

"Call me Promo," he said, scraping salt onto the rack of ribs. "Now what's this *iron* stuff these boys been telling me yer on about?"

CHAPTER 56

SHOCKING DEVELOPMENT

Before we could get the iron, we still had to grow our own shock sticks from eggs. Raiding a nest for larval tesla wasps meant finding a nest—and that's where the trouble *began*.

Luckily, Chuck and I had found one on our first recon to the bog, and we knew that general location. From that jumping-off point, it was a matter of spotting one of the wasps and following it back to its hidden home in a mound of peat drifting on the surface of the bog. There weren't any crocs in the area, and I had to assume it was because you could hear the faint *hiss* and *pop* of electricity in the nest from the dozens or hundreds of wasps hidden within.

Unfortunately, the crocs stayed away because the wasps seemed like the only thing in the bog grumpier than they were. The wasps were quick to attack the first goblin I sent out to verify the nest's exact location, and he'd been stung a half-dozen times by the time the hobbies pulled him, half-paralyzed, out of the water. He recovered quickly enough, but it would be easy for a goblin to drown if they were stung in a way that they couldn't keep their head above the surface.

"How you want to approach this, boss?" asked Chuck. He crouched on the shore, slinger slung over his shoulder. He stroked his chin. "Poppers?"

"Risks destroying the larvae," I said. I considered. King Ringo had thought he was being much smarter than me when he'd bragged about how they collected the wasps. But really, he'd given away his secret sauce. "The boglins came at them from under the surface."

"Well, that's all fine to *say*," said Chuck, "but I don't breathe mud."

It was a fair point. The boglins were clearly a subspecies of goblin specifically adapted to semi-aquatic environments. I had to assume they either had primitive gills or at least the ability to stay underwater for longer than a forest goblin. I went back to the edge of the shore and rooted around until I found some reeds, pulling the stems out and shaking out the interiors until I had several hollow tubes. I handed one over. "Try this."

Chuck looked down dubiously. "Done this in your old world, yeah?"

"No, but I saw it in a cartoon once."

My wrangler boss raised a fuzzy eyebrow. But he sighed and lowered himself into the water until he was fully submerged, except for the hollow reed just breaking the surface. It bobbed up and down, and I heard the subtle, hollow hiss of his breathing.

<Goblin Technology Unlocked: Sticky-Wet-Breather>

Thank you, clever fox. Insight flashed across the eyes of the rest of the goblins present, and in true goblin fashion, a few moments later they were all scrambling to find reeds of their own to try it out.

I had to imagine it was a similar situation back at the bog tower camp, and a wave of disappointment at Village Apollo, who were landlocked. I put a hand on Armstrong's shoulder before he could rush off.

"We're not going with them," I said.

"We're not?"

I shook my head. "I need to get used to exposing myself to dangerous situations less. The wranglers are animal-handling experts. Let them do what they do best."

The captain of my guard looked noticeably relieved. "Glad your 'ead's on right, King. Meanin' no offense."

"None taken," I said. "Besides, I've seen how capable our goblins are without my direct hand controlling things. We'll let them cook. This time."

I turned around at a *pop* and *snap*, and a thrashing splashing noise. It was just in time to see one of the hobbies cough into his tube, and the big, black, bulbous form of a tesla wasp that had crawled down his snorkel erupt backward out the other end. It arced through the air, prongs out, buzzing furiously, until it landed squarely in the backside of a goblin on the shore still getting his own reed sorted.

The unfortunate receiving goblin squawked, then went completely rigid as the electric sting from the wasp sent a jolt coursing through every muscle in his little blue body. He fell over, fur smoking.

<Goblin Technology Unlocked: Basic Bug Blastics>
<Your tribe has decreased to 136 members.>

Every reed currently sticking out of the water stopped moving momentarily.

"That's horrifying," I said.

"Erm, King? Can we go?" asked Armstrong.

I looked at the hulking hobgoblin wringing his hands and staring in the direction of the tesla wasp nest.

"Armstrong," I chided. "Are you afraid of bugs?"

"Just the ones what sting or bite," the big goblin confided. "Can't sneak attack a bug."

Aww. I actually found that somewhat endearing. "Don't worry, big guy. Let's head back."

"I'm still the strongest goblin in Tribe Apollo, you know," he muttered.

"I know," I said, patting his arm. "I saw you take on a javeline five levels higher by yourself."

The hobgoblin walked a little straighter at that—confidence restored. This king thing wasn't so bad sometimes, even when it was closer to being a camp counselor for a rowdy group of preteens.

We made our way back to the camp, where there was something of a commotion. It didn't take long to figure out why, when I found the boglin advisor George and six boglin bodyguards held at spearpoint by two dozen Tribe Apollo goblins.

I pushed my way through the crowd, angling spearpoints out of the way. "Stop, stop!" I shouted over the clamor. I spotted a couple of singed spots of fur, I'm guessing where the boglins had been forced to employ the shock spears. Promo stood with his big hooked pole, ready to crack heads. Hadfield glared from around the noblin's potbelly, a patch of blackened fur still sizzling. I moved up next to them.

"Woah, woah! Cool your jets, what's going on?"

"Found 'em sneakin' up to the camp, boss," said Hadfield, rubbing his singed spot. "Probably wot to steal more supplies."

"Lies!" said the boglin advisor. "This is a diplomatic delegation, and attacking it is an act of war!" He pointed at me. "We're here to see King Apollo!"

I crossed my arms. "What for?"

The advisor had a few singed spots himself from the debacle with the hydrocarbon spring. It was safe to say we were all a little burned out for the day. He broke eye contact and looked away. "The great King Ringo sent me. He recognizes the cunning of the claw-legged king, Apollo, and admits you are his *near* equal in intellect. Worthy of your crown of lame dry bones—"

That was the wrong thing to say, as a wave of fury rolled through the Apollo goblins present.

"Hey, hey, hey!" I shouted, regaining control of the situation before Ringo lost seven members of his tribe. Once things calmed down, I stepped into the circle so that I was face-to-face with the advisor. "I recommend not trashing the crown. It was their gift to me as their king. Get to the point."

The advisor cleared his throat again—or at least I thought that's what he was doing, until he hawked up a fishbone that had apparently been lodged in his throat. He fished it out of his mouth and discarded it. "The tribe has tasted cooked fish for the first time, and it resulted in a spawning bonus that greatly benefits Tribe Ringo. Ergo, the great King Ringo would like to officially open relations with Tribe Apollo and exchange more secrets of goblin technology, and hopefully some of whatever it is we're smelling in that smoke stack."

He leaned forward. *"And just between you and me, cooked fish tastes waaay better."*

I didn't need Ringo. I didn't need his tribe, I didn't need his tricks, and I didn't need his suspicion. I'd gotten tesla wasp taming and liquid fuels from him, which would, in turn, give me internal combustion and the power to fly over his silly little swamp village.

But I was a scientist, not a monster. And ultimately, neither was Ringo. The boglins were just a less resourceful tribe with fewer cards dealt to them that they had the ability to utilize. Ringo had been right when he said this world was unkind to goblins. I didn't want them to get wiped out if a group of humans or elves or whatever decided to cut through the swamp instead of going around to the west. More to the point, I wanted advance warning if such a group came gunning for *my* tribe from that direction. Besides, two goblin kings could progress faster than one by sharing branches of the Goblin Tech Tree. Though I had no doubt Ringo's suspicious nature would scrutinize such exchanges for any hint of imagined betrayal. I just had to hope future exchanges were less caustic than the trade for shock sticks and oil fire had been.

"Very well," I said. "Let it be known that Tribe Apollo recognizes Tribe Ringo as friends and allies under Raphina's watchful eye," I said, pointing up at the late afternoon moon just starting to illuminate from the sinking sun.

The gathered goblins of Tribe Apollo cheered and rushed to greet the boglins, who squawked in shock at suddenly being thrust into the air. I found myself caught up as well, lifted onto the top of the crowd and bounced across the hands of dozens of goblins.

"What is this? Betrayal!" shouted Ringo's envoy. I just laughed. "I demand you return me to Daytona at once!"

I stopped, a chill running down my spine. "What did you say?"

"I said unhand me!"

"No, about Daytona."

The goblins let George down and he dusted himself off. "Daytona Island, the domain of King Ringo."

Daytona?

Ringo . . .

I had thought it a funny coincidence that the swamp king had named himself after one of the Beatles. Hell, I thought myself clever by naming his advisor *George.* Great joke. Har har. But . . . what if the joke was actually on me? I never even stopped to consider the possibility, with the System all but confirming that my launch companions hadn't made it to Rava. But that didn't exclude the possibility that I was the only one who had ever made it here. Or, for that matter, the first . . .

"George . . . is King Ringo . . . from *Earth*?"

The advisor's ear twitched. "I'm sure I have no idea what you're talking about," he said, sniffing. "I've never even heard of a world called *Earth.* And if I had, my king would certainly not be from it."

Huh. The whole time I'd interacted with him, I had thought Ringo was a brain-addled, paranoid swamp creature native to Rava. Could he just be from Florida?

It . . . actually made a disturbing amount of sense.

What was more important was that I might not be completely alone as the only Earthling on this world. But I couldn't push things. Ringo already didn't trust us. Winning him over wouldn't happen overnight.

But it would happen. I'd make sure of it.

CHAPTER 57

HARVEST 2: ELECTRIC BOGALOO

<Your tribe has decreased to 154 members.>
<2 Hobgoblin Scrappers have been added to your tribe.>
<1 Hobgoblin Wrangler has been added to your tribe.>
<Your tribe has increased to 168 members.>
<Your tribe is consuming more food than it produces by 2.2 chooms per day. Your tribe will begin starving in 12 days.>

"Harvest teams, go!" I said.

All across the bank of the water, goblins began to wade out in teams of three. I would have liked to have been on the front line. I wasn't comfortable standing with the reserves in the back line.

It had taken a few days for the harvested larvae to grow into wasps capable of producing enough voltage to arc between their prongs. A few days also to stew over the fact that the boglin king of the swamp was very likely Florida Man reincarnated as a goblin, somehow. Why? The System had been utterly silent on the matter.

Ringo had refused all requests to meet again, despite my sending Hadfield to make our peaceful intents clear. Which seemed fair, since, you know, I'd tried to set him on fire and all. Still, I couldn't afford to stop trying to make contact. But it wasn't my top priority. We were pushing back into the swamp, and this time we weren't leaving without the iron. I held my heavy slinger at the ready, braced on the back of another goblin. Through the slit in my ceramic faceplate, I scanned the waterline, looking for signs our harvesters had been noticed.

The scrappers were in position and ready to give the signal, but there was always a chance one of the aquatic reptiles could slip our cordon and make it into the teams. So far so good, as the goblins waded through the water probing for iron nodules in the peat. I started seeing them pull ore from the peat and put it in their harvesting baskets. They were a blur of manic productivity, just like every other pursuit they tackled. With single-minded fixation, they scoured the peat bog in an uneven line for any trace of iron.

Several minutes passed, and the sun even drew behind Raphina's closed eye. A few especially industrious teams hauled ore-laden baskets back to swap for fresh ones, bolstered by the stone sloth totem's resistance to movement impedance. I began to wonder if we'd even have a croc-knocker attack—not that that was a bad thing. But . . . after I'd gone to all the trouble of getting captured by Ringo and having other goblins do the dirty work to steal larvae from the tesla wasp nest, it almost seemed a waste. A perverse part of me wanted to see how effective our counter-croc measures would be.

A low whistle sounded out in the bog, which was the scrapper signal that one of the big brutes had been sighted heading our way. I tightened my grip on the heavy slinger and sighted down the laths.

The goblins in the bog continued to work—if warier, now with a tighter grip on their shock sticks and slingers. I couldn't blame them. Croc-knockers had killed over a dozen goblins in as many minutes last time we tried to harvest iron. The only loss we'd managed to inflict on them had been when I'd sliced off the tongue of the biggest one. Maybe it had bled out after that? *Psh,* I should be so lucky.

I kept my eyes on the waterline—which was why I was the first to spot a dark shadow climbing toward the surface, and shouted a warning to the teams.

One of the harvesters turned just in time to see one of the extendable tongues breach the water and slam into his ceramic armor mask, sending chips and shards everywhere but leaving the goblin himself alive. The croc-knocker disappeared back underwater, and the beast broached a moment later, full of fire and ferocity. It spotted my gleaming white crown and diverted toward me.

"I've got this one," I shouted. "Get clear!"

The nearby harvest teams dove to the side, pulling the downed goblin away with them as I released the tension on my slinger. A clay ball launched forward with an angry buzzing. The hollow sphere exploded against the hide of the croc-knocker, and a half-dozen angry tesla wasps spilled out, keying in on the largest target in the area to express their outrage.

The croc roared as the wasps stung it. I hadn't been content to simply put larvae into the split poles to make shock spears. I had a whole arsenal of bio-electric weaponry now. Several other goblins launched wasp-tipped bolts from their own slingers in a wave of buzzing, popping artillery.

"Reload!" I called. Armstrong came up from behind me and started working the crank on the heavy slinger. "Wranglers up!"

Our bog wranglers pushed forward, insulated from the wasps with ceramic and leather armor from the waist up. Thin as it was, it wouldn't do much to deter the crocs. But the hobgoblins were able to enter the swarm of stinging electric wasps without being shocked into paralysis. They had their own spears—some with shock tips, and some with ceramic spearheads. We were going to kill this thing if we could. But, if not, we'd at least put the fear of Apollo into it.

A second low whistle sounded from the right side. Armstrong slapped another bug bomb into my sled just in time for the big one to burst out of the water. The alpha had come. When it roared, I could even see its severed tongue where I'd taken its knocker as a trophy. Well, I had something to trade for it, and no doubt. I swiveled the heavy slinger on my goblin pintle mount and let fly with my second bug bomb.

I'd made them by sealing clay half-spheres with large enough holes so the larvae wouldn't suffocate, but not big enough for the adult wasps to escape. The anti-croc bombs were a few steps up, technologically, from the simple shock sticks employed by Ringo's guards. But the principle was still the same: apply shock to croc.

Even without the iron knocker, the alpha was plenty dangerous with its powerful jaws and rending talons. On Earth, it would probably be the size of a large cayman, not even a true alligator. But to goblins? It might as well have been a T-rex for all the chance we had against it without technology.

I could tell the alpha was caught off guard when the sphere smashed into its side, releasing six more of the tesla wasps that proceeded to shock the big bastard of a croc as it bellowed its rage at us.

"Reload!" I called. Down the line from me, one of the slingers exploded in the gunner's hands, releasing its payload of wasps on the slinger team instead of the croc. But all the standard slingers with the specialized shock bolts had already sighted in the alpha and were pelting it with stinging darts.

With a final, hateful look, the alpha disappeared back below the water.

The goblins cheered, and not just because they'd chased off the alpha. The first croc was caught between a pair of sticky snatchers with one loop around its jaws and another around its rear leg as wranglers and goblins pulled at the poles. With the croc unable to move and unable to open its mouth, the other guards closed in and began to finish the job with their ceramic spearpoints. Even the harvesters lost track of their goal and leapt in with their ceramic bogging knives to help finish off the beast with the help of the night haunt totem boost. I held off on firing my next bomb.

In the grand scheme of things, the croc itself wasn't one of the bigger ones. In fact, it was only level 19, lower than the stone sloth alpha we'd killed. But it was the first one, and the tribe would be eating good tonight. Plus, it had a hunk of iron ore in its mouth the size of a fist. What was that worth? A knife? Two? One-fourth of a crankcase?

The goblins finished hauling the croc back onto the shore as I did mental math, trying to figure out the value of each croc-knocker between the food and the iron they harbored in their mouths.

I whistled for attention and got the group back on task. There was still work to be done.

CHAPTER 58

OIL AND ORE

<Your tribe has decreased to 162 members.>

The rest of the day wasn't bloodless. Other crocs tried to make a meal of the harvest teams, and not all of them failed before they were driven off. But by the end of the day, we'd managed to collect thirty-one chooms of iron ore, and I described the process of a bloom furnace to the ignis boss, Promo, over a dinner of roasted croc tail. It was, by far, the best thing I'd eaten since coming to Rava. Even if the igni couldn't work fire or ceramics or swing a hammer, they were worth it for the cooking alone.

I spent the rest of the daylight helping the goblins make large jars to store and transport the oil the boglins had brought to trade, which was currently held in several leaky skins that Ringo's advisor insisted were not part of the deal.

My goblins had figured out a pottery wheel of sorts—albeit one where the clay remained stationary, and the goblins spun around it on a greased bearing. It was quite fascinating to watch, really, especially when they got two or three goblins on the same wheel with different ideas about what they were trying to make.

We were up to twelve chooms of bog oil. The consistency was close enough to kerosene that I hoped it would burn in an engine without additional processing. But first, I still had to *make* the engine. Tomorrow we'd build our first furnace for smelting iron ore.

I sat back after dinner and watched the goblins. At some point, the little blue fuzz-balls had adopted graffiti based on the only reference imagery they had: engineering drawings. Flat surfaces within easy reach of a goblin were covered in iconographic schematics of the various technologies we'd unlocked so far. Parsing their art was like watching a chronological progression of our path through the Goblin Tech Tree. Strange way to start a cultural movement, but the engineer in me approved.

At this rate, it wouldn't be long before they developed a pictographic language. I didn't want to interfere with that process because any anthropologist would probably kill for the chance to watch it happen naturally. Not that anything about the goblins was natural, or even sensical.

A wave of cheers brought my attention around to several goblins trying to stand a pole upright that had been decorated with croc-knocker bones and capped with the skull of one of the beasts. Looking at the stripped skull, it looked less like a crocodile and more like an iguana or chameleon, or something. But the moniker was already lodged in my brain.

<Goblin Totem Unlocked: Croc-Knocker Skull. Goblins who appreciate this totem temporarily move 15 percent faster in wetland environments and can hold their breath 20 percent longer.>

The goblins present all took a collective breath and then, for the first time that day, none of them made any noise.

It was actually disconcerting. I looked out over a crowd of puffed-out cheeks and bugged eyes as the goblins stared one another down, each daring the rest to be the first to release their breath. I worried they were going to start to pass out.

Eventually, one of them cracked and let out a gasp, which propagated through the crowd, followed by jeers at the half of the goblins that gave up sooner—which then led to a minor civil war as the goblins who couldn't hold their breath as long began assaulting the rest. It all devolved into chaos within a few seconds as they forgot what they were fighting about and just started biting and punching anything that happened to be close by. Even Promo was wading through the crowd, laying into goblins with his hooked rod, and of course the hobbies were giving it their all even if they were overwhelmed by sheer numbers. In the end, the indivisible singular goblin was the great equalizer as their masses rolled over the variants.

All this over a skull on a stick. But, then, I'd never really understood *art*. I leaned back by the fire, watching the chaos unfold. Sometimes, it was good to be the king.

<Your tribe has increased to 179 members.>

"More heat!" I called.

Two goblins worked the impellers on the furnace by the light of the rising sun. Promo stood with the other igni that had been born at the bog camp (now Village Huntsville) the previous night and dumped baskets of charcoal into the bloom furnace. Smoke billowed out the top, along with an acidic tang that I surmised was the bacteria in the iron nodules within the furnace.

Making steel in a bloom furnace wasn't all that dissimilar to firing ceramics. You needed a chamber hotter than the hottest boil on Satan's big red behind, and you needed lots of air and heat.

It took hours for the furnace to melt down all the iron so that it could mix with the carbon, and I couldn't even check the progress of it. But we were following the book almost exactly—with a few modifications to account for differences in goblin methodology. We had to be getting close. I could feel the anticipation building.

<*Goblin Technology Unlocked: Boom Furnace*>

Don't you mean "bloom" furnace?

I felt a rumble start to mount beneath my feet. That wasn't anticipation shaking the dirt.

<*I said what I said.*>

My eyes went wide, and I whistled for everyone's attention. "Get down!" I shouted. "Now!"

Most of the goblins had learned pretty quickly that when I gave an order with urgency it was in their best interest to comply, so most of them dropped what they were doing and dove for the floor, pressing their hands over their heads to stop any imminent debris. The goblins working the impellers weren't fast enough, and when the furnace exploded, it took both of them with it, and knocked me to the ground.

<*Your tribe has decreased to 177 members.*>

Clay chips ricocheted off the brick tower and the trees, and rained from the sky for several seconds. When I looked up, the whole front face of the furnace had erupted outward, carving a path right through the cranking station while—amazingly—leaving the impeller assemblies completely intact.

While I felt bad for the goblins, impellers were a few orders of magnitude more rare. I picked myself up and dusted off my fur. The furnace was a mess. I grabbed a wooden pole and moved closer, ready to call the whole thing a disaster. But then I saw it: the red-hot glowing steel bloom at the bottom of the furnace.

I wedged the wooden pole underneath and dislodged the bloom. The metal rolled down the base of the furnace, shooting off sparks.

"Promo!"

"On it, boss!" shouted the ignis, grabbing a set of wooden tongs and examining the rough mix of steel and slag. He tipped it over to examine it from all sides. "To the stump!" he declared.

The goblins in the village cheered. They ran to the makeshift anvil we'd been able to scrape together. A stump sat in the middle of the area with a narrow wooden log sitting above. The goblins who had followed us from the furnace area raced to be the first to grab a series of ropes that fed into pulleys that were themselves attached to the pole. The goblins leapt up and hauled down, and the pole lifted from the stump.

Promo was quick to lever the steel bloom underneath the pole before the thing came crashing back down, compressing the iron and knocking off some of the impurities. The goblins on the lines were pulled off their feet, but they yanked back down and began a seesaw between their weight and the pole hammer. I watched as Prometheus got the billet turned every which way as they hammered it.

Shouldn't I get an unlock for the forge hammer?

<Still technically a sticky-hammer.>

I felt like there might have at least been *some* difference. But what did I know? I was only bringing my tribe into the Iron Age.

CHAPTER 59

DAWN OF IRON

It's a common misconception among people who play too many video games that technological progression always goes copper-bronze-iron, and then some sort of made-up stuff like *mithril.* In reality, bronze is actually pretty tough to get a hold of. On Earth, early sources of tin came from only a few places in Europe and Asia, and when those trade routes broke down, some societies actually fell back *out of* the Bronze Age for a while. For many applications, bronze was similar or sometimes even favorable. But one thing it *wasn't,* was a strictly necessary stepping stone into the Iron Age.

My tribe had its first steel bar. As I held the metal in place with wooden tongs, I watched the two igni cut and stack and continue to hammer it into a proper billet. We worked until midday, adding more heat from a charcoal fire when necessary, at which point the hobbies woke up and another iron-gathering expedition set out into the bog.

As in any case of development, the first thing we needed to manufacture was a tool to make more tools. In this case, a proper steel blacksmithing hammer. The oversized wooden mallets the igni were swinging looked more like the hammers you'd use at a carnival game. Luckily, the shaping and fixture of a hammer was pretty simple, as far as tools were concerned, and we had a hammer head by midmorning. Promo took a lunch break while he waited for his new toy to temper in the kiln.

<Goblin Technology Unlocked: Clangy Tools. All previously discovered tools may now be made with available metal variants.>

"Boss, I gotta say, it's an honor to receive our first steel tool," said Promo, spinning the hammer around while another hunk of iron heated in a boom furnace (with appropriate shielding for the impeller team this time).

"You'll need it, Promo," I said. "After all, it's not like we can go to the moon in a rocket made of wood. Metal is the future of the tribe. We'll need it to make an engine."

"Enn-jinn . . ." Promo said slowly, sounding out the word. "Sounds fun. What's it do?"

I thought for a moment, trying to describe it in fundamental terms for the primordial goblin. "It swallows fuel, makes heat in its belly, and creates internal pressure that translates to external force," I finally said.

"I get like that sometimes, too," said Promo, patting his rump.

I chuckled, shook my head, and pointed to the large jars of maybe-kerosene. "That stuff. An engine will let us use that to turn a wheel, spin a propeller, run a lathe, or charge a battery."

"You can use fire for that too, though, right?" asked Promo. "The balloons work off hot air. Can't you use hot air to move things?"

"Sort of," I said. "But not for the reason you're thinking. A hot air balloon rises because the hot air inside is less dense than the cool air outside. But, expansion of gases, or transition of liquids into gases, is a huge source of kinetic energy and a fundamental concept of most major forms of power generation where I'm from. What you're talking about is called steam power. And yes, we're going to make use of it. But we don't have large-scale energy problems right now. Almost all of our problems stem from a lack of materials."

"Like food," said Promo.

"Like food." I considered. "Did you just stop paying attention because I'd lost you and you got hungry?"

Promo started to giggle. "Sorry boss, you lost me 'round about *expansion of gases.*"

The other igni started to giggle, too, and held his hands up to his mouth to make a farting noise. I rolled my eyes as the goblins nearby started to do it, too. And then of course it propagated through the base. Not all of the goblins realized the others were using their mouths, either. When I'd mentioned material constraints, I'd been thinking more along the lines of manufacturing materials. Not just iron, either. We needed to start thinking about cloth, paper, properly cut lumber, more metal, more fuel, and a dozen other things. But I'd also been watching the food stores tick down from a safe margin to a few dozen chooms as the tribe continued to grow. Even assigning more hunters and fishers had done limited good. We needed a larger source of calories if we were to continue growing. If I was to support a population in the hundreds or thousands, we needed *kilochooms* of food. And we needed working engines to traverse enough area to secure large game. That had to be the next priority.

It didn't help that Neil's hunters were competing against the javeline for small game in the forest. Whatever else they were, the half-pigs were very effective hunters. But they also weren't in the forest exclusively to collect goblin trophies. If we buttoned up, they didn't risk losing too many of their own. But they were an ever-present threat. And they were coming sooner than I'd like. We'd spotted the occasional scouts near the base of the bluff, watching and probing for weakness.

I pushed to my feet, ready to get back to work. "I will say this: You and your noblin pals are going to have a lot of work coming your way. Are you up to it?"

"Trust, boss!"

We managed to get one more hammer ready by the time the harvesters returned with several more baskets full of raw iron, and not long after that, we heard the baying of hounds that announced Chuck and his wranglers making their daily visit. They reached us a few minutes later, and the wrangler swung down from his saddle with a grim expression.

I stood up. "What's going on?" I asked.

Chuck went to his saddlebags. "Javeline look like they're gearing up for a move on Canaveral," he said. "Eileen spotted a warband of them east of the springs."

I considered. "Canaveral is well defended, but if they attack during the eclipse, the goblins might be spread too thin to hold it." I looked to Armstrong. "Should we reinforce their numbers with an airdrop?"

Armstrong considered. "Could be a porkbelly trap, King. We send boys to Canaveral, and then the main force hits Apollo." He smashed a fist into his meaty palm. "That's what I'd do if I was them. But they ain't clever like me. Maybe it's just what it looks like."

I growled in frustration. Armstrong was probably right. There were eighty or ninety javeline in the forest that we knew of, though they'd taken to hiding their numbers from our overhead scouts because the scouts had a habit of dropping poppers on the javeline camps.

Village Canaveral had become an important source of food for the tribe thanks to the eclipse lizards having more meat than brains. As much as I didn't want to abandon Canaveral, even temporarily, I'd planned for this. There were gliders ready and waiting at Canaveral, enough to carry every goblin back to Apollo. But it would be a huge expenditure of sulfur to send them back.

"Evacuation protocol," I told Chuck. "Have everyone ready to pull back from Canaveral if the javeline attack during an eclipse. Let's head to Apollo and shore it up for an attack."

Promo stepped up, hefting his mallet. "Great, boss. Been missin' the old homestead. Ready to smoke some more javeline ribs."

"What about Huntsville?" asked Chuck.

The javeline hadn't shown any interest in the bog before, and any time Neil's hunters encountered them with overwhelming numbers, they simply withdrew—so I had to believe they acknowledged the threat Apollo goblins represented. Plus, Huntsville produced and consumed charcoal locally, and produced and consumed iron ore locally. The combination of the two was critical to smelting the iron, which was then hammered and purified into steel. All processes that benefitted from close proximity to each other. It was simply too much of a logistical burden to transport the raw iron *and* the charcoal to fire it to Village Apollo. The main village already had heating fuel sources, and I didn't want to strain that infrastructure either.

Beyond that, we had our tentative trade relationship with Ringo, and we'd even spotted a tethered balloon manned by a boglin hovering above Daytona. Emissaries sent by the boglin king still staunchly refused to confirm that the king was a reincarnation case.

"We'll leave the collection crews. Iron bar stock and oil will get sent to Village Apollo, like we always planned." I looked around. "This camp is going to be instrumental in defeating the javeline and securing the future of Tribe Apollo."

But until then, we might have to cinch up our belts and get cozy at Village Apollo.

CHAPTER 60

WELCOME HOME

I hardly recognized the bluff. It had changed so much in the time I'd been gone setting up operations in the bog. It seemed like Buzz hadn't spent a single minute idle, as wooden structures reached up above what few trees remained, with bridges and lattices crisscrossing disparate floors and intersecting structures at strange angles. The construction crew hadn't only built up, but also out and down, making the bluff itself look like it wore a lopsided hat at an angle that was less jaunty and more precarious. The sides of the bluff now played host to a plethora of cliffside dwellings and structures sprouting from the face of the cliff itself and anchored by thick cords. Freight traffic moved both up and down the bluff through a half-dozen elevators manned by dozens of goblins. The strange counterweight cranes stacked wood beams even higher, making odd, crooked buildings that swayed in the wind.

Over one hundred goblins called Village Apollo home, and it was about to get even bigger once the goblins of Canaveral withdrew. The airspace over the bluff was thick with smoke and crowded with the slow circling of personal gliders. We were spotted long before we reached the bluff, and a procession of goblins dropped out of the sky to join us, mimicking various noises of inventions I'd introduced. It was quite a bit of fanfare for having only been gone a couple of weeks. All of them wanted to see the hammer, or at least that's how I interpreted the hoisting of various wooden and stone mallets.

Promo handed over the first finished steel hammer and I hoisted it up so that it could catch the rays of the setting sun on its silvery surface. The goblins all cheered and raised their own tools in response.

Every goblin in the tribe was going to want steel tools. It was only natural. But most of them would have to settle for flint or make do with ceramic. All of the iron we had was earmarked for the igni to turn into hammers and engine parts. Well, *most* of the iron, I thought, looking down at my worn sloth-claw prosthetics. Engines were the ticket to jumping the developmental rail yet again. And in the next few days, I was going to work closely with Sally and Promo to get that technology unlocked. We had all the elements of internal combustion. Now, I just had to put everything together. Tribe Apollo was going preindustrial.

The route from the west took us through the paddocks that Chuck used for the cliffords and the livestock rounded up from the savannah. I spotted the stone sloth cub running among the meager herd, now at least twice the size of a goblin. Two wranglers in the pens directed it with whistles and shouts to corral the livestock into a new paddock.

"They're good," I said. "That cub is a regular sheepdog."

Chuck nodded, beaming like a proud papa. "Could use a dozen more like him."

"A few dozen more herd animals wouldn't hurt, either," I said, looking at all the empty space in the paddocks. "We could fit a lot of those 'lopes in here."

"Aye, but they're fast. The cliffords get tired easy. It's tough to drive a big group, so we settle for hooking a couple at a time." Chuck nodded to the cub. "Once he's trained up, we'll have a better shot. Maybe even at some big game."

Bringing down a big herbivore would be a huge boon for our food stocks. I watched the stone sloth circle up the few animals in the paddock and then barrel through them, despite the shouts of the handlers. Well, they still needed work.

We reached the base of the bluff just as a freight platform with a dozen goblins clinging to it hit the base, and all of them jumped off and ran around hooting and cheering. I practically had to start swinging in order to keep them from mobbing me.

"What is going on?" I shouted to Chuck over the racket of the tribe's manic clamor.

"They're glad to have their king safe and sound," said Chuck, laughing. "A king should be with his people. There's no other place you ought to be than surrounded."

"Fair enough," I said. I tilted my head upward at Raphina's waking eye. "I could think of one other place."

Chuck followed my gaze and grinned a mouth of sharp teeth at me. "We'll get there, boss," he said, reaching out and slapping my back. "You'll lead us. We all know it."

My wrangler boss handed our cliffords off to some of his assigned goblins and we scrambled onto the freight elevator, along with at least half the goblins who had joined us. There wasn't even room for most of them, they just clung to the sides and ropes, and the whole structure creaked worryingly as the platform slowly started to ascend under the load. As we gained altitude, I could really see the extent the western forest had been cleared.

Even as I watched, a small explosion rocked the base of a tree and the whole thing toppled over.

Goblins darted in to begin stripping the branches and bark with axes in a swarm of activity.

"So that's where all the bomb fruits are going," I mentioned.

"Getting drained for poppers and mixed with the icky-putty, too," said Chuck. "Grove of them popped up closer to the bluff where we'd stored 'em in holes, but goblins keep eating them before they get volatile enough to harvest."

"They're *eating* bomb fruits?" I asked.

Chuck nodded. "Not bad if you get 'em early. The igni squeeze 'em onto the meat for an extra kick."

Huh. I guess the explosive transition must happen during fermentation. It's an effective way to spread seeds, when you think about it, simply exploding and blasting them every which way. Still, it might make harvesting the juices safer if we collected them from stable fruit and stored them in vented containers to ferment.

One detour I had to make was visiting Sally and her engineers. I had hoped she hadn't spent the *whole* time I was gone building rocket boosters for the search effort. I needn't have been worried, as her engineers were banging out stacks of parts and shoving more clay into kilns.

Sally exploded with the most energy I'd ever seen out of her, which meant standing in front of me and reaching out to poke my chest before turning and running away. I figured she'd just expended her social battery with such a sensory overload, but she came back with six other goblins hauling a platform between them.

"Is that what I think it is?" I asked.

Sally chittered and shifted her weight from foot to foot. Before I left, I'd been sketching out drawings for a rotary engine case. My chief engineer, it seemed, had found them.

I looked at the two halves of the case, rendered in ceramic. They were . . . lacking, to put it lightly. Misshapen and different sizes, such that they could never actually be assembled. One of the reasons metal was ideal for this was that it was malleable, whereas ceramic couldn't be shaped once it was fired. But we had more clay than iron, and she'd still taken the first step.

"Well done," I said. "We'll make some molds and iterate when we can. We'll try both metal and ceramic. Still, I want to make sure we have a supply of raw materials for crafting munitions. Poppers are our best defense against the javeline, so I want to get more RPP rounds rolling."

"We've got the shockers and metal now," said Chuck. "Won't be long until we're tougher than the porkbellies." He looked south toward the savannah. "Just wish we were faster than them, too."

I grinned. "Give it time, my friend. I've got more surprises in store for you yet."

CHAPTER 61

BACK TO THE DRAWING BOARD

<Your tribe has increased to 192 members.>
<Your tribe is consuming more food than it produces.>

Village Apollo rang with the dulcet tone of metal on metal. Oh, that sweet sound of progress.

Under the supervision of Prometheus, the igni and their assigned assistants took to blacksmithing like a baby bird to the sky—eventually, and with much struggling. Even the heat-crafting specialists weren't born experts. I can't imagine how tough it would have been to get ordinary goblins up to a level of competence in smithing that would allow us to progress into the Industrial Age. Even though the Goblin Tech Tree granted them an understanding of the process, the igni needed time and practice to perfect their skills. They weren't quite at the point where they could bang out an engine block, so they were working up to it with knives, nails, gears, poles, and my newest set of prosthetics while we prototyped advanced pieces with clay molds.

I was partial to the spring-steel blades on my legs, especially. They were much heavier than the carbon fiber blades I'd used in races on Earth, but they were still a cut above the sloth claws. Buzz nearly fainted when the concept of iron nails was introduced to the GTT lexicon. Granted, no two came off the line in a similar shape or length, but neither did any of the structures Buzz built, so it was a start. Not every device would be as forgiving of defects. Poles would need to be smooth and true to eventually be purposed for axles, propeller shafts, and rifle barrels, though I doubted we'd see anything like a unified bore caliber. The gears being similarly disjointed had been a problem ever since we'd been making them by chewing wood into shape.

Standardization was a completely foreign concept to goblins, no matter how many examples and templates I tried to offer them. The only thing that *sort of* worked was making molds, and things somehow still came out of those wonky. Without the strange grease of the Goblin Tech Tree, I don't know that any mechanical devices produced in the village would work.

Piecemeal parts and soft fits weren't going to cut it for something with a pressure vessel and moving parts like an engine. Sure, we could handmake each one under my direct supervision, and that's how we were going to unlock the technology, but the Industrial Age meant industrialization. That meant factories and assembly lines and part tolerances. That meant guides and regs, and some method to record and keep track of them.

Bark and charcoal could only get us so far. We needed paper—actual paper. The method to make it wasn't complicated, and paper had other industrial uses as well. You take a finely woven screen and sift it through a pulp mass, then press and dry the result. Now, don't get me wrong. I wasn't so far gone as to think the average goblin had the attention span to read and write modern English. But the Egyptians had built the pyramids (and if you like conspiracies, the first battery, refrigerator, and UFO landing pad) with drawings of birds and cups. Or at least that's what it had looked like to me when my anthropology major then-girlfriend tried to educate me about early human cultures.

Huh. Maybe I should have paid more attention to her explanations instead of daydreaming about rowing away from the conversation. Anthropology was now much more relevant to me than it likely ever would be for her. Go figure.

I already had most of what I needed to make a basic paper factory, including one of the rainwater collection vats Buzz had been building to satisfy the village's drinking water needs. When the goblin-powered hammers weren't pounding the impurities out of iron stock, I instead turned them to mashing wood pulp. Fires were always going at Village Apollo now, so heating the pulp pool to break down the plant fibers was just a matter of putting rocks in the flames, then dunking them into the vat for a primitive heat exchanger. While that was working, I set two of Neil's hunters with the highest skills in basket and net weaving to making fine corded mesh screens.

Toward the late afternoon, I oversaw Javier's clothiers dunking the first of the mesh screens and applying pressure by jumping on flat, heated rocks. Turns out, paper pulp is a bit like milkshakes to goblins. We lost a half-dozen thirsty goblins to the papermaking process and tinted half the first batch of sheets blue. When the System said goblins could process nutrients from almost any organic matter, this was not what I pictured. I had to install a bunghole (don't laugh, it's a real thing) on the side of the vat so goblins could uncork the tub for a sip and quit trying to stick their heads into the pulp slurry between log hammer strikes.

<Goblin Technology Unlocked: Pulpy Scratch-Bark>

The eyes of most of the goblins in the village glazed over for about a half-second before they resumed what they were doing—except for Sally's engineers, who redoubled their effort. Paper isn't exactly the stuff of rock stardom. But the tribe would see soon enough what else they could use it for. At least the engineers seemed excited about it. Which, yeah, laugh all you want. I wasn't just an engineer, dammit, I was an astronaut. And I would be again.

I spent the afternoon relaxing as the hammers rang and the scent of wood pulp wafted through the village. I had to admit, I found it much more appealing as a goblin than paper mills had ever smelled as a human. But not quite appealing enough to take my turn at the bung. Still, if we could use wood pulp as a nutritional supplement, it might take some of the load off the hunters and fishers.

<Your tribe has decreased to 182 members.>

I had dozed off but was awakened by a loud shriek in the distance. A large number of goblins were streaming to the east side of the village, tasks dropped. I joined them and pushed my way to the edge of the bluff, hand sheltering my eyes from the sun. "What happened?" I asked. Of course, the goblins just chittered and squawked.

I needn't have bothered asking. A few minutes later, the eastern horizon filled with a dozen winged shapes. They were escape gliders from Canaveral. John had pulled the ripcord. The air controllers in the tower started making a fuss, clearing the landing area of the goblins napping or working in the open space.

One by one, the gliders came in, performing the goblin equivalent of a smooth landing (that is, a crash that wasn't completely catastrophic). The pilots and crew barely had time to bail from their craft before the next in line would plow into the back of the one before it, resulting in a pileup of gliders that clogged half the landing strip. One of the gliders didn't even make it onto the bluff, and instead crashed into the side.

<Your tribe has decreased to 180 members.>

At least *most* of the goblins bailed out ahead of the crashes.

The final glider came in, rough and ragged with several tears in the wings. I wasn't sure it would make the transition, but the pilot flared off and just got it over the edge of the bluff before dumping his altitude and crashing down.

I ran over to the landing strip and saw John, the martial taskmaster in charge of Canaveral, climbing out of the cockpit with his two hobgoblin lieutenants. He had a hide bandana tied around his forehead that was stained with blood, and his lieutenants were similarly festooned. All three saluted upon spotting me, and John stepped up to report.

"Sir, the porkbellies hit us at the same time as the lizards. A group of maulers, at least thirty of 'em, led by that big side of bacon you warned us about."

"Hrott?" I asked. Rotte's brother had threatened me at the river. I knew he'd be back eventually, after he finished with the other tribes in the area.

John nodded. "I commanded a withdrawal from Canaveral. I'm sorry, boss. We couldn't hold it."

"Damn!" I said, kicking a patch of dirt with my blade. Not only had it cost us goblins, but our most reliable source of food as well. I sighed and turned around, thinking. Bringing in more herd animals depended on engines. But we weren't going to get engines if the tribe starved before we could make them. We needed Canaveral. And I knew what I had to do to take it back.

"Follow me," I said.

I marched, John in tow, to the blacksmithing area where the ignis hammers still rang.

Promo greeted me, holding up a finished pinion gear and a rack with teeth that actually married up. "Success, King!"

"That's great," I said. "But we need to shift gears."

Promo looked at the gears in his hands.

"No, we need to adjust our priorities. Get the straightest, cleanest poles from the piles that you can find—as thick as your thumb. We're going to use them to make hollow tubes from iron."

"What are we doing with those tubes, boss?" asked Promo, scratching his belly.

I hated that internal combustion would have to wait. I hated that the javeline had pushed me to this point. But I supposed it was inevitable. Rava was a dangerous place. I'd only been here a few weeks, and in that time I'd been bitten, slashed, stabbed, and shocked. I'd seen a few dozen goblins come and go from the tribe with no mourning or even acknowledgment from the survivors. The planet was so dangerous that goblins were practically stamped with expiration dates. I needed something more than sharp sticks to level the playing field against the javeline.

"Making rifle barrels. We're going to war for Canaveral."

CHAPTER 62

GUNBLINS

<Your tribe has decreased to 179 members.>
<The majority of your tribe is not well-fed. A spawning bonus has been rescinded.>
<Your tribe has increased to 192 members.>

I'd never shot a gun on Earth. I didn't even like violent movies. I'd certainly never designed one—even as an engineering thought experiment. But, in principle, they were simple devices. And making a cowboy-style lever-powered gun receiver from ceramic and springs used mostly intuitive engineering principles. Actuate cocking lever: clear chamber, compress spring, set trigger, and load round. Pull trigger: release spring tension, strike primer, ignite propellant, *bang*. Repeat. That's why they call it a *repeater* rifle. Or so I had to assume.

We were skipping a few steps in firearms development. The earliest Chinese guns were more like the hand-cannons I'd originally tried to make when I was captured by the javeline, except made from bamboo. Early muskets were a function of shortfalls in material, chemical, and mechanical understanding. I could make up for one with a surplus of the other two, combined with the rapid iteration capability provided by ceramics and the Goblin Tech Tree.

I gave the initial plans to Sally, Neil, and Promo in the morning, and by afternoon, the igni assigned were pulling the first prototype receivers out of the kiln. Promo's smiths had provided us with spring wire, smaller gears and jigs, and other parts needed to create an internal magazine and receivers before they moved on to creating prototype ammunition.

Ammunition was another matter that I worried about. Until I remembered that we essentially had it unlocked already, and I didn't have to do everything myself. I brought Sally over and explained.

"I want tiny rockets that ignite when you hit the back of them." I held my forefinger and thumb up. "This wide, and about twice as long."

Sally held up her fingers and looked critically at the size. Then she nodded and started whistling for her engineers. They began hammering away, making molds and packing clay, while others started stoking the kilns. I watched batches of clay prototypes go in, and by the end of the eclipse, they came out as little ceramic cylinders, pointed on one end and hollow.

Of course, no two were precisely the same size or shape. And it was going to impact their performance and reliability. But as long as the bullets didn't destroy the ceramic receivers when they ignited—and that was a big *as long as*—then they should *somewhat* function, and they should be *somewhat* stable.

Who was I kidding? Half of them were going to explode on first firing. The others weren't going to fire at all. I handed them off to Neil.

He had some scat put on the top of the kiln to dry, and then had goblins grind it into a more powdery form of the putty before mixing it with the charcoal and sulfur.

<Goblin Technology Unlocked: Icky-Sicky Powder>

Once the bullets were cooled, some of Neil's hunters with his bonus to bomb handling carefully packed the compound into the back third and capped it with a small blob of bomb juice–infused icky-putty and a small dab of almost-dry clay.

"Looks good, boss," Neil reported.

<Goblin Technology Unlocked: Single-Stage Rockettes>
<Goblin Technology Unlocked: Miniature Goblin Blastics>

That was a good sign. When the System unlocked technology before it was even tested, it generally meant I was on the right track. I held one of the new micro-rocket bullets and inspected it.

"Nice work, Sally," I said. She beamed at me.

But now, it did still need testing. The easiest way was actually to use a modified slinger with a small pin at the front of the sled. It wasn't a rifle, of course, but I just needed to see how the ammo functioned.

I set up the slinger between two rocks with a cord tied around the release catch, got to a safe distance, and pulled the cord.

There was a shower of sparks, a fizz, and then nothing else happened. I frowned. I whistled to one of the other goblins and had him run up and reset the sled with a new round. Once he was out of the path, I pulled the cord again. This time, there was a *pop*, and the round whistled off, leaving a meandering trail of sparks as it flew through the air, twisted, bounced off an adobe wall, and tumbled over the edge of the bluff.

The goblins close to its flight path ducked, squawking in fear, and then rose, cheering. The dichotomy of goblins.

The third round exploded, destroying the entire slinger.

Armstrong laughed. "One outta three ain't bad, issit?"

"It's pretty bad," I said. "When we're going to be relying on volume of fire, accuracy is going to be a metric of how many shots we can pump out. They're not going to be reliable enough."

We tested the rest of the first batch and had six more successful ignitions and nine more misfires. I called Sally over.

"Besides the reliability, accuracy is the biggest issue. Rifling the barrels won't do much if the ammo isn't standard."

We needed a goblin solution to a goblin technological quandary. I watched a handful of goblins working at a pottery wheel—where they'd designed the clay to remain stationary while the goblins spun around it. *Hmm.* We couldn't spin the rifles around the bullets. But we could take the rifle barreling out of the equation.

"Alright. We're going to put spirals on the shafts in the clay before we fire them in the kiln. Can you take care of that?" Sally nodded.

I went to Neil next. "We need better than one in three," I said. We sat down to examine some of the dud rounds and figure out what went wrong. After some testing with expired rounds and very *careful* testing with some of the duds, I had it figured out.

"Clay is too thick at the back," I said. "It's acting like a pad instead of a cap. It needs a hole in the middle so the firing pin can actually strike the primer, yeah?"

"Onnit."

A commotion at the landing strip drew my attention, and I left Neil to his work as I went to see what was going on. One of Eileen's recon gliders had returned, limping home from Canaveral. I could see a few of the porcine crossbow bolts sticking out of the bottom of the frame, and part of the starboard wing was damaged. I waited as the pilot circled to bleed off altitude and airspeed before coming in and flaring off. Admirable piloting. I was unsurprised to see a hobgoblin wrangler pop out. With their heightened senses at high speeds, they were natural aviators. He chittered back and forth with Eileen, and she came to make her report.

"Piggies smashed up Canaveral, but only a few of 'em stuck around. Smoke from a camp farther north. Betting they want to keep us off their backs while they hit more villages. Reckon we could push what's left out of the Canaveral with a surprise attack."

"Well, they're in for a rude awakening," I said. "Get some supper. We've got an early morning."

CHAPTER 63

MARCHING ORDERS

<Your tribe has decreased to 189 members.>
<Your tribe has not been well-fed for multiple days. The spawning bonus for being well-fed has been rescinded.>
<Your tribe has increased to 199 members.>

While my taskmasters had their instructions to iterate on the designs for the rest of the day, I made progress turning copper wire, a spare metal shaft, and some permanent magnets into our first electric motor prototype. It wouldn't spin until I could rig up our first battery, but it felt good to have something to do with my hands. Around lunchtime, I heard a noblin's heavy footfalls approaching behind me and turned to see Promo with a tube carried over his shoulder.

"Alright boss, 'ere ye go!"

Promo handed down the first complete rifle with a barrel attached. I took it and nearly fell over forward with the weight of the thing.

"Oof!" I huffed.

"Need a hand, boss?" asked Armstrong.

I struggled to raise the gun level. "Just gotta get used to the weight. Going to be a two-goblin team, I think. Like the heavy slingers," I said. "Let's get this test fired."

My guard captain touched his fingertips together. "Maybe you ain't should be the one what does the testing? What if it blows up?"

"If it's lethal, it'll transfer to another member of the tribe anyway. But I'm not going to be anywhere near this thing for the test shots. We've got a setup with cord and I—" I looked up at the scrapper taskmaster. "You just want to be the first one to shoot it! You scoundrel."

Armstrong at least had the decency to look guilty. "Chuck's lads got the cliffies and Eileen's crew got the gliders, and she's not even a hobbie!

Even Neil's boys got their poppers. What do the scrappers got?" He opened his hands, empty palms up. "We dress up like bushes an' call out croc-knocker movements. I know it's importy, but I was just finking maybe my lads could get the first o' the boom-tubes."

I looked down at the heavy rifle of ceramic and steel in my hands. "Boom-tubes, eh?" I looked at him. "Well, these certainly suit your sneak attack bonuses."

"Whatcha say, boss?" asked Armstrong.

"I'm actually trying to hand it to you right now, but it's too heavy," I admitted.

Armstrong grinned, reached down, and plucked the rifle out of my hands.

"We'll make 'em lighter," said Promo. "Once we get 'em figured out."

While it wasn't exactly a feather for the scrapper, hobgoblins had substantially more mass, and Armstrong could swing the rifle and keep it somewhat level without help. He started aiming down the length of the barrel at a night haunt carcass the wranglers had managed to bring down in the night while the rest of us slept, making small explosion noises each time he worked the action. The gun wasn't loaded yet, but the action still gave a meaty *chunk* with each crank of the lever underneath, and a *thunk* with every pull of the trigger dropping the heavy hammer. I wanted the parts to be as robust as possible so that they'd be functional even if the goblins decided to use them as clubs instead.

"Ammo," I called. Neil brought over a basket of bullets, and I took a handful of the fired shells that looked close in size to the breech of the rifle. I didn't know if there were actual bullets made out of ceramic on Earth or if they would even work, but we didn't have lead yet. Heck, I didn't even know if these would penetrate the leather and rusty iron armor that the javeline maulers wore, so I'd set up an impromptu firing range with bits of salvaged porkbelly armor scraps and even a couple of roof tiles fired to ceramic plates.

Armstrong pulled the action on the rifle back, and I loaded a handful of bullets into the internal magazine. Once he closed the action, I retreated to a safe distance as he peered through the sight.

"Like this, boss?" he asked, swinging the muzzle around.

"Don't point that at us!" I shouted. He snapped the business end back downrange and sank into his shoulders in shame.

"Just take it slow. Breath in, out, aim, and shoot," I said, trying to remember any advice I'd seen on TV. I understood the inner workings of the rifle from a chemical and mechanical standpoint. But there's a big difference between knowing how to *build* a machine and knowing the proper way to *use* a machine—even one so simple as a gun. "Squeeze, don't pull, keep both eyes open, lead your target, relax, but hold tight, square your feet, an—"

Neil nudged me.

"Right. Just pull the trigger."

I hadn't expected it to work on the first try. And in fact, the *boom* was so loud and the gout of fire and smoke so great, I thought the rifle *had* exploded in my sapper's hands. But about a meter to the left of the piggy armor I'd strung up, a water cask at the other end of a spiraling smoke trail blew a leak and started pouring out its contents.

<Goblin Technology Unlocked: Gobby-Fingered Blast'ems>
<Goblin Component Technology Unlocked: Combust'em Chambers>
<Goblin Component Technology Unlocked: Gyro-Smoothed Grooves>
<Goblin Component Technology Unlocked: Pinny Sparkers>
<Goblin Component Technology Unlocked: Springy Mags>
<Goblin Component Technology Unlocked: Steely Bores>
<Goblin Component Technology Unlocked . . .>

Every goblin in the village dropped what they were doing. At least, the ones who had bothered still pretending to work. The first thing I heard when the ringing of my ears cleared was the roar of the horde flooding to the firing range faster than the penetrated water cask was flooding the end of the lane. Armstrong had to hold the rifle above his head, and even then goblins tried to climb up him or gnaw at his legs to bring the burly hobgoblin down.

"Back! Back!" I shouted over the noise. Amazingly, they listened. But they were *all* making *kr-pow!* noises and miming firing rifles of their own.

"No shortage o' willing hands, hoss," said Promo. He lifted his ceramic mask and rubbed the fur on his chin. "Got a few ideas what to make them manageable for the shorties."

For my part, I just wondered why I'd been so afraid of this. Guns were loud, fast, and explodey. Everything an astronaut/engineer needs in life. "Armstrong!" I shouted over the din.

The hobgoblin looked down at me.

"Shoot it again!"

Boom!

This time the round hit one of the piggy stand-ins. A smoking hole appeared in the leather jerkin.

"Again!"

Boom!

A support beam snapped above the ceramic tile, causing a bridge between two structures to sag and then splinter.

"Again!"

Click.

A dud. Armstrong cycled the action, ejecting the unspent round and cycling a new one.

Boom!

The thin ceramic tile cracked, and fragments of the bullet ricocheted off. Not a penetration, but it had certainly destroyed the integrity.

I nodded to myself.

System, how many of these can we make with current material stores?

<*You currently have enough steel, wood, and clay to make 22 blast'ems of various barrel lengths, and enough unprocessed iron ore in Huntsville for an additional 31. Ceramic barrels may be substituted for an additional 16 with slightly reduced reliability.*
You currently have enough clay, dung, sulfur, and charcoal to make 2142 rockettes, but metal may be substituted for ceramic for an additional 422.>

We couldn't dip so much into the clay that we wouldn't have enough for ceramic parts when the Ifrit arrived. But fifty rifles would arm a full quarter of the tribe. Combined with slingers, poppers, and cliffords, that might just be enough to push the piggies out of Canaveral, and maybe even out of our neck of the jungle for good.

Or until Habberport sent forces even more dangerous. The jungle forest was on our side, with thick growth being restrictive to traversing for anything larger than a dwarf. I imagined humans would have a tough time getting through the underbrush. But if anyone on this world was versed in human ingenuity, it was me. I didn't doubt they'd come eventually.

I waved Promo down. The noblin chief waddled over.

"Get the prototypes to the hunters so they can keep the tribe fed. I want us cranking these out as soon as we've got material for them."

"When will we take back Canaveral?" asked Armstrong.

I looked at Promo. "How many blast'ems can we make in a day?" I asked.

He did some counting on his fingers. "With the igni working on barrels and receivers exclusively? Twelve, thereabouts," he said. "More with more help."

I opened up the System window and transferred additional goblins under his team from Buzz and Sally. "You have it," I said. I looked back up at the scrapper. "Four days."

CHAPTER 64

PEPPERED PORK

<Your tribe has increased to 238 members.>

The piggies didn't give us four days. Two days after the first rifles came off the line, one of our hunters spotted a group of maulers scouting the paddocks on the west side of the bluff. A day after that, a recon glider spotted a group of at least twenty-five of them on a direct route to our woefully depleted livestock pens and bomb fruit orchard.

I handed out rifles and ammo to as many goblins as I could, with the scrappers each getting one and teams of two goblins getting one between each pair—one to shoot, one to act as a bipod in hopes that would give us a little more accuracy. The models we had for the non-variant goblins were lighter, shorter-barreled carbines, but they were still too heavy and we had far more goblins than rifles. I also gave some to the wranglers for them to shoot to effectively harry the javeline from the backs of cliffords. Every goblin going down the bluff had taken the time to appreciate the totems.

Armstrong and John led the infantry while Chuck led the cavalry. I had Eileen on the bluff above, ready to evacuate the igni and the non-combat taskmasters to Huntsville in the event we lost. All in all, it was still a motley assortment armed mostly with spears and slingers. Part of me worried the maulers would smash right through our resistance.

Having already damaged our food security by attacking Canaveral, forcing us down from the fortified bluff was a smart play by the javeline. They knew we couldn't afford to lose what little livestock we'd managed to corral. But the paddocks weren't completely defenseless, either. I watched as some of Buzz's boys finished up a small tower with a heavy slinger mounted. There were several such platforms at my best guess of strategic locations. But we were out of time. I could hear the javeline war party through the trees. I made to grab a rifle to join the line, and my taskmasters damn near tackled me.

"What is this?" I demanded, trying to wriggle free.

"You're a king!" said Armstrong. "Start acting like one!"

"No fighting," said Neil. "Leave it to us, boss!"

"Chuck!"

My wrangler boss looked conflicted. "I want you with us, boss. But . . . this is for the best."

"Unhand me!" I ordered.

All of my taskmasters were powerless to resist the direct order of my goblin king class. All except one. Armstrong, as captain of my guard, could ignore my orders if it meant keeping me safe, and that's exactly what he did when he stuffed me onto the freight elevator with three of his assigned goblins with orders to keep me from joining the battle.

I didn't like that I was asking others to fight a battle I wouldn't fight myself. But they were right. The risk of capture was too great, and then I'd be farther than the hot springs or the swamp. I'd be carted off to Habberport or wherever the javeline thought they could turn a profit for a talking goblin.

I made my way to the edge of one of the platforms on the west side of the bluff. My bodyguards chittered and looked ready to grab me, but I waved them off. "I'm not jumping," I said. "But I still want to watch."

My goblins had formed into loose ranks on the north side of the paddocks, while the clifford-mounted forces had melted into the forest to the west. The front-line group of almost 150 goblins, the greater share of my tribe, waited to receive the javeline with rifles, grenades, RPPs, shock spears, and more primitive weaponry. Behind them were the heavy slingers and flex-a-pults. Every bit of tech we'd developed was pointed squarely at the piggies. I just wished we had a good wall between us and not a paddock fence. But the javeline had forced our hand.

We didn't have to wait long. I smelled the first ones before I saw the first scouts dash out of the forest with spears raised high to throw. The first few goblins in the western half of the line cracked off shots and a piggy fell mid-stride. But his spear was already out and it landed among the formation. The sound was like listening to bottle rockets fire off on the next street over.

<*Your tribe has decreased to 237 members.*>

The second scout veered to the side and managed to avoid the shots, though several of the goblins tracked him and made to chase. I heard

Armstrong yell for order and watched as he got the excitable riflemen back in ranks and squared off.

<Goblin Technology Unlocked: Rockette Rally>

I could see the wave of understanding pass through the ranks. The goblins shifted their positions in subtle ways, a few meters here, a step back there, angling rifles over and through the paddock's northern fence. Somehow they seemed more ordered and less a gaggle—though they were still very excited goblins with new toys. Many of them cheered the fallen javeline and waved guns in the air. Luckily, only a few fired off shots that spiraled up into the air.

<Your tribe has decreased to 234 members.>

A loud mix of squeals and barks from the western forest alerted the gaggle to an incoming threat from that side, and several of the wranglers retreated. I spotted three of them without their gunners. The gun line shifted, and the main mauler force erupted from the trees.

"There he is!" I said, pointing at the largest of the pack. Hrott was leading the charge, big and broad with a spear raised overhead. Armstrong spotted him immediately, shouting back to the fixed positions.

The slingers on the towers let loose with sleds full of poppers, which landed on and around the force of armored javeline, causing a few to fall. Other positions flung rocks or shock darts, but they weren't effective at that range.

Armstrong held his rifle steady, tracking the incoming force. The maulers' hooves sounded like rolling thunder from where I sat on the bluff, and several goblins broke formation and ran in a panic for the southern forest.

<4 goblins have abandoned the tribe. Your tribe has decreased to 230 members.>

I froze. *What? They can do that?*

<They are not slaves, Apollo. They follow willingly because they believe you will lead the tribe to greatness. Until you give them a reason not to.>

What? This whole time I'd thought their loyalty was an in-baked biological imperative they had no choice but to follow. *Why now? They've faced death for me before.*

<You stood with them before.>

Ouch.

Still, most of the line held. Armstrong took his shot first, and then a wave of thunder echoed across the forest, cloaking the entire line in smoke and drowning out even the javeline charge. Several of the javeline fell. But not enough. The maulers split into two, one group charging straight into the fire with shields raised, and a smaller group circling around to strike at the pens with the livestock. Two more goblins threw down spears and ran for the trees.

<2 goblins have abandoned the tribe. Your tribe has decreased to 228 members.>

I grit my teeth. Even King Ringo had come into the swamp with his boglins instead of hiding in his wooden castle. I glanced at my bodyguards, who chittered to themselves, looking alarmed as the javeline reached the line of goblins and started to jump the fence.

The gun smoke was thick, and it wafted up to the bluff, smelling somewhere between the Fourth of July and a cow farm. It began to drift over the line, obscuring the goblins and javeline both from my view. From within, I saw the occasional electric blue flash of a tesla wasp or smoky burst of a popper along with the constant sound of supersonic cracks and whistles of the rocket rifle ammo.

<Your tribe has decreased to 220 members.>
<Your tribe has decreased to 215 members.>
<3 goblins have abandoned the tribe. Your tribe has decreased to 212 members.>
<Your tribe has decreased to 207 members.>
<5 goblins have abandoned the tribe. Your tribe has decreased to 202 members.>

Most of the goblins had held, and now the battle was joined. I had to hope they'd thinned the javeline group enough, because the maulers were absolutely deadly in melee combat with their strength, size, armor, and metal weapons.

Chuck chose that moment to bring the rest of his wranglers out of the woods in a red tide of barking and baying. And Chuck himself was on the back of the adolescent stone sloth as it roared and trundled alongside the drooling cliffords. They smashed into the back of the javeline. Chuck and several others broke off to take down the pigs that were in the paddock, laying wanton slaughter to our dwindling livestock supply.

I let out a whoop as the javeline squealed in the smoke, but a squawk from one of my bodyguards brought my attention around. He was jumping up and down, pointing and chittering and making snorting noises. I followed his finger just in time to see another two dozen lightly armored javeline rutters erupt from the forest south of the bluff.

The maulers had been conspicuous on purpose to keep our eyes north while their lightly armored cousins snuck around behind the bluff. It was a double attack!

CHAPTER 65

FLANK STAKES

The goblins who had abandoned the tribe encountered the new force coming from the south. They tried to turn around and run back for safety, but the second surprise attack of javeline was already too close. I didn't stay to watch the new force cut them down. There was no time.

I turned and ran to the east side of the village, where Eileen had the heavy gliders staged and ready for takeoff. My bodyguards squawked and chased after me.

"Eileen! Eileen!" I shouted.

My taskmaster turned in her pilot's seat and peered down at me. "How's the battle going?"

"The javeline brought up a second group from the south," I gasped between breaths. "They're going to hit the gunners from behind as soon as they deal with the stragglers. We have to do something!"

Promo lifted his ceramic mask. "So . . . we're not sticking to the evacuation plan?"

"No!" I said.

The noblin grinned at me and jumped down. "Good. Can't abide runnin' fer my hide." He raised his voice and his hammer. "Come on lads! Every dead pig is another taste of bacon!"

The evacuees cheered and rolled off the planes, but I held Eileen and her flight crews. "Not you," I said. I pointed to the rocket boosters that gave the heavy gliders enough thrust to gain altitude and soar between Village Apollo and Huntsville. "I wish I had a better idea, but do you think you can get this beast in the air with just one of those?"

Eileen glanced down. "Not very high. What are we going to do with the other one?"

<Your tribe has decreased to 199 members.>

"Point it at the porkbellies and turn it on."

"You realize that you do this, we no longer have an out," warned Eileen.

I nodded.

Eileen grinned and whistled for her crews to disconnect the safeties on all three aircraft. "Good. No blaze like a blaze of glory." They scrambled down, and within a few seconds, Eileen's heavy glider was ready.

I flashed her a thumbs-up. "Good luck!" I shouted over the clamor of every goblin still left on the bluff arming themselves and preparing to jump into battle. She reciprocated, and her aft crewman lit the portside rocket. The craft lurched, thrust vector uneven, and slid up the rails and into the air, much lower than I was used to seeing the heavy glider fly.

I ran back to the rest of the goblins who had grabbed whatever weapons were left—mostly slingers, spears, cleavers, and a few poppers that individual goblins had apparently stashed for a rainy day. One had a whole bomb fruit, despite the prohibition in the village. Some had their personal gliders. I took a glider and a popper and held them over my head, trying to think of something inspiring to say.

"*Come on, you apes! You want to live forever*?"

That got one hell of a cheer. And these guys had never even seen *Starship Troopers*, so they had no way to know I'd stolen it. But it did the job. The Tribe Apollo reserve howled, lifting their weapons over their heads. I ran for the west side of the bluff, followed by the whole gaggle of them.

<Your tribe has decreased to 197 members.>
<3 goblins have abandoned the tribe. Your tribe has decreased to 194 members.>

This time, my bodyguards made no attempt to stop me. They were just as caught up in the fervor. We ran, and like a furry blue waterfall, toppled over the edge of the bluff to join the battle.

The rutters had smashed through a handful of the deserters and were headed for a lethal flank attack at the rear of the wranglers' formation. My glider hit the wind and opened with a *snap* of hide pulling taut, and I heard the others behind me doing the same. The rest dropped all the way to the base. I glanced back. Most of the goblins were holding on to their gliders with one hand and held poppers in the other. The one with the bomb fruit was using both hands and holding the fruit with his *feet*. I had no idea how he'd managed to even deploy. Madness. I angled us southwest to intercept the wave of rutters.

The bomb fruit grove had slowed them down, as they had to carefully navigate around fallen fruit, lest they meet a pulpy end. I angled us north of it, just as they arrived and saw the second wave of goblins. Promo, with his steel hammer and hooked rod, was leading the charge. For all I knew, this was the first time the javeline had encountered a noblin.

"Now!" I shouted.

We dropped our ordnance on the rutters. Poppers and a bomb fruit erupted among them. Lightly armored as they were, the explosives had a greater effect than they'd had against their larger cousins. Several keeled over, unconscious or dead. The rest stumbled but got clear and began to sling rocks and light spears skyward. A few goblins squawked as they were knocked off their gliders, and I held on for dear life when a spear ripped through my left wing.

<Your tribe has decreased to 192 members.>

I turned north, quickly losing altitude, and saw a lumbering shape barreling toward me. I angled the glider toward it and had just enough distance left in it to drop onto the back of the stone sloth, where Chuck steadied me.

"Boss? What are you doing down here?" he demanded.

We rode past a trio of deserters that somehow managed to avoid the rutters, who looked up and saw me atop the sloth with Chuck.

<Your tribe has increased to 195 members.>

"Inspiring the troops, apparently!" I said. "Goblins won't fight for a king that won't fight for them."

Chuck barked out a laugh. "Then you're right where you ought to be! Let's give the piggies what they came for!"

He spurred the sloth cub on, maintaining his footing. Two sidesaddles had been rigged up on the flanks of the beast for goblin gunners, and I slid to one that had lost its gunner at some point. A carbine had been tied to a mount, so I worked the action back just enough to see the round still chambered. A basket of bullets jostled at my feet as the stone sloth bounded across the paddock.

The javeline rutters came at us, spears raised against the stone sloth, which was now substantially heavier than even one of the piggies. I screamed and fired as we trundled along, working the lever on the rifle and watching the tiny smoke trails smash basically anywhere *but* into the rutters. Marksmanship was apparently not one of my skills. I could lead a tribe, but not a target. I opened the action and stuffed another handful of bullets in.

We reached the line and the sloth reared up, sweeping its long claws into the first rank of javeline. It was all I could do to hold on as the enormous creature twisted and slashed. It spun us around, and I spotted a familiar face.

"Rotte!" I shouted. "Come and face Apollo!"

The javeline scowled. He still bore the scars on his face and chest from his fight with Armstrong. And, I hoped, on his backside from where I'd hacked him with the scrapper's knives. He leveled his spear and leaned into a charge. "I make talking goblin sorry!" he shouted.

I yelped and ducked as Rotte drove his spear forward. The wide, leaf-shaped blade trimmed the fur on the top of my head and skipped off of one of the sloth's clay plates. I popped back up and angled the rifle over the edge of the basket, and at this range even I couldn't miss. I fired as fast as I could work the action. The porkbelly who had captured me blew back, staggered by at least one successful hit as blood spurted from his shoulder.

But he wasn't done. He swept his spear in a broad arc, and the blade caught the ropes binding the basket to the side of the stone sloth. I ducked again as the basket fell and rolled on the ground, watching the world spin through the opening. The butt of the rifle smacked me in the face every time the barrel caught on the ground, until it came loose and the basket finally stopped.

I pulled myself out of the basket, stumbling, barely able to walk—only to see the rutter charging at me with his spear, Chuck chasing him on the stone sloth. I scrambled for the rifle and basically tripped over it, falling on my ass with the gun in my hands. I opened the action and grabbed a handful of rockettes that had spilled out of the basket with me, barely managing to stuff them in the right way around and close the action before the rutter was on me. I pointed it up at the hulking shadow and fired.

Boom, Boom, Boom, Boom!

Rotte slowed, hit several times. "I make . . . talking . . . goblin . . . sorry . . ." he said, words slowing. Chuck and the stone sloth caught up. The wrangler taskmaster reached down with his cleaver and finished the job with a clean slash to the side of Rotte's throat. Too humane for what the cruel creature deserved, really.

"Nicely done, boss!" he shouted down. I was too dazed and dizzy to reply.

With their leader dead and their own forces out of reach, the line of rutters began to falter. We'd met the flanking attack and stalled it out, and now the reserves from the bluff were about to swing around for a pincer movement. Chuck pulled us back out of danger so the sloth could catch its breath. The only thing missing was . . .

A loud shriek drew my attention around. Eileen had brought the heavy glider and ignited the second booster, only the lines were so jumbled that there was no way to separate pig from goblin at the front lines. Eileen and her crew bailed out of the heavy glider as it picked up speed, rocketing toward the front line.

Do javeline have blast resistance?

<I still won't tell you that was a good idea.>

The glider struck, and a bright flash and shockwave knocked me right over and sent me tumbling.

<Your tribe has decreased to 183 members.>
<Goblin technology Unlocked: Bigger Goblin-Guided Blastics>

I rolled upright, looking at the roiling cloud of smoke and dust. Shapes spun every which way through the air, and some of them landed near me. It was *raining goblins.* And less savory bits of javeline (unless you *are* a goblin).

"What was it you said to us, boss?" shouted Chuck over the echo of the explosion. "Pork rinds to the ionosphere? Whatever that is?"

A grin split my face. I laughed and laughed.

<Goblin Technology Unlocked: Strategic Bomb'ems>
<Goblin Technology Unlocked: Shock and Awe>

I glanced behind. What few rutters were left had turned tail. I saw one fall as a goblin landed on its head and bounced away, still screaming. All in all, I was surprised the blast had only killed twelve goblins in the thick of things. I'm sure there would be more needing prosthetics in the near future.

CHAPTER 66

THE TAILS OF TWO PIGGIES

I found Armstrong dusting off his fur near the blast site. The other scrappers held a javeline mauler that I recognized.

"I know you," I said. "You're Hrodd."

"*Hrott*," he snarled. "What is become of Rotte?"

I glanced back toward the reserve that I'd led down from the top of the bluff. "Dead," I said. "He'll trouble me no more."

Hrott surged against the scrappers, and very nearly got loose. He was in his teen levels, after all. Quite a force to be reckoned with. It was no surprise he'd survived the blast.

"I kill talking goblin for this!" he roared, spittle flying from under his helmet. "Lord of Habberport pay big for your capture, but I will bring him only your head! Will slaughter your—"

"Armstrong!" I said, holding my hand out. He dropped his rifle into it, and the weight of it very nearly drove me to the ground. I swung it around, struggling to lift it to point at the mauler chief's chest.

Boom!

A red button blossomed on Hrott's chest armor. His words choked off as the realization took him. The javeline leader's legs gave out under him, and he sagged to the ground, head drooping forward. His captors tentatively let his arms drop. They fell limp at the javeline's sides.

I handed the rifle back and raised my voice. "Take his helmet, and their tails! We're making a new totem to commemorate this day!"

A resounding cheer erupted from the surviving goblins. They pulled out knives and cleavers, each one eager to be the goblin that claimed the prize. They swarmed in, and I backed out of the press to take a breath.

The brothers Rotte and Hrott had menaced my tribe almost since the day I arrived on Rava. They were responsible for hundreds of goblin deaths, including several that had happened through lethal wounds dealt to me personally. More than that, they were disgusting traffickers of goblin parts. This wasn't like Ringo and his undereducated swamp boglins. I wasn't here to make friends with the javeline. They'd lost that chance. I wanted them out of my forest.

There were other survivors, of course. But we had no cells to hold them and the tribe had a food shortage. Seemed like an easy two-birds-one-stone kind of situation.

System, how many days can the tribe subsist off the fallout from this battle?

<Approximately 18 days' worth of javeline meat at current population exists on the battlefield or captured, with another 2 days' worth scattered to the area beyond by the blast.>

We'd lost enough goblins and gained enough piggies to stave off our immediate food concerns. A little pork goes a long way, and I had no doubt the igni would stretch every meal out of it that they could. But they'd be back to hammering iron soon enough. Industry awaited. And now, the biggest obstacle to our tribe's growth had been soundly defeated.

I summoned my taskmasters for a quick meeting while the tribe began the task of collecting anything of value from the battlefield—a task that would likely take the rest of the day and a good portion of tomorrow.

"I know you all wanted to keep me safe," I said. "But it's clear that I can't just sit back and let the tribe do the dirty work. I can't just be a king, I have to be a *leader.* Starting tomorrow, we're restaffing Canaveral. Now that our tribe is safe, the next priority is food security, and then unification of the other bluffs."

"And tonight?"

"Tonight we're going to friggin' party!"

Turns out goblins can get drunk off fermented bomb fruit juice if you get at it before it goes explosive and boil the volatile bits out. Thank God for the igni bonus to heat-based crafting. The moon was fully lit by the time I stumbled over to the cuddle puddle and collapsed on top. But before I could go to sleep, the System notification window popped up. I squinted and waved it away, but it was insistent.

<Your tribe has won a great victory! For successfully winning your first war and creating a commemorative totem, you have earned the following bonuses:
A one-time spawning bonus.
A new skill has been unlocked: War Chief. Your presence within 100 chooms (plus 10 chooms for every 100 members of your tribe) now increases the combat power and crafting speed of all goblins by 10 percent.
You have unlocked an additional variant choice based on your deeds. You may choose between Obblyn Partizans or Noblin Canoneers.>

Well, seeing as we'd just won a huge victory in large part thanks to firearms, some bigger goblins specialized in carting around some heavier firepower seemed prudent. If I had to guess, the rounds we were using were about equal in power to a small pistol round, or maybe a varmint rifle. That was enough for goblin-sized threats like the javeline, who were only slightly taller than we were. But it was only a matter of time until we came across something needing more oomph. Goblins being only a meter tall and about as strong as a six-year-old somewhat limited their proficiency with higher calibers.

Give me the Noblin Cannoneers.

<Error. Please select a valid option. Your choices are Obblyn Partizans or Noblin Canoneers.>

The Cannoneers, please.

<Error. Please sele—>

Christ, the second one!

<Approved. Noblin Canoneers will now spawn as part of your tribe.>
<Sleep well, King Apollo.>

"The spell was a success."
"But where are they?"
"The stars are blind in this matter."
"The Great Spirit is silent."
"We will scour the globe."
"There is no need. If the stars are blind . . ."
". . . then they are shadowed . . ."
". . . by Raphina's watchful eye."

ABOUT THE AUTHOR

Scott Warren is the author of the reincarnation LitRPG series My Big Goblin Space Program, originally released on Royal Road. He has written more than a dozen books in between working as a submariner, helicopter pilot, and international military instructor. While his day job takes him around the world—sometimes in the most austere of conditions—he is never far from a book in progress. Warren lives in Maryland with his wife and their cat, Lady.